A Mother's Love

Rosie Harris was born in Cardiff and grew up there and in the West Country. After her marriage she resided for some years on Merseyside before moving to Buckinghamshire where she still lives. She has three grown-up children, and six grandchildren, and writes full time. *A Mother's Love* is her thirteenth novel for Arrow.

Rosie HARRIS

A Mother's Love

arrow books

Published by Arrow Books 2007

6 8 10 9 7 5

First published in Great Britain in 2006 by
William Heinemann
Random House, 20 Vauxhall Bridge Road,
London, SW1V 2SA

www.randomhouse.co.uk

Addresses for companies within The Random House Group Limited
can be found at:
www.randomhouse.co.uk/offices.htm

The Random House Group Limited Reg. No. 954009

A CIP catalogue record for this book
is available from the British Library

ISBN 9780099502968

The Random House Group Limited makes every effort to ensure that the
papers used in its books are made from trees that have been legally
sourced from well-managed and credibly certified forests. Our
paper procurement policy can be found at:
www.randomhouse.co.uk/paper.htm

Printed in the UK by CPI Bookmarque, Croydon, CR0 4TD

To all the staff at Chalfont & Gerrard's Cross Hospital, especially the wonderful nurses on Memorial Ward

Acknowledgements

A big thank you to the wonderfully supportive team at Heinemann/Arrow, especially to Georgina Hawtrey-Woore. Thanks also to Caroline Sheldon for her on-going cooperation.

Chapter One

Julia Winter stood transfixed; her turquoise-blue eyes wide with surprise, completely mesmerised by the reaction registered on the faces of her parents in response to her simple statement, 'We want to get married.'

She had thought they might make some sort of protest, probably try to talk her out of it even, especially since Bernard was due to go to the Front any day now, but she hadn't expected either of them to look quite so shocked and outraged, especially since it was 1915 and the War had been going on for over a year. After all, she was the eldest daughter, and so it was surely expected that she would get married someday soon.

Apprehensively, she linked hands with her cousin, Bernard Winter, who was standing soldier-straight at her side and looking very handsome in his officer's uniform.

The silence in the room, broken only by the stentorian ticking of the grandfather clock, seemed to last for ever.

Julia bit hard on the inside of her cheek as the panic that had begun to build up inside her became an ache deep in her chest. She felt

Bernard's grip tighten on her fingers, and knew he was suffering as great a torment as she was.

When her father finally spoke, his voice was so harsh and censorious that Julia's heart thudded with fear. He was a broad, heavily built, middle-aged man and now, in his red-faced anger, George Winter seemed gigantic.

'It's quite out of the question, Julia. I am amazed that you and Bernard should even consider such a step,' he told her angrily, his intense blue eyes gleaming reproachfully behind the gold-rimmed glasses. He breathed deeply, his florid face sombre as he stared fixedly at her.

'But why . . .'

She knew her father still liked to think of her and Lillian as 'his little girls', but surely he didn't think that he could hold on to them for ever, she thought resentfully.

Lillian, with her big grey-blue eyes, and dimpled round face framed by golden curls, was four years younger, and might still be content to be treated as a child, but Julia certainly wasn't. At nineteen she was eager for independence. Some of her friends were already married, even though they were not yet twenty.

'Why? Surely you know the reason why, my girl?' her father rasped, scowling darkly. He half turned to his wife who stood a few paces behind him, nervously pleating the edge of the white lace apron she wore over her ankle-length, dark blue, silk dress. 'Haven't you told her?' he demanded.

'No . . . no, dear. I had no idea that Julia and Bernard wanted to get married . . . not until this moment,' Mabel Winter said in a perplexed voice, her grey eyes accusing as she looked across the room at her eldest daughter.

'You must have seen what was happening?' he persisted in a hard voice. 'Bernard's been mooning round the place for months. You should have recognised it was "calf love", and nipped such foolishness in the bud and sent him packing.'

'Yes, dear, if you say so,' she agreed submissively. 'To tell the truth, I always thought Bernard came to the house to see Lance more than Julia.'

With a disgruntled snort, George Winter walked over to the window. He stood there gazing out unseeingly at the well-kept garden beyond, absently twisting the waxed ends of his moustache into sharp points, until Julia's voice brought him back to the matter of the moment.

'Can't you understand, Father?' she pleaded. 'We're in love – desperately in love with each other.'

'Stop being so ridiculous! Love doesn't come into it,' he admonished, rounding on her angrily.

'Is it because of the War, sir?' Bernard questioned stiffly. 'Would you like us to wait until the hostilities end?'

'Now, or when this wretched war is over, doesn't change the situation in the slightest,'

3

George Winter boomed. 'You can't marry Julia. She's your first cousin, dammit!'

'Whatever difference does that make?' Julia asked, raising her eyebrows in astonishment.

'All the difference in the world,' her father exclaimed. 'Do you want your children to be imbeciles? It's against the laws of God, and man, to make such a marriage. You're so closely related that it is positively indecent!'

Bewilderment registered on Julia's face at his words. Her eyes became blue shields, masking her deep love for Bernard, as she faced her father.

'I don't care a jot about that, and neither does Bernard,' she told him defiantly. Her chin jutted determinedly. 'If I can't marry Bernard, then I won't marry anyone.'

'Julia! You must not speak to your father like that! What he says is quite right, my dear,' her mother said placatingly. 'Had I realised that you thought yourself to be in love with Bernard, then I would have been the first to point out this very same fact to you both.'

'This isn't just some crazy whim, you know, Aunt Mabel,' Bernard protested. 'I can assure you that we are very much in love.' He placed his arm protectively around Julia's slim waist, and drew her close to him.

'Even so, you can't possibly marry each other, my dear,' Mabel Winter told him in a shocked voice. 'For one thing, the Church wouldn't permit it.'

'Then we will get married in a register office,' Julia announced rebelliously. 'As long as we have a certificate to say it's legal for us to live together, that will do.'

'It would still be immoral. You can't marry each other, and that is final, so let's hear no more about it,' George Winter declared irately. 'You'd better go now, Bernard. And I don't want to see you round here again. Understood?'

'If Bernard goes, then I go with him,' Julia told her father, tossing her auburn head defiantly.

'You will go to your room, young lady, and stay there,' her father thundered. He advanced towards her and grasped her by the shoulder, pulling her away from Bernard's side and thrusting her unceremoniously towards the door. 'Upstairs, immediately,' he ordered.

Her cheeks flaming, Julia stood her ground. With an angry twitch of her shoulders she shook her father's hand away, her eyes smouldering.

'Please, Julia, do as your father asks,' her mother interposed agitatedly. 'Leave the matter for the moment; we can talk about it later, perhaps.'

'We'll do no such thing! There is nothing more to be said.' His face set, George Winter walked over to the chiffonier and selected a cigar from the ornate silver box that stood there. Then he settled himself down in his high-backed leather armchair and ignored them all.

'But—' Julia opened her mouth to argue

further against his decision, but her mother held a warning finger to her lips, and signalled with a movement of her head for Julia and Bernard to leave the room.

She followed them out, and ushered them both into the morning room, closing the door behind her before starting to speak.

'Julia, how could you upset your father like that?' she said reproachfully. 'And you, too, Bernard. You should have known it wasn't permissible for you to marry Julia. Whatever do you think your own father would say if we had agreed to your request!'

'He likes Julia; both my parents are very fond of her!' Bernard said stubbornly.

'Of course they are . . . she is their niece. They like her in the same way that we like you, my dear. But they still wouldn't give their approval for the two of you to marry!' She shook her head sadly. 'It really is quite out of the question, Bernard. Why, your father and Julia's father are brothers . . . it just wouldn't be right,' she repeated in shocked tones.

'Mother, do stop being so old-fashioned. It's just a silly superstition, and there's no truth in it.'

'Julia is quite right, Aunt Mabel. There is no scientific or medical basis for stopping cousins marrying. Europeans, even their royalty, have been doing it for generations. The Bach family produced twenty-eight distinguished musicians in five generations, and all of them were

6

the result of cousins marrying,' Bernard told her.

'Please, Bernard.' Mabel Winter pressed a hand to her head, a look of bewilderment on her face. 'You've heard what your Uncle George has to say on the subject so let that be an end to the matter.'

'Did he really mean it when he said I wasn't even to come to the house?' Bernard asked, running a hand through his close-cropped fair hair, his broad, handsome face perplexed.

'I'm afraid so, dear.'

'You mean we can't see each other any more?' Julia demanded, staring aghast at her mother. 'That's not fair! Father wouldn't stop Lillian from seeing her friends whenever she wanted to, now would he?'

'That is a slightly different matter, Julia,' her mother laughed nervously. 'Lillian is still a child, and not likely to get any fanciful notions about marrying any of them!'

'Fanciful notions!' Julia exclaimed exasperatedly. 'You don't believe I'm serious, do you? You, and Father, are making a terrible mistake. I'm in love with Bernard, and what is more we intend to be married.'

'Then, Julia, I'm afraid it is you two who are making the mistake,' her mother warned. 'Your father will never give his consent and I am equally sure that Bernard's parents won't be in agreement either.'

In that she was right. The argument was

short-lived. The decision on both sides was unanimous. The thought of first cousins marrying was utterly abhorrent to both families, and nothing either Bernard or Julia could say would dissuade any of them.

'If they won't give us their permission, then we'll simply have to elope,' Julia stormed when she and Bernard met secretly the next day.

'Give it time, dearest, they may come round,' Bernard consoled her.

'But there is less than a week of your leave left and once you return to your unit you could be sent to the Front at any time,' she pointed out, her voice trembling.

'That's true!'

'They might even recall you from leave,' she went on dramatically.

'Hush, darling!' Bernard gathered her into his arms, pressing his face against her sleek chestnut hair. 'We'll think of a solution before I have to go back to my unit.'

The remaining five days sped by. Not only did their problem seem insurmountable, but the situation was made worse by the fact that George Winter issued strict instructions that not only was Bernard not to visit, but also that Julia was to be confined to the house.

'Who does he think he is, one of the Huns we are supposed to be fighting?' Julia raged.

'Not another word, Julia,' her mother

begged. 'If your father hears you talking like that he will—'

'He will what? Have me put away? Lock me in my bedroom on a diet of bread and water? The world is changing, Mother. I'm grown-up, and I have a mind of my own. I'm not a fifteen-year-old like Lillian, content to be tied to your apron strings.'

'Until you come of age at twenty-one you have no alternative but to do as your father says,' her mother pointed out.

'You made that crystal clear last May when you refused to let me go up to London with Alice Sandford to the Suffragette meeting in Trafalgar Square,' Julia reminded her huffily.

'And a good thing we did,' her mother replied spiritedly, 'otherwise you might have ended up in prison like Mrs Pankhurst and her daughter.' She sighed, her grey eyes clouding. 'Perhaps you should have gone; a touch of force-feeding might have brought you to your senses, and made you realise how lucky you are to have a good home and a loving family.'

'You really don't understand, Mother, do you?' Julia told her impatiently. 'It's because there are so many others who are not as fortunate as me that I felt the need to support the Suffragette movement. It's time women had a say about the way their lives are run. The days when they were chattels, dominated by their father, or their husband, are gone . . .'

'Please, Julia,' Mabel Winter held up her hand,

her eyes pleading, 'no politics, I beseech you. Such talk makes my head ache, and it does no good at all. I hoped all that dreadful militancy was brought to a close when war broke out—'

'Simply because those women who were in prison were released doesn't mean it's the end of the Suffragettes' fight,' Julia interrupted scornfully. 'Women will get the vote – you'll see.'

'Julia! That will do!'

'No, Mother, you really must listen. Women will get the vote, and then they will be able to have a say in how the country is run. Some day there will be women in Parliament even.'

'A woman's place is in the home, caring for her husband and children,' Mabel Winter told her daughter emphatically.

With a self-satisfied smile she looked around the drawing room of their well-appointed house in Warren Drive, one of the most sought-after areas in Wallasey, admiring the richly patterned Axminster carpet, red velvet drapes and deep, comfortable armchairs.

'Only if that is what she wants and if she is allowed to marry the man of her own choosing,' Julia retaliated.

'That's quite enough! I might have known that was what all this was leading up to,' Mabel Winter said crossly. 'Well, the answer is still the same. Neither your father nor I, nor Bernard's parents, are going to condone a marriage between first cousins, so put the idea right out of your mind. All this nonsense only started when Bernard went into the army. I'm inclined to think it is the glamour of that khaki uniform he wears these days that has turned your head.'

'Mother! How could you say such a thing?' Julia protested. 'I agree he looks very handsome in his officer's uniform, but it is Bernard himself I'm in love with, not how he dresses. I love him just the same whether he's wearing his uniform, a business suit or a tweed jacket.'

'Well, in future, you'll have to regard him with brotherly love, in the same way as you do Lance. Now run upstairs and fetch my smelling salts, I feel quite faint with all this upset,' she added breathlessly, holding a hand to her heart.

'What I feel for Bernard is nothing at all like I feel for Lance,' Julia retorted scathingly as she went to do her mother's bidding. 'I think the world of Lance, but they're totally opposite in both looks and manner.'

The very thought of comparing Bernard's manly physique with that of her lanky brother was ludicrous, and irritated Julia immensely.

'Give Lance another year or two, and he'll fill out. He is only sixteen, remember,' her mother reminded her.

'Even so, they're not comparable. Bernard would never be content to be a dogsbody in father's office.'

'Julia, really! There is no call for you to speak so disparagingly about your brother. Your father says he shows considerable promise.'

Julia shrugged her slim shoulders in an exaggerated manner. 'I'm not interested one way or another.'

Although, outwardly, Julia appeared to have accepted her father's ruling, inwardly she was seething with resentment, but she knew better than to openly defy him.

George Winter was a strict authoritarian, and perpetuated the Victorian principle that he was head of the household, and must be obeyed in all things. This, as much as anything else, was what had fired Julia's interest in the Suffragette movement.

It infuriated Julia to see the way her mother always bowed to his decisions whether she agreed with them or not. His word was law, and he brooked no contradiction. Only Lillian, with her wide-eyed, innocent look and simpering smile, could get her own way with him. He never scolded Lillian, or sent her to her room, not even when she pouted or threw a tantrum.

When she was a child, Julia had borne punishments, such as having her ears boxed, or being caned, with fortitude. Lance had never been able to hold back his tears, but she had bitten hard on the inside of her cheek to keep herself from crying out, refusing to let her father see that he had won. As she became a young woman, with views of her own, she resented being chastised. Even more, she hated to see the way her gentle, pretty mother kowtowed to his authority, and never made a decision of any importance without consulting him first.

Although she was a very loving mother, Mabel Winter was first and foremost an obedient wife; she rarely voiced her own personal views, and never showed any temper or anger towards him. She carried out his orders to the letter – especially when it came to disciplining their children.

Their home was run to a strict timetable. They sat down as a family to breakfast at eight-thirty, luncheon was always at one o'clock precisely, and they assembled for their evening meal at half past six.

As a child, Julia had accepted this as the natural order of things. Then, as she grew older, she realised that her father's chauvinism had completely undermined her mother's self-confidence and, above all else, she discovered that he was not always right.

Their first major clash had come when she had discussed the Suffragette movement. Her father had been purple in the face with anger when she had repeated propaganda gleaned from her friend Alice Sandford.

After that, she had been forbidden to bring Alice to the house, but it hadn't affected their close friendship. As time passed, Julia had become more and more convinced that what Alice and her friends were fighting for was justified.

Nevertheless, she had felt relieved when Alice

13

had left home to take up nursing. She had hated deceiving her mother about her meetings with Alice, but she refused to be dominated by her father.

Now, or so it seemed, the subterfuge was to begin all over again if she was to go on seeing Bernard.

Chapter Two

The night before Bernard returned to his unit, Julia retired to her room early, complaining of a headache. She waited until her mother had brought her up an infusion of valerian to make her sleep, and then dressed again. She was so nervous that she could hardly fasten the tiny pearl buttons of her high-necked, cream blouse or the waistband of her dark blue skirt. Wrapping a black woollen shawl over her head and shoulders, and knowing the rest of the family would be gathered round the fire in the sitting room, she cautiously sneaked down the stairs and slipped out of the house.

Dusk had already gathered and there was a light rain falling. Feeling scared, yet resolutely determined, Julia picked her way between the puddles. As a sharp easterly wind whipped at her hair, which she had pinned up, threatening to undo it, she drew the shawl more tightly around her head and shoulders. March had come in like a lamb, but it was certainly going out like a lion, she thought shivering.

She had arranged to meet Bernard at the end of the road. For a second her heart pounded, and sweat rivered down the nape of her neck, as she saw a dark figure loom up beside the hedge. Cold fear gripped her in case it wasn't him. Then he spoke, calling her name softly. Breathing a sigh of relief, she ran towards him and flung herself into his arms.

'You're trembling,' he exclaimed, his voice husky with concern.

'I should have come to the house to meet you – how could I have been so thoughtless. It was just that I was afraid someone might see me hanging around and guess what our intentions were.'

'It doesn't matter, we're together,' she whispered. 'Don't let's waste a second of our time. Do you still have to go back to your unit tomorrow?'

'I'm afraid so, my darling,' he murmured as he gently stroked her hair.

She clung to him, pressing her face against his jacket so that he wouldn't know she was crying. He held her firmly for a moment, and then, gently taking her hand, led her down the road and on to the promenade. Two minutes later they were in the shelter of one of the beach huts, and she was once more enveloped in Bernard's arms.

'Are you really quite sure no one will find us here?' Julia asked with bated breath as, tremulously, she returned his passionate kisses.

'We're quite safe,' he assured her as he tenderly stroked her face and neck. 'My father has gone to a council meeting and Mother is entertaining some of her own friends. As long as I am back in the house for supper they will never miss me. What about you?'

'I told mother that I had a headache and I went up to bed early. I begged her not to let Lance or Lillian come up to my room and disturb me.'

'Then we have a couple of hours all to ourselves,' he breathed, his lips trailing kisses across her brow. 'Let down your hair,' he begged, his fingers deftly removing the pins that held it coiled high on her head.

As he fumbled to unfasten the buttons on her blouse, exposing the creamy flesh beneath, she made no protest. With her hair flowing over her bare shoulders, she felt as though all the barriers between them had been removed.

Quickly Bernard removed his jacket and grabbing a blanket that was on the wooden seat he spread it on the floor for them to lie on. She found her own fingers straying to the buttons on his shirt, toying with them, then undoing them, and slipping her hand inside to caress the warm smoothness of his hard body.

Their desire for each other was mutual. His breathing quickened as their caresses became more and more intimate, tension mounted until need overcame common sense.

Julia gasped with shock as their bodies were completely united for the very first time. The feeling of sublime sweetness that followed left her afraid to speak for fear of breaking the magic aura that surrounded them. She was highly aware that what they were doing was morally wrong, but she refused to listen to her conscience. Bernard would be going overseas any day now and she was as eager as he was that they should commit themselves to each other.

She felt tears of happiness trickling from the corners of her eyes as, passion spent, they lay there blissfully content in each other's arms.

Julia felt so deliciously alive that she wished time would stand still so that she could lie there safe in Bernard's arms for ever, but she knew that was impossible. Since it was the last evening of his leave, his mother would be expecting him to be home at supper time.

Reluctantly, they dressed and tidied themselves.

'One last kiss and then I'll walk you back as far as your front door,' he murmured, hugging her close to his long, lean body and pressing his lips gently against her brow.

'It might be safer if we said goodbye here,' Julia whispered huskily. 'Whatever happens we mustn't be seen together.'

'We won't be. There's no moon tonight so it will be pitch dark outside by now. I'll come with you as far as your gate.'

As they walked hand-in-hand, even their forthcoming separation couldn't dim the wonderment of the evening for Julia. Now, she and Bernard truly belonged to each other, and nothing her father or her mother said could ever take that momentous happening away from them.

'Are you sure you will be all right if I leave

you now?' Bernard asked anxiously as the Laurels suddenly loomed up in front of them, the curtained windows of the downstairs rooms glowing through the darkness.

'Yes, quite sure. I left the side door on the latch.'

His parting kiss was brief, ears strained for the sound of footsteps. He stood concealed by one of the laurel bushes from which the house took its name until he judged she was safely indoors, then he turned and walked away.

Julia found the first few weeks after Bernard had returned to his unit quite unbearable. Even hearing his name mentioned brought a flush to her cheeks and sent waves of burning heat through her. Her throat ached with the strain of holding back the tears which threatened to spill over at any moment as she waited anxiously for his letters, unable to understand why none came.

Hesitantly, she asked her mother if Aunt Agnes had heard from Bernard yet.

'She hasn't said so, but then I expect his days are full. When a crowd of young lads get together, they've far more to think about than writing home.'

Her words did little to set Julia's mind at ease. Uncertainty began to cloud the wonderful memories of the last evening they had spent together. Her elation gradually faded. Had she cheapened herself in Bernard's eyes by giving herself to him so readily, she wondered?

In her heart she knew this was not so, but in

the cold light of each new day, it was one of the many guilt-induced suspicions that tormented her.

As the April days lengthened, and flowers and trees burgeoned in the garden of the Laurels, Julia grew more apprehensive, and more wan and listless.

Her mother patted her arm consolingly whenever Julia enquired if there had been anything for her in the morning post. Mabel Winter couldn't bring herself to openly lie, and she wondered how long they could continue to withhold the letters and cards that arrived almost daily from Bernard.

George had promised his brother and his sister-in-law that they would destroy all correspondence the moment it arrived. But Mabel didn't feel justified in taking such a drastic step, so she had secreted away the unread letters, and all the daintily embroidered silk souvenir cards.

Both Agnes and Gregory Winter had been outraged at the thought of Bernard and Julia marrying. The consensus of opinion was that if they intercepted all letters between Julia and Bernard then both of them would think the other had lost interest and the affair would come to an end. Mabel hoped that in time Julia would think that Bernard had lost interest in her and so give up writing to him.

George was less optimistic. 'You should have done as I said in the first place and forbidden her to keep in touch with him.' He scowled as

Julia became more and more nervy and depressed. 'Then things would never have reached this stage.'

It broke Mabel's heart to see the affect all this was having on Julia, and she longed to be able to say or do something to help her. When Julia refused breakfast, she would take away the untouched food without a word so that her husband's attention wasn't drawn to it. Her eyes were full of understanding as she warned Julia, 'Don't let your father see you moping around the place. Why don't you and Lillian go for a nice walk?'

Walking with her younger sister, and having to listen to her girlish prattle, was the last thing Julia wanted to do. She spent every moment she could alone in her room, reliving the last precious moments spent with Bernard, reliving the thrill of his kisses, the wonderment of their love-making, those magical moments they had spent in each other's arms. Sometimes she asked herself if it had really happened, or was it a mere flight of fancy on her part?

At the end of the second month she knew it wasn't her imagination playing tricks, but that it was something far more serious. Each morning she found herself heaving at the sight of porridge and the smell of sizzling bacon.

She ached to confide in her mother about her condition but her courage always failed her. She was well aware of how horrified she would be because of the shame and disgrace it would bring on the whole family.

With each passing day, her problem became more acute. Her breasts felt sore and even seemed to be enlarged. She was sure, too, that she could detect a thickening of her waistline because her skirt was becoming uncomfortably tight.

Her mind in turmoil, she even toyed with the idea of committing suicide. She only held back because she thought the disgrace of that might be even greater than having a child out of wedlock.

There was only one other alternative, she told herself. She could run away!

But where could she go? Her savings amounted to only a few pounds, and if she went to family friends or relatives they would be bound to ask questions and, in no time at all, her parents would know about her predicament.

Julia decided there was only one person she could confide in, her friend, Alice Sandford. She wondered why she hadn't thought of her earlier. Alice had trained to be a nurse and might even know how to go about terminating an unwanted pregnancy.

The moment the thought entered her head she was swamped by guilt. Abortion, like marrying your first cousin, was a sin in the eyes of God, and illegal in the eyes of the law. It would be compounding her offence!

That night, when she undressed for bed, before she put on her night-dress, Julia studied her naked reflection in the full-length cheval mirror in her bedroom. She was still slim, but she must do something quickly, she resolved. In another month or two it would be impossible to hide her condition, no matter how tightly she laced her corsets.

The visit to see Alice wasn't quite the success she had hoped it would be. Alice was so involved in her new life that she hardly listened to what Julia was trying to tell her. Far from sympathising, or offering a solution, she seemed to think that Julia was intimating that she, too, wanted to become a nurse and encouraged her to enroll right away.

Thinking about it afterwards, Julia decided that perhaps becoming a nurse might be the perfect solution. If she could persuade her father to agree to let her do so then she could leave home without any explanation, or any of them ever knowing that she was pregnant.

She rehearsed what she would say to him. She would have to choose her time carefully. Perhaps one evening after dinner, when he was relaxed and mellowed by food and wine. She would wait until Lance and Lillian had left the room and then speak out in front of both her parents.

The telegram arrived a few nights later as they were finishing their evening meal. Hesitantly, her mother held it out to Julia who felt her heart pounding as her father intervened and took it from his wife's hand. He adjusted his gold-rimmed spectacles so that he could read the writing on the outside of the buff envelope.

'I think you'll find that it is addressed to me, Father,' Julia protested.

George Winter frowned. Using his table knife, he slit it open and drew out the small sheet of paper inside.

Julia bit down hard on the soft inside of her cheek to keep herself from screaming at him. What right had he to open it, or read it, she thought furiously. If the telegram was addressed to her, then it could only be from Bernard.

Her mind churned with all the promises Bernard had made the last time they had been together. Her heart raced. Perhaps Bernard had managed to get special leave so that they could be married before he actually went to the Front. Suddenly it made sense why she hadn't heard from him since he went away; he had been waiting until he had something positive to tell her.

Happiness and relief drowned her anger. The baby would be their secret. Once they were married there would be no scandal. Some people might consider it was premature, but there would be no harsh censure, no talk of illegitimacy.

Her father's next words stunned her. 'It concerns Bernard,' he said, looking over the top of his spectacles, first at his wife, and then at Julia. 'I'm afraid it's rather bad news . . . he's dead . . . killed in action at Ypres.' He frowned in Julia's direction. 'Terrible news . . . terrible.'

Julia felt as if the whole world seemed to be spinning wildly. A kaleidoscope of colours blurred her vision. Her mother's exclamation of dismay floated on the air, receding and advancing, over and over again, as though echoing through a long, dark tunnel. Griping waves of sickness filled Julia's mouth with bile. I mustn't faint, I won't faint! Determinedly, she willed herself to take deep, slow, breaths to quell the panic that threatened to envelop her.

'May I see?' Her voice croaked and her hand trembled as she held it out towards her father.

Without a word, George Winter passed the scrap of paper down the table to her. No one else spoke or moved.

'His poor mother,' Mabel Winter murmured, pushing back her chair and standing up. 'I must go to Agnes right away . . . would you like to come with me, Julia?' she asked gently.

'You may go after we have finished dinner, my dear,' George Winter said, authoritatively. 'However, I think it would be better if you went alone.'

'But Father . . .'

'I hardly think your Aunt Agnes will wish to be reminded of the discussions that went on between our two families the last time Bernard was at home,' he informed her coldly. 'I am most surprised that this telegram has been addressed to you.'

'Bernard told me he was going to put my name on his army documents as next-of-kin,' Julia admitted, flushing scarlet, and avoiding her father's eyes.

25

'Oh no!' her mother sank back on to her chair, pressing her hand to her lips in dismay. 'That means that the authorities may not have informed Gregory and Agnes that poor dear Bernard has been killed . . . only you!'

'I don't know about that.' Tight-lipped, Julia shrugged helplessly. She couldn't bear to think about Bernard being killed, much less talk about it. The thought of him lying dead in some muddy field in France, and knowing there was nothing she could do about it, stunned her senses. He might not even be able to have a proper burial!

'Oh, my poor dear sister-in-law, she will be heartbroken. And so will Gregory,' Mabel Winter gasped. 'Bernard was their only son . . . their heir!'

Julia tried to shut out the sound of her mother's wailing voice and the sight of her reddened eyes. No one seems to be concerned about how upset I am, she thought, resentfully.

When she'd not heard a single word from Bernard after he went back from leave, she had suspected that he had been sent to the Front. She had avidly scanned the newspapers, reading the accounts of the battles in France, to see if there was any mention of his regiment.

She wished she'd thought of writing to whoever was in charge of his regiment. Now it was too late, she would never have another chance. She would never see him again, never feel his arms around her. The sheer misery of knowing they would never make love again filled her with an anguish she couldn't bear.

In the days that followed, as the rest of her family openly mourned Bernard's death, Julia became more and more withdrawn. She stayed mute, grieving inwardly while presenting an almost indifferent manner. She felt estranged from everyone around her. It was as if a great tide of sympathy lapped round her mother, her aunt and her uncle, without ever touching her.

She wanted to scream, and shout aloud to the whole world, 'I loved Bernard more than any of you . . . and he loved me,' but she held back; stayed mute.

Although her mother and Lillian went into full mourning, and even her father and Lance wore black armbands, Julia refused to do so, claiming that Bernard had always hated seeing her dressed in black. She had more than Bernard's death to worry about. Their last night together, when for the first time they had completely given way to their deep passion, made Bernard's untimely death even more poignant for her. She remained tight-lipped, and dry-eyed, and retained a stoic silence whenever anyone mentioned his name in her presence.

'Really, Julia, you are behaving very badly, behaving in this way,' her mother chided. 'People are talking, you know. You might consider how the rest of us feel. After all, my dear, he was almost like a son to us.'

'Bernard could have been a son to you, he would have been your son-in-law,' Julia told her resentfully. 'You and Father didn't want that though, did you?'

Only when she was alone in her bedroom did Julia give full vent to her feelings. She sobbed into her pillow at night, not only because Bernard was dead, and she was expecting his child, but because she was faced with the dilemma of knowing that she was going to find it impossible to bring up her child single-handed and her need to get rid of the baby she was carrying was now more urgent than ever.

Forced by her family to accompany them to the remembrance service held for Bernard on the last Sunday in May, Julia knew that decision time had come. She could no longer pretend, not even to herself, that he would ever come back.

She wondered what Aunt Agnes would say if she told her that she was carrying Bernard's child. Even though it would be considered illegitimate, would it in some way comfort her for the loss of her only son? Could she depend on Aunt Agnes to support her through her pregnancy and help her raise Bernard's baby if it meant she supplied them with an heir? The thought of being subjected to Aunt Agnes's strict routine sent a shudder through Julia and she knew it would be foolish to even consider such a proposition and that she would have to find some other way out of her predicament.

She mulled over the matter for days, before

deciding that the only solution was to leave home. Uncertain about what her parents' reaction would be, she decided it was pointless to ask for their permission.

'I'm going to train as a nurse because I feel it is my duty to do so,' she announced boldly.

To her surprise, neither of her parents made any attempt to change her mind or to try and stop her. Her mother even went as far as to voice her approval. 'It's probably the sort of distraction Julia needs to help her to get over Bernard's death,' she told everybody.

Julia remained in a trance-like state as she made the necessary arrangements. She was accepted immediately. So many men had been wounded at Passchendaele and at Ypres, where Bernard had been killed. They were being brought back to England so there was a tremendous shortage of nurses.

On the day she left home to start her training, as she kissed her mother goodbye, the need to confide in her was overwhelming, but the words refused to come.

The moment passed. She turned away, choked by emotion, knowing that her familiar home life was finally over; nothing would be the same ever again.

Chapter Three

Had it been wise to let Julia leave home? Mabel Winter wondered as she went into her daughter's bedroom a week after Julia had announced her decision to become a nurse.

The room seemed cold and impersonal. It had already been thoroughly cleaned and aired, the bed stripped and covered by a dust sheet. It was as if she had gone for ever, Mabel thought sadly, the first of her chicks to leave the nest.

When Julia had announced her intention so quickly after the terrible news about Bernard, she had been too taken aback to argue. Her first thought was that it was an excellent idea for her to be doing something that would take her mind off her immediate grief, but after spending a number of sleepless nights thinking about it, she wasn't so sure. She was surprised that George had been so amenable to the idea. It was unlike him to give in to what merely seemed to be a hysterical whim on Julia's part.

When Julia had said she was going to become a nurse, he probably hadn't realised it meant that Julia would have to leave home. Like herself, he had no doubt been under the impression that

Julia had meant that she would be working at the local cottage hospital.

She had forgotten that Julia's friend Alice Sandford had left Wallasey after her training and so Julia would probably have to do the same. And, on top of that, Julia's decision to go immediately had been so upsetting. If only she could have persuaded her to delay her departure for a few weeks or so and go into mourning like the rest of the family. Openly flaunting convention was so unseemly; she knew Agnes was feeling it very deeply.

They had all been so distressed by the news of Bernard's death that, at the time, none of them was thinking or communicating too clearly. When Mabel realised exactly what was happening it had been too late. Julia had rushed into her enrolment with such haste that there was no time for any of them to counsel her and persuade her to think again.

Mabel crossed to the wide bay window and stood looking out at the peaceful scene beyond. Julia's room looked directly down on to the paved terrace where in summer, when the weather was warm, they took afternoon tea, or sat sewing or reading. Beyond that, there were sand dunes and the river Mersey, and in the far distance the misty purple outlines of the Welsh mountains.

The view was so idyllic that it was hard to believe that to the south, on the other side of the English Channel, a war was being waged;

a war that was taking from them the very cream of their young men.

Her heart ached for all those women who, at this very moment, were wondering exactly where in France their sons or husbands or brothers were, and if they were safe. Most of all, though, it ached for Agnes.

Life was hard, she thought sadly. Agnes had already lost five children. Two had been stillborn; the others had died within a few weeks of birth. Bernard had been a puny baby, but he had managed to struggle through a sickly childhood to become a strong, good-looking young man.

He was such a great solace to both Agnes and Gregory that it was too soon to know what effect Bernard's death would have on them both. For the moment, they were stunned, still unable to believe what had happened, or to fully comprehend that they would never see him again. She had watched her sister-in-law's face during the Remembrance Service, alert in case Agnes should suddenly faint, or break down and need to be helped from the church, but she had registered no emotion at all.

Having no body to grieve over put the whole incident into the realms of fantasy, almost, Mabel decided. She, too, found it hard to accept that someone as young and virile as Bernard should be lying dead somewhere in a trench in France.

Recalling their adamant refusal to even

consider letting him and Julia marry weighed heavily on Mabel's conscience. What they had determined was right and proper, but under the circumstances, perhaps they should have shown greater understanding. If only they had let him return to his unit filled with some hope for the future, then at least he would have died happy.

And Julia would have been able to grieve openly for him, not smother her feelings behind a mask of tight-lipped silence, Mabel thought sadly.

She suspected that Julia's decision to become a nurse was because of deep inward grief. She probably hoped that making a clean break would lessen the pain and help her to obliterate the memories.

She would find that exchanging the comforts of home life for the bleakness of a hospital dormitory was a daunting experience, but it was far too late now to change things, Mabel thought worriedly. She only hoped Julia would be able to handle the situation.

When she had mentioned it to some of her own friends at the weekly sewing circle, they had told quite harrowing stories of young girls they knew who had become nurses since the outbreak of the War. Most of them had been sent to hospitals full of men from the British Expeditionary Force who had been wounded in France, and they had been appalled at the horrors they had encountered. Their patients were often about their own age, young men who had been dreadfully maimed and injured. Some of these young soldiers were so badly shell-shocked that they were almost deranged.

With a deep sigh, Mabel Winter walked across to the wardrobe, opened one of the highly polished, mahogany doors and stood looking at the neat row of clothes hanging there. Wool and velvet winter dresses, bright crisp cotton blouses, silk and muslin summer dresses. Missing were her winter coat, navy skirt and a blue and white blouse which Julia had been wearing when she left the house, as well as a few of her everyday suits and dresses.

As she closed the wardrobe doors again it felt as if she were locking Julia out of her life. She went into her own bedroom, and from one of the drawers of the walnut escritoire, took out a bundle of unopened letters and cards that she had secreted there; correspondence from Bernard.

A deepening sense of despair because she and George had kept them from Julia flooded through her, and brought stinging tears to her eyes. As she spread them out over the quilted pink silk counterpane on her bed a feeling of guilt overwhelmed her because she had violated Julia's trust and privacy. She wondered what she ought to do with them. By rights, they belonged to Julia, of course, but to hand them over to her now would only reopen the wound. George believed she had already destroyed them, but she couldn't bring herself to do that, not even now.

Carefully, she rewrapped the cards and letters in a silk scarf that Bernard had once given her as a Christmas present, and locked them away again in her writing desk. Someday, when the war was over, and the pain of Bernard's death had blurred for all of them, she would perhaps ask Julia if she wanted them as a keepsake.

There was no knowing when that would be, of course. Far from the end being in sight, she thought sadly, the War seemed to be escalating. The battles at Ypres and Artois had cost the British Army dearly and they still hadn't taken Vimy Ridge.

Slaughter and carnage seemed to be uppermost in the minds of the Germany Army as they bombarded the French and British with guns and shells. Now that Italy was fighting against Austria–Hungary, and British troops were being diverted to Salonika, it looked as though the whole of Europe was to be involved in the bloodletting.

Mabel prayed the War would end soon, before Lance felt it was his duty to become a soldier. He was such a thoughtful, sensitive boy that now, with Julia enrolled as a nurse for war service, it wouldn't be long before he, too, would be wanting to do his bit for his country.

It was all very well the Government putting up posters of Lord Kitchener, resplendent in his uniform, pointing his finger and declaring 'Your

Country Needs You', but they seemed to be impervious to the heartache left behind when the young men did enlist.

Thinking of Lance brought her back to the present and the fact that he would be seventeen the next day. Normally they would have celebrated with a full-scale family party, but with Julia away, and Agnes and Gregory in mourning for Bernard, it didn't seem right to do so. Lillian would be disappointed, of course, since she loved dressing up in her prettiest dress, and having an excuse to thread coloured ribbons in her hair. Perhaps it would be all right if they celebrated quietly between themselves, Mabel decided. She would roast a plump chicken and make one of Lance's favourite puddings.

When they sat down to dinner there were three packages beside Lance's plate. As he unwrapped the one from his parents, and took the engraved silver wristwatch from its dark red velvet case, his blue eyes gleamed with pleasure. Lillian's present was a silk cravat which he admired immensely, going round the table to kiss her laughing face.

'Hurry up and open the other one,' she urged excitedly.

He picked up the long white envelope, and as he slit it open, a white feather dropped out on to the table. Lillian's eyes widened in dismay at the sight of it.

'Isn't that what they hand out to cowards?' she murmured, aghast. 'Does that mean someone thinks you are a coward, because you haven't joined the army, Lance?'

'Of course he isn't a coward,' her mother told her severely as their father carved the plump, golden chicken that Mabel had set before him. 'Now let's hear no more about it.'

For a moment there was a stunned, uneasy silence, then Lance pushed back his chair, his blue eyes filled with anger. Before anyone could say anything to pacify him, Lance had stormed from the room, slamming the dining-room door behind him.

Mabel jumped up from the table and rushed after him, but George called her back. She hesitated in the doorway, startled by the venom in Lance's voice as he shouted at her over his shoulder to leave him alone.

'Let him go!' George ordered curtly. 'The boy's becoming paranoid. It's high time he grew up and learned to accept criticism.'

Mabel sighed, but she returned to her place at the table without a word.

The moment they'd finished their meal and she'd cleared everything away, Mabel went to look for Lance, but he was not in his room nor anywhere else in the house, and she had no idea where he might have gone.

Mabel collected a warm shawl from her bedroom and went out into the garden to wait for him to return. Darkness shrouded the borders and a thin, crescent moon rose high over the laurel bushes that surrounded the front garden of the house. She was still there when George came looking for her and insisted she should come indoors right away.

'He's run away . . . to join up . . . I'm sure of it,' she said, voicing her fears aloud.

'Rubbish! Sulking somewhere, more likely. He's been inattentive in the office of late, so I'm given to understand. Restless, careless with his figuring, so my chief clerk tells me. I've been meaning to speak to him about it for days, but I've been too damned busy,' George Winter growled.

'Lance isn't sulking,' Mabel told him, her gentle face drawn with worry. 'He's so very unhappy. Bernard's death, and Julia leaving home to become a nurse, have made him feel he's not playing his part. Now this business with the white feather . . .'

'Poppycock! Stop imagining things,' her husband interrupted sharply. 'Damned nonsense! I don't wish to talk about it. If he has no more sense than to take notice of something like that, then let him go. A spell in the army might make a man of him,' he added, his voice rough with decision.

'Or, he might end up dead like Bernard!'

George Winter didn't answer. He took out his gold hunter and began to wind it up, as he always did before he retired for the night, comparing the time on the face of it with that of the clock on the mantelpiece.

'It's time we were all in bed,' he pronounced.

'Is the house locked up?' he asked as he returned the watch to his waistcoat pocket.

'I'm not going to bed until Lance comes home,' Mabel said in a small, determined voice.

'I see!'

For a moment she thought George was going to forbid her to wait up and braced herself for an argument. She had never in her life defied him, but on this occasion she felt she would be justified in doing so. Julia had already set an example.

Watching her daughter, head held proudly, not asking for their permission, but boldly telling them both that she intended to become a nurse, had made her realise that she was much too meek and humble. She had decided then that she ought to assert herself sometimes, express her opinions in a more decisive manner and not allow George to have the final decision over everything.

Sitting there on her own by the dying fire after George had gone to bed, Mabel began to think once more about Julia and her brave decision to become a nurse. It was so commendable that she was putting her own heartache behind her and not only making a fresh start, but also helping with the war effort. However, she couldn't help feeling anxious for her eldest daughter, and now there was this business with Lance. Her heart ached for both of them.

Chapter Four

The military hospital where Julia was told to report at the end of a brief training session at her local hospital in Wallasey seemed like another world.

The local hospital had been a pleasant two-storey building with flower beds on either side of the gravel drive that led up to the entrance. The place Julia had been sent to on the outskirts of Liverpool was a grim, three-storey building in red brick with narrow, barricaded windows and drab green paintwork. There was no garden, no flower beds, only a tarmac forecourt where the ambulances parked.

Julia felt that nothing was turning out like she'd expected. Her training had lasted only four days and consisted of a series of lectures in a temporary hut at the rear of the Wallasey hospital. A harassed middle-aged woman, who claimed to be a retired matron, had checked out her skills in bandaging and First Aid, asked one or two simple routine questions about hygiene, and then told her she was to be sent to a temporary military hospital midway between Liverpool and Southport where she was to report for duty on the men's surgical ward.

Tears pricked at her eyes as she put on the regulation dress of stiff, blue cotton, which chafed underneath the arms and around the neck, and fastened on the crackling white overall. She looked round the narrow, cell-like room that she was to share with another girl with distaste and felt homesick for her own spacious, comfortable bedroom.

As she struggled to fold the starched white square of linen into a regulation-style cap and pin it into place on her head, she wondered if perhaps she had acted rashly. The way things were turning out it looked as if she had made an even greater mistake than if she had told her mother the truth.

Anger and frustration against the whole world swamped her as she grappled with hairpins, trying to fix her cap in place. For one wild moment, she wondered what they would do to her if she walked out of the hospital and went back home to Wallasey.

No matter how carefully she folded and pinned it, the white square would not conform to regulation shape, nor stay in place. She was still struggling with it when a plump girl with shiny black hair came bouncing into the room.

'Hello, you must be the new arrival. Sister Granville sent me to look for you. You should have reported for duty over five minutes ago. Here, let me help.' She snatched the white square from Julia's fingers, deftly folded it, and was busy pinning it into place before Julia could even return her greeting.

'I'm Bridget Kelly,' the girl told her. 'I've been at this place for three months so if there is anything at all you need to know, then come and ask me.'

Her wide grin and infectious laugh lifted Julia's spirits. By the time she had answered Bridget's quick-fire barrage of questions and learned that Bridget came from Dublin, and that she was the eldest of six brothers and sisters, she felt as if they had known each other all their lives.

'Come on, you'll do. We'd better be getting back to the ward or Sister Granville will have the hide off both of us. Stickler for time, is Sister Granville, otherwise you can get away with murder, so you can.' She grinned, her blue eyes sparkling.

As they hurried down the corridor, the over-powering hospital smells made Julia feel queasy. Her first two hours on duty seemed to be spent handing out bottles and bedpans or collecting them up and emptying them.

On her first excursion into the ward, wheeling a metal trolley piled high with bottles and bedpans, she didn't know where to look and was glad that Bridget was with her.

Collecting them after they had been used was even more embarrassing, especially since some of the more seriously injured had to be helped off their bedpans and cleaned up before they could be tucked up in bed again. Despite the liberal use of carbolic everywhere, especially in the sluice room, the smell of urine, and worse, made Julia want to retch.

Her initial feeling of revulsion was soon forgotten, however, when she discovered that many of the men were not much older than she was, and that they were equally embarrassed at having to ask her for help.

Bridget Kelly was a tremendous support. No matter how many times Julia did things wrong, Bridget's smile never wavered and she never grew impatient.

When Bridget went off duty at midday, Julia wondered how she would get through the afternoon.

The rest of the day, however, was comparatively quiet compared to the morning rush when baths and dressings had to be fitted in as well as bed-making and the daily round by the surgeons and their retinue.

Once lunch had been cleared away, and those in need of bottles or bedpans attended to, the men rested until their evening meal was served. This was the last duty of their shift for the day staff. The night staff administered medicines when they came on duty and made the patients comfortable for the night.

By the time Julia came off duty at the end of her first day, she felt as if she had used every muscle she possessed and that every bone in her body ached.

As she followed the others to the hospital canteen for their evening meal she was sure she was too tired to eat. All she wanted to do was to lie down and sleep. Even the knowledge that the narrow bed was as hard as a rock, and that she would be sharing the small room with another girl, no longer seemed to matter. She had intended to write home and send her mother the address of the hospital, and explain that she'd not had time to come home on a visit, but once she had finished her meagre meal all she could think of was sleep.

The first three days were unbearable. A strident bell wakened them at six o'clock each morning. Then came the scramble to share the primitive washing facilities, and to get dressed before rushing to the canteen for a breakfast of lumpy porridge, bread and margarine and a mug of strong tea.

At seven o'clock sharp, there was an inspection by the Ward Sister before they started work. Such strict discipline made Julia feel more like a prisoner than a nurse.

Being the newest recruit, she found herself assigned to the more menial tasks. She soon overcame her revulsion of handling bottles and bedpans. Sorting out the putrid dressings, so that the bandages could be sent to the laundry, and the wads of cotton wool, stained with blood and yellowish-green suppurations, taken to the incinerator, was quite another matter. No matter how much she screwed up her eyes to cut out the unpleasant sight of what she was handling, the stench would assail her nostrils and make her stomach heave.

As the days passed, however, she found there were some compensations. One thing she liked was that when she wasn't on duty her time was her own to do as she pleased. No one enquired where she had been, or was even interested whether she went to her room and slept, or went off on her own somewhere.

For the first few days all she wanted to do was sleep, but once her system grew used to the hard physical work, and the new routine, her youthful energy returned and she looked forward to her free time just as the rest of her companions did.

'Why don't you come out with me and some of the other girls?' Bridget invited her, the first Saturday Julia was at the hospital. 'We often go into town together.'

'Thank you. Where are you going?'

'Oh,' Bridget made a wry face, 'here and there. First, we'll go into town and walk around the shops, looking at all the things we'd like to buy if only we had the money!'

'I see. And then?'

'It depends.' She crinkled up her dazzling blue eyes. 'Sometimes we get talking to some of the soldiers and go off for a drink with them. Or we might go to the NAAFI for something to eat, or even to a dance at the Catholic Church Hall. They hold them every Saturday night and they always let soldiers and nurses in free.'

To Julia it all sounded rather daring but she didn't say so. Instead, she accepted Bridget's invitation, secretly excited at the thought of flaunting convention so boldly, and wondered what her parents would say if they knew.

The evening wasn't a success. Julia was far too shy to mix freely with the young men they met, and seeing so many happy couples was a poignant reminder of her own loss. It was almost as if, for the first time since the telegram had arrived, the full impact of Bernard's death hit her forcibly. She couldn't believe that she would never see him again, never feel the warmth of his lips on hers, or his strong arms holding her close.

When Bridget and her friends said they were going on to the NAAFI canteen with the party of young soldiers they had been dancing with, she declined to go with them.

'My head is aching and so are my feet,' she explained apologetically. 'If you don't mind, I think I'll make my way back to the hospital. See you all tomorrow.'

They didn't try to persuade her to change her mind. Instead, they gave her instructions on how to find her way back to the hospital and laughingly called after her to remind her not to speak to any strangers.

It was beginning to grow dusk outside as she left the dance hall and goose bumps came out in a rash on her arms as she hurried along the streets, passing little knots of men and boys, many in uniform, who whistled, or called after her. She was almost at the hospital gates when a young sailor, who had drunk rather more than he could take, lurched up to her and tried to take her arm.

Terrified, she fought him off and began to run towards the hospital gates. Not to be put off he chased after her, grabbing at her arm so that she stumbled and almost fell.

In a blind panic she lashed out at him, but she was so frightened that her limbs felt as though they had turned to water. She had no idea what would have happened next had not a tall, imposing man intervened and beat the sailor off with his walking stick.

The sordid incident left her shaken and unnerved. Gulping her thanks, she looked up and recognised the angular raw-boned face of Sir Edward Wilberforce, a friend of her father's.

'Great heavens! Julia . . . is it you? What on earth are you doing here at this time of night?' he barked, his dark eyes questioning.

'I'm working at the military hospital.'

'You mean you're one of the new nurses? Your father never mentioned it the last time we had lunch together, and yet he knows I'm a surgeon there. I haven't seen you when I've been doing ward inspections.'

'I – I've only been here about a week. I haven't even had time to write home and let them know which hospital I've been sent to yet,' she explained.

He frowned. 'Well now, this is not a very good start, is it? You mustn't let it put you off being here, though. We need all the young nurses we can get. Are you sure you are all right now, or would you like a drink to steady your nerves?'

'No, Sir Edward, I'm quite all right now, really I am,' Julia assured him.

'Well, that's good.' His thin lips parted in a tight smile. 'Come, I'll walk back with you to the hospital to make sure you are safe. I don't like to think what your father would say if he knew you'd been molested. You really shouldn't go out at night on your own, you know.'

'I was with a group of other nurses only they were going dancing, but I felt too tired to go with them.'

'Hmm, I see! So does that mean you are you finding nursing hard work?'

'Yes . . . very hard,' she admitted with a rueful little laugh. 'I'm finding it's all very strange, especially having to share a room with another girl.'

'So you are feeling homesick?'

'A little.'

He left her at the entrance, raising his hat and giving her a stiff little bow before he turned abruptly on his heel and strode off into the night.

She fully intended to put the whole incident from her mind, and not to mention what had happened to Bridget. The next morning, however, after he had completed his ward round, and his retinue headed by the Ward Sister had dispersed, Sir Edward Wilberforce stopped outside the sluice room where she was working to ask her if she was all right.

Wide-eyed, Bridget cross-questioned Julia the moment he moved on. Covered in confusion, Julia explained that he knew her father and told her the whole story about what had happened after she'd left them all and set off to come back to the hospital.

Now that she knew that Sir Edward was working at the same hospital as she was, Julia found herself looking forward to his daily visits to the ward. She was far too unimportant to be in the retinue that accompanied him, but she would wait in the sluice room, or in the ward kitchen, in the hope of exchanging a quick smile, or receiving an encouraging word from him, as he left the ward.

Her early morning discomfort had disappeared since she had left home. She felt so well that sometimes she wondered if she had imagined herself to be pregnant and that missing a couple of periods had, after all, been a false alarm. She kept counting the days, hoping that perhaps she had been mistaken and that soon everything would be all right.

Her life had developed into a pattern that she was beginning to enjoy. Hard work by day, usually followed by a night of dreamless sleep, even though her narrow bed was like a rock and Bridget snored.

At the end of her first month at the hospital, when Sir Edward asked her if she would like to go for a drive into the country in his motor car, on her next afternoon off, she accepted.

It was a blazing hot July day, and even with the windows wound down it was stiflingly hot in the car as Edward Wilberforce drove his Morris Cowley away from Liverpool and they headed towards Southport.

'Come along, we'll walk along the promenade from here,' he told her when they reached the sea front. 'I know a delightful spot where we can sit and enjoy the view.'

As she looked at the expanse of dappled sand spread out before them it reminded Julia so much of home that she had a sudden feeling of panic about her situation. She realised there had been no reprieve and that already her figure was beginning to change. In sheer desperation, she told Edward Wilberforce of her condition and asked his advice.

For a moment he stared at her as if he couldn't believe his ears. Even when she went on to tell him that she and Bernard had been planning to be married on his next leave, he still seemed astonished by her news.

'Great heavens! What on earth were you and your parents thinking about allowing you to become a nurse if you are in that condition? When is it due?'

'I'm four months pregnant, but my parents don't know anything at all about it,' she added hastily. 'I couldn't tell them . . . not after Bernard was killed.'

'Then the sooner they do know the better. In fact, I feel it is my responsibility as a friend of your family to inform your father and tell him to come and collect you immediately,' he told her firmly.

'No! Please,' Julia begged him, 'you mustn't do that! I don't want them to know.'

'Nonsense! Of course I must tell them, it's my duty to do so,' he stated in a cold, pompous voice. 'Come,' he took hold of her elbow and began to steer her back to where his car was parked, 'I'll drive you over to Wallasey and you can do it right way.'

'Oh, no!' She pulled free. 'If I do decide to tell them, then it will be in my own way, not under pressure like this.'

He stared at her, his eyes hard and angry. 'Can I trust you to do so? If you haven't done so up until now, how can I believe that you will?'

Chapter Five

Julia spent a sleepless night. She was suddenly feeling rather fat and uncomfortable. Repeatedly she ran her hands over her stomach, conscious that her shape was changing and she no longer had an hour-glass figure. Her waist was now so much thicker that it was more or less the same size as the rest of her body.

Repeatedly she counted the months and days since Bernard's final leave when they had made love in the beach shelter on the Wallasey foreshore.

It had been March, late winter, now it was mid-summer. Four months ago; three months since the telegram had arrived saying that he had been killed at Ypres, almost two months since she'd left home to become a nurse.

If only she hadn't been sent to the military hospital where Edward Wilberforce worked, or if she simply had never encountered him, then things might have been very different, she thought resentfully. So far, no one there, not even Bridget Kelly, had the slightest idea that she was pregnant. With any luck, she could have stayed there for at least another couple of months which would have given her a chance to save up some money.

She realised that it had been very silly of her to blurt out to Edward Wilberforce that she was pregnant. He was bound to tell her father about her condition even though she'd asked him not to do so. He'd seemed to feel that it was his duty to do so, especially since she had admitted that her family knew nothing at all about it.

Perhaps it would be a good thing if he were the one to tell them, but she doubted it. It certainly meant that she couldn't go home now. They'd been outraged when she and Bernard had said they wanted to get married. To learn that she was having his child, out of wedlock, would be regarded as an even greater disgrace.

Even if she went crawling back and told them how sorry she was it was doubtful that they would let her stay there. It was too late now for them to insist on her having an abortion, but they certainly wouldn't allow her keep her baby. No, she thought wryly, they would send her away until after the baby was born and then they would arrange for it to be adopted. In their eyes it would be the only way to deal with the unbearable shame and to hide the truth from Lance and Lillian.

Julia remembered the fleeting idea she'd had at the memorial service they'd held for Bernard when she'd wondered what Aunt Agnes would say if she confided in her that she was pregnant with Bernard's baby. Was it now too late to throw herself on their mercy?

She toyed with the idea as she drifted in and out of sleep. Each time she surfaced she found herself trying to decide which were the dreams and which was the reality. There were times when she fantasised that she had told them. Not only that, but they'd welcomed her with open arms and told her that they were delighted. They'd insisted that she could stay with them until the baby was born . . . and live with them afterwards for as long as she wished.

Then, in the next drift of sleep, she was back in her own home, both her parents berating her over the disgrace she had brought on them and the rest of the family. They were insisting that the baby must be adopted, that there was no possibility at all of her keeping it, not even if she did have Aunt Agnes and Uncle Gregory's blessing.

One thing she wouldn't do under any circumstances, she resolved, was give up her baby because it was her last link with Bernard. They'd refused to let her and Bernard marry, despite the fact that they both loved each other so very much. They couldn't stop her from cherishing for ever the wonderful memories he had left behind, though, or the baby they'd made together.

What would their child look like, she pondered. Would it be a sturdy little boy with Bernard's square face, blue eyes and thick curly fair hair? Or would it be an auburn-haired, sombre-faced child with turquoise eyes like her?

It didn't matter, it was their baby, hers and Bernard's, and no one was going to take it away from her. She'd fight tooth and claw to keep the child, and bring it up. Her mind was pulsating with all the stories she would tell it about Bernard, a war hero, a man to be respected and with a reputation to live up to.

The problem of how she was going to do all this haunted her. It was all in the future and she had no idea what Fate had in store for her. If only she could go back home, stay there until the baby was born. More than anything she wanted to provide it with the sort of childhood she had enjoyed at her comfortable home in Warren Drive. Common sense told her that was out of the question, she'd burnt her boats and she had to make her own way in future.

She knew she couldn't stay at the hospital. Edward Wilberforce was bound to tell Matron about her condition. He would also ask her next time he saw her if she'd done as she'd promised to do and told her parents. She could lie, of course, but that was taking a great risk because he would be bound mention it to her father. He might already have done so, in fact, and told him where she was, she thought worriedly.

For how long could she manage to avoid Edward Wilberforce? She'd have to find excuses to ensure that she was well away from the ward when he was doing his rounds so that he had no opportunity to interrogate her and discover that she had not contacted her parents.

She wondered if she would be allowed to go on working there once Sister or Matron learned the truth. When they did it was more than likely that she would get her marching orders from Matron and be sent away in disgrace.

Perhaps, she thought, it would be better if she took matters into her own hands and left before they could drum her out.

She said nothing to Bridget as they got ready for night duty but decided to slip away without a word to anyone. She had only very few possessions so it would be easy enough to pack her holdall without anyone noticing what she was doing.

She would have liked to have waited until she'd been paid, but was convinced that wasn't practical. Fortunately, she still had most of the money she'd brought with her when she'd left home. It amounted to less than twenty pounds and unless she managed to find work right away it wouldn't last her very long.

She'd have to find somewhere to live and because she'd never had to do anything like that in her life before she had no idea how to go about it. She didn't even know how much it would cost her for a room in a hotel or even for bed and board in a lodging house.

She wouldn't go back to Wallasey, she resolved, but would stay on this side of the

Mersey. Liverpool was such a big city that it would make it much harder to trace her whereabouts. She'd find a place down by the docks to live. It would not only be easier to hide there but it would also be cheaper, too, so her money would last longer. She'd have to find work, perhaps some sort of casual job in a shop or some place where they didn't ask too many questions. It wouldn't be easy because she had no real skills or training of any sort.

For the rest of the night, instead of concentrating on her work on the ward as she should have been doing, she elaborated on her intentions like a spider weaving its web, deriving a feeling of hope and safety from planning the detailed intricacies.

Quite soon now the days would be getting shorter and in next to no time it would be autumn. She must get settled before winter set in because her baby was due in December, as far as she could work out.

She knew so little about these things. Perhaps she should go and see Alice again and ask her to explain what she ought to expect in the weeks immediately prior to the birth as well as afterwards.

She wasn't sure how long she would be able to go on working. She'd heard talk of women working right up until the minute their child was born, but they were usually the strong, brawny type. She didn't think that description fitted her. She was already beginning to feel tired and bulky and awkward. She didn't dare think what it would be like in a couple of months' time when she was really big.

Each time those thoughts came to her she pushed them firmly to the back of her mind. From now on she must take each day as it came. The important step was to get away from the hospital without anyone being aware of her intention to do so.

She imagined there would be a hue and cry when they found out that she was missing, but it would soon die down, she wasn't that important.

Apart from the inconvenience it might cause because it left the duty rota one short, no one would be very interested. She hadn't made any real friends, apart from Bridget.

Sneaking away from the hospital next morning was easier than she'd imagined it would be. When she and Bridget came off night duty she made sure that she ate every scrap of her breakfast. Porridge, toast with a scraping of margarine and a teaspoonful of marmalade. She thought longingly of the bacon and eggs, or kedgeree, that she could have had if she'd been at home. It was wartime, she reminded herself, and food was in such short supply that she was lucky to be as well fed as she had been while at the hospital.

'I'm so tired that I'm going straight to bed,' Bridget told her. 'It seems a wicked waste of a lovely August day because it looks as though the sun is shining and that it's going to be glorious out of doors. If we wake up early enough, shall we go for a walk before we have to go back on duty?' she yawned.

'That sounds like a good idea,' Julia agreed, yawning in unison with Bridget.

She waited until Bridget was snoring; a gentle rhythmic sound, then she pulled out the ready-packed holdall from beneath her bed and cautiously made her way out of the room, closing the door quietly behind her.

'Going home on leave, luv?' Julia jumped nervously as the soldier on duty at the hospital entrance gate grinned at her and nodded towards the holdall she was carrying.

'No, I'm taking my washing home,' she told him.

'Lucky to be living so close that you can do that,' he commented. 'Where is home, then?'

Julia hesitated, acutely aware that she must be very careful what she said.

'Between here and Southport.'

He nodded. 'If you hurry, you should catch the next bus, there's one due in about five minutes.'

'Thanks.' Julia smiled and headed for the bus stop a few yards up the road. The moment she was out of sight she crossed over the road and was just in time to catch a bus going in the other direction, not towards Southport, but towards Liverpool. She had no idea where to get off so she told the conductor, 'As far as you go.'

'Where's that then, luv? Do you mean the Pier Head?'

Julia nodded and handed over half a crown, not sure how much the fare would be.

The conductor punched out a ticket and then delved into the leather satchel strapped across his chest for the change, counting it out carefully into Julia's outstretched hand.

As the bus rattled its way through the centre of Liverpool and began to head downhill towards the Mersey, Julia stood up impulsively and made her way towards the door.

'I thought you said you was going all the way to the Pier Head, luv,' the conductor muttered indignantly, pulling on the overhead wire to signal the driver to stop.

'This is near enough,' Julia told him.

'Well, if you'd said it was the Exchange Station you wanted, then you should have said so and it would have cost you a penny less. Don't blame me that you've been overcharged.'

'I won't.' Julia smiled.

As the bus lurched to a stop she ran down the steps and out on to the road, heading blindly towards the station. Then she stopped in dismay. She had no idea why she was there or why she had suddenly decided to get off the bus.

For one fleeting moment she toyed with the idea of taking a train to the Wirral. If she did, then in ten or fifteen minutes she would be at Wallasey Village station. From there she only had to walk along Harrison Drive and in no time at all she would be back home in Warren Drive.

Was that the right thing to do? She took a deep breath, should she return to the fold, to the safety of her family home, the companionship of her brother and sister, go back to the safety of the sort of life she had always known?

There would be a heated scolding from her parents, but she would be taken care of until the baby was born and they'd arrange for the child to be adopted. In six months' time her own life would be back to normal. She could put it all behind her like a bad dream and start 1916 as though nothing untoward had ever happened.

She was tempted. It was such an easy way out. There would be no more discomfort or hardships, no money problems. She could pick up the threads of her own life so easily.

Then the memory of being in Bernard's arms, of their love for each other and the precious memento he had left behind in her care, stiffened her resolve to stand on her own two feet.

Picking up her holdall, she hurried away from the Exchange Station area into Great Crosshall Street and then turned left, trudging along the busy street and staring around her at the tightly packed, scruffy-looking houses. It was the sort of area her family would describe as slums, she thought wryly, and the very last place they'd think of looking for her.

All she had to do was find a small hotel. Her parents only ever used the imposing new Adelphi or the Stork Hotel in Queen Square so they would never dream of looking for her in this part of Liverpool.

Chapter Six

'Is something the matter, Sir Edward?' Sister Granville enquired anxiously when, for the third time during his ward inspection, Sir Edward Wilberforce mopped at his brow with a crumpled white handkerchief.

'No. No!' he rasped. He stared at her balefully, his dark eyes hooded as he wondered how to broach the subject of Julia Winter's pregnancy that was uppermost in his mind.

'I . . . I thought that perhaps you, too, might have fallen victim to gastritis. Another of the nurses, Nurse Winter, has gone down with it this morning. She has not been here very long, Sir Edward, but I think you know her?' she added as she looked at him questioningly.

'And you say she is suffering from gastritis?'

'Well, I can only assume that is why she didn't report for duty. Bridget Kelly, the nurse who shares a room with her, had the same problem yesterday, and this morning I was told that Nurse Winter was unwell, so I assumed—'

'Assumed . . . you assumed that was what was wrong with her! For heaven's sake, it could be the start of an epidemic,' he retorted scathingly as he strode out of the ward.

As he stalked down the corridor he silently cursed himself for making an issue of Julia's absence with Sister Granville. The bush tele-graph would already be relaying his outburst and making what they could of it.

He knew only too well that gossip and tittle-tattle spread like a prairie fire. By now, Sister Granville would already be scuttling off to Matron to inform her that he was in a foul mood. She'd report not only what he had said, but the tone of voice he had used when speaking to her as well, he thought grimly.

In all probability Matron would take it upon herself to go along and check if Nurse Winter really was suffering from gastritis and what would happen if she found out the truth?

Sir Edward scowled darkly, thrusting his clenched fists deep into the pockets of his white hospital coat. It really wasn't his problem, but he couldn't help feeling some responsibility since Julia was the daughter of one of his oldest friends.

He could only trust that Julia would have the courage to do as she had promised and return home and explain her condition to her family. He chuckled inwardly. Gastritis indeed!

He checked his watch. It was almost eleven o'clock. Perhaps if he joined Matron when she took her mid-morning coffee he would have an opportunity to broach the matter. At least it would give him a chance to clear the air about the way he had spoken to Sister Granville. Perhaps he had been a little harsh.

Without giving himself time to change his mind, he strode down the corridor that led to the administration offices and knocked on her door.

Matron made no secret of the fact that she was quite surprised to see him. Her welcome was cordial, but she looked at him questioningly. They were colleagues of long-standing, but they could hardly be said to be friends. She was a strict disciplinarian and approved of his methods because they dovetailed neatly into her way of doing things. She was also impressed by his title and now she visibly preened because he had deigned to visit her office without an invitation.

He felt his spirits reviving as he sipped his coffee and ate two of the digestive biscuits she offered him.

After they had exchanged trivialities, it was obvious she was curious as to why he was going out of his way to pay her a social visit.

'Sister Granville tells me there is an outbreak of gastritis amongst her nurses,' he began.

Matron froze. Her hard brown eyes became glistening beads beneath her frowning brows.

'I know nothing of this.' She pushed aside her coffee cup, picked up a sheaf of papers from her desk, and riffled through them. Her frown deepened.

'Is she referring to the two nurses absent from duty on her ward this morning?' She looked down at the paper. 'Nurses Kelly and Winter?'

'I believe those were the names,' he said blandly.

'Gastritis, you said?'

'She could be wrong.' He shrugged deprecatingly. 'I hope she is. With so many sick men . . .' Deliberately, he left the sentence unfinished. His stare held Matron mesmerised for a moment.

'I must look into this.' She consulted her list again. 'They share the same room . . .'

'Quite so!'

'I wish this had been reported to me earlier, when there was a house-doctor free.'

'Please, Matron!' He held up a hand. 'I'm the one who has raised the question, so the least I can do is check the situation out for you.'

'You, Sir Edward!' Her amazement showed in her wide-eyed surprise.

'Why ever not? I am a fully qualified doctor,' he said with a touch of irony.

'I'm sorry, Sir Edward.' She bit her lip in confusion. 'That must have sounded very rude . . . especially when you were trying to be helpful. I'll investigate the matter immediately,' she told him crisply.

He stood up smiling. 'I'll come with you,' he stated, walking towards the door.

'There's really no need!' She held up a hand to stop him accompanying her, but Sir Edward was adamant.

'I've taken up quite enough of your morning as it is, and this may be a false alarm,' he murmured as they set off in the direction of the nurses' quarters.

Matron's knock was brusque. She flung open the door without waiting for an answer. Bridget, who was just getting out of bed, gawped, her bare legs dangling in mid-air, as she clutched the bedcovers to her chin.

Sir Edward's gaze raked over her dismissively as he looked around the room.

'Where is she, then?' he demanded.

'You mean Julia – Nurse Winter?'

He nodded. 'She reported sick. Gastritis, the same symptoms as you are complaining about.'

Bridget shook her head, looking bewildered. 'No, I don't think so. She told me she had asked for a day off so that she could go home and visit her mother,' she said quickly, hoping that the sudden rush of colour to her cheeks didn't give away the fact that she was covering for Julia. 'It was her mother who was unwell, not Julia,' she gabbled.

Sir Edward gave a short, hard laugh, turned on his heel, and walked out. Julia had fooled them all. He frowned as he strode down the corridor alongside Matron as they headed back to her office. He wondered if he ought to explain to her the probable reason for Julia's absence; at least it would set her mind at rest if she knew there was no fear of a gastritis epidemic breaking out in the hospital in the immediate future. Why the hell had Julia Winter turned up at his hospital? he thought irately.

He was due to lunch at the Club with Julia's father later in the week and before then he'd have to reach a decision about whether or not to tell him exactly what was going on. Knowing George Winter as well as he did that wasn't going to be easy. With his high moral standards he was going to be absolutely outraged when he was told that Julia was pregnant.

Edward thought back to a conversation they'd had a few months earlier when George Winter had been deeply concerned about Julia wanting to marry her cousin Bernard. He'd never seen a man so incensed. The matter had resolved itself when Bernard had been killed in battle. That had been a sad state of affairs, but in some ways quite fortuitous as far as George and Mabel Winter were concerned.

Now this, the fact that Julia was pregnant, would be a devastating blow for them. Thank God he himself had never married so he had no children of his own to worry about, Sir Edward thought wryly. Even so, he felt it was his duty to acquaint his lifelong friend with the facts as he knew them, whether it meant betraying Julia's confidence or not.

He only hoped that Julia really had done as her room-mate had told him and that she had taken the day off to go home. With any luck she would have broken the news to them herself which would make his task that much easier. In fact, he wrestled with his conscience, perhaps he need do nothing at all. She was hardly likely to mention his name to them so they need never know that he knew. Or would she?

Matron was tight-lipped when he told her the real reason why Julia Winter hadn't reported for duty that day.

'This is quite outrageous, Sir Edward! She has broken every one of my rules and told lies into the bargain.'

'She's very young, and this is her first experience of being away from home,' he said placatingly. 'She was probably very homesick, as well as overcome by guilt at not having told her family about her condition.'

'Nevertheless, she has still flaunted the rules,' Matron expostulated. 'Pregnant indeed! She probably only decided to become a nurse to get away from home so that her family wouldn't know the truth.'

'You are possibly right, but I think she should be treated leniently, however. The chap she was planning to marry, and who is without doubt the father of the baby she's carrying, was killed in battle a few months ago.'

'Really? Are you sure about that, or is it just a trumped-up tale she's spread around?'

'It is quite true, Matron,' he affirmed gravely. 'I am a close friend of her father's.'

'Oh!' Her hand flew up to cover her mouth. 'You should have said so earlier, Sir Edward. I may have unwittingly said some things about Nurse Winter which were better left unsaid.'

He smiled graciously. 'Don't give it another thought, Matron. Quite rightly, you spoke your mind which is understandable when your authority has been flouted.'

'I do apologise, Sir Edward. I wouldn't dream of criticising any friends of yours.' She stood up and moved towards a cupboard and brought out a bottle. 'Perhaps you'll join me in a sherry,' she suggested tentatively.

He assented affably. 'That would indeed be most acceptable, Matron.'

He smiled inwardly as he noticed that her hand was shaking as she placed two glasses on the desk and filled them.

He drained his glass and smiled acceptance as Matron took it from him and raised her eyebrows enquiringly.

'A delightful amontillado,' he murmured as she refilled his glass with the pale amber liquid. He held it up and watched as the sunlight gilded it.

'You know, Matron,' he murmured thoughtfully, 'I think it might be to everyone's advantage if Nurse Winter doesn't return to this hospital. There are bound to be rumours. The nurse she shared a room with may well have been aware of her condition and might even have been covering up for her.'

Matron sipped her sherry thoughtfully. 'We are very short of nurses.'

'I agree, but she wouldn't be able to work here for very much longer, now would she?'

'No, that is very true.'

'It might be detrimental for the reputation of this hospital to let her stay,' he added in a more determined tone when he saw she was about to dissent.

Matron gulped her drink. 'I'm sure you are right, Sir Edward, we'll do whatever you think best. After all, our wards are full of young soldiers and, as you say, we don't want any scandal. The only problem is, where can we send her?'

Sir Edward drained his glass and stood up. 'I don't think we need trouble ourselves about the outcome, Matron. I'm sure that if Nurse Winter has gone home today then once she has explained her condition to her family they certainly won't let her come back here. I am sure we can rely on them to take good care of her and sort things out in their own way.'

Chapter Seven

Mabel Winter was far more worried about Julia than she cared to admit. She knew her eldest daughter was headstrong and liked her own way, but she was also aware that she had very little experience of what living in the real world was like.

How could they possibly allow her to marry Bernard when they were not only cousins but first cousins! Surely, if either of them had thought seriously about the matter, they would have realised that it was quite impossible for them to do so.

As it was, Fate had stepped in and the matter had been taken out of their hands. It was such a terrible solution, though, that Mabel wished she could wipe it all from her mind. Bernard had been only three years older than Julia and to have his life snuffed out so brutally was cruel beyond words.

She leaned closer to the mirror as she patted an extra dab of powder to her cheeks. She frowned, dissatisfied with the result. No matter how hard she tried, or how much make-up she applied, it was impossible to cover up the puffiness of her eyes, or the fact that they were red-rimmed from crying.

George seemed to be able to put the fact that they'd had no news of Julia since she'd left home completely from his mind, but she couldn't. She was sure that Julia's disappearance was related to something more than Bernard's death.

If only there was someone she could talk to about it, somebody she could open her heart to, knowing they would understand the stress she was under.

George would be horrified if he found that she mentioned the matter to anyone outside the family. Which meant the only person she could confide in was Agnes and she was already consumed with grief over Bernard so it would be cruel to burden her any more.

Yet, in some ways, it concerned Agnes almost as much as it did her, Mabel reflected. Her mother's instinct told her that Julia was in some sort of deep trouble and she sensed that could only mean one thing . . . that Julia was pregnant!

She had no idea how it could have happened. Julia had always been chaperoned whenever Bernard called. They hadn't been left on their own for a single moment. If she hadn't been in the room with them herself, then either Lillian or Lance had been there. The same applied if Julia and Bernard ever went for a walk; they'd never been allowed to do so on their own.

If only George would discuss the matter with her.

To some extent she could understand Julia's reaction. She was sure that dashing off to become a nurse was her daughter's way of dealing with her terrible loss, but it was foolhardy nevertheless.

She could understand Julia feeling she wanted to do something to help the war effort. She even felt like that herself some days when the news from the Front was particularly grave.

If only she had talked things over with them in a rational manner, they could have worked out some sort of plan that would have been acceptable and far less harrowing.

To defiantly declare her intention to take up nursing in the way she had done, almost daring her father to oppose her decision, had been foolhardy and Mabel was still surprised that he hadn't opposed her action.

From what he had said when he heard Julia had left, she gathered that George was quite certain that the underlying influence was Alice Sandford. She had been a bad influence on Julia since the day they'd met. All her silly chatter about the Suffragette movement, trying to make out that women should be regarded as equal to men, was flying in the face of tradition.

'Everyone knows that a woman's place is in the home, looking after the family, nurturing and caring for children, not out in the workplace demanding recognition and equality with men,' he'd stated forcibly. 'Such revolutionary ideas turn the world upside down and only result in bad feeling between men and women. Furthermore, they undermine the man's sense of responsibility. As head of the household it is a man's job to earn money to keep his family in comfort. A woman is expected to be in the home where she can nurture her loved ones. They are two completely separate roles.'

Saying she was going to train to be a nurse, of course, was a devious move on Julia's part. Nursing was considered to be women's work; there was no argument about that. Julia was very aware of this and no doubt had relied on it to avoid an argument with her father, knowing that he could hardly object to her doing good work of that kind. Using that and Bernard's untimely death she had managed to get her own way as usual, Mabel thought despairingly.

Was she nursing, though? That was the question Mabel Winter kept pondering. Somehow she didn't think so. Even though she had reported for training at their local hospital she wasn't there now and there had been no word from her to let them know where she had been sent.

Mabel had made numerous enquiries, hoping to find out Julia's whereabouts. She'd intended either to write to her or visit her in the hope that perhaps she would be able to persuade her to reconsider her rash decision and to come back home again.

'Yes, Mrs Winter, she certainly reported here to Victoria Hospital, but she was here less than a week and then posted to a military hospital,' she was informed.

'Without undergoing any proper training!'

Her gasp of surprise had brought a wry smile from the sister. 'She was given four days' training, that is all the time we can spare. There is so much carnage in France; our boys are coming back by the shipload. Some of them are so horrendously wounded, that we need all the nursing staff we can get – whether they are fully trained or not.'

Trying to repress her shiver of horror, Mabel had asked which hospital Julia had been sent to, but that was something the sister refused to divulge.

'I'm afraid that is something I can't disclose,' she was told firmly. 'You'll have to ask the military authorities for that sort of information.'

Mabel realised she should have done this in the first place, but she also knew that she had already overstepped the mark, and if George found out that she'd been making enquiries, he would be furious.

'She's taken her life into her own hands, so her future is entirely up to her. I don't wish to discuss it any further,' had been his final words the night Julia had left home.

Mabel knew better than to argue with him, or even plead. She needed more subtle methods if she was to glean the information she wanted.

She'd waited patiently for the right moment and his announcement over breakfast a few weeks later that he would be lunching with his friend Sir Edward Wilberforce had provided her with a tremendous opportunity, one she'd taken full advantage of.

'You won't forget to ask him how his new military hospital is coming along,' she prompted.

'Yes, yes! It's not *his* hospital, though, you know, Mabel. He's only the head surgeon.'

'Oh, I thought he was on the Board of Governors.'

'It's a hospital, woman, not a school; they don't have a Board of Governors.'

'I should have said "Trustees",' she corrected herself meekly. 'My mind was wandering. I was wondering if perhaps that might be the military hospital where Julia has been sent to work.'

'Julia!' He frowned, almost as if he didn't know whom she was talking about. 'I doubt it,' he said irritably. 'It's far more likely that she's chased off after that Alice Sandford.'

'Well, perhaps Alice is there as well, it might be worth asking him.'

George had scowled, but she was sure that deep down he was as concerned as she was about where Julia was and whether or not she was safe. She suspected that he, too, would like to have her back home with them.

Nevertheless, he dismissed her suggestion out of hand. 'Good heavens, Mabel, a man in

Edward's position isn't going to know the name of every nurse who works in the hospital. They're minions, nothing else.'

She didn't argue, but she knew she'd sowed a seed and that now it was implanted it would fester. He'd mention it to Edward, she was quite sure. All she had to do was be patient.

George Winter was late arriving at the Wirral Club in Liverpool's Rodney Street. Edward Wilberforce had already ordered himself a dry sherry and was ensconced in one of the luxurious leather chairs in the club's well-appointed Members' Room.

They were lifelong friends, having first met at the age of ten, when they were both shy little new boys at their preparatory school.

During their early years they'd been inseparable; it was only after they left the school that their paths had started to diverge. There had been a gap of several years while Edward had been away at medical college, years during which George had been absorbed into the business world associated with shipping and exports and imports. The bond forged in their youth had remained, however. The moment Edward had taken up a post of junior doctor at Liverpool University Hospital they'd re-established contact. Ever since then their monthly luncheon had become an almost unbroken ritual.

They occasionally met at other functions as well. From time to time Edward enjoyed a social evening at George's home in Warren Drive. They were, in fact, almost as close as brothers and, although Edward had never married, he had taken a cordial interest in George's family.

Normally, it was one of their first topics of conversation. Edward would enquire after the family and George would recount the latest news, changes, developments and the state of their health before they went on to other more interesting and diverse topics.

Today, however, George sensed that Edward was more withdrawn than usual, almost taciturn, as if he had his mind on other things.

George put it down to problems caused by the War. It was challenging all of them in one way or another. Trade was fluctuating by the minute. Shipping was affected in so many ways. Loss of key men, loss of cargoes, even loss of ships. It should have been over long before now instead of which it seemed to have accelerated. More and more lives were being lost in France as well as those involved in shipping.

Although supplies of food were somewhat curtailed because of the War, they were still served with an acceptable meal at the club. The well-stocked cellar, built up over many years, was not yet depleted and so they were not only able to enjoy their favourite wine, but also a glass of vintage port to follow.

Well mollified by the food and drink, George remembered his wife's veiled suggestion that he should ask Edward if Julia had joined his new military hospital as a nurse. Now mellow and relaxed, he decided there was no harm in doing so although he was sure that if Julia was there, then Edward would have mentioned it as soon as they'd met.

Or perhaps he was not supposed to disclose such information and that was why he was so edgy, he thought shrewdly.

He approached the subject in an indirect way, leading their talk round to Edward's increased duties as chairman of the trustees responsible for the new hospital.

'We all have to do what we can,' Edward said dismissively, sipping at his port.

'Some take on a heavier load than others,' George commented. 'This patriotic spirit seems to be dominating all our lives.' He gave a forced laugh. 'Why, even my own daughter has felt the call of duty.'

Even as he uttered the words he realised that, for the first time ever, Edward had not enquired about his family. Simultaneously he sensed his friend's unease as he drained his glass of port and prepared to leave.

Despite his own brusque dismissal when Mabel had suggested that Edward might be able to give them news of Julia, he was alerted by his friend's demeanour. They'd known each other too long and too closely for him to hide his unease.

'Come on, Edward, out with it, man. Tell me what's on your mind . . . what you know. Is Julia working at your hospital? If she is, then it would set Mabel's mind at rest. She finds it extremely distressing not knowing where Julia is.'

Edward cleared his throat. 'Well, she was there,' he admitted uncomfortably.

'Was?' George Winter frowned.

Sir Edward nodded. Words of explanation seemed to lodge in his throat as he stared uneasily at George.

'Was?' George repeated. 'Where is she now, then?' he persisted.

Edward shook his head. 'I've no idea. No one at the hospital knows,' he added quickly. 'She left without a word of explanation so it is no good asking anyone else there.'

George scowled. 'Why on earth should she do a thing like that? Was she in some kind of trouble? Come on, tell me what you know. Julia never was very good at obeying orders. What did she do? Ruffle Matron by answering her back? Something of that sort, I'll be bound.'

'No, it's far more serious than that, old chap! Your daughter is pregnant . . . I take it you didn't know,' he said sharply as he saw George's mouth drop open in shock.

George Winter spent the afternoon locked away in his office, pacing the floor as he tried to sort out in his mind the news Edward had given him about Julia.

He'd never been in such a quandary in his life. How could he go home and tell Mabel such shameful news?

He could understand now why Julia had been so keen to marry Bernard before he went back to France. Young blackguard! He should have been horse-whipped. Taking advantage of a young innocent girl was unforgivable.

He found it hard to believe. He wondered what his brother Gregory was going to make of the situation. Agnes would be devastated, he thought gloomily.

What made matters even worse was that Bernard was dead. He couldn't even defend himself or explain how things had reached such a disastrous state.

George blamed Mabel that they were in this predicament. She'd been far too lenient with Julia. She should have explained these things to her, made her aware of what danger she could be in from a hot-blooded young man like Bernard.

Young Julia had been so unworldly. Thinking herself to be in love, she'd probably had no idea what was going on, not until it was too late and the damage was done.

Young rogue! Picked up his kit-bag and was on his way once the deed was done!

Though that wasn't completely true, he reminded himself. Bernard had begged to be allowed to marry Julia. They'd been the ones who'd turned him away. He'd been outraged by the idea because they were first cousins, but they had all been equally shocked.

He delved into his waistcoat pocket and

brought out a slim gold case. Selecting a cigarette, he brought out a matching gold lighter from another pocket and lit up. He drew on it deeply, savouring the flavour, feeling its steadying effect on his jaded nerves.

This was only the tip of the iceberg, he reminded himself. He might know the truth but no one else in the family did. Should he tell them, or should he keep the revelation to himself? He could visualise the impact it would have on his brother and his wife, not to mention Mabel, who'd be absolutely hysterical.

He paced restlessly, trying to resolve the best way of dealing with the situation. It was unlikely that Edward would say anything. He had been embarrassed, so much so that he didn't think Edward would come to their home for many a long day, so there was no fear of him relaying the news to Mabel. Gregory and Agnes barely knew Edward. Gregory, being almost five years older than him, had never mixed with his brother when they'd been boys.

By the end of the afternoon, George Winter's mind was made up. The chances of Julia coming back home were pretty slim, he reasoned. If she'd intended to do so, then she would have returned immediately after she'd left the hospital. According to Edward, that was at least two weeks ago.

He wondered fleetingly where she was and how she was managing, and then he hardened his heart. The girl was trouble. She'd defied him as she so often did and she deserved whatever was coming to her.

As far as he was concerned, she was gone from their lives for ever. From now on he'd forbid the rest of the family to ever mention her name too. Mabel might be heartbroken by his decision but she'd obey him, she always had. Julia had been the rebel, the only one who'd ever dared to oppose his wishes.

Well, that was all in the past, she'd defied him for the very last time, he resolved.

Chapter Eight

There were so many side streets that in no time at all Julia found herself utterly lost. She wasn't even sure if she could find her way back to Exchange Station. She would need to ask directions from someone.

She'd noticed that the further she wandered the more grim and depressing the houses seemed to become. Some of the side streets seemed to be little more than alleyways. Many of the courts, as they appeared to be called, had high tenement houses built around three sides of a small paved yard.

Most of them were cluttered with litter and had strings of washing stretching across the yard from one side to the other. Men and women were sitting on the doorsteps of many of the houses, or leaning against the grimy walls, gossiping or smoking, while raggedy children played at their feet.

Occasionally Julia was aware that someone was looking her way and a frisson of fear went through her in case they asked her what she was doing there. No one did, they only stared disinterestedly and carried on with whatever they were doing.

Finding a small hotel, Julia decided, was not going to be as easy as she'd anticipated. Perhaps it would be better if she returned to the Exchange Station where there were bound to be plenty of small hotels.

She didn't want to go anywhere near Lime Street because the Adelphi Hotel was so close by and that was where her father frequently went for lunch with his business associates. It was in the same area as the Wirral Club used by Edward Wilberforce and he was someone else she was anxious to avoid.

They certainly wouldn't frequent any buildings in this area, Julia thought wryly as she started to walk along Everton Road.

It was at that moment that she spotted it: the Darnley Hotel. The notice outside claimed that it was a Commercial Establishment catering for Families, Travellers and Businessmen.

The hotel had a stuccoed front that had once been cream, but was now so grimed by soot and smoke that it was as grey and depressing as the sky overhead. Julia studied it for several minutes before she plucked up the courage to walk towards the stone steps leading to the black front door that was wide open as if ready to welcome all comers.

'It's better inside than it looks from out here, luv,' a man's voice said encouragingly.

Julia swung round, startled to find that a tall, skinny young man, wheeling a bicycle with what looked to be a pair of ladders, a bucket and an

86

assortment of chamois leathers tied on to the crossbar, was watching her.

He gave her a lopsided grin. 'I thought I'd mention it because you seemed unsure about whether to go in there or not,' he explained, his brown eyes twinkling.

'So, you've stayed here have you?' Julia asked.

He pushed his cap to the back of his head and his face turned red with embarrassment. 'No, I haven't exactly stayed at the Darnley, but I have been cleaning the windows here for Paul and Eunice Hawkins ever since I was a nipper so I do have a pretty good idea about what the rooms are like and so on.'

Julia smiled. 'You're a window cleaner!'

'That's right. Looking after the business for my old man,' he told her with a touch of pride in his voice. 'Reynolds and Son, but my dad went into the army almost eighteen months ago so I'm carrying on single-handed. I'm Bob, by the way, Bob Reynolds. I expect I'll be called up any day now,' he went on garrulously, 'so I don't know what will happen to the business then.'

'This war has changed all our lives,' Julia said sadly.

'Yes, even for young ladies like you,' he answered with a cheeky grin. 'When us men go into the army then you have to take over our jobs. I've not seen any women becoming window cleaners, well, not as yet, anyway. You're not by any chance looking for a job are you, miss?'

'I am, but not as a window cleaner,' Julia

laughed. 'I'm also looking for somewhere to stay while I look for work. Have you any suggestions?'

Bob Reynolds puffed out his cheeks. 'Whew! That's a tall order, luv. Well, as I said, this place is first class, but you might find it a bit pricey.'

Julia nodded thoughtfully.

'Probably have to pay as much to doss down here for one night as you'd pay for a whole week in a room in one of the streets around Scottie Road.' He looked her up and down appraisingly. 'I think this would suit you better, though.'

Julia frowned. 'Well, I can afford to stay a couple of nights here and that will give me a chance to have a look around the area. Thanks anyway for your help.'

Picking up her holdall, she moved decisively towards the hotel. What on earth was she doing having a heart-to-heart with a window cleaner? she asked herself.

The entrance lobby opened into a medium-size foyer with a high-fronted reception desk. It was unmanned, but there was a brass bell on the counter top and a printed card propped up against it that read 'Ring for Assistance'.

Julia hesitated. On the counter top there was another printed card giving details of the facilities available. Tentatively she studied it, trying to work out how many nights she could afford to stay there. A single room was two pounds a night, but she had no idea if that was reasonable or not.

The only way she could find out would be to go along to somewhere like the Adelphi or the Stork and see what sort of rates they charged. Remembering the plush interior of the Adelphi when her family had all been taken there for dinner on the occasion of their parents' Silver Wedding celebrations, she was pretty sure that their charges would be a great deal more than they were asking at this place.

'Can I help you?'

Julia jumped. A middle-aged man wearing a grey pin-stripe suit which emphasised his portly figure had suddenly materialised from nowhere and was standing there, fingering his thin pencil moustache and looking at her enquiringly.

Julia took a deep breath. 'Yes, I wanted a room,' she stated.

'I see. And would that be a single room?'

'Correct.'

He hesitated. 'We normally accommodate businessmen or families.' He frowned, running a finger around the stiffly starched collar of his white shirt. 'How many nights would you be staying?' he asked when she made no comment.

'I'm not sure.'

His thick eyebrows lifted questioningly. 'I assumed you were only staying overnight, that you were possibly in transit between Liverpool and . . . ?' His voice trailed off as he waited for her to complete the details.

He seemed to be discomfited when she made no answer.

'Being wartime we do occasionally get the unaccompanied wife staying for one or two nights while waiting for her husband to return from overseas,' he commented.

Julia remained silent. She resented his probing, then, in a sudden rush of exasperation, she decided to give him a reason why she was there. 'I'm thinking of moving to Liverpool to live,' she told him primly, 'so I need somewhere respectable to stay while I take stock of things here.'

'I see.' He pursed his lips. 'So you'll be staying for several weeks, then?'

Julia looked uncertain. 'I'm really not sure. Your hotel was recommended by . . . by a friend, Mr Hawkins. I was planning to find a job first and then somewhere permanent to live,' she explained. 'I imagine it will be easy enough to find employment; so many men have been called up there should be plenty of openings.'

Again Paul Hawkins's eyes narrowed as he studied the expensive cut of her clothes. 'It depends on what sort of position you are hoping to find. You don't look like the sort of young lady who would want to work in a munitions factory.'

Julia drew herself up stiffly. 'If I consider that to be the sort of work that is most suitable, then naturally I shall take a pride in helping the war effort,' she said pompously.

Paul Hawkins nodded solemnly. 'It wasn't what you had in mind, though, was it?' he asked.

'No,' Julia admitted, 'I was thinking more of working as a replacement for a man who had been called up. Serving in a departmental store, or as a clerk in one of the shipping offices, something like that.'

'You have experience of that sort of work?'

She frowned haughtily. 'Does it matter? At the moment I'm looking for somewhere to stay, so I hardly think my employment qualifications are of any importance.'

'Forgive me.' He smiled ingratiatingly and reached down to a shelf under the highly polished counter and brought out the hotel register, laying it with a flourish on the counter top.

'Perhaps you will be good enough to sign this and add your name and address, if you please.'

Julia frowned. 'Is that necessary? I am only renting a room for a couple of nights.'

'I'm afraid it is compulsory.' He reached behind him and took down one of the keys hanging on a board. 'Perhaps you would you like to see the room? It will be two pounds a night. All meals, including breakfast, are extra.'

Julia did some quick calculations. She'd have to eat, and from the prices she'd seen on the menu, if she ate here, she would only be able to afford to stay three or four nights. Would she be able to find suitable work in that time?

'Provisionally I'll say two nights. If I wish to stay any longer, then I'll let you know.'

He nodded gravely and held out his hand for

her holdall which she had put down by her feet. Then he paused. 'If you will sign the register first, I will show you up to your room.'

Julia picked up the pen, her mind working overtime. She dare not give her Wallasey address in case anyone decided to come looking for her. Hurriedly she signed her name and then added an imaginary address in Southport.

The room was small and sparsely furnished. A single brass bedstead covered with a beige candlewick bedspread was pushed up against one wall and what little space remained was taken up with a tallboy and a matching wardrobe in dark oak. There was also a cream Lloyd Loom chair and an oblong nondescript rug in dark blue the same colour as the plain cotton curtains at the small narrow window.

'Is it to your satisfaction? You'll find the bathroom and the lavatory further along the landing,' he told her as he handed over the key to the room.

Julia nodded. 'Thank you, Mr Hawkins. It will do quite nicely for two nights.'

'Then perhaps when you have acquainted yourself with the facilities, Miss Winter, you will come back to the reception desk so that I can show you where the dining room and the guests' lounge is situated.'

'Thank you.'

As soon as he had gone, Julia sat down on the edge of the bed and took stock of her surroundings. It was smaller than the room at the hospital but at least she wouldn't be sharing it with anyone else. She wondered what was happening back there. By now Bridget Kelly would have raised the alarm that she was missing and everyone would know.

She didn't think that anyone would be very concerned about her absence. Matron or Sister might be annoyed because it would mean that they were a nurse short and their rota was ruined. Apart from that, Bridget would be the only one who would really be concerned about her. And Edward Wilberforce, perhaps. She hoped that he would think her absence was because she'd gone home to explain everything to her parents.

As far as she knew he only met her father about once a month so, with any luck, she would have found work and moved into a place of her own before her father learned that not only was she pregnant, but that she had also run away, she thought confidently.

In order to do that she'd better start looking right away, she told herself briskly. First, she must get a job and then she must find somewhere permanent to live. Or should it be the other way round. She frowned at her reflection in the small cheval mirror standing on top of the tallboy as she smoothed her hair into place, noticing the worried expression on her face.

What on earth had she got to worry about, she asked herself. She was free of them all now. No one knew where she was, and apart from Edward Wilberforce, neither did they know that she was expecting a baby. He might never mention the fact to her father. After all, it was none of his business and now that she had left the hospital he might decide that it would be better for all concerned if he didn't become involved.

The future was in her hands. It was up to her to find work and somewhere to live. Once that was taken care of then she'd have to make all the necessary arrangements for the baby and for caring for it after it was born.

Perhaps that was why she looked so troubled, she thought ruefully. She had absolutely no idea how she was going to go about doing all those things and there was no one at all she could ask for advice.

Which was most important? she asked herself again. She'd thought getting a job, but now perhaps it was finding somewhere to live. The sooner she economised on what she was spending on accommodation the better. From what the window-cleaner chap had said, she could probably rent a room for a month on what she was paying to stay here for even one night.

Bob Reynolds kept thinking about the girl he'd spoken to outside the Darnley Hotel and wondered if she had decided to stay there or not.

If she hadn't looked so worried, she'd have been a real smasher with her bright russet-coloured hair and those vivid blue eyes, he mused.

Dressed in such smart clothes and with her

posh way of speaking she wasn't a bit like any other Judy he'd ever met and he wished he could see her again and get to know her better.

He'd never had a real girlfriend, he reflected as he turned into Old Hall Street and began to set his ladders up against the windows there, leastways, not one he'd ever taken home. He knew his mam would fly off the handle if she thought he was serious about any of the young bints in the Scottie Road area.

Even though he'd lived there all his life, she seemed to think that their family was a cut above the rest. Believed in keeping herself to herself, did his old lady, preferring the cat for company rather than any of the neighbours.

She'd been in service out at Blundelsands when she'd met his dad. He'd called to clean the windows at the house where she worked as a parlour maid and for some unknown reason she'd accepted his invitation to walk out.

His dad had been a bit of all right in those days; he'd seen a snapshot of them both all togged up in their Sunday best and looking like real toffs.

The trouble was that his mam still seemed to think she was a toff. Bit of a snob and no mistake. No one was good enough for her. Daft, really, to have airs and graces like that and still be living in Skirving Street.

Mind, their house stood out from the rest, it always had with its starched net curtain and donkey-stoned step. She was so damned house proud that she even put down newspapers on the Axminster runner in the passageway, from the front door to the living room, if there was the merest spot of rain outside.

Indoors, everything had to be just so. She was fanatically tidy; everything had its right place and had to be in it, including him and his dad.

That's why he'd never taken a girl back home. His mam would have grilled her all about her background until the poor bint was stiff with fright. His mam would be watching everything the girl did, from drinking a cup of tea to putting her coat on, and would then comment about it afterwards.

Now this one, though, he reckoned she'd be the apple of his mam's eye. She looked the part and spoke as though she'd been educated like a proper lady.

He looked at his reflection in the window he was cleaning and laughed to himself. A Judy like that was hardly likely to be interested in a scruffy window cleaner, even if he did wear a clean shirt every day and his boots were always polished. No, she'd be looking for an ambitious office chap dressed in a smart suit and stiff white collar, someone who worked from nine to six and came home looking as dandy as when they'd left in the morning.

Still, he thought as he moved his ladders to the next window, he could always dream.

Chapter Nine

Julia didn't unpack. She stowed her holdall away in the wardrobe, locking the door for safety and taking the key with her.

Paul Hawkins was back at the reception desk when she returned to the foyer. 'Right, Miss Winter,' he greeted her effusively as she handed in her room key, 'I'll introduce you to my wife, Eunice, and she'll show you the dining room and—'

'Later, if you don't mind, Mr Hawkins. I am already late for an appointment.'

'Very well, Miss Winter, when you return, then. Dinner is served at seven-thirty. We would like to know in advance if you wish to join us,' he added, looking at her expectantly.

Julia frowned, remembering the prices she'd seen on the hotel menu. 'I'm not sure if I will be back by then. Probably not,' she added apologetically.

She turned away quickly before he could reply. She needed air, fresh air. There was a claustrophobic atmosphere about the hotel and she wanted to be outside, away from this pompous, pretentious man and his rather ingratiating manner. She wanted to be able to think through the steps she had already taken and plan what her next move was going to be and to do that she needed to be on her own.

Once outside, Julia found the keen breeze coming off the Mersey helped to clear her head. The jumble of thoughts about what she'd done and her future slowly began to divide into tidy heaps. She'd told nobody at the hospital that she was leaving, so hopefully no one from there would be able to trace her whereabouts.

Concentrating on the months ahead was of paramount importance. Soon, very soon indeed, everyone would be able to tell at a glance that she was pregnant, so her first necessity was to find somewhere permanent to live. She also needed a job, but who was going to employ her if they realised her condition?

She tried to think what she was going to be capable of doing. She wouldn't be able to manage heavy work, or lifting of any kind. Even stacking shelves in a shop or factory was probably unwise since it was bound to involve lifting heavy boxes. Serving behind a counter might be acceptable, for a few months. An office job would be far better. Somewhere where she was sitting down most of the time and where she didn't have to come into contact with any customers would suit her nicely.

Julia had been so engrossed with her thoughts that she'd paid no attention to where she was walking. Now she found herself in a maze of small streets. Most of them appeared to be dirty, dingy-looking streets and dreary litter-strewn courts even worse than the ones she'd seen earlier in the day.

Panic-stricken, she looked for street names, but none of them meant the slightest thing to her. The faster she walked the more she realised that she had lost her bearings completely and that she seemed to be walking in circles.

Shivers ran through her as she realised she had no idea how to get back to the hotel. She knew it was in the region of Tithebarn Street and Crosshall Street, but how far away was that? This was such a mixed area. She shuddered as she saw the sort of people who lived in the grim houses and the sordid courts that were built cheek by jowl with stinking factories. They were all so shabby, the men with mufflers around their necks and the women with black shawls wrapped around their shoulders. Most of the children were either barefoot or wearing scuffed old boots with their toes hanging out.

For a poignant moment she had an overwhelming longing to be back home in Wallasey's Warren Drive with its imposing detached houses divided by neat hedges and the pleasant views of the Mersey just beyond the sand hills.

Even her mother's constant fretting, her father's overbearing manner, Lillian's peevish jealousy and Lance's youthful brashness suddenly seemed to be merely endearing traits.

Scrubbing away the threatening tears with her gloved hand, she pulled herself together and tried to concentrate on the street names. There was no need to panic, all the streets must lead to a main road sooner or later. And all the main roads led down to the Mersey. All she had to do was decide which was a main road and then follow it downhill to the Pier Head. Once she reached there it would be easy to walk back up Tithebarn Street and locate Exchange Station and her problem would be over. She wasn't lost, only slightly disorientated.

Finding a main road was not as easy as Julia had expected it to be. Panic was once again building up inside her. People were looking at her rather strangely as she hurried from one street corner to the next, peering up at the name plates, hesitating and then setting off again.

She felt a tremendous relief when she spotted a man with a bicycle that had ladders balanced precariously on it making his way up one of the side streets. She hoped it was the window cleaner, Bob Reynolds, the young chap she'd spoken to earlier and who'd recommended the Darnley Hotel. In desperation she called out to him.

Hearing his name shouted, he turned his head, hesitated, waved back to her, and then continued on down the road.

'Bob, Bob Reynolds! Wait for me, please. I need to ask you something!' she yelled breathlessly, breaking into a run.

'Hello, I thought you were staying at the

Darnley, so what are you doing around here?' he asked in surprise as she caught up with him.

'I . . . I came out for a walk, to take a look round, but . . . but I've lost my way,' Julia gulped.

'I'll say you have.' Bob grinned. 'So what do you think of what you've seen up to now?'

Julia's mouth tightened as she sensed he was laughing at her. 'I'm looking around because I want to find somewhere to live,' she told him primly.

Bob pushed his cap further back on his head and looked puzzled. 'I thought you'd found somewhere. Don't you like it at the Darnley, then?'

Julia shrugged. 'It's quite suitable, but I can't afford to stay there permanently. Mr Hawkins charges two pounds a night and that doesn't include breakfast.'

He nodded solemnly. 'That is a bit steep. I'll ask around tomorrow when I'm on my rounds and see if there is anything going,' he promised. 'Just a room, is it?'

Julia nodded. She hated the idea of having to live and sleep in the same room, but she knew that it was all she could afford, for the moment. 'I want somewhere clean and respectable, remember,' she stated firmly.

He grinned. 'I get the picture, you don't want any bed-mates!' He laughed at her bemused expression. 'I'm talking about bedbugs,' he explained.

'So what time will you come to the hotel to let me know what you've found?'

Bob hesitated. 'That's not such a good idea. Mr Hawkins is a good customer. Me and me dad have been cleaning his windows there for four or five years. He mightn't like it if I gave one of his clients another address.'

'He knows I'm only staying for a couple of nights while I look around for somewhere permanent.'

'Yeah, but even so . . .' Bob said reluctantly.

'Oh all right, I'll meet you somewhere away from the hotel. What about outside Exchange Station?'

'Yes, that sounds fine!' Bob gave her a cheery smile. 'Say five o'clock, then, shall we? That'll give me most of the day to see what's what.'

Julia smiled gratefully. 'Now, can you tell me how I get back to the hotel from here?' she begged as Bob swung his leg over his bike ready to ride off.

'Are you telling me that you are lost?'

'I am,' Julia admitted.

His lips shaped into a soundless whistle. 'And I thought you were calling after me because you liked me,' he teased. 'Come on, then, I'll walk with you as far as the corner of Tithebarn Street and you'll be able to see the hotel from there.'

He looked at her sideways as they began to walk along the road. 'If you don't know anything at all about the Scottie Road area, then why on earth do you want to come and live

102

here?' he asked in a puzzled voice. 'You don't look like the sort of Judy who lives round this way.'

Julia's mouth tightened into a thin straight line. She was on the point of telling him that it was none of his business, but in the nick of time common sense stopped her from doing so. He was the only person she really knew in Liverpool to talk to so it wouldn't do to antagonise him. It had been an incredible stroke of luck finding someone so kind and helpful.

Paul Hawkins was still behind the reception desk checking over a pile of invoices when Julia walked back into the Darnley. He greeted her effusively.

'Ah, Miss Winter, you are back! Does this mean that you will be joining us for dinner this evening after all?'

Julia hesitated, conscious of her need to make her money go as far as possible. Then, as a feeling of hunger assailed her and she remembered that she'd had nothing to eat since breakfast at the hospital almost twelve hours earlier, she nodded. 'Yes, I will be eating dinner here,' she agreed.

'Good!' He beamed at her. 'Then please come this way and allow me to show you where the dining room is and which will be your table.'

He came from behind the reception desk and led the way towards a door at the far end of the room, which he opened with a grand flourish. The dining room was quite small. There were four round tables, all large enough to seat four or five people and six smaller ones each laid for two diners.

Julia noticed that the white tablecloths were crisply starched, the wine glass at each place setting sparkled and the cutlery was neatly aligned.

She nodded approvingly. 'Very nice.'

He pointed to a small table at the far side of the room. 'That is your seat, Miss Winter. Table Number Five, the same as your room number. All right?'

'Yes. Thank you.'

'Seven-thirty promptly, Miss Winter, we'll see you then. Now, I would like to show you the lounge where coffee will be served after dinner.'

The lounge was much larger than the dining room. There was an assortment of individual armchairs and two-seater settees. Some were upholstered in moquette and a couple of them in dark green leather.

At the far end of the room was a fireplace and halfway down the room was a piano. Some rather dull oil paintings, mostly seascapes, adorned the walls and there were heavy brown velvet curtains at the two bay windows. The floor was carpeted with Axminster patterned in brown, yellow and dark green. Someone had attempted to make the room inviting but there was an air of stiff formality about it that was far from welcoming.

Julia suppressed a shiver of distaste as she looked around and there was no enthusiasm in her voice as she once again murmured, 'Yes, very nice.'

Upstairs, in her single room, Julia wondered what she was doing there. She felt unbearably homesick. Nothing was turning out as she had hoped. At that moment she would have given anything to be back home in her own bright sunny bedroom with its pretty flowered curtains, its soft feather bed and all her treasures collected over the years.

She lay down on the bed and rested her head on the lumpy pillow, closing her eyes and shutting out her dreary, unfamiliar surroundings.

Back at home her mother would be clearing away the dishes after their high tea and Lillian would be helping her to wash up. Her father would be sitting in his favourite chair, reading the *Liverpool Evening Echo* and smoking his one cigar of the day. Lance would probably be upstairs in his room doing his homework or strumming discordantly on the guitar he was learning to play.

Well, she was freed now from all that stifling routine, she told herself. She was living her life in her own way, able to do exactly what she wanted without anyone commenting, criticising or offering opinions that she didn't want to hear.

She didn't dare contemplate what her parents would have said if they knew about her condition. Well, by leaving home, she'd avoided having to hear all that, she told herself. Anyway, it was more than probable that they would have sent her away because of the disgrace the moment she'd told them about the baby, so all she'd done was forestalled them.

Memories of Bernard flooded her mind. He'd been so handsome with his shock of fair hair and eyes as blue as the sky on a summer's day. She would never forget their last meeting when, for the first time, they had overcome their scruples and given way to the passion that had been so powerful that they could no longer deny their urgent need to make love.

She'd never dreamed that she'd become pregnant right away. It seemed impossible since it was the one and only time they'd gone the whole way.

Why, oh why had Bernard been sent overseas so soon after returning to his unit? To be killed within weeks of reaching France was so cruel. She wondered what he'd had to endure during that time. She didn't know if he'd had to live in a hut or in a muddy trench. There might even have been shells exploding all around him. Perhaps that was why he had never written to her, not even sent a postcard.

She wondered if he had been frightened, whether she had been in his thoughts. Had he recaptured the wonder of those precious moments of their last night together, had their lovemaking meant as much to him as it had to her? Above all, she kept wondering what

Bernard's reaction would have been if he'd known that he was to be a father.

If only her parents had tried to be more understanding. She'd never forgive them for the things they'd said or the many obstacles they'd put in the way when Bernard had told them that they wanted to be married.

Pulling herself together, she stood up and fished around in her handbag for the key to the wardrobe. Taking out the holdall she'd stowed away in there, she unpacked her toiletries and went to look for the bathroom.

She felt refreshed after washing her face and cleaning her teeth. Back in her room she changed out of the clothes she'd been wearing all day and into the smartest of the dresses she'd brought with her, even though it was creased. Then she combed her hair and applied fresh make-up, daringly outlining her mouth in bright red lipstick.

She studied her reflection in the full-length mirror in the wardrobe door, noticing how good she looked in her pale blue silk dress. At the moment no one seemed to have guessed her secret, and she intended to try and keep it that way until she had found herself a job.

Chapter Ten

Dawn was painting iridescent streaks of blue and grey light over the rooftops before Julia finally fell asleep.

She had been so utterly weary that she'd expected to fall asleep the second her head touched the pillow. The moment she closed her eyes, though, her mind seemed to become incredibly alert. All her many doubts and fears for the future surfaced like fish jumping for flies.

She refused to admit, even to herself, how foolish she'd been to have burned her boats quite so hastily. She even wondered whether, if she had told her parents about the baby, they might have accepted the situation after all. Aunt Agnes and Uncle Gregory would possibly have welcomed the thought of a grandchild, someone to carry on Bernard's name.

Common sense told her that such a solution would never have worked. Aunt Agnes would have taken control and Julia would have been pushed to one side, told she was too young, too inexperienced to know how to bring up a child. Without Bernard there to take her part and convince them that she was quite capable of doing so, what would she have been able to do? She hated not being the one in control and her frustration in a situation like that would have been unbearable.

Repeatedly, she kept telling herself that she had done the right thing. Taking matters into her own hands, leaving home and letting them think whatever they wanted to about her had been by far the best course.

Her father always claimed that she was head-strong and would have had no sympathy with her predicament. She was not like his precious little Lillian, who, in his eyes, was the perfect daughter; petite, sweet, lovely to look at and docile. She'd watched him stroking Lillian's shiny fair hair almost as if she was a kitten or a pet rabbit.

Lance was too young to understand all the implications so it was unlikely that he would have supported her. No, she assured herself, she'd done the right thing. Everything would look brighter and sort itself out once she'd found a job as well as somewhere to live, and she was self-sufficient.

The morning was overcast and Julia wondered what she should wear to go job hunting. She had changed her mind and decided to look for a job first. The trim black costume that she wore when she went to work in her father's office, though rather formal, seemed to be the most suitable – although she was afraid it might make her appear rather conspicuous.

As she'd walked round the nearby roads the previous evening she'd noticed how shabby everyone was. Most of the women, even quite young ones, were wearing shawls instead of jackets. Some had even been bare-legged and many of the kiddies who'd been kicking a ball around had even been barefooted.

Bob Reynolds, the window cleaner, had been wearing grey trousers, a grey flannel shirt open at the neck and with the sleeves rolled up to the elbows, and a sleeveless knitted waistcoat on top. She wondered if he always dressed like that or whether he smartened up when he wasn't cleaning windows.

She hunted through the few clothes she had brought with her and finally settled on a light blue cotton skirt with a matching jacket which she teamed with a plain high-necked white cotton blouse. It was neat, but not too smart.

She picked up her handbag and her gloves, then paused and put the gloves back into the drawer, smiling to herself as she did so. She didn't think that many of the people living around here wore gloves, especially white ones.

Before she left the room she checked how much money she still had. Two nights were the maximum she could afford to stay at the Darnley. Once again she decided that finding a room was even more important than finding a job.

For almost two hours she tramped from one street to the next, but there wasn't a 'Room to

Let' sign to be seen anywhere. Back in Wallasey, there had always been plenty of 'To Let' signs. Not in Warren Drive, of course, but in many of the less imposing streets, especially in the Liscard and New Brighton area.

She had no idea what else to do. She'd asked at one or two of the corner shops if they knew anyone who might let out a room, but the moment she started speaking she was met with hostile stares almost as if she was a foreigner.

By midday she felt footsore and hungry. A mug of tea and a bacon butty in a small greasy café in Scotland Road partially revived her and strengthened her resolve to find both a job and somewhere to live. Since she'd had no success in finding a room, Julia decided that she would concentrate on getting a job.

She tried to work out what she was capable of doing and glumly admitted to herself that it didn't amount to very much. She'd worked as an office clerk but it had only been spasmodically and for a short time. Since it had been in her father's office it had been in a very minor role. She'd done some nursing, but even taking into account her training, it had only been for a few weeks and she'd only been doing what other people told her to do. She had no references and there was no one to recommend her in any way.

She walked over to the greasy counter, paid for her food, and, squaring her shoulders, walked out into Scotland Road. She stood there on the pavement taking stock of the shops that lined the road on both sides. There was every sort of business imaginable; shoe shops, milliners, ladies outfitters, pawn shops, butchers and bakers. Surely one of them had a vacancy, she told herself. She started systematically working her way down the road.

After making eight fruitless calls and being told that either they couldn't afford an assistant because trade was bad, or that it was a family business and they didn't employ any outsiders, Julia felt desperate.

She wandered along aimlessly, unsure of what to do next. Since there seemed to be no vacancies at any of the shops in and around Scotland Road, factory work was the only alternative. She had no idea what was involved, but then, she told herself, she hadn't known what working as a nurse was going to be like and yet she had managed to cope with it. She'd still be there if it hadn't been for Edward Wilberforce, she thought bitterly.

She paused for a moment to sit down on a wooden seat inside Chapel Gardens while she decided what to do. The sun was blazing overhead and she felt both weary and drowsy. Once again she felt tempted to go back to the pleasant life she'd enjoyed at home and throw herself on the mercy of her family. Then the thought that her baby might be taken away from her if she did, made her resolve to stay away from them and stand on her own feet.

The sound of bird song brought her out of her reverie and she looked round her in surprise. She couldn't see any birds at all in the few trees in Chapel Gardens.

Rousing herself, she started to walk in the direction of the sound and found herself standing outside a building surrounded by trees. Hanging from their branches were a number of cages full of little greyish-brown birds.

Puzzled, Julia looked to see if it was some sort of botanical building connected to Chapel Gardens and was surprised to read *Throstle Nest Hotel* inscribed above the door. She smiled to herself, remembering that the word throstle was the old name for the song thrush.

'Sing well, don't they, luv?' a man commented. He was carrying a glass jug and proceeded to walk from one cage to the other, filling up the water dishes inside each one.

'They're lovely. Are they yours?'

'I suppose you could say that. There've always been throstles here, that's why the hotel's name is what it is.'

'And you own the place?'

He shrugged his wide shoulders. 'I'm the landlord. Why do you ask?'

'I was wondering if you had any vacancies . . . for staff, I mean,' she blurted out, colour rushing to her cheeks.

He shook his grizzled head. ''Fraid not, luv. You looking for work, then?'

Julia nodded. 'Yes. I thought it would be easy

to get a job, but I've tried at dozens of shops and they all say trade is bad or that they're family businesses.'

He looked at her speculatively, his sharp brown eyes studying her shrewdly. 'You don't look the right sort to work in a factory, but that's where the jobs are at the moment. With the men being called up they've had to take women on to replace them.'

Julia frowned. 'Are there any factories round here looking for staff?'

'I'm sure there are, but I couldn't really say. I do know, however, that Cairn's Brewery a few streets away have started taking on women. You could give them a try.'

'Thank you.'

'Ask to speak to Mrs Barker,' he called after her, 'she's the forewoman there.'

It took Julia all her courage to walk into Cairn's Brewery. The huge red brick building, with its central tower rising like a massive chimney, was very noisy and there was an overpowering smell of malt.

'Whatcha want, chuck?' A brawny woman wearing a sacking apron over her own floral apron, the sleeves of her drab grey dress rolled up to the elbow, demanded in a loud voice.

'Are you Mrs Barker?'

'What's it to you?'

'I was told to ask for her because she's the forewoman and I'm looking for work.'

The woman sniffed disparagingly. 'Ever worked in a brewery before then, luv?'

'No,' Julia admitted reluctantly, involuntarily squaring her shoulders.

The woman looked her up and down disdainfully. 'You don't look as if you know what work is, certainly not factory work. It's hard graft here and can be pretty mucky if you're in the mashing room. That's where the grain or malt's crushed up and mixed with water before it goes into the fermentation tanks.'

'So what would I have to do in there?'

The woman threw back her head and laughed so that her huge breasts and belly wobbled. 'You won't be in there, luv. That's men's work. If you get taken on at all, then you'll most likely be on the bottling belt.'

Julia had no idea what she meant or what was entailed but sensibly she kept quiet. She hoped that since the woman was so garrulous then given time she'd be enlightened.

'You look as though you're dressed for a day out in the park, not working in a brewery or anywhere else for that matter,' the woman commented. 'You sure you want to work here, or are you just wasting everybody's bloody time?'

'No, I really do want a job,' Julia told her earnestly.

'If you're sure, then I'll take you to see Mrs Barker and she'll deal with you. Come on, then, chuck.'

'What's your job here, then?' Julia asked as they made their way across a paved yard which, at one end, was stacked high with wooden barrels.

'Clear up everyone else's bloody mire, don't I? As fast as I mop up one load of dirt then someone else makes a fresh mess. Smashed bottles, overturned tuns and vats, leaking pipes, spills, you name it and they yell out for Jane Higgins to come and clean it up for them, the lazy buggers. Bloody Mrs Mop, that's me.'

Jane Higgins led the way down a red brick passageway towards a green door at the far end. She rapped loudly then pushed the door open. The jangling noise of hundreds of moving bottles assailed their ears. Raising her voice, Jane bellowed, 'Mrs Barker, there's someone here looking for a job.

'Go on,' she said, giving Julia a sharp shove and pushing her into the room.

Julia stumbled forward aware that the eyes of all the women working at the narrow table that ran the full length of the room seemed to be fixed on her.

Mrs Barker was in her early forties and had a thin narrow face, peroxide-blonde hair pulled back into a pleat, and cold grey eyes. She looked up fleetingly as Julia walked towards where she was perched on a high chair behind a high wooden desk.

'Well?' she demanded expectantly.

'I'm looking for work and I was told there might be a vacancy here,' Julia told her.

'Oh yes? Who told you that?'

'The Landlord of the Throstle Hotel.'

'Have you ever done any of this kind of work before?'

'No, I'm afraid not, but I learn things very quickly.'

'So what sort of work have you done?'

'I've been an office clerk and I've done some nursing.'

Mrs Barker frowned. 'Did you leave those jobs or were you sacked?'

Julia bit her lip. 'I left both of them for personal reasons.'

Mrs Barker's thin lips tightened. 'Oh yes, what sort of personal reasons.'

'I'd rather not go into details,' Julia told her. 'It concerned one of the doctors.'

'You sound to me like a bit of a fly-by-night, so think on, we don't want any trouble of that sort here. We don't encourage mixing with the blokes. Your job will be in the bottling room and you keep right away from the brewery men. Understood?'

'Perfectly! Perhaps you should tell them to keep away from me,' Julia told her spiritedly.

Mrs Barker laughed cynically. 'Most of them are in their dotage, or else they're just out of school and too young for the army, so you shouldn't have any trouble . . . always providing you don't encourage them.'

'Does that mean I have the job?'

'One week's trial. Start tomorrow morning

at eight o'clock. Finish at six. You'll get a half an hour break at midday, but you take turns with the others. The belt keeps going, it doesn't stop for any breaks. If you need to leave your place for any other reason during the day, you ask permission and someone takes over your job. Do you understand?'

'Yes, I think so.'

'Eight o'clock, then. You'll be issued with an overall and cap which you will wear at all times while you are at work. Have you got that?'

'Yes. Thank you. Will someone show me what to do?'

Mrs Barker stared at her in silence. 'Eight o'clock. Right? The way out is through that door over there, turn right and the door to the yard is at the end.'

Julia hesitated. 'You haven't told me yet what my wages are going to be.'

'You haven't done any work yet,' Mrs Barker snapped. 'The rate is ninepence an hour so, if you work a full week, that will be two pounds a week.'

Julia frowned as she did a quick mental calculation. 'Surely it will be more than that. It's a ten-hour day and five hours on a Saturday, so it should be at least two pounds five shillings . . .'

'Less half an hour each day lunch break, your insurance, company fund and the cost of your overall. There will also be stoppages for any breakages or spillage.'

'I see.'

'Furthermore,' Mrs Baker went on, her voice becoming more authoritative and more calculating by the minute, 'since you won't be starting until tomorrow, that means you will be a whole day short this week so you will not be receiving a full week's pay.'

Julia's head whirled as she did some revised calculations. She'd certainly have to find somewhere to live that was cheaper than the Darnley. But how was she going to do that if she was working until six o'clock each day? she wondered.

Her only hope was that the window cleaner, Bob Reynolds, would be able to find her somewhere to rent. Or, perhaps one of the women she'd be working alongside next day would be able to tell her the best way to go about finding a room.

Walking away from the brewery in Blackstock Street, Julia didn't know whether to be pleased or disillusioned. She'd got a job, but it wasn't the sort of work she'd ever expected in her life to have to do. She had no idea what being on the bottling line involved, though doubtless she'd find out soon enough when she reported for work at eight o'clock the next morning.

Chapter Eleven

It was the longest week that Julia could ever
remember. She was still staying at the Darnley
because she hadn't had time to look for
anywhere else. The early morning start didn't
bother her, she had become accustomed to early
shifts at the hospital, it was the conditions she
was working under that made it seem to stretch
out for ever.

The work was so uninteresting, so repetitive,
that at times she felt like screaming. Yet there
was no let-up. From the moment the belt was
switched on at eight o'clock in the morning
there was a never-ending stream of bottles
coming through. Hour after hour they passed
along it until the whistle sounded at six o'clock
and the belt finally ground to a halt.

Ten hours of never-ending bottles going past
and she had to stand there as part of a team. If
she didn't keep pace with the other girls on the
line, then the bottles would start piling up in
front of her and the others would start shouting
at her and blaming her for being slow and
causing a jam.

She didn't know why she couldn't keep up.
All she had to do was one small task each time

a bottle came past her. Each of them had only one repetitive task to perform, but they had to work as a team to keep up with the stream of bottles.

The first task when the bottles began to come along the belt was to fill them; the next was to add the special screw top; after that the labels had to be stuck on.

The bottles started out absolutely plain, then one girl stuck on the neck label, the next one attached the main label, and the third added a label on the reverse. The next woman on the line made sure that the top was properly screwed on and the last woman placed the bottle into a crate which one of the men carried away.

The first day she was there Julia had been given the easiest job, simply to pack the filled and labelled bottles into the crate. They'd arrived so fast, though, that in next to no time she'd found them piling up everywhere. When two of them fell off the belt crashing on to the floor and sending a stream of beer everywhere, Julia knew from the outburst of laughter that everyone had noticed. Then Mrs Barker, looking very irate, marched over and began packing the bottles into the crate herself until the backlog was cleared.

After that Julia didn't even look up, but worked as fast as she possibly could, ignoring the chatter going on all around her. She wondered how the others could manage to take their mind off the job long enough to talk about what they'd done at the weekends and what they were planning to do that evening, or about the goings-on in their families.

She even wondered if, although it looked simple and she'd been told it was the easiest job on the belt, they were in fact fooling her and she had been given the hardest job of all.

Next day she'd ask Mrs Barker if she could do one of the other jobs, she resolved.

'All new girls are put on crating for the first couple of weeks,' Mrs Barker told her frostily. 'You have to take your turn like all the others. A week on each stage, that's the rule.'

'I'll do a swap with her if you like,' one of the women interrupted.

'Shut your gob, Margaret Parsons, this is none of your business,' Mrs Barker said crisply.

'I know that, Mrs Barker, I was only trying to help. Sticking on labels is easier in my opinion.'

'She's right, there's no argument about that,' another woman agreed, 'that's God's truth, so it is.'

'Oh very well,' Mrs Barker sighed exasperatedly. 'Change over tomorrow.'

Julia tried to thank Margaret Parsons, but it brought guffaws of laughter from the other women.

'She only wants to be on that end of the line so that she can chat up Jake Williams when he's collecting the crates,' she was told.

Julia didn't mind what her reason was; she

was relieved to be free of the mountainous pile of bottles.

'Labelling is a doddle,' Margaret confided. 'All you have to do is stick it on. It's easy graft, a kid could do it.'

A kid might be able to do it, but she couldn't, Julia realised after a couple of hours. Sticking on a label sounded simple enough, if only it would stick. She applied the glue, as she'd been told to do, and carefully pressed the label into place, but that wasn't the end of it. The moment the bottle had passed along to the next girl, the label seemed to develop a life of its own and either dropped off or slipped so that it was on crooked and was therefore unacceptable when it came to the final inspection.

There were so many spoiled bottles that once again Mrs Barker decided to change the job Julia was doing.

'Since you can't stick on labels, and you can't pack the bottles into crates, then do you think you can manage to fill them?' she asked with a tinge of sarcasm in her voice.

'I'll try,' Julia promised.

That move proved to be even more disastrous. There was no way of controlling the flow of beer that came down the rubber tube. Theoretically, all she had to do was to insert the tube into the neck of the bottle and then withdraw it the moment the bottle was full and insert it into the next bottle. The skill lay in transferring the pipe a split second before the bottle was full. If she moved it too soon, the bottle wasn't a full pint, if she left it too late, the beer spilled over on to the belt, or over her. The smell was heady and permeated her clothes so that even when she left the belt, the smell hung round her in a haze, choking her, making her head ache.

Dragging herself to the brewery each day became a form of torture. It was only the realisation that she needed the money in order to pay for her hotel room at the Darnley that kept her going there each day.

There was a further problem. The smell of beer clung to her clothes even after she left the brewery and Julia was afraid that Mr Hawkins might notice and comment on the fact.

He wouldn't know where she was working so he might think that she spent all day in a pub drinking. Either way he might decide to ask her to leave and she still hadn't had time to look for a room.

On Friday morning, Mrs Barker called her over the minute she arrived. Julia's heart thudded. As she picked up her overall and walked over to the high desk a sixth sense told her what was afoot even before the forewoman had a chance to say a word.

Mrs Barker snatched away the overall Julia was about to put on and tossed it to one side. 'You won't be needing that any more,' she pronounced as she handed her a small buff envelope. 'You're fired, Miss Winter!'

'You said I would have a week's trial, Mrs Barker,' Julia challenged, 'and I've not been here a full week, not yet!'

'You've been given a fair trial and your work is not up to standard,' the forewoman told her.

'By the end of the week I'll have mastered things,' Julia protested lamely.

'We can't afford to wait and find out,' Mrs Barker told her caustically. 'You've interrupted the flow and created havoc, you've also caused too many breakages. The other women are unhappy with the situation. There's no easy solution. If I let you stay, then the other women will leave.'

'I need the job in order to earn some money,' Julia said desperately.

Mrs Barker's mouth tightened. 'My instructions are that you are to leave the premises right away. I have arranged for you to receive a full week's pay in lieu of notice. You will find two pounds in that envelope, Miss Winter. Now bugger off.'

As she heard the titters of laughter from the women on the line, Julia snatched the envelope Mrs Barker was holding out and stalked off without another word.

Outside, although the August sunshine was blazing hot Julia couldn't stop shivering, she felt so angry. She'd been treated disgracefully, she fumed. Two pounds would only pay for one more night's accommodation at the Darnley.

She was back to square one, she thought, as

she walked through the brewery gates into Blackstock Street. She still had to find both a job and somewhere to live.

She walked as far as Chapel Gardens and sat on the seat there to try and collect her thoughts. She studied her hands. The skin of her fingers was wrinkled because of the constant immersion in liquid. Her nails, which had always been so well cared for and buffed to a shine, were broken, and the cuticles ragged.

She wasn't going to make it on her own, she thought despondently. All her life she had been pampered and cosseted, safeguarded from life's realities. She had no idea that women had to work like they did on the bottling line at the brewery. Was it any wonder that they cursed and blasphemed worse than any man she had ever heard?

She had thought that some of the nurses at the hospital had been hard and brusque, and that some of the language used by the injured men was shocking. It was nothing, though, to the things the women on the bottling line said or the sort of intimate matters they openly joked about.

She fingered the brown pay-packet that she'd thrust into her pocket as she left the brewery. She would have liked to have been able to refuse it, toss it back at Mrs Barker and walk away with her head held high, but common sense had prevailed even though two pounds wasn't very much.

As she stood up she felt a small fluttering movement and a wave of faintness swept over her. She sat back down again quickly, thinking it was the heat, then realisation dawned on her, filling her with awe about what had just happened. It was the baby moving, she was sure of it. It was proof that it was alive and she found the knowledge overwhelming. She'd known her waistband was getting tight, and that she was putting on weight, but this was so positive.

A tremendous feeling of joy swept through her. There was no doubt at all that it had moved. She felt elated. Her baby, hers and Bernard's, was sending her a signal, reminding her of her commitment. It made her all the more determined to do as she had planned and to make an independent life for herself and her unborn child.

As she walked out of Chapel Gardens into Newsham Street she spotted Bob Reynolds walking towards her, ladders balanced on his bike, a bucket jangling against the framework.

He greeted her with a broad, friendly smile. 'I thought you must have decided to leave Liverpool when you never turned up to meet me like we agreed.'

'I'm sorry about that, but I found myself a job and didn't finish work until six o'clock each evening.'

'Then what are you doing skiving off and sitting out here enjoying the sunshine?' he said, grinning at her.

'I've just been sacked,' she confided.

'Flippin' 'eck! That's not too good! What happened? Some sort of argy-bargy? Where were you working?'

'At Cairn's Brewery.'

He looked puzzled. 'Never! Doing what?'

'I was on the bottling line, but I couldn't do anything right and I couldn't keep up. The forewoman said she either had to sack me or all the other women would walk out.'

'Fugginell!' Bob threw back his head and laughed. 'So what are you going to do now?'

'Find another job, of course,' she told him defiantly. 'Do you know anywhere where there is one going?'

Bob looked thoughtful. 'I do, as a matter of fact, but I don't know if it is the sort of thing you would want to tackle.'

'Why, what sort of work is it?'

He pushed back his cap and ran a hand through his thick brown hair. 'What did you say you were doing before you came here? Was it nursing?'

'That's right.'

'Mm! In that case, then, I suppose this job could be right up your street.'

'You mean it is in a hospital?'

'Well no, not exactly.' He hesitated uneasily. 'It's at an undertakers.'

'Undertakers! Are you having me on?' Julia bristled, her eyes glittering angrily.

'No, luv! A chap I was at school with has been

turned down for the army because he's not fit and he's gone into partnership with another bloke and they're running a funeral parlour.'

'So what is the job?'

'They want someone to make the bodies look good after they pop them into their coffin. You wouldn't have to lay them out,' he added hastily. 'Usually the family have already arranged to have that done, but, as undertakers, they are expected to tidy them up for their family and friends to take a last gander at them before they screw down the coffin lids. Could you do that or does it sound a bit too gruesome for you to tackle?'

Julia hesitated. It certainly did sound gruesome, but if she could nurse men who had been badly injured and disfigured, then surely it would be no worse than that.

She shrugged. 'I think I could manage to do that,' she said coolly. 'I'll give it a try anyway.'

'Come on, then, the funeral parlour is only around the corner in Great Homer Street. I'll walk there with you, if you like, and introduce you to the two blokes who run it.'

'You said you'd find me somewhere to live,' Julia reminded him as they walked along the street. 'I can't find anywhere. No one seems to put a card in their window around here to say they have a room going,' she explained.

'That's true. I do know of one that's for rent, but it's in one of the courts and it's a pretty rough sort of area.' He glanced sideways at

Julia, taking in her neat appearance. 'It wouldn't be like staying at the Darnley!'

'No, well, I definitely can't afford to stay at the Darnley any longer,' Julia said ruefully. 'I'm rapidly running out of money and I don't suppose the undertakers will be paying very much.'

'Let's see if you decide to take the job there first, shall we?' Bob Reynolds parried. 'They might offer you more than you expect and then you could look for somewhere a little bit better than Frederick Court to live.'

'It would help if you told me something about these two chaps. You haven't even told me your friend's name, nothing except that he's gone into partnership with someone and that the two of them are running a funeral business.'

'Sorry!' Bob Reynolds gave her a huge grin. 'I forgot that you weren't from around these parts and that you wouldn't have heard all the gossip about it. His name is Danny, Dan McKee. His mate's name is Paddy Finnegan.'

'So they're both Irish,' Julia murmured.

'Their mams and dads came from somewhere in Ireland. But Danny and Paddy are both Scousers, born and dragged up in Liverpool. They're a wily couple; you could even say a pair of wheeler dealers, the way they go about things.'

'Rather a strange sort of business for them to go into, then, isn't it?' Julia frowned.

Bob looked at her sharply. 'Yeah, yer probably

right, luv. Still, that's what the pair of them opted to do. Danny had worked there and when the old chap who owned it decided he was giving up and wanted to get rid of the business, he let Danny have it dirt cheap. Paddy simply jumped on the bandwagon, more or less. As far as I know they're making a go of it.

'Well,' he paused and turned to look her in the face, 'now that I've put you in the picture and told you all I know, are you sure you still want to go after this job?'

'Of course I am. Anyway, if this Danny McKee is a friend of yours, then he can't be all bad, I suppose,' she said, smiling.

'He was a shy kid when we were at school, but then he was always sickly. He caught tuberculosis when he was about six and it left him with a gammy leg so he couldn't run and kick a football as good as the rest of us. That meant he got bullied quite a lot.'

'You stuck up for him though?'

'I don't think he likes people all that much,' Bob went on, ignoring her remark. 'That's probably why he prefers dealing with the dead 'uns rather than those that are living.'

'What about Paddy Finnegan?'

Bob Reynolds looked uncomfortable. 'I'm not too sure about him. He's sharp and a bit of a smart arse. He brags a lot. Personally, I wouldn't trust him as far as I could throw him. He has a strong Irish accent, by the way, but I reckon it's put on. He looks like an Irishman, mind.

Dark shiny hair, bright green eyes. He's brash-looking and oozes charm and fine words. It's all a great big act, though. He's as sharp as a needle and he'd do himself down if he thought it would pay off,' he added with an uneasy laugh.

'I take it you don't like this Paddy Finnegan very much.' Julia smiled.

'True, but you'll probably be bowled over by his good looks and Irish charm.'

'I might be,' Julia teased, 'but we'll decide about that later, after I've met him, shall we?'

'Yes, well, there's the place.' He stopped as they turned into Homer Street. 'It's three doors down on the right, you can't miss it. It's got the name on the door and the window is decked out with a bloody big black urn as well as festoons of black and purple crêpe and a couple of vases of artificial white lilies.

'I'll meet you back here in about half an hour. Don't worry if it takes longer, I'll still be waiting for you and then I'll take you to look at this room in Frederick Court . . . That's if you still think you want to go and live there.'

Chapter Twelve

The room Bob Reynolds took Julia to see in Frederick Court sent shudders through her. The court itself was depressing enough: a dark, damp area with terraces of high houses on three sides. The stone steps leading up to the front doors were cracked and chipped and they were littered with all sorts of rubbish. Rusting iron railings down the sides of the steps divided one house from the next.

Julia let out a small scream as something furry ran across her feet.

'It's only an old moggy,' Bob chuckled as a mangy tabby cat slinked away from them.

A pall of smog hung over the court, blackening the stonework, brickwork, slates, and even the cobbles. As she looked up at the cracked and dirty windows, Julia felt the area was so revolting that she wanted to walk away. Then common sense prevailed. She couldn't afford to stay at the Darnley. Her savings were almost gone and from now on all the money she would have was what she managed to earn.

Her hopes that the wages she'd be offered at the funeral parlour would be enough for her to look for somewhere more salubrious had not materialised.

Although Bob's friend Danny McKee and his partner Paddy Finnegan had been keen for her to take the job, they were quick to point out that they were still building up the business and managing on a shoestring themselves.

Danny was even living on the premises in a room no bigger than a store cupboard. They stressed that having to find her wages was going to be a further drain on their resources. At first, they'd claimed that the most they could afford to pay her was only thirty shillings a week.

Indignantly, she told them that she'd walked away from her previous job at the brewery because they'd only pay her two pounds, so she wouldn't dream of taking on a job that paid less.

After a heated discussion they agreed to a salary of two pounds, three shillings. Once again she found herself on a week's trial. She was confident, though, that this time she would be able to cope with the work even though it appeared to be much more involved than Bob Reynolds had led her to believe.

'We're not just popping them into a box ready to bury them,' Paddy explained.

'Oh, no! We want to make them look happy and comfortable and even more lovely or handsome than they did in real life,' Danny told her gravely.

'You will be the one who must explain all this

to the grieving relatives when they come to make the funeral arrangements,' he added.

'You expect me to talk to the relatives!'

'Indeed we do! It's an important part of your job. It is up to you to persuade them to buy the most expensive coffin they can afford, and not to simply settle for the cheapest,' Paddy enthused. 'Encourage them to take pride in choosing the most highly polished one in top quality wood; one with machine-turned gleaming brass handles and perhaps a brass plate on the lid engraved with their name. It doesn't stop there, either,' he went on exuberantly. 'Always make sure they select the most luxurious lining from our range of samples. We can also offer the choice of a silk or satin pillow, and supply all sorts of other trimmings.'

'Right!' Julia nodded. 'I think I understand all that, you've made it all very clear.'

'Then there's the actual funeral itself,' Danny went on. 'People think that our gleaming black and glass hearse drawn by black horses with their headdresses of waving black plumes is a truly magnificent sight. We can also supply a professional mourner; a man dressed in sombre black, from his shiny top hat to his highly polished black boots, who will walk in front of the hearse.'

'That part is played by Danny, or so I understand,' Julia remarked.

'Yes, I am the one who undertakes that responsibility,' Danny acknowledged gravely.

'Always try and persuade them to have our pall-bearers rather than using members of their own family,' Paddy went on. 'Point out that our pall-bearers are not only experienced, but they are all the same height, and they have had considerable training so they know the right way to carry the coffin. No matter how big it is, or how heavy its occupant might be, they will never drop it or mishandle it in any way.'

Danny's lugubrious face suddenly lit up. 'Never overlook the importance of flowers. We can arrange for the wreaths to be collected from the florist. If they wish, they can tell us what they want and we can have them made up for them. We will transport them from our premises to the house when we collect the coffin of the deceased and ensure that they are tastefully arranged.'

'In other words, you offer a complete service.'

'We most certainly do. From the moment they summon us to the house to measure the deceased, until we transport the last of the mourners back to wherever the wake is held, we guarantee that everything is done to their utmost satisfaction.'

Julia was impressed by their sincerity, but aghast at the amount of organising involved when they told her that she would be expected to keep a list of all the services that were provided and also for writing out an account afterwards for the customer.

Afterwards, when she was relating to Bob

Reynolds what had gone on at her interview, she probed, 'If there're only the two of them, Bob, then how on earth do they manage to provide enough men to be pall-bearers to carry the coffin as well as a mourner to walk in front and lead the procession?'

'Well, they've got plenty of out-of-work chaps they can call on who are willing to put on a black suit for a couple of hours and earn some beer money. And, as you know, it's Danny who acts as the professional mourner.' Bob laughed. 'He looks the part, doesn't he, with his long white face and that sad droopy moustache. Being tall and thin and slightly hunched makes him look even more solemn as he limps along. Touches people's hearts, so I'm told.'

'So what part does Paddy play? Is he the one who organises everything?'

'He charms the bereaved with his Irish blarney, making them spend far more than they can afford. When he finds they can't pay him, he puts them in touch with a moneylender. That way he gets his fee right away and the poor sods go on paying off the debt he's talked them into for years and years to come.'

'So why do I have to try and sell them all the accoutrements, then?' she asked in a puzzled voice.

'You soften them up and Paddy will be there in the background ready to put the pressure on if they start to waver. He's very good at being persuasive.'

'You seem to know a lot about it,' Julia commented.

'Danny tells me all about it and how Paddy works,' Bob told her. 'Danny would be no good on his own, but his gloomy manner is just right for dealing with the bereaved in the first instance. They seem to take comfort from his sombre appearance and melancholy manner. Wouldn't do for me now, would it? They don't want someone with a grin like a Cheshire Cat all over their face, not when they're feeling sad and dejected because they've just lost a loved one.'

Sad and dejected was exactly what Julia felt like as she had her first glimpse of Frederick Court.

'I did warn you it was pretty grim,' Bob told her when he heard her sharp intake of breath and saw the look of disillusionment on her face. 'Do you want to go inside, or would you rather turn back now and reconsider the idea?'

Julia squared her shoulders. 'No, of course not. I was taken by surprise for a moment, that's all. It's all I can afford so can I take a look at the room, please?'

'You'll have to meet Martha Smith first. She's the landlady. She lives in the basement and lets all the other rooms out.'

'What is she like?'

Bob puffed out his cheeks. 'A bit like the house.' He grinned. 'Rather old, run down and grubby. She's got a heart of gold though. Her husband was in the Merchant Navy. He was drowned at sea years ago and she was left penniless with four kids to bring up. She persuaded the owner of the house to let her stay on rent-free in exchange for keeping the rest of the tenants in order, collecting the rents and so on. With a roof over her head she worked at whatever she could get so that she could earn enough to feed them all.'

'What a terribly hard life she's had,' Julia murmured sympathetically.

'It was! The kids went barefoot most of the time and had patches on the patches on their clothes. She managed to bring them all up though. One girl is in service over in Wallasey, one is married and living in Birkenhead, and the two boys are now both in the army. There you are, now you know everything. Don't let on to Martha that I've told you all that about her or she'll have my guts for garters. She might wear a shawl and be a scruffy, elderly working class woman, a Mary Ellen, in fact, but she's got her pride.'

'I'll make sure I remember that,' Julia told him quietly.

'You do and you'll be fine. She'll make you welcome and keep an eye out for you,' he assured her. 'I went to school with two of her kids so I know what I'm talking about.'

'Is there anyone you don't know around here?' Julia asked, touched by his thoughtfulness.

Bob grinned. 'Lived here all my life, haven't I, and me mam and dad the same. Dad's been a window cleaner for almost thirty years so of course we know a lot of people.'

'I wouldn't have thought that there would have been very much call for a window cleaner around here,' Julia commented dryly.

'No, that's true! Not many of them can afford us,' he admitted sadly. 'Most of our work is shop windows. Shops and, of course, the windows of some of the big shipping company offices in Tithebarn Street and Old Hall Street.'

'Not the Liver Buildings?' Julia teased.

'No.' Bob shook his head. 'Our ladders aren't long enough to clean those windows,' he chuckled.

Martha Smith greeted Bob affectionately. She was in her sixties, wizened and wrinkled despite being overweight. She scrutinised Julia appraisingly and looked very surprised when Bob told her that they had come to see her because Julia was interested in renting the room that had become vacant.

'Are you quite sure about that?' Martha Smith sniffed. 'She looks to be a bit too much the lady to want to live in a slummy old place like this,' she stated forcibly.

'Does that really matter, as long as she can pay the rent?' Bob quipped.

Martha frowned uncertainly.

'She's going to start work at the Homer Street Funeral Parlour on Monday so she wants to get fixed up before then,' Bob explained. 'Now then, can she have the room or not?'

Martha shrugged. 'That's up to her. She'd better take a look at it first.'

She struggled out of her chair, then hesitated. 'Why don't you take her upstairs and show it to her. While you are doing that I'll brew us all a nice cuppa,' she suggested.

'As you like,' Bob agreed. 'Come on, then,' he held out a hand to Julia.

The staircase was dark and narrow and had a strange, musty sort of smell. The room that was to rent was on the second floor at the front of the house and it was much bigger than Julia had expected.

There was a single bed at the far end and, halfway down the room and in front of the black-iron fireplace, there was a peg rug, a wooden table, two upright chairs and one rather rickety rocking chair. Opposite the fireplace there was a grimy window, hung with thick red curtains, which looked out over the court. The paintwork in the room was all dark brown and the cracked lino on the floor had a dark green and brown swirling pattern.

The room was stuffy and completely airless. Bob pulled aside the heavy red curtains and, after a struggle, managed to push the sash window up. The minute he moved his hands away it fell back down with a heavy thud.

'I'm afraid you'll have to wedge it open; the sash cords have rotted,' he said, shrugging apologetically.

Bob watched uneasily as Julia looked round

the room speculatively, trying to assess everything in as reasonable a way as possible. Apart
from the furniture there was a built-in cupboard
for clothes and another which seemed to have
some cracked dishes and a few chipped cups
and saucers in it.

'So where do I cook?' She frowned.

'You share the kitchen with Martha. And the
lavatory is outside in the yard,' he mumbled.

Julia pulled a face. 'That's rather primitive,
isn't it?' she questioned.

'I did tell you that I didn't think this place
would be right for you,' Bob warned.

Julia sighed, knowing that she really had no
choice but to take it. 'Have you any idea how
much the rent is?' she asked, playing for time
before she had to make a decision.

'I think Martha told me it was seven shillings
and sixpence a week.'

Julia looked shocked. 'For this! One room,
and I have to share a kitchen! Where do I have
a wash?'

Bob looked round uncertainly. Near the bed
was a table with a large floral washbasin and
matching jug standing on it. 'Over there, I
suppose,' he told her, pointing to it. 'You'll have
to bring water up in the jug and there's a bucket
underneath for you to tip the dirty water into
afterwards, and you carry it back down to the
kitchen and empty it.'

He walked over to the cupboard where she'd
noticed the cups and dishes. 'There's a kettle

and a saucepan in here so you could probably boil water to make a cup of tea on the trivet at the side of the fireplace,' he added cheerfully.

'And where's the coal for the fire?'

'That will be down in the cellar, or out in the yard, I suppose.' Bob frowned. 'You'll have to check with Martha Smith about all those sorts of things.'

Over a cup of strong tea, laced with conny milk and accompanied by a lump of wet nelly, Martha Smith confirmed all that Bob had told her.

Her mouth tightened when Julia queried her about the rent, and she looked taken aback when she began to try and persuade her to lower it. Julia was as determined to get it down as Martha Smith was to keep it at seven shillings and sixpence. They finally reached a compromise of six shillings and Martha agreed that Julia could move in immediately.

As she left Frederick Court, Julia looked back uncertainly, doubt written all over her face. The room was cheap and she felt that Martha Smith would be a fair landlady, but that was about all there was to be said in its favour.

There were approximately sixteen weeks before her baby would be born Julia reasoned. If she could bring herself to put up with such sordid accommodation for the next three months then she might manage to scrape enough money together to move into something better before the child was born.

That, of course, was always assuming that Danny and Paddy would let her go on working at the funeral parlour right up until the very last minute.

She didn't see that there would be any real problem about them doing so. The dead wouldn't mind her being pregnant and the people she had to deal with would be too concerned with their own sorrow to worry about her condition.

The only ones who might raise objections were Danny and Paddy, but as long as she could carry out the work they wanted her to do she didn't think they would object either; not with the miserly salary they were paying her.

Chapter Thirteen

Julia was up early on Saturday morning. She'd washed, dressed, packed her few possessions into her holdall, handed over her room key to Paul Hawkins, and was walking towards Frederick Court before nine o'clock.

There were so many things she wanted to do over the weekend that she didn't know where to begin. This was going to be a completely new start, she told herself. No more thinking about the past and hankering after all the things that she'd been forced to give up. She'd made the choice and she intended to stick by it and carve out a new lifestyle for herself.

Renting a room of her own was what she had planned to do right from the moment she'd walked out of the military hospital – in fact, ever since she'd left her comfortable home in Warren Drive. Well, with Bob Reynolds's help she'd now managed to do just that and, even though it was little better than a slum, it was up to her what sort of place she eventually made of it.

If only she had some money to spend on decent pieces of furniture and other things to make it look nice, she mused. As it was, she could barely afford the bare necessities like coal and food. Still, she told herself optimistically, she had a job to go to on Monday and if she was very prudent then she'd manage to get everything she needed given time.

She was so engrossed in her thoughts that she was startled to hear someone calling out her name.

'Miss Winter! Julia . . . hang on . . . wait a minute, I want a word with you.'

Bob Reynolds was breathless by the time he caught up with her. In addition to his usual paraphernalia he was carrying an extra bucket, a couple of tins of paint and a canvas bag crammed with an assortment of brushes.

'That room of yours in Frederick Court,' he said awkwardly. 'I thought it might look a bit better if it had a fresh coat of paint. I knew we had some odds and ends left over from when my dad did our own place, so I thought . . .' He paused, stumbling for the right words and looking rather sheepish.

'Bob, that's very kind. You're right; it's just what the place needs. Painting it might get rid of those horrible smells of stale cabbage and something else that smells even worse, but I can't work out what it is,' Julia told him with a warm smile.

'The smell is probably bugs,' Bob told her. 'Whitewash on the ceiling and some emulsion paint on the walls and a bit of varnish on the woodwork, and that'll drive the little blighters on their away,' he told her confidently.

'Bugs?' she looked at him puzzled.

'That's right; those places in Frederick Court are alive with 'em.' He grimaced. 'Bed bugs, fleas and cockroaches, not to mention all the flies, bluebottles, spiders and the like. The little beggars can't stand the smell of paint and varnish, though, so once we've done the room over then you'll be shot of them.'

'We?' Julia stopped walking, a blank look on her face.

Bob blushed. 'I wasn't sure if you'd ever done any decorating before,' he mumbled, 'so I thought perhaps you might like me to give you a hand.'

'You thought right,' Julia told him. 'The only thing is, I don't think I can afford to pay you, well, not right away. Once I get my wages next week, then—'

'I'm not asking you to pay me!' Bob exclaimed. 'I was offering to give you a hand, that's all.'

It was Julia's turn to feel confused. 'That's jolly kind of you,' she smiled, 'but are you quite sure you shouldn't be cleaning windows?'

'It's Saturday, so I can manage to spare a couple of hours,' he told her disarmingly as they continued towards Frederick Court.

By the time they were outside the front door of Martha Smith's place, Bob was whistling cheerfully as though he was really looking forward to the painting job ahead of him.

'I'll carry my bag up and come back down

and help you with the tins and stuff, if you like,'
Julia volunteered as he propped his bicycle
against the railings and began unloading it.

As she pushed open the door of the room
she'd rented, Julia caught her breath. There was
a rustling and a scuttling and she knew Bob
had been right; the room was alive with unwel-
come visitors. Gingerly, she placed her holdall
on top of the table and looked around. It was
so dank and dreary that she wondered if she'd
been in her right senses when she'd agreed to
pay Martha Smith six shillings a week for it.

The more she looked, the less she liked what
she saw. The wallpaper was so grubby that it
was impossible to tell if it was patterned or not.
She noticed, too, that it was peeling away from
the wall in places. She looked up at the ceiling
which was grey and, in the corners, festooned
with cobwebs. There was a brown stain in one
place as though at some time there had been a
leak from the room above.

'I thought I could do the ceiling and give the
walls a first coat, then go and get on with my
own work while it's drying. I can come back
and do the second coat later on today or
tomorrow morning,' Bob told her as he followed
her into the room.

'It certainly needs it,' Julia agreed. She could
hardly credit her good fortune as she helped him
to bring up the rest of the tins of paint and the
brushes. She would never have been able to
tackle something like this on her own and she

certainly didn't have money to spare to call in anyone to decorate it for her.

For the next hour they worked side by side, Bob issuing the orders once he saw she had no idea what to do. He did it in such a pleasant way, accompanied by the odd quip or amusing banter so that she did all he asked without feeling the slightest resentment at being ordered around.

By mid-morning there was an overpowering smell of whitewash and emulsion, but the place was already looking so different that Julia's heart lightened.

'I'm off now to clean some windows,' Bob told her as he paused by the door to look round and admire his handiwork with a smile of satisfaction. 'I'll be back later on,' he promised. 'Keep the window propped open and mind you don't brush up against the walls until they are dry.'

'Is there anything I can do while you're away?'

'You could have a bash at varnishing the woodwork,' he suggested. 'You'll have to wash it down first with some hot water and soda to get rid of the dirt and grease.'

She frowned. 'I haven't any cleaning stuff, not even any old rags.'

'Hang on, I'll nip down and see if Mrs Smith has some you can use,' he told her.

He was back in a matter of minutes with a large enamel bowl half full of hot water, some cloths, a scrubbing brush and a jam jar of soda crystals.

'Here you go, luv. Now mind you wait until the woodwork is dry before you start to put the varnish on it. Use this two-inch brush and only dip the tip of the brush into the tin. You only need a little on it at a time, remember.'

'You mean I mustn't try to rush things.' Julia grinned.

'That's right. It's a bit painstaking, but you'll probably do a better job than me,' he laughed. 'I prefer to be using a big brush and doing the walls rather than fiddling around with one of them little ones.'

By late on Sunday the room at Frederick Court had been transformed from a dirty, drab hovel into somewhere clean, and reasonably habitable.

As soon as Bob Reynolds left Martha Smith lumbered upstairs to satisfy her curiosity and see how Julia was getting on, under the pretext of inviting her to come down and join her for something to eat. She stared round the room transfixed, as if she could hardly believe her eyes.

In addition to the whitewash on the ceiling, the cream distemper on the walls and all the woodwork freshly varnished, the dusty red curtains had been given a good beating, the lino on the floor had been scrubbed, the furniture polished and the grate blackened so that it now gleamed.

'Bloody hell! You've made a little palace out of the place,' Martha exclaimed in disbelief. 'If I'd known it could look this good, I'd have charged you double the rent, I certainly wouldn't have let you barter me down to six bob.'

'I should be charging you for all the cleaning and scrubbing I've had to do to make the room liveable in. I should also be asking you to pay for all the paint and for all the work Bob Reynolds has done,' Julia responded, scowling. 'Filthy, dirty hole – I wonder you had the nerve to rent it out.'

Martha and Julia stared at each other antagonistically, and then, in unison, they both burst out laughing.

'Reckon we're as bad as each other, luv,' Martha Smith puffed. 'I came up to ask you to come down and have a bite of supper with me. Do you fancy some tasty Manx kippers, a bit of apple pie and custard and as much Rosy Lee as you can drink? Or there's even a glass of stout or a drop of gin, if you prefer it.'

'Thank you. Give me ten minutes to clean myself up and I'll be there,' Julia agreed. 'Now you've mentioned food I feel absolutely starving.'

'Then I'll get back downstairs and start cooking the kippers,' Martha Smith said. She paused and took another look round the room, shaking her head from side to side in disbelief. 'I can't belief what a transmogrification you've managed to make here, luv. I really can't.'

151

'I didn't manage to do it all on my own, you know,' Julia reminded her.

'No, of course you didn't. I saw that Bob Reynolds here, I wondered what he was up to spending so much time up in your room,' she added slyly.

'Well, now you know,' Julia told her tartly.

'Between the pair of you you've certainly done a good job, so you deserve a bit of a celebration.'

'Yes, we have, but I want to have an early night,' Julia warned her. 'I am starting work in the morning.'

She didn't really want to go down to Martha's place, but she felt that it would be unwise to refuse the hand of friendship that was being held out. She hoped it would also give her a chance to find out something more about Bob Reynolds and perhaps even about the Homer Street Funeral Parlour.

Meeting up with Bob Reynolds had been a real stroke of luck since it was thanks to him she had managed to find both a job and somewhere to live, Julia reflected as she prepared for bed.

He might be something of a rough diamond and merely a window cleaner, but he was one of the nicest men she had ever met. He was good-looking, too, with his warm brown eyes, generous mouth and mop of thick brown hair. She loved the way that it flopped down over his brow when he took off his cap, making him look very young and vulnerable.

She wondered exactly how old Bob Reynolds was; it was something she'd forgotten to ask Martha. He'd said that he'd been at school with Danny McKee, but she found that difficult to believe. Danny seemed to be years older.

Bob, with his tall, slim figure and weather-beaten skin, looked so fit and healthy. He seemed to be completely happy with his life. Whistling cheerfully most of the time he even made pushing a loaded bike, shinning up and down ladders and putting a shine on windows seem enjoyable.

He had a wonderful carefree attitude to life, and he had the most infectious laugh she had ever heard. Yet, from what Martha Smith had told her about him, he didn't have all that easy a time at home. Now that his father was in the army he was trying, single-handed, to keep their business going. That couldn't be easy; in fact, it was quite a responsibility and yet he seemed to be making a very good job of it.

That wasn't the only problem, it seemed. From what Martha had said, Bob's mother was a bit of a tartar. She idolised Bob, but although he was a very good son and did everything he could for her, it wasn't enough. She actively discouraged him from having any girlfriends because she was afraid he might get serious with one of them and want to get married.

'She's dead scared that if that happened, then

he would up sticks and leave home,' Martha confided.

'You mean he doesn't ever go out with girls?'

'Once or twice, I hear, he's taken some young Judy home to meet his mam, but never the same girl more than once.'

'Why is that?'

'Because old Mother Reynolds makes sure they won't want to come a second time,' Martha cackled. 'She's that bloody rude to them that the thought of having her for a ma-in-law frightens the living daylights out of them.'

'So the next time Bob asks them to go out with him they turn him down.'

'Turn him down! They take to their heels, luv. They can't get away fast enough; you can't see them for dust.'

'So it's goodbye, Bob, don't ask me again,' Julia said sadly.

'That's right, and can you blame them. They know there's plenty more fish in the sea; ones without an old shark for a mother.'

'Poor Bob!'

'Damn shame, I call it. Selfish old bitch. He's such a lovely fella and he'd make some nice girl a wonderful husband.'

Julia felt that was true. Bob was extremely kind and caring. He'd certainly gone out of his way to help her and she'd been a complete stranger. The day she'd bumped into him by Exchange Station he'd never seen her before in his life.

She'd never forget how he had taken it upon himself to come along with paint and stuff and help her to decorate the room he'd found for her. He'd done it out of the goodness of his heart because he knew she couldn't afford to pay him.

She wished there was something she could do for him in return because he was such a nice person in every way. She'd like to get to know him better.

She was curious about his mother, though, and she felt she'd like to meet her. It would be interesting to find out what sort of woman could persuade such a handsome, outgoing man like Bob to stay by her side instead of being married and having a home and family of his own.

Thinking of marriage took her mind back to the wedding she and Bernard had talked and dreamed about. Even if he'd still been in the army and serving in France by now, if things had gone the way they'd planned, they would have been married, and would have known that one day soon, hopefully before their baby was born, they'd be together again and looking forward to a wonderful future for the three of them.

Her thoughts returned to Bob Reynolds. It seemed so sad that although he was alive and well, and probably had similar dreams, for different reasons, they could never be fulfilled.

Perhaps one day he'd manage to overcome his mother's hold on him and satisfy his dream.

She sighed enviously, imagining herself as the lucky girl standing there at his side in a flowing white wedding dress.

She smiled inwardly, picturing what would happen if Bob took her home to meet his mother in a few weeks' time when it was really obvious that she was expecting a baby. Poor Mrs Reynolds would have a fit, especially if she thought it was his.

Julia scolded herself as she settled down to sleep: Julia Winter, I think you must have a touch of the sun, or you are becoming slightly delirious from lack of food, to think such mischievous thoughts.

Chapter Fourteen

Nothing Martha Smith had been able to tell her about Danny McKee and Paddy Finnegan came anywhere near the truth of what the two men were really like.

Julia arrived at the funeral parlour promptly at half past eight on Monday morning as she'd been instructed to do. The door wasn't open and when she rang the bell nothing at all happened. In response to her persistent knocking, Danny McKee eventually appeared. His sandy hair was tousled and standing on end and he was clutching a grubby counterpane around him. His feet were bare and it was obvious that he had scrambled out of bed in a hurry. It took him several minutes of fumbling with the locks before he managed to open the door and let her in.

'What's the time?' he muttered, running a hand over the stubble on his face.

'You told me to be here at half-eight so that everything was ready to open up at nine o'clock,' she reminded him.

'Sorry, I seem to have overslept. Forgot to set the alarm clock,' he mumbled apologetically. 'Paddy will be here any minute. Can you sort yourself out while I go and have a wash and shave?'

'I'll do better than that, I'll make us both a cuppa and it'll be ready for you the moment you've got yourself together.'

'You will!' He looked taken aback. 'Thanks, chuck!'

Paddy was loud with his praise when he arrived ten minutes later and found a pot of tea already brewed and waiting.

'Sure, now, and it's a little gem we've found,' he enthused. 'Milk and two sugars in mine. Danny only takes one sugar. While you're pouring it out I'll nip next door and pick up a lardy cake. Danny likes nothing better for his breakfast.'

By twenty past nine they'd 'fed their faces' as Paddy put it and Julia had washed up their cups and plates and whisked all the traces away.

'Now, shall I be the one to show you round the place or do you want Danny to do it?' Paddy asked.

Julia shrugged uncertainly. 'Depends which of you knows the business best,' she said tactfully.

'Boy! we've got a right one here.' He grinned. 'Looks as though we're going to have to toss for it.'

'I can think of a better way,' Julia told him.

'Oh yes?' He frowned. 'What's that, then?'

'For today, why don't you leave me to get my bearings and watch how you do things, and I'll ask questions when I need to. At the end of the day you can add whatever else you think I need to know. I'll probably pick things up much more quickly if we do it like that,' she said with a disarming smile.

'I'm happy to give it a whirl,' Paddy enthused. 'Now, what about you, Danny? Do you agree that it's the most sensible way for us to be doing things?'

Danny nodded nervously. 'Sounds quite a good idea to me,' he agreed.

'I know more or less what is required of me,' Julia explained, 'but I'd like to see how my job fits in around what you two do.'

'We're hoping you are going to take on some of the things we attend to, remember,' Danny reminded her.

'Yes, so if I follow you around, then this will give you a chance to point out which duties you want me to take over, and I can see exactly how they are done.'

By the time the Homer Street Funeral Parlour closed for the day Julia's head was whirling with all the new things she had seen and learned.

She found the smell of formaldehyde, coupled with the sickly smell of lilies, quite overpowering, and she was glad to get outside into the fresh air.

Danny, once he was dressed and had recovered from the shock of her arriving before he was out of bed and properly dressed, had primed her on how they handled all the arrangements.

'It's important that when someone comes in and says that they want to use our services that they have brought along a death certificate. They can only have one of those if the death has been registered. In order to do that they have to obtain a medical certificate from their doctor confirming the death and to take it along to the local Register Office of Births, Deaths and Marriages.'

'Yes, I do know that. I've worked at a hospital, remember,' Julia told him.

'Then you know how you have to be careful about the way you talk to the relatives of someone who has just died,' he said pedantically. 'They're pretty touchy and often, because they're so upset, they don't make sense when they're trying to tell you something. It takes a lot of patience, luv, so do try and remember that and be patient and make allowances for them,' Danny persisted, shaking his head dolefully.

'Of course I will.'

She felt irritated when Danny looked at her questioningly, almost as if he either didn't believe her or he didn't trust her to be caring enough.

'The registrar's certificate will tell you the name, age and when the death took place. You have to ask them when they want the funeral to take place, and the name of the church and the clergyman who is to officiate. Is that clear?'

'Yes, Danny, that's all perfectly clear.'

'You also need to ask them if they have some idea of the number of people who will be attending the funeral and how many of those are going to need transport to get there. Understand? Mind you, most of them will probably make their own way there,' he added dejectedly.

Julia nodded.

'Sure, now, and you must always remember to ask if they want a mute to walk in front because that's Danny's special job,' Paddy interrupted. 'Wait until you seem him in his grand funeral attire! Begorra, he looks the part, I can tell you!' he guffawed. 'Morbid, sombre and with those hunched shoulders and his limp he looks as though he is bowed down by all the grief imaginable.'

Julia felt at a loss for words. Having encountered Danny when he'd been only half dressed, his hair standing up on end, clutching a counterpane round his bony figure and with his scrawny legs protruding from beneath it, she could hardly imagine him playing the part of chief mourner.

'The first thing you need to do is to find out the religion of the deceased and then what sort of service the relatives want,' Danny went on, ignoring both Paddy's presence and the comments being made as he continued to acquaint Julia with what her duties were to be.

'Some want their loved ones embalmed,' Danny said dourly. 'That's an extra, of course.'

'Sure it is, and I will tell you more about that later on,' Paddy promised her.

'I understand.'

'Next,' Danny went on, listing them off on his fingers, 'you must find out if they already have a plot in the cemetery. After that, check whether they want us to keep the body in our mortuary until the day of the funeral or whether they want us to take the coffin to their home and leave the body there with them until the day of the funeral.'

'If they're Irish, then like as not they'll want the body at home because all their friends and family will want to pay their respects and also to keep a vigil,' Paddy butted in. 'Some of them may even want us to provide a lyke wake. That's someone to go and sit at the house and watch over the body,' he explained to Julia.

'I see; and I suppose a lyke wake will be charged as another extra.'

'Sure, so it will be! Don't you ever forget that! Extras are what bring in the profit.'

'I would have thought that would be taken care of in the price of the coffin?' Julia commented.

'The coffin does play an important part and is certainly the most essential item. The cheapest sort is elm; it's light, clean-looking and good value. Some people, though, go for oak, or if they really want to splash out, then they might ask for mahogany. There's a wide choice of handles and they can be made of brass or even of silver if that's their wish. The lining inside the coffin is usually satin or silk, but if they don't mind the price, then it can even be velvet.'

'Am I supposed to try and talk them into choosing the most expensive?'

Paddy gave her a lopsided grin. 'Sure now, you catch on quick, luv. We're in this business to make a living so the more we can persuade them to spend the better.'

'You must be very tactful,' Danny said worriedly. 'Don't push it, but don't go thinking that the poorer they look the cheaper they will want the funeral to be. Often it's the other way round.'

'Sure and that's the truth,' Paddy agreed. 'Danny himself is a right stingy Proddy, whereas a lot of our customers are fervent Cat'lics. The poorest of them often have the grandest funerals. You get a sixth sense about these things the moment they walk in the door,' he confided.

'Danny's too kind and soft-hearted, I imagine,' Julia said thoughtfully.

'Too sentimental by far,' Paddy agreed. 'He believes in giving them the cheapest deal possible, but that's not what all of them want. They want to show off. They insist on the lilies, the candles, the procession; in fact, all the trimmings, even if it puts them in hock for years to come. They want everything to look grand in the eyes of their friends and neighbours, as well

163

as in the eyes of God. The bigger the display the more chance the man or woman in the coffin has of being received at the Pearly Gates by St Peter himself.'

'Are you a Catholic yourself, Paddy?'

'Born and bred, so I am. I was an altar boy from the time I was knee-high to Fr O'Grady, but here I am anything I need to be,' he added cryptically. 'The thing is, I've taken the trouble to study the requirements of all the religions under the sun and I go out of my way to give each and every one of our customers exactly what they need. I've even been known to take the nails out of the coffin when we reach the burial site, immediately before lowering the coffin into the ground, you understand, so that the person inside can get free more easily on the final day of judgement. It's an old Irish custom,' he added hastily when he saw Julia raise her eyebrows disbelievingly.

'Is that it? Everything I need to ask them about?'

'No, you also need to find out if they want a notice to be published in the *Liverpool Echo* or the *Liverpool Daily Post*, or anywhere else. Some of them might even want it in a newspaper in some other part of the country as well.'

'All these additional services are regarded as extras and they all go on the bill, I take it?'

Paddy nodded. 'Some folks take burial very seriously. They save up for a good end through clubs of one sort or another for years. Some save all their lives just so that they can die well. Those who haven't saved leave it for their relatives to get into debt on their behalf. Tally men, the varmints they are, appear on the doorstep the minute someone dies. Then it's not just the cost of the funeral the poor souls have to pay out for, but double or treble that amount because of all the interest they incur on the money they borrow.'

'So how much does an average funeral cost?'

Paddy shrugged. 'It can be as low as twenty pounds, if they pick an elm coffin, but a really grand funeral can cost whatever they want to pay. A really big wreath, for example, can cost as much as a working man earns in three months. If the church service includes an organist and a choir they are all extras and have to be paid for, remember.'

'What about embalming?'

Paddy's eyes narrowed. 'Well, that's a special extra, but there's not much call for it in Liverpool. It's still not anywhere near as popular in this country as it is in America.'

'So are you trained to do it?' Julia queried.

Paddy crossed himself and then nodded very solemnly. 'Well, let's say that I do it whenever I am asked. It's not one of the duties I would expect you to take over,' he added gravely as Julia suppressed a shudder.

'Finally there's the question of the headstone and the inscription they want to have engraved on it', Paddy went on. 'Like the funeral, the choice is wide. We work closely with a monumental stonemason, so there's a tremendous selection. They can be plain or marbled, pink, white or even black, and they can be engraved in black or gold leaf. There're also the most wonderful statues and these include beautiful angels and cherubims as well as magnificent crosses.'

'Certainly it is all far more complicated than one would think,' Julia commented.

'Yes, and I've not even mentioned children's funerals,' Danny said gloomily. 'These call for special attention. If the child is under two years old, then we always select a white coffin.'

'Indeed, and unless the family want a full-scale funeral, the coffin is carried by our Danny, the mute,' Paddy pointed out. 'He heads the procession from the house to the church with the family, led by the child's parents, walking behind.'

'There's also funeral stationery. Black-edged cards giving details of when the funeral will be. We supply those, in collaboration with a local printer.'

'In fact, one way or another, you handle everything,' Julia commented dryly.

'This is a dedicated business, Julia, so never forget that the more services we can undertake for these people then the better living we make for ourselves!'

'The bereaved are in a state of shock so they welcome the convenience of being able to put everything in our capable hands when they are beside themselves with grief,' Danny exclaimed dourly.

'It's a responsible task we carry out so we expect you to look the part, the same as we do,' Paddy said hesitantly. 'We don't encourage any laughter or bright chatter in front of our clients and we would like you to wear black and to appear serious at all times. As far as those coming to us for professional help are concerned, we are in mourning at all times.'

'That's right,' Danny pointed out, 'even the background music we play is either pastoral chanting, hymns or something similar. The whole atmosphere of the place has to be as sombre as a church. Our manner must at all times convey sympathy and compassion.'

Julia could understand this and appreciated the necessity for levity to be avoided, but she felt Paddy was taking things rather too far. As the weeks passed and she saw the smarmy way he dealt with people and how he glibly talked them into doing things on a grand scale, whether they could afford to do so or not, she began to feel outraged.

Surely, she reasoned, it was better for the widow to buy shoes or boots for her barefooted children than to buy an expensive coffin and have it lined with velvet and then bury it in the ground to rot.

Bob Reynolds felt dog-tired as he pushed his loaded bicycle along Newsham Street into

Scotland Road, heading for his home in Scrivener Street. He'd had an exceptionally busy Monday and he knew he had no one except himself to blame. Part of the trouble was that he'd had to bust a gut to squeeze in three extra jobs. They were ones he'd missed doing on Saturday because he'd been so busy decorating the room in Frederick Court for Julia Winter.

He smiled to himself. It had looked smashing when they'd finished, though, and she'd been as delighted as a dog with two tails.

He'd been so pleased with what they'd achieved that he'd started to tell his mother all about it when he'd got home, but the minute she'd picked up on the fact that he'd done it for nothing she'd blown her top.

She'd got so het up that he wished he'd kept his mouth shut. He should have remembered that she had a jealous, possessive streak and that she didn't even like him seeing girls, let alone helping one as much as he'd been doing since he'd met Julia.

If she'd known that the emulsion and white-wash he'd used were what had been left over from when his dad had done their place out before he went into the army, she'd have made an even bigger scene!

He grinned to himself. He was becoming a proper bloody knight in shining armour where Julia Winter was concerned. He'd now managed to fix her up with both a job and somewhere to live.

The trouble was, he couldn't put her out of his head. She wasn't like any of the Judys he'd ever know before. It wasn't only the way she looked and dressed; she even spoke different.

He didn't know much about Wallasey, but he loved the sound of her posh accent. He'd been over on the ferry boat for a day trip to New Brighton and he'd even heard of Warren Drive where the nobs hung out and had their big houses.

It was easy to see that Julia wasn't used to slumming it. What's more, she had no nous at all when it came to slapping on a bit of varnish. She'd been willing to give it a go, though! He admired her for that and she'd made a neat fist of it once he'd shown her how.

That's what he liked about her, he reflected. For all her posh accent and swanky ways Julia Winter didn't mind a bit of hard graft.

She was a looker, too. When she turned those turquoise-blue eyes of hers on him he could feel his ticker racing; thudding like a hammer in his chest. She stirred his blood, there was no getting away from that! He'd never known a girl with hair the colour of hers. It was neither red nor brown but somewhere in between, like the rich auburn colour of the leaves in autumn. And it was so sleek and shining that it was all he could do to keep his hands to himself and not start stroking it.

If he'd done as much to help any other girl as he had Julia Winter he'd have expected at least a kiss and a cuddle afterwards, he told himself. In her case, though, he'd felt that the smile of approval on her face as she'd looked round the room when they'd finally finished was reward enough.

He'd still like to put his arms round her and kiss her, but he wasn't too sure how she'd react if he took such a liberty. He was afraid to risk it because he couldn't bear the thought of her storming off in a huff and him never seeing her again.

As far as he was concerned she was someone special. At the moment her manner was friendly and affable so perhaps, if he played his cards right, then one day she'd let him take her out. If she felt the same way about him as he did about her, then one day his dream might come true.

He wondered how she'd fared on her first day at the funeral parlour. He didn't think that it was really up her street, but she'd probably find it better than working in a factory.

From what she'd told him they'd given her a pretty hard time at Cairn's Brewery, but then, that was only to be expected. The type of women who worked there would be able to tell the moment she opened her mouth that she wasn't one of their sort and would try and take her down a peg or two. At least Paddy and Danny wouldn't do that though he'd bet his next pair of bootlaces that they'd make her work damned hard for her money.

Chapter Fifteen

Julia knew she should be both happy and contented. She now had a fairly decent room and a reasonably paid job, but even so, she felt both uneasy and unsettled.

Although her living arrangements were squalid compared to the sort of home life she'd known in Warren Drive, they were adequate for the moment. It was more her job than anything else that left her feeling so worried, and this was mostly because of Paddy Finnegan.

Paddy was always the last one in attendance. It was always Paddy, never Danny, who undertook to nail the coffin down after all the relations had viewed the corpse for the very last time and tearfully said their farewells.

Paddy always requested to be left alone to do this solemn task, insisting that it upset him so much that he couldn't bear for anyone to be in the room with him.

At first Julia had respected his sentimentality, until one day, when she had been working there for about three weeks, a grieving widower came in and handed her a rosary, asking her to place it in the coffin with his wife.

As she hurried into the mortuary to carry out

the man's request before the coffin was nailed down, she found Paddy already in there. He was so intent on what he was doing that he didn't hear her approaching. As she reached his side she stared in disbelief, horrified to see that he was struggling to remove the rings from the dead woman's fingers.

There was a startled silence as Paddy looked up and turned to face her, his green eyes blazing as he realised that he'd been caught in the act.

'Her husband asked me to do this,' he blustered. 'He said they were family heirlooms and wanted them returned to him so that he could pass them on to his eldest daughter.'

Julia shook her head. 'I don't think so!' She held out her closed hand palm upwards and then slowly opened her fingers, displaying the rosary that she had been asked to place with the body. 'He's only just this minute left here and he came to ask that this should go in the coffin before it was finally nailed down.'

Paddy opened his mouth as if about to argue further, but as he looked into Julia's face he realised that it was pointless to bandy words with her so, with a shrug of his shoulders, he capitulated.

'How could you steal from a dead body?' she said, her voice heavy with disgust.

Paddy scowled. 'Well, the stiffs don't want rings or any other bits of jewellery any more now, do they? Sure and it's wasteful for them to be buried,' he blustered.

'So what on earth did you intend to do with those rings?' Julia persisted. 'Sell them and pocket the money?'

'I wasn't doing it for my own gain,' he exclaimed defiantly. 'I was doing it to help get this business on its feet. We've a lot of overheads such as rent, the horses, and so on, not to mention salaries,' he added meaningfully.

'The way you cajole people into having the most expensive funeral, even when you know they'll end up in debt for years to come, should cover all your overheads and leave you with a handsome profit,' Julia retorted.

Paddy craftily changed his tactics and looked contrite. 'Sure now and I've made a terrible mistake. You won't be mentioning this to Danny, now will you?' he pleaded.

'Are you saying that he knows nothing about what you're doing? That he's not in on this with you?'

'Danny! With his conscience! He'd have to confess to Father Bunloaf on Sunday now, wouldn't he, and he'd be doing penance for the rest of the week,' he chortled.

'I thought you said he was a stingy Proddy and that you were the one who was a Cat'lick,' Julia taunted, mimicking Paddy's voice.

Paddy's green eyes narrowed. 'You know something, you're too soddin' smart for your own good, Julia Winter. So damn sharp, in fact, that one of these days you'll end up cutting yourself if you're not bloody careful,' he told her spitefully.

'Smart enough to have got your number, Paddy Finnegan, that's for sure. I think you're absolutely contemptible,' she raged. She was so worked up that she was trembling with anger.

'Begorra, and that's a great shame, so it is,' he sighed, 'because I was going to count you in and give you a share . . .'

'How dare you!' Julia turned on him like a wildcat, her face flaming. 'You are so utterly despicable I can hardly bear to talk to you.'

'Then perhaps it would be best if you didn't, and even better if you forgot what you've seen going on. Understand? Keep it inside your bloody nut unless you want to lose your nice cushy job here,' he added ominously.

Julia bit back a sour taste in her throat as without a word she turned on her heel and walked away.

Julia was in a complete quandary about what she ought to do. By rights, she knew that the matter should be reported to the police, but could she afford to do that? Furthermore, it would be her word against Paddy's and she wasn't at all sure which one of them the police would believe.

Paddy had such a gift of the gab that he could convince most people about almost anything when he turned on the charm. She would be so nervous and tongue-tied that they'd probably dismiss whatever she said as being either of no account or else a figment of her imagination.

Yet what Paddy was doing was so reprehensible that she really couldn't stay silent. She wondered who on earth she could confide in.

She wrestled with the problem for most of that night, but she still had no solution. She needed to talk to someone, but she knew she daren't breathe a word to Martha Smith because she was far too garrulous. Julia could imagine how her sharp eyes would widen and her jaw drop if she breathed the merest hint to her about what she'd witnessed.

Even so, Julia wondered what Martha would advise her to do if she did know. She seemed to have no time for the police, nor, indeed, for authority of any kind. Yet Julia was sure she would be horrified to think of anyone stealing from a corpse. Such desecration would be considered a heinous sin.

She knew the right person to tell was Danny, but his shoulders were already bowed with so many worries, real and imaginary, associated with running the business that she felt reluctant to burden him any further.

Julia sighed. Which left only Bob Reynolds.

Over the weeks that she'd been working at the funeral parlour she'd got to know Bob's routine and almost automatically she found herself taking a route next morning which she knew would ensure their paths crossed.

He was always pleased to see her and ready

to stop for a few minutes and catch up on how she was getting on. Usually she had minor daily happenings to recount. She was always careful what she said because she knew that Danny was Bob's friend, but there was usually some small incident to laugh and joke about.

That morning it was different; the moment they met and exchanged greetings, Bob seemed to sense that all was not well and that she was worried about something.

'So what's wrong then, luv?' he challenged when she seemed to be making no effort to tell him what was on her mind.

Julia frowned. 'Heavens, is it that obvious?'

'Well, either that or you've been tucking into Martha Smith's bowls of scouse too often.'

'Scouse?' Julia pulled a face. 'That's certainly not my favourite food, I can assure you.'

Bob grinned. 'Then it must be the other reason.'

For a moment Julia didn't understand, but the moment it dawned on her what he was talking about colour flooded her cheeks. She was finding that most of her clothes were getting tighter, but she didn't think it was that obvious to anyone else that she was pregnant. She certainly hadn't mentioned her condition at all to anyone, so she was surprised that Bob knew.

'When's it due, then?' he asked conversationally. He cocked his head on one side and studied her critically. 'About the end of November?'

Julia couldn't believe her ears and Bob laughed at the look of consternation on her face.

'Have you and Martha Smith been gossiping about me?' she asked sharply.

Bob shook his head. 'No, as a matter of fact I guessed over a month ago that you were in the pudding club.'

'You did! But how?' she asked indignantly.

'It stands to sense. A posh bird like you doesn't come slumming because she wants to. There's bound be some good reason.'

'Yet you said nothing?'

He shrugged. 'I didn't want to put the boot in. I thought you'd tell me when you were good and ready to do so. I didn't know that Martha knew.'

'She doesn't.'

'That figures. She wouldn't have let you have the room if she'd known.'

'Why ever not?'

'She can't stand screaming kids; they are the last thing she'd want under her roof.'

'There are plenty of them all around her. Frederick Court is full of barefoot young children with streaming noses.'

'That's one of the reasons she doesn't want any in her house,' Bob pointed out. 'A really young baby is even worse. Squalling, puking and crying day and night. Anyway, how can you manage to look after it in one room when you have no kitchen?'

'Lots of other women around there seem to be able to do so,' Julia pointed out dryly.

'You're not like them though, are you! They've grown up in the place and are used to those sorts of hardships. I don't really think you are.'

Julia felt uneasy. Her original reason for seeking Bob out was temporarily forgotten as she thought about the predicament she might be faced with in the not-too-distant future. Where she was living was certainly no paradise, but now that it was cleaned up, it was relatively comfortable and it suited her well enough.

She felt guilty about not telling Martha what lay ahead. It was only in the last few weeks, though, since she had felt the first movements like a butterfly fluttering inside her, that she had really started to think at all seriously about the coming baby and to acknowledge it as a real person.

'So what was it you said you wanted to talk to me about?' Bob asked, interrupting her wandering thoughts.

Brought back to the present, Julia hesitated. Was it wise to stir things up at this moment, she wondered? If she told Bob about Paddy desecrating the corpses and Bob took the matter up with Danny, then she might find herself out on her neck. Without her wages she'd not be able to afford her room. Even though, by the look of things, if what Bob had told her about Martha Smith was true, she might have to start looking for some other place to live she didn't want to find herself out of work as well.

'I haven't time now,' she prevaricated. 'It's

not all that important so I'll tell you next time I see you.'

'When will that be?'

Julia looked uncertain.

'I tell you what.' Bob grinned. 'Why don't I take you to the pictures?'

Julia hesitated. It was on the tip of her tongue to ask him why he should want to take a pregnant woman out for the night. Then, as their eyes met and she became aware of the warm, caring look in his gaze, she relaxed. Bob Reynolds was really the only friend she had in Liverpool, she reminded herself; the only one who was interested in her welfare and what might happen to her.

'Thank you, I'd like that, but we must go Dutch.'

Bob frowned and for a moment she thought she'd offended him. Then he gave her one of his big grins. 'OK, if that's the way you want it, luv. See you tonight, seven o'clock outside the Rotunda. You do know where that is?'

Julia shook her head. 'No, but I'll find out. I'll be there.'

'I'll give you a clue,' Bob chuckled. 'Try the junction of Stanley Street and Scotland Road; you can't miss it.'

At the end of the evening she'd tell him about Paddy and ask his advice, Julia decided. She'd stress that she was sure Danny wasn't implicated and that he knew nothing at all about what was happening.

* * *

179

Julia arrived at the Rotunda with only a couple of minutes to spare. Bob's directions on how to find the place had been easy to follow and the building itself was so unusual that she couldn't have missed it even if she'd wanted to.

It was her conscience that had delayed her. Right up to the very last minute she'd been debating with herself whether or not she should go. Even though she kept telling herself that it wasn't a proper date, it was simply two friends going to the pictures together, it still didn't seem to be the right thing to do.

There were a number of people standing around outside obviously waiting for friends to arrive, but she couldn't see Bob. For one uneasy moment she wondered if, like her, he'd had second thoughts, but in his case decided not to come.

Her heart flipped as she caught sight of a tall young man dressed in dark grey flannels and a lighter grey tweed jacket. Although his hair was a different colour, from the back he reminded her so much of Bernard that it brought a lump to her throat.

When he turned round and saw her staring, then came hurrying towards her, she felt so embarrassed that she wanted to turn and run. She felt even more flummoxed when she saw that it was Bob Reynolds and that she hadn't recognised him out of his working clothes.

His face lit up when he spotted her. 'For a moment I was worried in case you couldn't find the place!' he greeted her. 'Got yourself all dolled up I see.' He grinned, his brown eyes studying her appraisingly.

'I didn't recognise you, either, not without your bike and ladders,' she quipped.

Julia hesitated when they were shown to the back row of the cinema, into one of the double seats usually claimed by courting couples. She soon found she had nothing to worry about, though. Bob was attentive, buying her a small box of chocolates, but he didn't encroach on her space.

They were both highly entertained by the amusing antics of Charlie Chaplin in *The Little Angel*. Several times Julia found herself giggling at Bob's uproarious laugh almost as much as at the comic's behaviour.

She'd enjoyed herself so much that as they walked home along the lamp-lit streets, Julia was loath to spoil such a pleasant evening by telling Bob about Paddy Finnegan. She'd resolved to leave it until another time when Bob himself raised the matter by reminding her that she'd said that there was something she wanted to talk to him about.

He listened in silence to Julia's revelations. He was shocked by what she told him and as uncertain about what ought to be done about it as she was.

'I can't believe it,' he said, shaking his head in dismay. 'I'm damned sure Danny has no idea about what's going on. I'd stake my life on that.

He'd be terribly upset if he discovered that anything like that was taking place.'

'I think you're right,' Julia agreed, 'but I think he should be told, don't you?'

'It will break his heart when he hears about such skulduggery. He's not only as honest as the day is long but he gets upset over the slightest wrongdoing,' Bob said worriedly. 'When we were at school, if he thought anyone was cheating, or copying another lad's work, he'd not rest until he'd had it out with them.'

'You mean he told on them!'

'No, no, he wouldn't dream of doing that. He'd tackle them himself and tell them what they were doing was wrong. He'd try and make them stop doing it by pointing out that cheating and pinching another boy's work wasn't right.'

'Danny did that?' Julia stared at him in astonishment. 'There's nothing of him; he wouldn't stand a chance against any boy bigger than himself!'

'No, he was always getting beaten up. That's where I came in.' Bob grinned. 'I was a real tiger when I was a kid and I was always in fights. I had more black eyes and bloody noses than anyone else in the school.'

'Mainly from defending Danny?'

'Well, I knew he meant well and that he was doing the right thing, so I stuck up for him.'

'All of which means you wouldn't want to be the one to tell him about what Paddy is up to,' Julia said quietly.

'Most certainly not, and you should think twice before you do anything more about it.'

'Why, what do you mean?'

'If you spill the beans, then Paddy will get rid of you, sack you on the spot,' Bob pointed out.

'Would Danny let him do that?' Julia questioned uneasily.

'He's more likely to believe Paddy than you,' Bob explained. 'He hardly knows anything about you really, now does he? I know he thinks you are a big asset to them, but he's in partnership with Paddy, remember.'

'What about if it comes to light in some other way; if someone discovers that Paddy has stripped the rings from their loved one's hands? What happens then?'

Bob ran a hand over his chin. 'I don't know. It's important that you think about yourself, though.'

Julia frowned. 'I don't understand.'

Bob looked uncomfortable. 'When's that baby of yours due?' he asked bluntly. 'Not all that far away, is it, so I imagine you need the chance to save as much money as you possibly can before then.'

Julia stiffened. 'I don't see how that is any business of yours and I don't understand what it has to do with what Paddy Finnegan is doing.'

'If you get the sack, where do you think you'll find another job unless you go back into a factory – and I don't think from what happened before that you're cut out for that sort of job,' Bob pointed out.

'You mean that I should sit tight and say absolutely nothing so that I can go on working there for another couple of months,' she said scornfully.

'I'm only thinking about you and your baby,' he told her. 'You've got a mountain of problems ahead of you as it is. Once old Martha finds out that you're preggers then she'll want you out. That could mean you'd be out of a job and without a roof over your head both at the same time.'

Julia bit down on her lower lip. Bob was right. If that happened, then how on earth was she going to manage? By retaining such a stony silence ever since the day she'd left home she'd burnt her boats and couldn't go back there.

'I suppose you're right, Bob. I'd better mind my own business, hadn't I?'

'It's the wisest course for the moment,' he agreed reluctantly. 'Give yourself time to look around for another job and somewhere else to live and then decide what you want to do about Paddy.'

'I don't like it, though. I think it's an absolutely dreadful thing that he's doing.'

'So do I, which is why I think it might be better if you found somewhere else to work,' he repeated.

'That's not going to be easy, not the sort of job I'm able to do,' Julia said worriedly.

184

'No, you're right there!' He paused as they reached Frederick Court. 'Look, try not to worry; I'll keep my ear to the ground.'

Julia placed a hand on his arm. 'Thanks, Bob. I know you managed to find me the job I've got now, but I can hardly expect you to perform another miracle.'

He grinned. 'I'll try my best. Perhaps we can have another night out to celebrate when I do.'

Julia smiled non-committally. 'Tonight's been great, thank you for taking me.'

'That's until next time, then,' Bob said, as he kissed her awkwardly on the cheek.

Chapter Sixteen

Julia dreaded going into work on Monday morning, unsure of how Paddy would react now he knew that she was aware of his nefarious activities.

For most of the morning she managed to avoid him. At midday, when she went into the back room that was used for storage and as a general purpose room to brew up the tea for the three of them, she found him waiting there and she started to retreat.

'Julia, are you trying to avoid me?' he called after her.

She hesitated and then turned and went back. 'No! Why should I be?'

Paddy's green eyes narrowed, but he said nothing. He remained staring intently at her as if waiting for an answer. When she made no response, he walked over to her and put an arm around her shoulders, squeezing her towards him, completely ignoring the way she tried to pull away.

'Come on!' With his free hand he jerked her head around to face him. Before she could prevent him doing so his mouth came down on hers, kissing her so hard that she was gasping for breath by the time he released her.

Angrily Julia pushed him aside and moved as far away from him as she could. 'What on earth do you think you are doing!' she exploded wrathfully.

'Sure now, me darlin', and you've been waiting for me to do that ever since you came to work here. I've seen the look in your eyes. I've been well aware of the way you watch me, eyeing me up whenever we're in the same room.'

'You're mad!'

'And you're beautiful! Especially when you're in a temper and your eyes blaze like dazzling gems. Now then, my pretty little colleen, what about coming out with me tonight?'

'Stop talking utter rubbish, Paddy,' Julia snapped, smoothing her hair down and straightening the collar of her trim black dress.

His eyes narrowed. 'Don't act all uppity with me. I saw you smooching with that window-cleaner fella, Bob Reynolds, in the back seats of the Rotunda.'

'What on earth has that got to do with anything?' Julia asked, her colour rising. 'Keep away from me,' she added angrily, as he started to edge closer to her.

'Come on, now, we could be really good friends,' Paddy said.

'Friends! After what I witnessed last week

you are the last person I would want as a friend.
You . . . you're despicable!'

'Begorra, you're a real little tease, so you are,'
he chuckled. 'Come on, let's forget the past and
enjoy ourselves; we're made for each other, I
know we are.'

When she looked at him contemptuously and
made no reply, he came towards her again, a
huge smile on his face. 'Let's spend some time
together, get to know each other better. I can
show you a good time, Julia, and a pretty young
girl like you deserves to be taken out and shown
a good time,' he cajoled.

'You'd take me out and wine and dine me on
money you've got from selling the rings you've
taken from dead women's fingers,' she said in
disgust.

He shrugged. 'You're not going to let me
forget that one little incident, are you?' he said
in mock penitence. 'If I told you that it was the
first and only time it ever happened—'

'Save your breath! You've done it countless
times, I could tell from the way you manipu-
lated them off her hand. You even oiled her
fingers to make them slip off more easily,' she
said disparagingly.

'Very observant!' Paddy sneered. 'So what are
you going to do about it?'

'I don't know. I've thought about it all over the
weekend. I know what I ought to do, but—'

The colour drained from Paddy Finnegan's

cheeks. 'You haven't mentioned what you thought you saw to anyone else, have you?'

Julia didn't answer.

'Well, have you?' he hissed angrily.

Julia clamped her mouth tightly shut. She knew she shouldn't be enjoying putting him under such a strain, but she felt exultant when she saw the torment on his face. She could hardly believe that someone who could be so callous and unfeeling towards the deceased could be so frightened.

'Please, Julia,' he begged, grabbing at her arm and drawing her so close to him that she could feel the heat from his body. 'If I promise you that I'll never do anything like that ever again, that I'll start afresh, will you forget all about what you thought you saw? Please, Julia, come on now, put me out of my misery.'

She stared at him hostilely, full of distaste, as she turned away.

'You could help me, Julia,' he said softly. 'With you by my side as . . . as my wife, I'd be a different fella. Begorra, it would be a new life for both of us. I'd treat you like a queen, darlin'.'

Julia looked at him with contempt. No one could ever fill the void in her heart or the gap in her life that she'd known ever since the telegram arrived with the terrible news that Bernard had been killed in action, certainly not a brash, wily scoundrel like Paddy Finnegan.

She knew that she'd been silly to let her heart

rule her head and to run away from home as she'd done, but she still felt that it was the right decision knowing her parents' strong principles about such matters and it was the only way she could be sure of keeping her baby.

At the time she'd had no idea how difficult it was going to be to stand on her own two feet, and in the last few weeks she'd been left in no doubt that the comfortable, sheltered life she'd led had not prepared her for earning her own living. She was now facing up to the fact that it would get even harder once the baby was born.

Bob's remark that Martha Smith would want her out of Frederick Court the moment she discovered that she was expecting a baby had frightened her, but she was determined to try to talk her round and persuade her to let her stay there.

Even so, it would still be tough going. In the few weeks she'd been living at Frederick Court she'd seen the struggle some of her neighbours had in trying to bring up their families on very little money.

Foolishly, she'd spent so much on buying things to make her room comfortable that she had hardly any money left so it was important that even though Paddy's advances were objectionable she mustn't antagonise him too much. This was her third job in as many months and it was certainly far better than the first two, so she didn't want to lose it.

When she didn't answer, Paddy pulled her into his arms again. 'Come on, you're driving me crazy.'

Breathing heavily, and ignoring her struggles, his mouth came down on hers again, bruising her lips in a savage kiss. His hands began caressing her, feverishly roaming over her body despite her frantic protests, cupping her breasts, sliding up and down her back, pulling her ever closer to him. Suddenly he stopped fondling her and gave an explosive guffaw. 'Mother of God! I don't believe it! You've got a bun in the oven!'

He ran his hand over her belly again in disbelief. 'You have! You're bloody well preggers, aren't you? What the hell is going on?'

Angrily Julia pushed him away, smoothing down her mussed-up hair and straightening her dress.

'My God! You've been hoodwinking us! I could have ended up marrying you and providing you with a father for your little bastard.'

Julia felt stunned and outraged by his attitude. 'How dare you insult me like that,' she said furiously. 'If anyone is in the wrong, it's you! You were trying to molest me and take advantage of me even though I was trying to push you away.'

When Paddy didn't answer she realised that Danny had walked into the room and was standing with his mouth agape listening to their exchange. She saw his eyes widening in consternation as he studied her shape and his face reddening as he looked hurriedly away.

Paddy remained on the defensive, desperately struggling to remain in control.

'You'll have to leave, we can't have you working for us in your condition,' he went on relentlessly. He looked across at Danny. 'I'm surprised that your friend Bob Reynolds would foist this bint on to us and tell us that she was reliable, yet not say a sodding word about the problems she was bringing to the place,' he blustered.

'What a load of rubbish you're talking,' Julia interrupted defensively. 'Trouble? Problems? I might have both ahead of me, but I don't see how it affects either of you in any way!'

'Unmarried and in your condition and dealing with the bereaved in a predominantly Catholic area! What do you think Father McGuire would say if the news reaches his ears?' Paddy exploded. 'We'd lose business hand over fist, that's what would happen,' he rushed on when neither Danny nor Julia said a word.

'No, Danny,' he drew a big breath, 'even if it upsets your friend Bob Reynolds, I'm afraid she has to go immediately.'

Danny nodded in silent agreement, rubbing his receding chin agitatedly.

'Hold on a minute,' Julia demanded. 'I'm not denying I'm pregnant, but I don't see what concern that is of either of you. I do my work efficiently, and no one else has any need to know or see me if you don't want them to do so.'

Paddy shook his head, his mouth pursed in a silent whistle. 'No, it's completely out of the question. It would be deception,' he said solemnly. 'It would be unfair to our clients.'

'Unfair to your clients!' Julia retorted. 'It's not nearly as unfair as your despicable behaviour of pinching the rings off dead bodies before they're buried.'

'What was that you said?' Danny gasped, his pale eyes bulging in horror.

'You mean you are not in on it with him?' Julia sneered. 'Your partner here takes off the women's rings before he nails down the coffin lid. What he does with them afterwards is anybody's guess, but I bet there are plenty of pawnbrokers and back-street jewellers around here who could enlighten us.'

The colour drained from Danny's long face making him look more gloomy than ever.

'I don't believe a word of what you're saying,' he stuttered. 'I've known Paddy all my life, he's my partner, he wouldn't dream of doing anything like that.'

'I caught him doing it last week,' Julia told him calmly. 'Ask him if you don't believe me, though I'm sure he'll try and wriggle out of it and deny doing it.'

'Take no notice of her silly accusations,' Paddy blustered. 'She's upset because I've found out she's pregnant.' He shuddered. 'Trying to throw herself at me, the minx,' he went on. He gave a harsh laugh. 'You know what she was after. She's looking for a husband. Someone to give a name to her little bastard. Watch yourself, Danny. She hasn't been able to pull the wool over my eyes so she'll probably have a try at cajoling you into marrying her.'

'You're a liar, Paddy Finnegan, you're just trying to avoid the truth about the shameful things you've been up to coming to light,' Julia retorted furiously.

'You want to warn your friend Bob about what she's up to in case she makes a play for him,' Paddy went on ruthlessly. 'She managed to get him to take her to the Rotunda the other night, canoodling with him in the back seats, so she was.'

Danny shook his head despondently. 'You'll have to go, Julia. We can't have you working here, not in your condition,' he told her reluctantly.

'Begorra, thank the Lord you've seen sense,' Paddy said exultantly. 'You must leave right now, to be sure, mustn't she, Danny? Right this very minute.'

'I'll go,' Julia told him calmly, holding her head high and looking at him defiantly. 'The first place I'll be going to when I leave here, though, will be the police station.'

Julia watched as the two men exchanged glances and she smiled inwardly; satisfied that she had them both worried as she saw the consternation on their faces.

'You silly bint, surely you don't really think that any self-respecting scuffer would take any notice of your silly accusations,' Paddy bluffed scornfully.

'That remains to be seen,' she said cryptically.

'You've no proof, none at all,' Paddy argued confidently.

'True, but I'm sure the police will be able to get some fast enough. Once the accusation becomes public knowledge you'll have the bereaved up in arms. Dozens of them will be demanding that the bodies of their loved ones should be exhumed so that they can check for themselves. When they do . . .' She left the sentence unfinished.

They looked at her startled. 'Holy Mary, Mother of God!' Danny exclaimed with a shudder. He crossed himself and looked askance at Paddy, who shrugged exasperatedly.

'So, when's this baby you're having due to be born, then?' Danny asked uneasily.

Julia shrugged. 'Trying to change the conversation all of a sudden, aren't you? Anyway, what's it to you? I thought you wanted me to leave right away.'

'We've been trying to explain the problems about you working here,' he told her uncomfortably. 'You see, Julia, this is a mainly Catholic area and—'

'They've no time for unmarried mums or their

little bastards,' Julia interrupted bitterly. 'Then neither do the Protestants or Methodists or Baptists.'

'Your family kicked you out, did they?'

Julia shook her head. 'They know nothing at all about it,' she stated firmly.

'I see it all now; you got yourself knocked up and then you didn't want your family to know so you ran away,' Paddy exclaimed.

'If you want all the details I'll tell you,' Julia said wearily. 'The man I was planning to marry was killed on active service. It was at Ypres, in the second battle, the one that took place in May, to be exact. I didn't even know I was pregnant when the news arrived. The moment I realised that I was, I packed a bag and left home.'

'And came here?'

'Not right away. For a while I was nursing at a military hospital outside Liverpool.'

'So why didn't you stay there? It would have been handy when the baby was born,' Paddy guffawed.

Julia gave him a supercilious look. 'There was someone else working there who knew my family and I was afraid he would tell them about my condition and where I was.'

As the two men looked at each other uncertainly, Julia seized her chance. 'I don't see how any of this affects my work here,' she repeated quickly. 'No one else knows.'

'Not at the moment, perhaps, but what about in a month or two's time!'

'And these accusations you've made against Paddy,' Danny protested. 'I don't think we can trust you to go on working for us after something like that.'

'Trust *me!*' Julia flared. '*He*'s the one you can't trust. I wasn't making it up. Every word was true. I caught him at it last Friday. From the way he was acting it was something he'd done many times before,' she declared contemptuously.

Danny shook his head. 'I'm sorry, Julia, but I'm afraid I don't believe you. Paddy wouldn't do a thing like that so, as he said, you'd best get your coat on and be on your way. The sooner we part company the better it will be for all of us.'

'If you sack me, then I'll report what I saw happening to the police,' she threatened.

'You'll be wasting your time, luv. They won't believe a word of it and neither will anyone else around these parts. Most of the local scuffers were at school with us or have known us all our lives. Think about it, they're not likely to take your word over ours,' Danny told her gently.

Chapter Seventeen

Julia didn't go back to Frederick Court, but went to her favourite seat in nearby Chapel Gardens. Sitting there in the late September sun she tried to collect her thoughts and reason out what she must do next.

She pushed the temptation to give in and return home to Wallasey from her mind. By now, she mused, if Edward Wilberforce had lunched with her father, then her family might already know the predicament she was in.

She could picture her father's disbelief and anger and her mother's tight-lipped refusal to discuss the matter. Both of them would be extremely displeased that their eldest daughter could have let them down so very badly.

If it had been Lance or Lillian who was in any sort of trouble, her mother would have been eager to help, but not in her case, Julia thought sadly. On reflection she was now convinced that it had been her mother's fault that there had been such a strong objection to the idea of her marrying Bernard. She had been so insistent that it would be considered scandalous in the eyes of the law as well as by everyone who knew them.

Even so, it took tremendous will-power to put them completely out of her mind and not to consider the possibility of going home. It was only after she'd left Warren Drive that she'd begun to fully appreciate what a wonderful, carefree life she'd enjoyed there when she'd been growing up. Her mouth watered at the recollection of the delicious meals her mother had served up, so very different from what she could afford now, or Martha's standby of scouse or kippers.

She'd always had her own prettily furnished bedroom, a wardrobe full of smart clothes and, as a child, all the toys and games she could possibly want. The irritations of having a younger sister and brother were so trivial compared with what she'd endured since then that she could readily dismiss them.

The horrors of the sights she'd seen in the hospital flooded her mind. Most of the patients had been extremely young and some of their injuries had been so gruesome that she'd only coped by shutting her mind to them. She dare not allow herself to think that Bernard might have been as seriously injured as some of them for fear of losing control and giving way to tears.

She found it hard to convince herself about that, though, because she knew instinctively that Bernard's injuries must have been even worse than any of theirs since he had died on the battle-field. If only he'd been brought back home to

England. Even if he had been badly injured, they would have been able to spend some time together. She was sure that once he knew that she was expecting his baby he would have managed somehow to persuade both her parents and his into allowing them to marry.

The scandal if they hadn't agreed and given their blessing would have been too much for such upstanding prominent people to bear. He certainly wouldn't have let her mother, or his, or anyone else, force her to have the baby adopted.

She sighed. Bernard wasn't able to help her fight the enormous battle that faced her now and so she had to start planning for the future.

She mustn't let Martha Smith know that she was no longer working at the Homer Street Funeral Parlour, not yet, anyway. She'd have to try and find another job before either Martha Smith or Bob Reynolds heard the news that she'd been sacked.

If Martha knew she was out of work, she might be worried about the rent and want her out, even before she discovered that she was pregnant. When she finally found out about that, then if what Bob had told her was true, and Martha Smith really couldn't stand the noise of a baby in her place, it would be the last straw.

If, however, Julia reasoned, she was working and able to pay her rent on the dot, then perhaps Martha would overlook the fact that she was pregnant, at least for the immediate future, and that would give her time to find somewhere else to live.

Finding work was going to be a really big problem. Shop work was out now that her pregnancy was becoming obvious. This left only some sort of cleaning job or factory work again, she thought gloomily. Although they were short of workers because so many men had been called up for the army and the navy, those in charge at the factories were still demanding competent workers. They only had to take one look at her and they seemed to be able to tell that she couldn't do the work they wanted. She'd now lost three jobs in less than three months, she thought despondently.

She shivered as a keen wind sprang up, blowing the multicoloured leaves from the trees so that they fell in swirling clouds around her. Autumn was here, the days were not only getting shorter but colder, too. Winter wasn't all that far away and nor was the birth of the child she was carrying.

Sitting here in Chapel Gardens, wasting time was not getting her anywhere, she told herself sternly. She had to pull herself together and get on with things. She'd find a new job; what she'd done once she could do again.

For the next few days she continued to leave Frederick Court soon after eight o'clock each morning and by not returning until after six o'clock in the evening, Julia hoped that Martha would not realise that anything was amiss.

Filling in the long day was not so easy. She scanned all the newsagent windows to see if there were any vacancies advertised that she thought she could go after. Sadly, the ones she found were for work that she knew she couldn't do. She went into every type of shop imaginable to see if they had any vacancies only to be told that there were none available.

Despondently, she accepted that it would have to be factory work again after all. She decided to start with the biscuit factory on the corner of Dryden Street. It was within walking distance of Frederick Court, so she wouldn't need to spend any money on tram fares. It would be clean work, the sort of job they needed women to do. It wouldn't be as noisy or as smelly as bottling beer. The pay would probably be about the same, but there might even be perks in the shape of broken or misshapen biscuits which would be a welcome treat.

Buoyed up by all the positive aspects she made her way to the factory office. If she could get a job there and get taken on right away, then there was still time to save the money towards future expenses after the baby was born.

'Go through that door and across the yard and then tag on to the end of the line of women, they're starting this morning,' the clerk instructed her, writing down her name and address after she'd confirmed that she'd worked in a factory before.

Already daunted by memories of her previous factory job, coupled with the knowledge that they would probably object to the fact that she was pregnant, her spirits and hopes sank even lower when she saw how many women there were already in the line that was moving through the door. Nonetheless, she joined the end as she'd been told to do and hoped for the best.

To her surprise she found herself being shepherded inside the building along with all the others by an enormous middle-aged woman who made her feel slim by comparison. At the entrance to a long, low building they were each issued with a white overall coat and a white cap and told to put them on.

Her spirits lifted as she saw how the long white coats completely covered them almost down to their ankles. Wearing one of these she could be any size or shape, so no one would know she was expecting. As long as she continued to feel as well as she did at the moment then no one need ever know. With any luck, she would be able to work right up until the baby was born.

By her second day at the biscuit factory, it was obvious to Julia that it was unlikely that she'd be able to stick it out for a full week, let alone the next three months. The heat was oppressive, the flour-laden air made her sneeze, her clumsiness made her slow. Worst of all, her lack of knowledge of what she was supposed to do caused her to hold up the assembly line time and time again.

'I thought you said you'd done this sort of work before,' the forewoman ranted.

'I have,' Julia assured her. 'I worked at Cairn's Brewery on the bottling line.'

'And I bet they bloody well sacked you?' she guffawed.

'As a matter of fact, I moved to a much better job,' Julia informed her haughtily.

'Oh yes, and what was that? Cleaning out the public loos in Lime Street?'

'No!' Julia bit down on her lower lip. 'It was working at the funeral parlour in Homer Street.'

The forewoman suppressed a shudder. 'That place is full of corpses, isn't it?'

'Of course it is. It is an undertakers!' Julia affirmed with a humourless smile.

The forewoman looked at her curiously. 'My God! How could you work there? What were you doing, for heaven's sake?'

'I made sure that they looked their best before they were buried.'

'Pity you didn't stay there, then!' She laughed raucously. 'At least the poor buggers couldn't complain about your ham-handed ways.'

'What on earth do you mean by that?' Julia questioned in an irritated voice.

The forewoman glared at her. 'You've certainly

done nothing right here. You've caused more disruption in two days than anyone else has ever done before.'

Julia sighed. 'I'm sorry, I will improve, I promise.'

'Well, we'll never know if you can keep that promise or not,' the forewoman said sarcastically, 'because you're leaving us right this very minute.'

'Do you mean you're sacking me?'

'Too right I am, luv. Better to be short-staffed than have some bloody nincompoop like you working on the line.' She held out a small brown envelope containing Julia's pay. 'Here's your ackers, now be off.'

They glared at each other antagonistically. Snatching the pay-packet from the forewoman's hand, Julia fought back the sour taste in her throat. She couldn't believe that she was being sacked yet again. Tears stung her eyes as she headed blindly for the door. 'Hey, you! That overall is company property,' the forewoman yelled after her.

Without stopping, Julia unbuttoned the long white coat and threw it down on the floor as she reached the door. She left the biscuit factory with her emotions churning. She seemed to be completely unemployable and she had no idea what to do now. The few miserable shillings she'd earned there would hardly pay for a week's rent.

Even the weather had turned against her, she thought dourly as she trudged through the grey drizzle, shivering as its clammy coldness enveloped her.

She was so engrossed in her own misery that it wasn't until Bob Reynolds grabbed her by the arm that she realised he was walking alongside her and trying to catch her attention. Her tear-stained face told its own story.

'What's wrong now,' he asked, frowning. 'I've been looking for you for days. Danny told me you'd left their place.'

'Left! I didn't leave, I was sacked!'

'That's not what Danny told me.'

'He wouldn't, would he? He and Paddy Finnegan are playing holier than thou because both of them are trying to cover up for what's been going on.'

'I did tell you it would be better if you said nothing,' Bob warned. 'Paddy and Danny are lifelong friends so it's only natural that Danny would take his word and not yours.'

'It did happen, though, Bob. It really did. I saw Paddy stripping those rings off a dead woman's fingers. I really think I should report it to the police.'

'Move on, Julia. You've no proof. It's only your word against both of theirs.'

'It could be proved,' she argued stubbornly.

'How?'

'If the bodies were exhumed and the rings were found to be missing then the police would know that I was telling the truth,' Julia insisted stubbornly.

Bob shook his head. 'People wouldn't want their loved ones to be dug up from out of their graves, not even to prove if what you are saying is the truth, so forget about it.'

'I don't know if I can do that,' she muttered, looking at him sideways. 'Anyway, what does it matter to you?'

'Danny is my friend and I'm positive he wouldn't dream of doing anything wrong. I'm also quite sure he had no idea that Paddy has been doing anything he shouldn't be, like you told me he was.' He paused and held up a hand. 'I wasn't looking for you so that we could argue the point about all that,' he said quickly. 'I wanted to see you on an entirely different matter.'

'What's that?'

'I didn't know you'd been sacked or that you'd found another job, but I had an idea you wouldn't be staying at the funeral parlour for much longer. I wanted to tell you that I know where there is a job going that I think might suit you.'

Julia's face brightened. 'Really! What sort of job is it?' She caught hold of Bob's arm excitedly.

'It's office work. Writing letters, keeping the books and all that sort of carry on.'

'Work I know I could do,' she told him eagerly, her eyes shining. 'Is it still going?'

'I'm not too sure because it was a couple of day ago that I heard about it, but it might be.'

'Why didn't you come and tell me? You know where I live.'

He looked at her with raised eyebrows. 'And let Martha know you were out of work?'

She shrugged. 'So where is it?'

'At the Darnley.'

'The Darnley!' Julia looked puzzled. 'Do you mean the hotel where I stayed?'

'That's right. Mrs Hawkins has always done the books and looked after that side of things, but she's not too well . . .'

'So it's only a temporary arrangement?'

Bob shrugged. 'I don't rightly know. It would be for a year or more, I'm pretty sure of that.'

'Heavens! Whatever sort of illness has she got, if she's going to take that long to get over it?' Julia gasped.

'She's pregnant. The baby is due at the end of November, but I'm pretty sure she won't be ready to come back to work again before next Easter at the earliest.'

Julia stared at him bewildered. 'Mr Hawkins is hardly likely to think I'm right for the job since I'm expecting my baby in December, now is he?' she said despondently.

Bob ran a hand through his mop of hair. 'I don't know. You seem to be fit, she isn't. From what I've heard it seems she's lost a baby before, so this time she wants to take special care of herself. She's a lot older than you,' he added by way of explanation.

Julia nodded thoughtfully. 'Maybe you're

208

right. It's worth giving it a try. Do you think I should go along there right now?'

'Well, the sooner the better. It's taken me a couple of days to find you. Martha Smith thought you were still working at the funeral parlour and neither Danny nor Paddy knew where you'd gone when I dropped by.'

'I'll go now, right away. Thanks, Bob.' Her spirits soaring, she began to hurry off in the direction of the Darnley.

'Hold on, Julia,' Bob called after her. 'There's something else I wanted to suggest.'

She paused impatiently as he caught up with her. 'What's that? Can't you tell me some other time?'

'No! I wanted to suggest that if Mr Hawkins does offer you the job, then perhaps you should try and persuade him to let you live in at the hotel.'

'Live in?' Julia looked bewildered. 'I don't understand.'

'Well, as I warned you, Martha won't want you living at her place in Frederick Court once you have a baby. If you can persuade Paul Hawkins to let you have a room at the Darnley, then that would solve the problem for you, wouldn't it?'

Julia frowned. 'Yes, but that would mean telling Paul Hawkins that I am expecting a baby and that might jeopardise my chance of getting the job.'

'Not necessarily. Much better to tell him now,

right at the outset when he is interviewing you. If you leave him to find out for himself, he might feel so annoyed that you've held out on him that he turns round and sacks you.'

'But I don't want to tell him,' Julia protested.

'You'll have to do so!' Bob exploded. 'Have you looked in a mirror lately? A blind man can see you're in the club, so you can hardly hide the fact for very much longer.'

Chapter Eighteen

Despite her initial eagerness, the nearer Julia got to the Darnley the more nervous she felt. She had serious doubts about going after the job when she knew that it meant telling Paul Hawkins she was pregnant.

Bob Reynolds thought differently and he was so insistent that very soon everyone would know anyway that in the end she capitulated.

'I think it is a waste of time so I'm only doing it to stop you nagging me,' she told him indignantly.

He grinned, pleased as Punch that she was doing what he asked. He kissed her on the cheek and offered to walk along to the Darnley with her.

'I won't stand a chance of getting it, not when I tell him that I'm expecting a baby,' she grumbled when the hotel came in sight. 'I'm only doing it to prove that I'm right and you're wrong,' she said in exasperation.

'The fact that you are pregnant might be the one reason why he will take you,' Bob argued.

'How do you make that out?'

'His wife, Eunice, is a really jealous cow. She'll have the final say on who gets the job and she won't want any pretty young Judy who might take his fancy working there. Taking you on will be safe enough.'

Julia pulled a face. 'Thanks for that! It's all I need to give me confidence.'

Bob chuckled good-naturedly. 'You know what I mean, and what I'm trying to say. Now go on! In through that door and don't come back out until you've got the job,' he told her firmly, giving her a little push, and smiling encouragingly as he did so.

'Are you going to be here waiting for me when I come out?' she asked with a provocative smile.

Bob hesitated, then shook his head regretfully. 'No, I can't spare the time, I've work to do. Tell you what, though,' he said quickly when he saw the look of disappointment on her face, 'why don't we go out tonight and celebrate properly?'

'Celebrate?' Julia frowned. 'What makes you think we have anything to celebrate?'

'Nothing at the moment,' he grinned, 'but by tonight we'll be able to celebrate that you have a new job at the Darnley and that you will be living there once again.'

'Living there!' She looked at him scornfully. 'Dream on, I very much doubt it.'

Bob shrugged. 'Well, we know you can't stay in Frederick Court . . .'

'Shush! Don't say another word.' She placed a finger over his lips. 'I'm very superstitious! If we take it for granted, then it won't happen.'

'You are funny!' he said with an amused smile. 'Never mind. I won't say another word, but I wouldn't mind betting that we will be celebrating tonight.'

Julia found it strange to be back in the hotel where she'd spent her first few nights after taking her decision to stay in Liverpool. She looked around the foyer and reception area, this time much more aware of how clean, comfortable and well appointed it all was.

Paul Hawkins, looking as portly and suave as she remembered him, was behind the reception desk. For a moment Julia thought that he hadn't recognised her. Like all good hoteliers, however, he had a very retentive mind for names and faces.

He welcomed her with an ingratiating smile. 'Good morning. It's very nice to see you again. How can I help you? Do you wish to book a room?'

'No, thank you.' She hesitated uncomfortably. 'I've come about the job of bookkeeper ... that's if it is still available.'

Paul Hawkins's florid face was a picture of bewilderment. 'Really! I haven't advertised it yet! How did you know about it?'

'A little bird told me,' Julia told him coyly.

'I see.' He stared at her as if suddenly remembering her more clearly. 'Miss Winter, I seem to recollect that you left here rather suddenly.'

Julia nodded. 'I did, didn't I?' She sighed. 'I'm afraid it was a family emergency. Everything is settled now,' she said ambiguously. 'I do need to find a job, though, and as soon as I heard that you were looking for a bookkeeper it sounded the perfect answer. I'm sure I can provide the sort of service you are looking for,' she told him with a winning smile.

'You have worked in an office?'

'Oh, yes.' She smiled confidently. 'As soon as I left school.'

Julia sat with her fingers crossed, praying he wouldn't ask for details. She didn't want to reveal the name of her father's firm, nor the fact that her working experience there had been extremely limited. She didn't think he would be very impressed if he found out that she'd only been there for a very short time as the office junior who was expected to stamp the letters and make the tea.

'Right.' He tugged at the points of his waistcoat. 'Well, if you'll take a seat and wait a moment, I'll call Mrs Hawkins. She'll want to meet you and ask some questions,' he explained. 'Up until now she has been the one running that side of things, you see, so she would be instructing you in your duties.'

Julia nodded. 'I understand.'

Eunice Hawkins was in her late thirties and she sailed into the office rather like a schooner under full sail. She was overweight and not very tall. Despite her cleverly designed flowing black dress her pregnancy was far more obvious than Julia's. Her peroxide-blonde hair was piled up high on her head and her plump cheeks were brightly rouged, making her look like a life-sized porcelain doll. She was puffing away breathlessly as she lowered herself down on to the chair her husband held steady for her.

As they were introduced Julia noticed that although her light blue eyes were sharp and intelligent she constantly deferred to her husband and rarely questioned anything he said.

'You can see that it's no longer possible for me to go on working,' she exclaimed exhaustedly after Paul Hawkins had introduced them.

'We want someone who can start right away so that my wife can initiate them into what is required before it's too late for her to be able to do so,' Paul Hawkins added.

'My doctor says I need to have more rest from now on, until the baby is born,' Eunice explained.

'I quite understand.' Julia nodded. 'You see, I'm pregnant myself.'

She bit her lip worriedly as she saw them exchange glances. The moment the words were out she wished she'd not told them quite so soon. She should have waited until after they'd completed the interview and agreed to give her the job, but it was too late now.

'My baby's not due until December,' she said quickly. 'That's ages away,' she added with a tight little laugh. 'Probably you'll have had your baby and be back running the office before mine arrives,' she gabbled on.

She felt anxious as, once again, Mr and Mrs Hawkins exchanged glances with each other.

'So you are Mrs Winter, not Miss Winter, and your husband – where is he?' Paul Hawkins asked.

For a moment Julia felt too choked to speak. Then taking a deep breath she said in a low voice, 'The man who was to have been my husband is dead. He was killed at the second battle of Ypres.' She raised her head proudly and dabbed at her eyes at the same time.

'My dear,' Eunice Hawkins leaned forward and patted her arm. 'I am so sorry; it must be terrible for you. Your family must be so concerned about you.'

Julia shook her head, still wiping the tears from her eyes. 'I have no family now,' she confessed in a voice only a little above a whisper. 'They turned me out when . . . when they heard about the baby, so I am all on my own. My baby will be my family when it arrives,' she added with a brave little smile.

'You poor girl!' Eunice murmured in a concerned voice. 'So where are you living?'

Julia chewed on her lower lip and lowered her eyes, looking down at her lap uneasily. 'I have a room in Frederick Court,' she said in a low voice.

'Frederick Court?'

'It's in one of those alleyways off Scotland Road, my love,' Paul Hawkins told her quickly.

'Good heavens!' Eunice Hawkins held her

hand to her mouth. 'Are you comfortable there?'

Julia gave a little shudder. 'No, not really, but it is all I can afford.'

Again the Hawkinses looked at each other questioningly, then Paul Hawkins cleared his throat noisily. 'You can have a room here – if that would help,' he said brusquely.

Julia's turquoise eyes widened in affected surprise. 'I could never afford to do that!' she gasped.

'It would be one of our staff rooms, not quite like what you enjoyed when you stayed here as a guest,' he explained quickly. 'It would be clean and comfortable and quite pleasant, I can assure you. What is also important is that you would not have to pay for it or for heating and lighting.'

'In fact, you could also have your meals included in the package as part of your wages. We'll work something out,' Eunice Hawkins promised.

'It sounds wonderful,' Julia breathed with a grateful smile. 'I would need some wages, though. I must save for things I will need for the baby.'

'Yes, we quite understand about that,' Paul Hawkins assured her quickly, then added cautiously, 'I think we are all rushing ahead far too quickly. Let my wife show you the work we will require you to do and then we can settle all these other matters, if we think you are suitable and if you still want the job.'

Julia went out of her way to impress them both and convince them of her ability not only to do the work Eunice outlined, but to carry out any other tasks they might require her to do. She was quick to realise how much she had missed the sort of comfort the Darnley offered. Now, she not only wanted to work there but also to be able to live there as well.

When, after Mr and Mrs Hawkins had consulted together in private, and confirmed that she had both the job and a room there, she couldn't wait to tell Bob the good news and to celebrate with him in style.

The only thing that remained to do now was to tell Martha that she was giving up her room. She didn't think it would upset Martha too much because she would have no trouble at all in letting it, and at probably double the rent now that, with Bob's help, she had spruced it up so well.

Julia knew she should be overwhelmingly grateful for all the help and concern she was receiving from Eunice Hawkins. In actual fact, she felt both overwhelmed and stifled by all the attention. Eunice always seemed to be close by, watching her, as if noting every movement she made.

Sometimes Julia felt that Eunice appeared to be almost as concerned about her health and welfare as she was about her own.

'She advises me about my meals and what I

should be eating and drinking and she even tries to tell me how to spend my free time,' she told Bob resentfully. 'Every day she checks to make sure that I not only get plenty of exercise, but that it's the right kind. It wouldn't be so bad, but she also supervises me all the time while we are working.'

For all that, Julia had to admit that she was enjoying being at the Darnley. She found it quite easy to understand the hotel routine and to cope with the bookkeeping on a day-to-day basis. She kept telling Eunice and Paul that she could manage quite well on her own and that it was time for Eunice to rest more.

Neither of them seemed to take any notice of what she said, though, and much to her annoyance, Eunice continued to shadow her all the time.

'You need to have plenty of rest – just as much as I do,' Eunice insisted. 'I know all about these things and I understand exactly how you must be feeling, my dear, and how tired you must be at the end of a busy day.'

Julia kept assuring them both that she felt fine, that she didn't have any backache or swollen ankles or anything else wrong with her. She would have liked to point out to Eunice that this was because she was so much younger than her and in much better physical shape. She wasn't overweight like Eunice, but she couldn't tell her that, in case she hurt Eunice's feelings.

Julia was aware that Eunice had gone out of

her way to make sure that her room was comfortable. She had insisted on installing a well-upholstered armchair and a padded footstool. She had also brought along cushions and added so many other little touches to make the room more attractive. Julia had also brought all her personal belongings from the room she'd had in Frederick Court so that what had once been an austere staff bedroom was transformed into a cosy little nest.

It was Paul, though, who suggested that instead of having to take time off in order to visit a local doctor Julia should be seen by the doctor who came to visit Eunice each week.

Dr Christopher Wiseman was middle-aged, tall and suave with a highly polished bedside manner. He arranged to see Julia even though she told Paul and Eunice that she felt it was unnecessary. She felt embarrassed by so much solicitude. When she tried to protest there were such hurt expressions on the faces of her benefactors that she tactfully withdrew her protestations and expressed gratitude instead.

Bob Reynolds was highly amused when she told him all about what was happening and teased her good-naturedly about the fuss they were making of her.

'Fallen on your feet, I'd say,' he laughed. 'You should be pleased that they are so good to you, especially after the sort of harsh treatment you received from the bosses in the factories where you tried to get work.'

Julia sighed. 'Yes, I know I should be. It's just that both Mr and Mrs Hawkins seem to be doing far too much for me. I'm only an employee after all.'

'Well, repay them by doing a good job, especially when Eunice Hawkins can no longer work.'

Julia remembered his words when, towards the end of November, Paul told her that Eunice was not too well.

'Doctor Wiseman has insisted that she must stay in bed. He wants her to stay there until after the baby arrives, so I do hope you are going to be able to manage things on your own,' Paul said worriedly.

'Of course I can! I've had ample time to learn your routine. I have told Eunice that she should rest more,' Julia responded. 'May I go and see her?'

'Well, the doctor said she was to have complete rest and that she was not to have any visitors at all for a few days,' Paul said awkwardly.

Over the next few days he seemed to be distracted, almost distraught. He seemed to spend more time in his private quarters with Eunice than he did in the hotel itself.

Julia felt most concerned and wondered if there was anything more she could do to help. Whenever she asked he shook his head firmly and dismissed her enquiry about his wife almost as if he resented her curiosity.

'Dr Wiseman has recommended a highly qualified nurse who has also been trained as a midwife,' Paul explained. 'She will be living in and taking care of Eunice so we must all accept her rulings about visitors as well as everything else.'

Julia still had no idea what the problem was, but Dr Wiseman seemed to be in constant attendance. He always looked very grave as he left the hotel. In addition, he also seemed to be in complete agreement with the nurse that no one, other than Eunice's husband, was to visit her.

Although Julia accepted his ruling she still felt very puzzled and questioned Dr Wiseman when she next saw him for her own check-up.

'Complete rest is essential for Mrs Hawkins,' he told her firmly. 'I hope everyone is obeying the strict instructions that have been imposed,' he added unsmilingly.

Julia was surprised by his attitude. The polished bedside manner seemed to have vanished. He seemed to be treating her almost as if she was a stranger.

Bob was as nonplussed as she was when she told him about the strained atmosphere at the Darnley. To try and put her at her ease, he came up with all sorts of excuses.

'Becoming a father at his age is probably quite an undertaking for Paul Hawkins,' he pointed out. 'He must be in his fifties if he's a day, and even though Eunice is quite a bit younger than him she's no spring chicken either.'

'Do you think they really want a baby at their time of life?' Julia asked, puzzled.

'Oh there's no doubt about that. Paul has made no secret of the fact. Eunice has tried to start a family several times, but it has always come to nothing.'

Julia frowned. 'What do you mean?'

Bob looked uncomfortable. 'She's miscarried, hasn't she? That's why they're making all this fuss about her staying in bed from now until this one is born. They want this baby so badly that they don't want to take any chances.'

Once she understood how important it was that Eunice must have complete rest, Julia accepted her exclusion from Eunice's bedside as philosophically as she could. After all, she kept reminding herself, she was only an employee.

She also kept reminding herself that with her own baby's birth so imminent it was more important than ever that she remain on good terms with Eunice and Paul Hawkins, as well as with Dr Wiseman.

Chapter Nineteen

Eunice Hawkins felt extremely uneasy. She was almost at full term in her pregnancy and she knew she should have felt both excited and relieved. Instead, there was an undercurrent of concern in her mind about what the outcome was going to be.

This was her fourth pregnancy in fifteen years. So far, nothing untoward had gone wrong, but she kept remembering all her previous confinements and their tremendous disappointments. Consequently, a strong feeling of foreboding hung over her like a grey cloud.

Christopher Wiseman kept assuring her that all was well and that very, very soon she would at last be holding a baby in her arms. She hoped he was right. At the back of her mind, though, there was the constant reminder that with her history there was always the chance that something might go wrong.

She knew that because of her age this was probably the last time she could ever risk being pregnant again. The desire for herself and Paul to have a child, preferably a son, was so much more important to her husband than it was to her. His hankering for an heir was overpowering.

She sometimes wondered if it was the main reason why he had married her.

She'd been twenty-one and Paul had been over forty when they'd first met. In those days she'd been slim and pretty and was already working at the Darnley Hotel as a receptionist when he'd taken over as the manager. He'd been intrigued by her youthful gaiety and she'd been impressed by the dark, handsome man and fallen for his mature charms.

She resented the fact that her doctor was insisting that she must rest, preferably in bed, from now until her baby was born, but she knew better than to argue with him, at least in front of Paul.

On her own, though, and confined to her bedroom, it meant many hours of solitude. With nothing to do except read she found herself spending a great deal of time brooding and remembering the past. Normally this was something which she preferred not to do because it left her feeling depressed.

She'd not been much older than Julia Winter when she'd first come to work at the Darnley Hotel. That was sixteen years ago, years that had at first been extremely exciting, but which now had deteriorated into a dull monotony.

After her parents had died within two months of each other, she had needed not only a job, but also a roof over her head. The opportunity to work at the Darnley Hotel had been a dream come true, especially as it meant she could also live there in the staff quarters.

At first she had been terribly lonely then, gradually, she'd begun to make friends. At first it had been joining other members of the staff to go dancing or to the pictures. Then it had been dates with young unattached businessmen who visited Liverpool on behalf of their companies and frequently stayed at the hotel.

She'd learned to make the most of herself: she'd dressed smartly and improved her already good looks with carefully chosen make-up and flattering hairstyles.

She'd not only attracted the notice of the clientele but also of the new manager, Paul Hawkins, when he took over the hotel a few months after she started work there, and she'd been highly impressed by the suavely handsome man with his sleek dark hair, grey eyes, dynamic personality and boundless energy.

He was almost twice her age, a man of the world, and a successful businessman. She was flattered by his interest and flirted with him outrageously. She tantalised him, weaving a magic spell of promise until he was so besotted that he was unable to resist her charms.

Paul Hawkins had plenty of money and he was ready to spend it freely in order to give her a good time. He took her out, bought her countless attractive presents, and gave her beautiful flowers. Outside their working environment he treated her as though she was on a pedestal.

At first she wasn't serious about their relationship. To her he was a middle-aged man, but she basked in his attention. She also played on the fact that Paul was extremely flattered to have a young girl interested in him. Even though he probably suspected that she was merely looking for a good time and a bit of fun, he wanted more than that.

When they met, it was the start of a new century. Queen Victoria had just died and the new king, Edward the Seventh and his attractive wife, Queen Alexandra, had brought a breath of excitement, heralding the start of a new era.

Paul Hawkins's arrival at the Darnley opened up a new and exciting life for Eunice when he responded to her flirtation and started paying her a great deal of attention. In next to no time he had swept her off her feet with his smooth tongue and overpowering charm.

He'd told her that together they'd be the perfect team. With his business experience and her youthful exuberance and spontaneous enthusiasm they could make the Darnley one of the best hotels in Liverpool.

She was impressed and excited, and she believed him. She hung on his every word, did everything possible to please him and help him fulfil his highest dreams.

Paul was her first lover, indeed her only lover. The first time she found herself pregnant she was overjoyed. So was Paul. He couldn't do enough for her. If he'd put her on a pedestal before, now he cocooned her in cotton wool.

She was his princess. All his deep-seated dreams of having a family, a son to follow in his footsteps, were about to come true, thanks to her.

In those days she'd been bubbly as well as attractive. Over the years, and as the result of three abortive pregnancies, she had put on weight. She'd also lost her light-hearted, frothy approach to life. Gradually, her charms depended on her mature ripeness and experience rather than on glamour.

The first time she'd become pregnant, Paul had proposed and insisted, without a moment's hesitation, that they should be married right away. He'd been overjoyed at the thought of a boy, a son and heir, someone to carry on his family name.

There'd been an expensive wedding. The elaborate reception had been at the Darnley. They'd been toasted and fêted by all their staff and also by many of their regular clientele and all those who had been specially invited for the occasion.

When she'd seen the wedding photographs, however, she'd been horrified. She was very conscious about the difference in their ages, but in their wedding pictures it was so startlingly evident that she wanted to cry. It was a case of beauty and the beast, she'd thought bitterly. Paul appeared middle-aged and so pompous in his morning suit and grey topper that he looked more like her father than the bridegroom. On the other hand, she looked young and innocent in her fairytale white satin dress and floating white veil.

Six months into her pregnancy she'd miscarried. Paul had been absolutely devastated. Once she was over the initial shock she'd been secretly relieved. She felt she was too young to be tied down with a child. She wanted to go dancing and to parties; she still had a lot of living to do.

A month or so later, when she was ready to work again in the hotel, Paul had already replaced her. She'd been disappointed, but Paul told her that he wanted her to be a full-time wife. He was confident that she'd be pregnant again in next to no time.

She knew it would be no good arguing with him, but she'd been determined to keep working, so she'd started to help behind the scenes in the hotel.

Initially, it had amounted to little more than organising the day-to-day routine. Then, gradually, he'd agreed to her taking over the bookkeeping. It had been pretty dull work so that when she became pregnant for the second time, she'd felt almost relieved.

She'd lost the baby again, though. This time she'd only been five and a half months pregnant. Paul had been aghast, but she'd been the one who had stayed optimistic. To her amazement, she found that she was now the one who wanted a baby even more than Paul did; she couldn't wait to become a mum.

Almost two years passed before she'd been able to breathe a sigh of relief, confident that everything was going to be all right. She was going to be a mother at last. Paul was over the moon and insisted on cosseting her almost as if she was an invalid, pandering to her every whim.

The months seemed to crawl by, and the waiting was interminable. She was so scared remembering her previous pregnancy, when she reached five months. To her great relief, that milestone passed successfully and her hopes soared. She indulged herself in new clothes, good wines and delicious food. She was bursting with enthusiasm; she wanted to celebrate every night of the week. She would have done so, if Paul hadn't restrained her because he was so concerned that it wasn't good for the baby.

Two months before she was due to give birth, the inevitable happened. Paul panicked at the sight of blood, fearing the worst was once again happening. He had been right. A week later and it was all over. The baby arrived early, and it was far too premature to survive the ordeal of being born.

After that, because, once again, she compensated for her loss by over-eating, her figure suffered, but her spirits were so low that she no longer cared how she looked.

She and Paul quarrelled constantly. She pushed him away, determined not to make love whenever he tried to take her in his arms. She never wanted to go through the ordeal of becoming pregnant ever again, convinced that it was highly unlikely that it would result in a healthy, live baby.

Paul, tired of her rebuffs, spent more and more time chatting up the younger members of the staff. Finally, out of jealousy, and knowing that she'd lost her youthful looks, her figure and her charms, she welcomed him back to her bed again.

They agreed that it would be a completely fresh start for them both. Knowing that she would never see thirty again, she changed everything about her appearance, from the colour of her hair to the style of clothes she wore.

Paul indulged her and even though she now looked plump and a little bit brassy, he made no comment. He'd put on considerable weight himself and, even though he still had quite a commanding figure for a man in his fifties, he couldn't conceal his paunch or his florid complexion.

Eunice once again found herself pregnant. Since she was now in her late thirties they were well aware that there was an even greater risk that she would lose the baby than there had been before.

Paul immediately engaged the services of a

private doctor, Christopher Wiseman. He'd been recommended because he specialised in difficult childbirth cases and he'd promised that there would be a live baby at the end of her pregnancy. To achieve this, of course, she must do exactly as he told her to do and follow his advice and the regime he imposed to the letter.

For all his suave bedside manner, Christopher Wiseman was a hard taskmaster. He regulated her food and drink and imposed a carefully designed exercise rota. He even told her how many hours' sleep she must have each night and recommended rest periods during the day.

He wanted her to give up her work in the hotel completely from the time she was five months pregnant. It wasn't easy to comply because of the War. Men, and even women, were still being recruited for the armed services or to work in armament factories. Hiring suitable staff was not easy so they had kept deferring the decision until Julia Winter had applied for the job.

Eunice had been surprised to learn that Julia was pregnant, especially when she claimed that her baby was due at the same time as her own. Julia looked incredibly fit and well. Yet, at the same time, it had been rather encouraging. Somehow, it had made the likelihood of her own pregnancy being successful seem more possible.

When she had told Dr Wiseman about the surprising coincidence, he had suggested that perhaps he should look after Julia as well as her.

She had liked the idea and, to humour her, Paul had agreed. It had been comforting to be able to compare notes and to share symptoms with Julia, and this had taken a lot of the anxiety out of her own waiting.

At least it had until now. As a precaution Dr Wiseman had insisted that she gave up work completely now that the baby was due within only a matter of weeks.

'What about Julia? Can we rest up together?' she asked, when Dr Wiseman insisted on her stopping work.

'Julia doesn't need to rest,' he told her. 'She's not only younger and a lot fitter than you, but her baby isn't due until two weeks after yours.'

At first, she'd sulked and tried to persuade him to change his mind, but Dr Wiseman would not be moved. He not only didn't think Julia needed to rest, but he wouldn't even allow her to come up and visit. Furthermore, he'd even convinced Paul how essential it was that she didn't do so.

She felt annoyed that he was keeping them apart because in the short time they'd been working together Julia had become a friend. 'We've shared our progress, she understands me and she knows how I feel and what I'm experiencing like no one else can possibly do,' she repeatedly told Paul and Dr Wiseman.

Both of them remained adamant.

'You can talk about it afterwards, after your babies are born . . . that's if you still want to do so,' Dr Wiseman told her firmly.

At the time, Eunice had thought them heartless, but later she realised that she should have known better, and she was glad that Paul had insisted that she follow their advice.

Now, as she looked down at the precious bundle cradled in her arms, she could understand Dr Wiseman's reasoning and, with hindsight, she couldn't fault him. He had been so right, of course, in the way he had handled things.

Under the circumstances she didn't want to talk to Julia about the baby; it wouldn't be fair to do so, not yet, at any rate.

Chapter Twenty

Incredulity and shock mingled on Julia Winter's face as she listened to what Dr Christopher Wiseman had to say at the end of his customary check on her progress.

'Are you quite sure there is something wrong?' she protested. 'I feel absolutely fine!'

'It's not you who is stressed, Julia, it is the baby,' he explained abruptly. 'Unless you come into my clinic immediately and your baby is induced right away, then I am extremely concerned about what might happen.'

The colour drained from her face and she was shaking. 'You mean it could die?'

'I'm very much afraid that is a possibility.'

She shook her head in disbelief. 'Why is it stressed, what has happened? What has suddenly gone wrong? I've been so careful,' she gulped, tears spilling down her face. 'I've done everything you've advised me to do.'

'Don't upset yourself, please,' he warned. 'It's not your fault. It occasionally happens. The baby is constantly moving and sometimes ends up lying in a position where it manages to twist the umbilical cord around its neck.'

'And when that happens what does it mean? Is it dangerous for the baby?'

His eyebrows rose and he let an ominous silence convey the risk that was involved.

Julia shuddered and covered her face with her hands. The possibility of losing the baby was too dreadful to contemplate and something she'd never even thought about the whole time she'd been pregnant.

If that happened, then all her endeavours to get away from home, to be independent so that she could keep this one last memento of Bernard, would be gone for ever. It mustn't happen. She wouldn't let it.

'So what do I have to do? Can you help me, Dr Wiseman? You must save my baby,' she implored.

'My recommendation is that your baby should be induced as soon as possible. As I've already suggested, if you come into my clinic right away, then the necessary procedure can be commenced immediately.'

'You mean today?' she gasped. 'My baby isn't due for another couple of weeks.'

'Yes, I am well aware of that,' he frowned, consulting the papers in front of him, 'but I cannot recommend too strongly that you take my advice immediately, that's if you want to save the life of your baby.'

Julia looked bewildered. 'You want me to come right away? Right now!'

'That's what I advise,' he repeated impassively.

236

'Of course I want to do what you say,' Julia agreed, 'but I don't see how I can. Mrs Hawkins is confined to her room so it would mean leaving Mr Hawkins in the lurch. He's expecting me to cover for her, you see.'

'I am quite sure he will understand my concern and want you to do as I suggest.'

Julia shook her head uncertainly. Her mind was in turmoil. She was torn between her need to do what was asked of her for the baby's sake and her reluctance to cause Paul Hawkins any inconvenience.

'I don't know what to say,' she explained ruefully. 'Mr and Mrs Hawkins have both been so kind and considerate to me ever since I came to work here that I hate the idea of letting them down.'

Dr Wiseman sat drumming his long white fingers on the table impatiently and humming tunelessly to himself as he waited for her decision.

'Perhaps you would you like me to speak to Paul Hawkins and explain the situation on your behalf,' he offered.

A look of relief lightened Julia's face. 'Would you?' she breathed gratefully. 'If he feels he has to say no, I shall quite understand,' she added quickly.

'I'm sure he won't do that. He is bound to realise how important this baby is to you. Now don't worry. Run along and pack a bag with the things you are going to need for a week in my clinic while I speak to Paul. I'm sure he will give his consent and then I can drive you straight there.'

When she returned ten minutes later with a bag packed with her own things and those she had prepared for when the baby was born, she found Dr Wiseman waiting for her.

'Paul Hawkins has been most understanding and has accepted my diagnosis without any quibbling,' he told her.

'That is very considerate of him.'

'He seemed to be most concerned about your predicament because he realised how serious the situation is for your baby. Furthermore, he understands that this is an emergency and that there is no time to lose, so shall we go?'

Julia hesitated. 'I must see him for a few minutes before I leave. There are things he needs to know,' she explained.

Dr Wiseman took his gold hunter watch out of his waistcoat pocket and studied it, frowning impatiently. 'Five minutes, no longer,' he said brusquely.

'I'm very sorry to hear this news, Julia,' Paul Hawkins told her, his face full of concern. 'The final weeks can be a very worrying time; I know only too well from Eunice's previous confinements. That is why I have been so concerned about her condition these last few weeks. It's why I've insisted that she follows Dr Wiseman's edict to the letter and has complete rest. Now I shall expect you to do the same. Put yourself in his experienced hands and do whatever he tells you. Believe me; you can rely on him to take care of things.'

'Thank you. I'll do my best. I'm sorry if it is inconveniencing you . . .'

'Not another word! Come along now,' he said, as he propelled her towards the door. 'Let's not keep the doctor waiting. You are very fortunate that he became aware of your dilemma in good time. You are also very lucky that he is able to accommodate you in his clinic at such short notice so that he can deal with the matter.'

'Yes, I suppose I am, but I feel rather frightened,' Julia admitted, letting the tears come at last.

Paul puffed out his cheeks. 'I can assure you that you have nothing to worry about and that you will receive the very best treatment and care,' he assured her.

Having been given Paul Hawkins's permission, as well as having his support and concern, Julia felt a lot better about accepting whatever Dr Wiseman might tell her was necessary.

Nevertheless, as he drove her from the Darnley to his private clinic in Bold Street, she became more and more apprehensive. She was puzzled about what had gone wrong and how it could possibly have happened. She had been so careful. She'd followed all his instructions and listened to Eunice's good advice about all the things she should and should not do. She still felt so well in herself that she'd been positive,

239

until this moment, that she would have a healthy baby when the time came.

More than anything she wished Dr Wiseman had given her enough time to let Bob know what was happening. They'd been seeing quite a lot of each other recently and he would be worried when he heard the news from Paul Hawkins.

Surely this is merely a precautionary measure that Dr Wiseman is taking, she told herself over and over again. As she sat in the back of his car as it nosed its way along Whitechapel, through the busy traffic in Church Street and turning left into Bold Street, she tried desperately to convince herself that everything was going to be all right.

Julia huddled beneath the crisp white sheet desperately trying to come to terms with what had happened. She had no idea how long she had been in Dr Wiseman's clinic. It had been the middle of a cold morning, bright with early December sun, when she'd left the Darnley. Now it was grey and dank outside, so it probably wasn't still the same day.

Everything had happened so swiftly from the moment she'd arrived at Dr Wiseman's clinic that she felt bewildered and disorientated. She'd barely been inside the building before she found herself divested of her own clothes and decked out in a white clinical gown.

After a careful examination Dr Wiseman had confirmed that his initial fears were justified.

'The baby is in a serious state of distress and immediate intervention is necessary,' he told her. The next thing she knew was that she was being whisked away to the operating theatre.

She dimly remembered there'd been several gowned figures alongside her all talking to each other but not to her. She recalled a sweet, sickly smell and the pressure of a pad of some kind being placed over her face. After that there was nothing but complete oblivion.

Now, waking up and finding herself in bed in an austere room with a nurse sitting at her bedside, she still wasn't sure where she was or what had taken place.

The moment the nurse saw her open her eyes and try to speak she leaned over the bed, murmuring soothing words. She took Julia's hand and checked her pulse before saying she would summon Dr Wiseman.

Julia tried to ask her what had happened, but though she mouthed the words her voice seemed to fail her.

Dr Wiseman looked very grave and formal as he, too, checked her pulse. In a subdued voice he explained that despite all their efforts to save her baby it had been stillborn.

'I did tell you that it was in considerable distress and was lying in a dangerous position,' he reminded her as she stared at him in disbelief and covered her face with her hands. 'As I feared, your baby was strangled by the umbilical cord,' he explained. 'Even though we operated the moment you reached here it was too late. I am so sorry. I know what a terrible loss this must be for you.'

She didn't want to believe him. She was sure he had made some serious mistake, so she shook her head, refusing to believe what he was saying.

She slid her hands down under the bedclothes and felt the flat void of her stomach. Her baby had been born, there was no doubt about that, so it must be around somewhere. They'd bring it in to her any minute now so that she could feed it, she told herself.

'Julia, are you listening to me? Do you understand what I am saying?'

She turned her head away; clenching her teeth, refusing to meet Dr Wiseman's stern, dark eyes. Again he told her that they had been unable to save her baby and that it had been stillborn.

His words reverberated inside her head. Dead, stillborn; your baby is dead, it was stillborn.

She felt so devastated that she didn't want to think about it, far less talk about it.

In her mind's eye she'd visualised it as a boy, a living replica of Bernard. A little boy who would grow up sturdy, intelligent, and every bit as handsome as his father had been.

She'd seen Baby Bernie as being the centre of her life, her universe. He was to have been her entire future, her whole reason for living.

Now there was no baby and the future looked bleak. She felt sad, lost and very lonely. She didn't even want to think about the days ahead; days that would stretch into months and then into years. Her life would be an enormous vacuum because all her plans had come to nothing. No one needed her; no one would care what happened to her. From now on she was nothing but an empty shell; a piece of flotsam to drift or be blown around at will.

She dragged herself back to reality, aware that Dr Wiseman was still at her bedside. 'Can I see my baby?'

'No Julia, I don't think that is advisable,' he murmured. He shook his head regretfully. 'There is no point in distressing yourself any further, my dear,' he added consolingly.

'Was it a boy?'

He remained non-committal. Taking one of her hands he held it between both of his. 'For the moment it is better not to try to talk about it or even think about what has happened,' he said firmly. 'I want you to put the entire incident out of your head as though it never happened,' he counselled.

Julia closed her eyes wearily. She felt bruised and sore both physically and mentally. This couldn't be happening. It was like a nightmare, even her mind was cloudy. She felt too exhausted to argue with him. Perhaps he was right and she should put it all behind her. What possible good would it do to dwell on what had happened?

Pregnancies did go wrong. Look how many Eunice had endured which had ended in tragedy.

It reminded her that Eunice's baby was due about now. Making a supreme effort she forced herself to ask how Eunice was.

'Mrs Hawkins has a baby daughter,' he told her. 'It was born the day before you came in here. Didn't you know?'

'How could I, when you kept her isolated in her room and everyone was forbidden to see her?' she said irritably.

'I thought perhaps Mr Hawkins may have mentioned it.'

'He probably thought it was better to say nothing when he heard that my pregnancy was not going well,' she murmured. 'She's been very fortunate,' Julia sighed enviously.

'Yes, indeed. A splendid result, especially after so many disappointments,' he agreed.

'I would have thought that my chances of having a safe delivery and a live baby were far greater than hers,' Julia protested peevishly. 'I'm young and healthy and I've had a trouble-free pregnancy. Eunice has had several miscarriages and she has needed bed rest for the past few weeks.'

Dr Wiseman smiled wryly. 'One never knows how things will finally turn out.'

Julia's eyes filled with tears. She began to whimper, softly at first, then rising to a hysterical crescendo. The bitter torrent of tears racked her body.

Dr Wiseman placed a hand firmly on her shaking shoulders, murmuring words of condolence and comfort, but they fell on deaf ears.

Her despair was so pathetic that it filled him with a deep-seated feeling of remorse which troubled him. He knew that only time would erase the mental bruising that she was suffering.

'I am going to give you a sedative, Julia,' he told her compassionately. 'Something to soothe your nerves and help you to sleep. When you waken you will feel calmer and stronger, and hopefully you will be able to accept the inevitable.'

Julia had no idea how long she slept. She felt as though she had lost all sense of time. She hovered between sleep and reality for so long that everything around her became blurred and she was unable to work out what was happening.

Whenever she stirred and opened her eyes, nurses supported her and held cups of liquid to her lips, gently encouraging her to drink.

When she eventually surfaced back to normality she discovered that she'd lost almost a week. Her bruised body had healed, but her mind was a blank about so many things that she felt completely disorientated.

It was not until she was allowed out of bed and could do things for herself, that everything around her gradually become more normal. She was anxious to get out of the clinic and away from all the bitter memories she now associated with it.

She knew it wasn't Dr Wiseman's fault. The nurses had all told her that these things happened. There were often complications, especially with first pregnancies, over which there was no control. They even went as far as to tell her she'd been extremely lucky because she'd been in such good hands and had received such first-class care.

When Dr Wiseman came to tell her that she was now well enough to be discharged, he tried to encourage her to put this very unfortunate episode behind her and to try and make the most of the future.

'Mr and Mrs Hawkins asked me to tell you that your room at the Darnley is still there waiting for your return. Your job is also there whenever you feel well enough to go back to it,' he reminded her.

The news was reassuring. At least she still had both a job and a roof over her head, so she wouldn't have to resort to asking Bob for help once again. Returning to the familiar routine might help to restore her confidence and give her time to sort out in her own mind exactly what she wanted to do next, she decided resignedly.

'You're very young, so you'll have more children,' the sister in charge reminded her as she left the clinic. 'Try not to brood about it. You're an attractive young woman and you'll soon find another boyfriend and get married and start all over again.'

Paul Hawkins said much the same thing when she returned to the Darnley. 'My word, you are looking very fit and trim,' he said admiringly as he welcomed her back. 'Do take some time off if you feel like it. Don't be in too much of a hurry to start work again,' he advised.

'Surely you must be finding it difficult to cope with everything without either me or Eunice here to help,' she countered.

'I've managed, but it's not been very easy,' he admitted. 'Our little daughter seems to demand a lot of attention. I would welcome the chance to be able to spend more time with her, because every moment is so precious.'

'Of course you must want to do that and I'm ready to start work right away,' Julia told him haltingly.

As she blinked away her tears his face became a patchwork of disturbed emotions. Suddenly conscious of how insensitive he had been in mentioning their new baby he touched her arm, shaking his head and looking embarrassed as he struggled to find the right words to tell her so.

Chapter Twenty-one

The rest of December 1915 seemed to pass in a complete haze as far as Julia was concerned. The week she remained in Dr Wiseman's clinic after the Caesarean operation she'd felt so dispirited that she didn't care if she ever recovered or not. Her baby was dead; the one final link with Bernard was gone for ever.

She still couldn't accept the fact that her baby had died or understand why it had happened, because she had felt so well all the way through her pregnancy. Remembering all the old wives' tales she'd heard, mainly from Eunice Hawkins, she'd taken care not to do anything particularly strenuous. She'd not even gone dancing. Apart from the occasional walk, and a trip to the pictures once a week with Bob Reynolds, her time had been taken up with working at the Darnley.

Dr Wiseman had been very solicitous and eventually he'd tried to talk her through what had happened and to explain everything, but none of it made any sense to her. He had prescribed medication to help her deal with her overwhelming despondency and to encourage her to put it all behind her and stop worrying since there was nothing now she could do about it.

By returning to work as soon as she was discharged from the clinic, she'd hoped it would help, but she so often found her mind drifting that she wasn't surprised when Paul Hawkins became impatient. He also told her to put the past behind her and to get on with her life.

'You're young and attractive, so look to the future. Most girls in your situation would have given a sigh of relief and thought of it as a chance for a fresh start. Go out and enjoy yourself when you are not working. Start the New Year as you mean to go on; think yourself lucky that you have no responsibilities.'

'You can afford to be optimistic,' Julia pointed out balefully. 'You and Eunice have a baby daughter. You've got everything you've ever wanted.'

Paul smiled and nodded, and then he frowned. 'No, not quite everything I wanted, Julia. I was hoping for a boy.'

'You've got a healthy, living baby,' Julia exploded, her eyes blazing, her voice husky with emotion, 'so both of you should think yourselves lucky.'

'Oh we do,' he assured her, smiling fatuously. 'She needs an awful lot of attention, but she's filling out and gets more lovely every day.'

'Have you decided on a name for her?'

'Yes, we have.' He nodded, his grey eyes lighting up. 'We're going to call her Amanda.'

'Amanda.' Julia nodded thoughtfully. 'It sounds perfect.' She smiled. 'When are you going to let me see her?'

He looked uncomfortable. 'Whenever you are ready to do so,' he told her. 'Eunice is longing to show her off, but' – he spread his hands helplessly – 'we weren't sure how you felt about it . . . if you were ready yet.'

Julia wasn't at all sure what her reactions would be when she saw Eunice's baby for the first time. As she walked along the thickly carpeted corridor to their private rooms her thoughts were in turmoil. There was such a tight knot of envy building up inside her that she wanted to turn tail and run.

There was an anxious look on Eunice's plump face as she opened the door of their living room and her pale blue eyes locked with Julia's misty stare. Then the closeness that had built up between them since Julia had come to work at the hotel managed to bridge the gulf. In the next moment, they were in each other's arms, exchanging a babbling chorus of congratulations and commiserations.

'Oh, Julia, I've been longing to see you,' Eunice exclaimed, 'but it didn't seem right, somehow, to ask you come and see me. I know how bitter and desolate you must be feeling, and I was afraid you might think I was gloating by showing off Amanda,' she explained in an embarrassed voice.

Julia nodded silently, squeezing Eunice's hands to show she understood.

'So are you going to show her to me or not?' she asked, fighting back her tears.

Together they walked over to the elaborately canopied cradle. As she looked down at the sleeping baby Julia felt a strange sensation. It was as if a surge of pure love for the sleeping infant hit her like a tornado. All the pent-up bitterness that had threatened to sour her mind for ever seemed to be washed away.

'She's angelic,' she breathed. She reached out and traced the delicate outline of the baby's face from brow to chin, almost reverently.

She'd been uncertain about what her feelings would be when she saw Eunice's baby for the first time. She'd imagine she'd be jealous, resentful and envious. Instead, she felt a tremendous love for the baby and a deep-seated wish to protect her and to ensure that she was always safe and happy.

After that, Julia thought about Amanda constantly. Every day there seemed to be a change in her. Soon she was becoming plump and pretty with a fuzz of reddish-gold hair which, together with her big blue eyes, looked enchanting.

Julia often wondered what her own baby would have looked like. Bernard had been fair-haired, and his eyes a bright blue, so would their baby have had his colouring, or would it have had more turquoise-coloured eyes and auburn hair like she had? Julia sighed, perhaps a mixture of both, she thought wistfully.

It was something she would never know, she thought sadly. It was pointless tormenting herself by building up an imaginary picture in her mind.

Trying to forget, putting all thoughts of their baby out of her mind and concentrating on her own future was not easy, no matter how hard she tried to do so.

She'd seen Bob Reynolds once or twice since she'd returned to work. At their first meeting he'd seemed to be embarrassed about the whole event, especially about her losing her baby, but he'd tried to cheer her up nevertheless.

'Look luv, you've got to start again. There's a lot of living still to be done. You mustn't let this ruin the whole of your life. From what you've told me about him, I don't think your Bernard would want you to do that, now would he?'

At the time she resented his words and they only made her feel worse. Then, in the depths of the next sleepless night, she suddenly saw the sense of his reasoning. The baby, like the wedding she and Bernard had been planning to have, was not meant to be. She must accept that.

Bob Reynolds nodded sagely when she told him this and assured him that that she had come to terms with what had happened.

'Good. There's less than a week before this year ends and a new one begins, so remember, 1916 is going to be not only a new year, but also a new life for you.'

'It will be, I promise. From now on I'm going to think only about the future.'

'I'm going to make sure you really mean that. I'm taking you out on New Year's Eve. Put on your glad rags and we'll celebrate in style! We'll go dancing, have a drink, and at midnight we'll join in all the celebrations and see the New Year in together. OK?'

'I can't think of a better way of spending a Friday night,' she told him.

'It's not any old Friday night. This will be one that you will remember for ever.'

In that Bob was quite right, but not in the way he had intended. Friday, the last day of December 1915, was a further landmark for Julia. A small news item caught her eye as she was scanning through the morning edition of the *Liverpool Daily Post*:

It has been reported that Private Lance Winter of Warren Drive, Wallasey, only son of prominent local businessman George Winter, has been killed in action . . .

Julia read it through three times before it fully registered. Lance, her young brother, had become another casualty of the War. She didn't want to believe it. Lance was much too young to die.

First Bernard, and now her brother Lance. When would this massacre end? She might have walked away from her family, but she still had fond memories of Lance.

She would never forget the day when she'd first seen him as a tiny baby. She hadn't minded the fact that because he was a boy her father thought more of him than he did of her, even though she was the eldest, and she'd always tried to protect him as they were growing up. Occasionally she'd even lied for him, covered up when he was in a scrape of some kind rather than let him appear in a bad light in their father's eyes.

In return, Lance had looked up to her, depended on her, believed in her. He'd even understood her feelings for Bernard. He'd been sympathetic when she'd tried to persuade her mother and father to let her and Bernard marry. He was the only one she'd confided in that she intended to run away.

He was too young to do very much to help her, but they'd embraced, promised to keep in touch, and to meet again sometime in the future. Now, he was dead and they would never be able to do so.

Lance had always admired Bernard and he'd wanted to be like him. He'd been envious when Bernard had joined up. He'd obviously emulated him the moment he was old enough to do so, and had joined the army. Just like Bernard, he had been killed in action, the pair of them heroes, but dead nonetheless.

War was so cruel, Julia reflected. It affected so many lives and brought grief that spread out its evil tentacles far and wide.

Her mother would be heartbroken about Lance, and her father would be devastated. For a moment she was tempted to return home, to offer them her support and to try and comfort them. Then she remembered her parents' attitude towards her and she hardened her heart.

She was not ready to be verbally berated for failing them any more than she wanted to be reminded that in their eyes she had brought disgrace on the family.

Julia was filled with bitterness and grief. Bob Reynolds was right when he said that the past was over and there was nothing she could do to change any of the things that had happened. There was only one thing she could do now and that was to try and start afresh.

Julia intended to go wild on New Year's Eve even though Paul wanted her to help at the hotel. He could sack her if he wished, she didn't care. He had no worries, so how could he understand how she felt? She needed to drink, sing and dance to excess in order to erase every fragment of the past and to start with a clean, new slate on the first day of January 1916. She was determined that it was to be the beginning of a fresh start for her.

On New Year's Eve, Bob Reynolds saw a side of Julia he had never seen before.

He had suggested that they should go out somewhere for the evening and see out the old year in traditional style.

'I'd love to, but I think Paul is expecting me to work; it's always a busy night at the Darnley, apparently.'

'That's a pity, but if you feel you must, then I understand,' he told her.

She looked at him with her head on one side as she thought about it. 'Why should I work?' she muttered rebelliously. 'No, I've said I'll go out with you, so that's what I'll do.'

'You can work most of the evening if you want to, because I must spend some time with my mother. We've always seen the new year in together. Mind you, she goes to bed the moment the ship's klaxons and horns have sounded. As far as she is concerned, five minutes past twelve and we are into the new year and she's ready for her bed.'

'So we don't start celebrating until after midnight, Right?'

'You won't be too tired by then, will you?' he asked solicitously.

'Not a bit of it, you wait and see. I thought you said we'd go dancing, though?' she reminded him.

'I did, but I wasn't thinking clearly,' he admitted. 'I can hardly leave my old mum on her own. It would break her heart.'

'So I suppose I have to kick my heels until after midnight, then, do I?' She pouted.

Bob ran a hand through his thick hair. 'Perhaps you could come and meet her,' he suggested tentatively. 'Then, once it's five minutes into the new year, we could go and enjoy ourselves.'

Julia nodded thoughtfully. 'Yes, I suppose we could do that. We could all go out and have a drink . . . take your mum with us. It might be a change for her, she might like the idea.'

Bob pulled a face. 'I doubt it; she's pretty set in her ways. I can't think of the last time she went out for a meal, let alone went into a pub for a drink.'

'Then perhaps it is time that she did!'

'Well, I'll ask her, but don't count on it.'

'No, don't you ask her, I will,' Julia told him. 'I'll come round to your place between half past eight and nine o'clock.'

'Well, let's see how she reacts when she meets you, and if things go well, then we can suggest we all go out for a drink.'

Bob's mother seemed to be rather put out that Bob had invited anyone to join them, especially when she realised that it was a young girl.

After five minutes of talking to Julia, however, she seemed to change her mind. She approved of Julia's good manners, liked the way she spoke, and approved of the red wool dress she was wearing under her full-length navy blue coat. She was smart but not showy, she decided. She spoke quite differently from any of the girls who lived round them on Skirving Street and she had quite a respectable, responsible job.

Mrs Reynolds mellowed even more when she saw Julia stroking Tiger, their tortoiseshell moggy and when she noticed the aged cat purring quite happily when Julia picked it up. After a few minutes of kneading Julia's lap the cat not only settled down but dozed off.

Even so, Mrs Reynolds remained aloof and openly quizzed Julia about her background and where she was now working.

Eventually, Mrs Reynolds served up a hot punch and some homemade mince pies and she nodded approvingly when Julia accepted a second mince pie.

However, she looked rather taken aback when, shortly before midnight, Julia suggested that all three of them should go down to the Pier Head and be in the thick of things when the celebrations were at their height.

'No, I'm too old for all that sort of carry on; you and Bob go on your own. I'll stay here and keep my old moggy company. All those hooters and klaxons frighten him stiff.'

Julia feigned reluctance but she was easily persuaded. Tucking her arm through Bob's, she hurried him down Water Street so fast that by the time they reached the Pier Head they were both breathless.

When the New Year celebrations there finally ended, Bob took Julia to a club near Lime Street where they drank champagne and danced until the early hours of the morning.

They were both unsteady on their feet as they made their way back to the Darnley. Bob wanted to come inside and see her safely to her room, but she was sober enough to know that Paul wouldn't like that and insisted he left her at the side door which Paul had left unlocked.

There was a flatness about the start of the new year. Julia woke on Saturday morning with an aching head, a foul taste in her mouth, and a black depression that swamped all her good resolutions.

She dragged herself down to the hotel office. Paul Hawkins recognised her problem, sent for a pot of strong black coffee, and insisted that she drink two cups of it before she made any attempt to work.

Julia accepted his cure in silence; her head ached too much to argue. Half an hour later she was feeling sufficiently revived to attend to her duties and express her gratitude to Paul for his patience and understanding.

'I think you'd better find yourself another boyfriend if this is the state you get into when you go out for the evening with Bob Reynolds,' he told her grimly.

'It wasn't his fault. He tried to stop me from drinking so much, but I'd just read in the paper that my brother had been killed in action. It got to me because he was so young. I have no one to blame but myself.'

'Julia, I'm so sorry!' Paul looked stricken. 'I had no idea. Do you want to take a few days off, give yourself time to grieve? You will want to go and see your family, they must be devastated and—'

'That would be turning the clock back,' she interrupted.

'I don't know about that, but I can understand what a terrible blow it must be after . . . after everything else you've been through in the past few weeks.'

'They say that things happen in threes, don't they?' she said dryly. 'Three tragedies – Bernard, my baby and now my brother – three jobs, and then I found this one. Things are going to be all right now, I'm quite sure of that.'

Paul let his hand rest on hers. 'You're very brave and gutsy and that's something I admire.'

Julia stared into his grey eyes. 'So have I still got my job, even though I overdid things last night and I was too hungover first thing this morning to come to work on time?'

'You most certainly have, Julia. What is more, I hope you will go on working here and making your home with us for many years to come.'

She smiled and withdrew her hand. 'Then perhaps I'd better start doing some work before you change your mind.'

'Go up and wish Eunice a Happy New Year first of all,' he told her.

Julia hesitated. Seeing Eunice meant seeing Amanda and she wasn't sure she wanted to do that while she felt so emotionally vulnerable. Every time she saw the baby she felt overwhelmed by her feelings for her.

Chapter Twenty-two

In April 1916, Julia once again found her life disrupted by the horror caused by the War when Bob received news that his father had been killed in action.

'He should never have been sent to France, not a man of his age,' Bob raged. 'Once you're past forty your reactions aren't the same. Men of his age are a liability on the battlefield.'

'No, they're cannon-fodder, the same as my Bernard and my brother Lance,' Julia said bitterly, her eyes misting as deep memories came flooding to the forefront of her mind.

Bob ran a hand over his face, brushing away the tears that had come into his own eyes.

'It's my mother I am worried about,' Bob explained, 'she's taking it very badly. At first she wouldn't believe the news. She even went as far as to say that the War Office had made a mistake and that it couldn't possibly be my dad.'

'They hadn't, though?'

'No, of course not! His army number, regiment and everything else was all written down there and they were all correct. There was no mistake.'

'It's so very sad,' Julia murmured. Reaching out she took one of Bob's hands, cradling it between her own. 'Is there anything I can do to help?'

He ran his free hand through his mop of thick brown hair. 'I don't think so, she's so cut up about it that she will barely listen to me,' he said hopelessly.

'Would you like me to come and see her?'

Bob shook his head. 'She doesn't really know you and so I think it might only upset her.'

'Surely she must know that we are close friends and that I want to help if I can.'

'I've never been much of a one for knowing any girls,' Bob said awkwardly. 'She'd still think it strange that I was bringing you to see her again at a time like this.'

'Not if you told her that I'd lost my younger brother Lance in action. You can tell her about Bernard as well, if you like. It might help her if she talked about her loss to someone who has experienced the same thing.'

'Maybe you are right, I don't really know. At the moment, she seems to spend most of the time huddled in an armchair by the fire, nursing our old moggy and staring into space with a vacant look on her face.'

'Brooding! Probably reliving memories from the past,' Julia murmured softly.

'I suppose, but I don't know, because she won't talk to me. She just sits there, hour after hour, stroking Tiger. I make cuppas for her, and cook some grub, but half the time she doesn't touch it when I put it in front of her.'

'She really needs to open up and talk to someone other than the cat.'

'I know that,' Bob agreed, 'but she won't. She refuses to say a word to me and yet we've always been so close.'

'You are too close to her, probably. She doesn't want to burden you with her grief. Perhaps she'd talk if I came to see her. She might find it easier to confide in another woman,' Julia persisted.

'She's never had any women friends,' Bob murmured. 'My dad and me have always been enough for her. She's always been against idle jangling. She's never had any time for women who spill all their family secrets to outsiders. Washing their dirty linen in public, is what she calls it.'

The picture of his mother which Bob was revealing troubled Julia. She seemed to have no friends of her own and with her life centred solely on Bob and his father she probably led a very isolated existence.

'I still think I might be able to help if you took me to see her,' Julia repeated stubbornly.

She was so fond of Bob and so grateful for all the help he had given her that she felt this was at last an opportunity to do something for him by way of repayment.

'I don't think so. If she won't talk to me then she's certainly going to clam up if a stranger comes into her home.'

Julia felt hurt but she didn't press the matter.

She could see how worried Bob was about his mother as well as being upset about losing his dad.

She remembered how she'd felt when she'd heard about Bernard. She'd wanted to hide away, to shut out the rest of the world, and even though she'd had both her family and Bernard's around her, she hadn't wanted to talk to them, or even to confide in them. It would seem that Mrs Reynolds felt much the same way about sharing her grief with anyone, even Bob.

The truth of this came home to Julia in the weeks that followed. Bob spent more and more time with his mother, trying to comfort her and help her to face the world.

Julia felt disappointed that he wouldn't let her help in any way. She even began to feel resentful when it meant that time and time again their regular weekend outings were cancelled because Bob felt guilty about leaving his mother on her own.

'Why don't we take her with us?' she suggested.

Bob looked shocked. 'Take my old girl dancing! Are you taking the mickey?'

'Not dancing! That wasn't what I meant,' Julia retorted. 'We could take her to the pictures with us, though, couldn't we?'

Bob shook his head. 'She doesn't approve of the cinema; she'd never agree to come.'

'Then let's take her for a walk. The weather

is nice; it would do her good to get out in the fresh air.'

Again he shook his head. 'I don't think so.'

'Perhaps we could take her on the ferry over to New Brighton one Sunday,' Julia went on, ignoring his objections. 'A leisurely stroll along the promenade, she'd love that.'

'I'll suggest it to her, but I don't think she will agree,' he sighed. 'I can't even persuade her to go out to the shops to buy food; I have to do it myself.'

Julia pondered over the situation. She really did want to help. She felt that in some ways Bob was being insensitive and didn't fully understand his mother's needs so she decided to take matters into her own hands.

She was only too aware that Bob was very reticent when it came to expressing his feelings. They had been going out together every weekend for several months now and the nearest he had got to letting her know how he felt about her was a quick hug and a hasty peck on the cheek when they said goodnight.

Sometimes she longed for him to take her into his arms and tell her how much she mattered to him. Then common sense prevailed, and she felt that it was better all round if they simply stayed close friends because she still felt that no one could ever take Bernard's place.

Without mentioning anything to Bob she arranged to have an afternoon off work. She chose a time when she knew he would be out working on his window cleaning round and would be nowhere near Skirving Street.

She dressed carefully for the occasion in a plain grey suit with a pale blue blouse trimmed with a white lace collar and used hardly any make-up. She took along a carefully selected bunch of spring flowers as an excuse for calling.

She knocked twice before Mrs Reynolds answered. When she did she opened the door a mere crack and peered out suspiciously. She looked even smaller and more wizened than Julia remembered her. She had on a dark print overall over the top of a plain black dress and her grey hair was pulled back into a small, tight bun on the top of her head. She looked so desperately unhappy that Julia's heart went out to her.

'Yes?' Her voice was harsh and unfriendly.

'Hello, Mrs Reynolds. I was so sorry to hear about your loss, I thought you might like these.'

Mrs Reynolds frowned and started to shut the door. 'You've got the wrong house, I don't know you,' she said dismissively.

'Yes you do! I know your son, Bob. He cleans the windows where I work, and we often talk,' Julia went on brightly. 'The Darnley Hotel,' she added lamely when Mrs Reynolds still didn't recognise her. 'He brought me to see you on New Year's Eve.'

Mrs Reynolds stared at her balefully. 'What's he been saying, then, for you to come here again now?'

'He told me about his dad being killed; he knew my brother had died in France on active service just a few months ago . . .'

'What good does gossiping about it do?' Mrs Reynolds snapped. 'Doesn't bring them back, does it?'

'Sometimes it eases the pain to talk about them, though,' Julia said gently.

'I got no time for people who waste time jangling,' Mrs Reynolds retorted. 'Is that all you have to say?'

'I'd hoped you would ask me in and we could share our memories over a cup of tea,' Julia said wistfully. 'However, I understand if you are too busy for us to do that, so I'll just leave these flowers and be on my way.'

Mrs Reynolds made no effort to take the bunch of flowers as Julia held them out to her. Instead, she opened the door wider. 'You'd better come in, I suppose,' she told her and led the way into a living room at the back of the house.

It was clean and comfortable rather than cosy. Julia noticed that an armchair was pulled up close to the fire and from the crumpled cushions in it she guessed that Mrs Reynolds had been sitting there brooding just as Bob had told her.

'Take a seat, then, and I'll go and put the kettle on,' Mrs Reynolds told her.

'Will you take these and put them in water?'

Again, Mrs Reynolds hesitated. 'I'm not much

of a one for flowers; they're a waste of money, if you ask me. I don't have a vase anywhere in the house.'

'I'm sure you have a jug you could use to put them in,' Julia suggested.

'Yes, I suppose I could do that with them,' the older woman said ungraciously.

Left on her own, Julia looked round the room, trying to imagine how Bob fitted into the drab surroundings. Everything was dark and gloomy from the dark green repp curtains at the window flanking the thick ecru lace ones, to the dark brown lino on the floor, and the homemade rag rug in front of the fire showed signs of hard usage. The well-worn, well-polished dark oak table and sideboard were plain and serviceable. There were no ornaments on the mantel-ledge apart from a heavy chiming clock under a brass dome.

Talk, as they drank their cup of tea, was desultory. Julia tried to explain how well she knew Bob, but Mrs Reynolds sniffed in disapproval.

'I've warned him often enough about talking to strangers and letting them know all your business,' she said in a disagreeable voice. 'Since his father hasn't been here to keep an eye on him he seems to talk to just about anybody.'

'He's very kind and helpful and well liked by his customers,' Julia protested.

'His job is to clean their windows, not have heart-to-heart chats with them. I keep telling him that if he talked less, then he could clean more windows.'

'Bob is only being polite and friendly,' Julia said, defending him.

'Telling them all his business,' Mrs Reynolds interrupted. 'What was he doing telling you about his dad? Nothing to do with you, you never met the man.'

'I told you, he knew I had lost my brother and the man I was planning to marry . . .'

'There you go, that's exactly what I was saying. He stands around, chattering to people like you, about things which don't concern him at all, when he should be working.'

'You make it sound like a crime,' Julia said defensively. 'I think of Bob as a friend, a very dear friend who several times has gone out of his way to help me.'

'Very dear friend, indeed!' There was venom in her voice and in the look she directed at Julia. 'I've warned him about getting mixed up with girls. He's got other things to worry about, so you can forget any fancy ideas you've got in your head about him. He'll be getting the sharp end of my tongue when he gets home for sending you here to try and soften me up about him and you seeing each other. Now, finish drinking that tea and be on your way.'

In the weeks that followed Julia's visit to see his mother, even more of Bob's time seemed to be taken up with trying to placate her. Because he was staying home and keeping her company, Julia found herself at a loose end.

Living and working at the Darnley she'd not made any local friends other than Bob and so she was now taking a much greater interest in the Hawkinses' baby. Amanda was now almost five months old and was beginning to recognise people and reward them with a beaming smile or an engaging, gurgling laugh.

Julia found her bewitching and was fascinated by her day-to-day development. Every time she saw Amanda she felt a small stab of jealousy. Eunice was so lucky to have such a gorgeous little girl. She couldn't help wondering what her own baby, who would have been the same age, would have been like if it had lived.

Paul and Eunice were both besotted by their little daughter. Eunice had intended to hire a nursemaid to care for Amanda so that she could return to work, but instead she was still looking after her herself.

'I can understand you feel you want to do that,' Julia agreed. 'I'm sure I would feel exactly the same if I'd waited so long for a baby as you have.'

'True, but it is such a different way of life for me,' Eunice pointed out. 'I've been so used to being at the centre of all that is happening in the hotel.' She sighed. 'Being up here away from it all, I really do miss all that.'

'I can understand that, too. But you could still be involved, of course,' Julia said thoughtfully.

'I can hardly bring Amanda down into the office, now can I?' Eunice laughed.

'No, but you could still come down and work for a few hours each day, or whenever you wanted to.'

Eunice looked thoughtful. 'You mean while Amanda was asleep? Yes, I suppose I could do that, but I'm not sure that I would be able to concentrate.' She frowned. 'I'd be listening all the time in case Amanda woke up or was crying.'

'What about if we tried sharing the work,' Julia suggested tentatively. 'You could come down and work in the hotel if I came up here and took care of Amanda.'

Eunice's face brightened. 'Do you mean that?' she exclaimed in astonishment.

'Of course I do! It needn't be every day. Just now and again, whenever you felt like it. Perhaps you could undertake some special job, like doing the wages. That would be one morning or afternoon a week and I could take care of Amanda while you were down in the office.'

Eunice frowned. 'Let me talk to Paul about it. He mightn't approve,' she said cautiously.

'Why ever not? You know the work inside out, so you are hardly likely to mess things up, are you?'

'It's not that! Paul is so concerned that Amanda is getting the right attention . . .'

'It will only be for an hour or so and I can always call you if I need you.'

'Yes, of course. I'm quite happy about that. I

know you'll look after her. I think it's a tremendous idea.'

Paul was surprisingly enthusiastic. He was fed up with hearing Eunice bemoan the fact that she was losing all contact with the hotel. They had worked as a team for so long that even though he found Julia efficient it wasn't quite the same. Having Eunice back at his side, even if it was only for a few hours a week, would help to restore and revive the working partnership that had brought them together in the first place.

For all three of them the arrangement worked well. Julia found her workload in the office lightened considerably, Paul liked having Eunice there and Eunice felt that her life had been transformed. In no time at all she was back to her busy, bustling self; well groomed and more smartly dressed than she'd ever been.

Julia liked the new arrangement for several reasons. There was less pressure at work, and she found it wonderful to be able to cuddle Amanda and play with her. It also meant that her days were busy and, gradually, as Bob's mother adjusted to widowhood, she was delighted to find that her regular outings with Bob were resumed.

Julia persistently asked him to take her to see his mother, but he always dodged the issue by saying she preferred not to have any visitors.

'You mean she didn't like me?' she questioned.
Bob remained non-committal and either

changed the subject or laughingly reminded her that he had warned her about what his mother was like.

Their own enforced separation seemed to have brought a new closeness. They were no longer merely good friends. Their goodnight kisses began to take on a new meaning, and their embraces were more passionate.

Julia experienced an inner glow when he held her in his arms. She looked forward to seeing him. He was constantly in her thoughts; she even dreamed about him.

The icy numbness that had enveloped her after Bernard had been killed began to fade. She felt more alive and vibrant than she'd done for years and she knew that it showed both in her face and in her demeanour.

All through the early summer she delighted in her new-found happiness and when, as they returned home after one of their Saturday night visits to the pictures, Bob asked her if she would marry him she accepted.

'I know I am only a window cleaner,' he said in an apologetic voice, 'but I'll make sure you'll never want for anything.'

'I wouldn't care if you were a road cleaner or a chimney sweep,' she laughed.

He took her back to Skirving Street so that they could break the news to Mrs Reynolds. Bob's mother didn't congratulate them, but regarded Julia with a suspicious gleam in her eyes. 'So you've got him in the end, have you?'

she commented sourly. 'I hope it's not because he has to wed you that he's asked you.'

Julia's face flamed and for a moment she wondered if Bob had told her about the baby she'd already lost. Then she felt the pressure of his arm around her shoulder, as if he was trying to calm her and reassure her.

'No, I'm afraid you're not going to be a grandmother, Mrs Reynolds. It probably won't be for a long time yet because we haven't even fixed the date of our wedding,' she replied quietly.

Bob's mother didn't answer, but her silent acceptance of the situation said more than words ever could.

Julia sensed the enmity between them and realised that Mrs Reynolds would probably do everything in her power to stop her and Bob from marrying.

She can try all she likes, Julia thought rebelliously, but I won't let it make any difference. This time there is no reason why I should be cheated out of marriage.

'How about a glass of sherry, then, so that we can drink to the future,' Bob suggested, smiling at his mother and trying to infuse some pleasure into the occasion.

'You two do whatever you like, but I'm off to bed,' his mother told him.

'That didn't go too well, did it?' Julia murmured quietly, as the living-room door closed behind Mrs Reynolds.

'Better than I had expected.' Bob grinned, pulling her into his arms and kissing her. 'Give my mam time and she'll get used to the idea.'

Chapter Twenty-three

In August 1916, when Bob was called up for military service, Julia was devastated. It seemed that Mrs Reynolds's morbid warning, 'You haven't got him to the altar yet, my girl,' was coming true.

Determined not to let anything ruin her future with Bob she tried to persuade him that they should get married before he had to report for duty.

'I thought you'd want a fancy do, white dress, flowers and all the rest of it,' he said in surprise.

'In wartime!'

'So you'd settle for a quiet wedding and a bit of a bash at the Darnley afterwards?' he asked, smiling.

'We could certainly celebrate there,' Julia agreed. 'Paul and Eunice would love the idea. Do you think we will be able to persuade your mam to come?'

'It's worth a try. She seems to have come round to you visiting lately.'

'You mean she hasn't barred me,' Julia admitted grimly. 'She doesn't exactly greet me with open arms though, does she?'

'That might be because she still isn't sure that we are serious about each other.'

'You mean she thinks I'm just some stray Judy whom you've picked up for a bit of fling.'

Bob looked hurt. 'No, of course not!'

'I think she does. Whenever we meet she makes some cryptic remark or other. It really hurts, Bob.'

'Come on, she doesn't really mean it. She's still grieving about my dad, remember. She's always gone out of her way to protect me, you know that.'

'Protect you!' She looked at him wide-eyed. 'Are you saying she's trying to protect you from me?' She laughed indignantly. 'She doesn't need to do so; we haven't even had a chance to sleep together yet. Whenever I come to your house she makes sure we are never left alone for more than five minutes.'

Bob ran a hand through his hair. 'She is afraid of losing me. She's guessed how much I love you and she's worried that she's going to have to take second place.'

'So what are we going to do about it?'

'Go and see her and tell her that we are getting married sooner than we originally planned, I suppose.' He grinned.

Mrs Reynolds seemed to shrink inside her black dress when they told her what they intended to do.

'Get married before you go into the army!' she exclaimed startled.

'That's right,' Bob said firmly. 'We were planning to do so quite soon so it simply means that we are bringing the date forward by a few months, that's all.'

'Is this your idea or hers?' she asked, shooting a venomous look at Julia.

'Well,' Bob looked taken aback, 'we've talked it over and we're both agreed that is what we want to do.'

'What she wants to do, you mean,' Mrs Reynolds said bitterly. 'Making sure that she's your next-of-kin so that she gets your army allowance and I'm left to starve,' she sniffled.

'How dare you say such a thing!' Julia exclaimed. 'I never even thought about that.'

'Now then, you two!' Bob interrupted, looking embarrassed and trying to calm the situation. 'You both mean a lot to me, but in different ways.'

Mrs Reynolds ignored him. 'You're a lying little bint,' she declared, wagging her finger at Julia. 'Of course you did. The only reason you've run after my Bob is because he has his own business and you think he can afford to keep you in luxury. Take my word for it, there isn't going to be any wedding; I won't stand for it.'

'You're a bitter old woman,' Julia responded contemptuously. 'I don't have to stand here and listen to your rubbish.'

'Go on, then, get out. My son knows that his dad would turn in his grave, wherever that is, if he was to leave his poor old mum to fend for herself at my age,' she said triumphantly.

*   *   *

With Bob away in the army, to take her mind off her chagrin that Bob had given in to his mother's demands, Julia spent even more time with Amanda both during the day and after work.

Amanda was now nine months old, a beautiful baby with a winning smile, golden curls and huge blue eyes. She was already crawling and needed constant supervision.

The more work Eunice undertook in the hotel office the more time Julia spent with Amanda. As well as caring for her at home she now regularly took her out for a walk in her pram whenever the weather permitted.

Eunice was not too fond of pushing the big Silver Cross pram but Julia liked nothing better. Most days she took her for a walk around St John's Gardens with Amanda sitting up and taking notice of the flowers and birds.

As December arrived, the memory of losing her own baby a year earlier made Julia feel despondent. She found herself constantly going over and over in her mind how things might have been.

She consoled herself by concentrating on Amanda. She would soon be walking; by the spring Amanda would be a toddler and her big high pram could be replaced with a pushchair. When that happened she'd be able to travel with her on the bus or boat, so they could even go over to New Brighton.

Sometimes she wondered if Paul Hawkins

noticed that she was spending less and less time in the office. If he did, he said nothing and, since he'd recently given her a pay rise, she assumed that the arrangement suited him as much as it did her and so he didn't question it.

Once a week she wrote a long letter to Bob, telling him what news there was, but mostly relating incidents to do with Amanda. His letters were short and stilted and very erratic. He didn't like army life and when he described the conditions they had to live under she could well understand why.

Several times he had asked her if she had been to see his mother, but he never made any comment when she failed to answer that question.

Bob had been in the army for almost a year, serving in France for most of that time, when she received a brief note written by one of his fellow soldiers to say that he had been seriously injured at Ypres and expected to be sent home.

The very mention of Ypres brought memories of Bernard flooding back; bitter-sweet thoughts that she had tried so hard to put out of her mind.

It seemed so uncanny that Bob should be injured while serving at the same place. What worried her almost as much was that the news had reached her from someone she didn't know. The brief scrawl was signed by someone called Alan Patterson and there seemed to be no address on the paper. He claimed he was a friend of Bob's and that because he knew Bob wrote to her regularly he thought she would want to know what had happened.

She did, but she found that receiving the news in this way was very ominous. It implied that Bob was too seriously injured to contact her himself.

There was no date at all on the letter so she had no idea when it had been written or even when Bob had been injured. It might only have been a few days ago or it could even have been weeks, she thought worriedly.

She searched through back copies of the newspapers to try and find out if there had been a battle there recently. She knew the first one had been in October 1914. There had been another battle at Ypres in May 1915, and that date was permanently engraved on her mind because that was when Bernard had been killed. Now, or so it seemed, a third battle had taken place at the end of July.

It was now almost the middle of August so where was he? He could be in a military hospital, either over in France or back in Britain, but where? He might even have been sent home to convalesce and Mrs Reynolds hadn't let her know.

She wrestled with the problem all day. If he'd been sent home, then why hadn't he been in touch with her? Surely he would have done so, unless his injuries were such that he couldn't manage it.

Somehow, she couldn't bring herself to mention

it to either Paul or Eunice Hawkins. She let three more days go past, hoping against hope that she might hear from Bob himself. Then, when she didn't, she finally made up her mind that she would have to go and see his mother.

As Bob's official next-of-kin, Mrs Reynolds would be the first to hear if he had been injured she reminded herself. If she already knew, then she may have sunk into depression again like she did after Bob's father had been killed. If Bob had been sent home, then she could even be struggling to look after him and would welcome someone to give her a hand.

Later that day on her way to see Bob's mother, Julia racked her brains trying to think of what to say to her. If only his mother had accepted her and they'd got to know each other, it would be so much easier.

When she reached Skirving Street, their house stood out it was so well kept with its pumiced front door step and window sills and polished brass knocker and letter box.

The thick ecru lace curtains at the front window were tightly closed and the heavy drapes behind them also appeared to be drawn. Julia's heart thudded uncomfortably as she wondered what that signified. They could be drawn merely to keep the sun off the furniture and the carpet she told herself. She hoped that was the reason.

Her heart in her mouth, she knocked on the front door and waited. The noise echoed down the hallway but no one came to answer. She knocked again, but there was still no reply. She was about to turn away when she saw a movement and realised that someone was standing behind the front-room curtains watching her so she bent down and called through the letter box.

'Mrs Reynolds, it's Julia Winter. Can I speak to you for a moment?'

The silence lasted for such a long time that she was on the point of giving up and walking away when she heard footsteps approaching.

The door slowly opened halfway and Julia's breath caught in her throat as she faced Mrs Reynolds. She looked so sad that Julia's heart ached for her.

'Yes?' Mrs Reynolds peered out, looking questioningly at Julia and scowling. 'What is it you want this time?' she asked in a petulant voice.

'Hello, Mrs Reynolds. I was wondering if you'd heard from Bob lately?'

Bob's mother stared at her balefully then started to close the front door.

'Look, can I come in for a minute so that we can have a chat?' Julia begged.

Mrs Reynolds frowned heavily, accentuating her wrinkles and making her look very old and frail. 'Why, what is there for us to talk about?'

'I want to ask you about Bob, of course, and if you'd heard from him recently.' Julia smiled.

'He's not here. He'll be coming home soon I suppose, but I have no idea when,' she said wearily.

'If I came in, we could have a chat and you could tell me where he is now,' Julia persisted.

Mrs Reynolds shook her head undecidedly, then suddenly she seemed to make up her mind. 'Oh very well, then,' she muttered resignedly.

She opened the door wider and Julia followed her down the hall to the living room at the back of the house.

'I suppose you want a cup of tea?' Mrs Reynolds stated ungraciously.

'That would be very nice.' Julia smiled at her.

'I was going to have one when you started banging on the door. It's already made. Sit down while I go and pour it out.'

Julia shivered as she looked around at the changes in the living room which had been made since she was last there. Now there were framed photographs of Bob everywhere, on every available surface. They ranged from Bob as a baby and as a schoolboy right up to the very latest ones of him in his army uniform. The whole room was like a shrine to him. She longed to pick them up and study them, but she thought she'd better not in case it upset his mother.

Remembering how distressed Mrs Reynolds had been when her husband had been killed, she looked around again to see if there were any of Mr Reynolds, but there didn't seem to be any at all; not a single one.

They drank their tea in silence. Mrs Reynolds ignored her presence and sat there staring into the fire as if she was in the room alone. In

284

desperation to gain her attention, Julia started to talk about Bob.

'He's a soldier now, as you very well know, so why are you here?' Mrs Reynolds interrupted peevishly.

'What I want to know is whether or not you've heard from him lately,' Julia said quietly.

'Of course I haven't! How can the poor boy write to me when he's broken his arm? It's his right arm and that's the hand he uses to write with, isn't it?'

'I knew he'd been hurt but I didn't know he'd broken his arm,' Julia ventured.

'Broke his arm and lost one of his legs, poor boy. How's he going to come back and be a window cleaner? He won't be able to go up a ladder if he only has one leg, now will he? How can he carry a bucket or ride his bicycle with a broken arm. He's probably suffering from shell-shock as well; most of the soldiers are when they send them back home.'

Julia felt horrified, but she tried not to let it show. Now she knew why one of his friends had written to let her know that he'd been injured.

'Has Bob told you which hospital he is in, Mrs Reynolds?' she asked gently.

Mrs Reynolds shook her head. 'No, of course not. I've no idea.' She paused and wiped the tears from her eyes. 'They don't tell you that sort of thing. They like to keep it all hushed up. They're afraid we might turn up there and make a fuss, I suppose.'

'Would you like me to try and find out where he is?' Julia offered.

Mrs Reynolds's face brightened. 'Do you think you can do that?'

Julia didn't know, but she made a wild guess. 'I'm sure if I get in touch with the commanding officer of his regiment he will be able to tell me.'

'Oh, yes, and you know him, do you? A friend of yours, is he?' Mrs Reynolds commented acidly.

'Well, no, but I'm sure if I get in touch with Bob's regiment . . .' her voice trailed away as she realised the uselessness of trying to do so because she couldn't claim to be a relation.

'I'd have to say that I was asking on your behalf,' she pointed out. 'Would that be all right?'

Mrs Reynolds shrugged dispiritedly. 'Please yourself. I don't suppose they'll tell you anything even if you do.'

'I'm sure they will tell me whatever they can.'

'I doubt it! I tried to find out about my Wilf, Bob's father, when he was killed and it was like banging your head against a brick wall.'

'So you never managed to find out any details about what happened?'

'Not a peep! They never even sent his body back! He's still out there. Some place in France, I suppose, or wherever it was he was fighting when he was killed.'

'I'm sure they'll send you the full details in time,' Julia murmured.

'You got more faith in them than I have then,' Mrs Reynolds said bitterly.

'Perhaps when the War ends –'

'They took my husband away from me and got him killed and now they've turned my son into an invalid, and they don't give a damn!' Mrs Reynolds interrupted.

Julia wondered if she should tell Mrs Reynolds that she'd been working in the military hospital outside Liverpool, but the recollection of the terrible sights and injuries she'd witnessed when she'd been there stopped her.

Listening to Mrs Reynolds's ranting, she didn't think it would help her to understand any better what happened to those men who were injured at the front. Probably, instead of helping her to come to terms with what had happened, it might make her feel even more bitter.

'How's my lad going to be able to earn a living when he comes out of the army, that's what I want to know? They'll stop sending me his allotment so how are we going to manage?' Mrs Reynolds droned on. She rocked backwards and forwards on her chair, her spindly arms wrapped round her thin body almost as if she was holding herself together.

'With only one leg he won't be able to ride his bicycle or climb up his ladders to clean windows, now will he?' she repeated.

Julia tried to answer, but it was pointless. Mrs Reynolds was so full of her own grief that Julia knew she wasn't listening to a word she said.

She went on bitterly bemoaning what had happened to Bob until Julia began to wish she'd never come. She could understand now why Bob was always so evasive when she asked him in her letters if he'd like her to go and see his mother.

As soon as she could make a reasonable excuse she left, but not until she had promised that she would make some enquiries about where Bob was.

'See if you can get them to send my poor boy home so that I can take care of him,' Mrs Reynolds urged as she saw Julia out. 'I'll look after my Bob far better than they will if only I can have him back here.'

Julia promised she would but she felt uneasy about what coming home would do for Bob. Judging from the state of the living room, the house had already been turned into a shrine to him. He'd certainly be well nursed, and waited on hand and foot, but the atmosphere would be so claustrophobic that it would depress him.

She wasn't even sure if Mrs Reynolds would let her visit him if he was at home and now, more than ever, she wanted to be with him . . . as his wife. She wanted to be the one looking after him, but because of the strong hold his mother seemed to have over him she was not at all sure that she could get him to agree to that.

Chapter Twenty-four

There were several long months of waiting before Bob Reynolds came home to Skirving Street. Although Julia had done her best to find out which military hospital he was in, she'd had no success.

The War wasn't going well and there seemed to be a tighter control than ever on what people were being told. Because she wasn't classified as next-of-kin, or even family, no one in authority would tell her anything.

Even though she was desperate for news of Bob, Mrs Reynolds changed her mind and stubbornly refused to cooperate by giving her permission to say she was acting for her. 'Don't you try using my name and making out that you are some sort of relation of ours because it won't wash, my girl. I'll make sure it doesn't,' she told her sourly.

'We would have been married before Bob went overseas if you hadn't made such a fuss,' Julia reminded her.

'Yes, that's what you wanted, wasn't it? To get him to tie the knot and send his pay home to you so that you could go out and enjoy yourself. You'd have squandered it all with never a thought for me. He's been my mainstay, the breadwinner, ever since his dad was called up. You wanted to grab it all and take it away from me and leave me to starve. Oh, I know your sort, my girl. Little money-grabber with no thought for anyone else.'

Her voice rose to such a hysterical pitch that Julia put her hands over her ears to shut out the sound.

'You can put all ideas of marriage right out of your silly nut,' Mrs Reynolds went on. 'He isn't going to tie himself to some flashy bint like you. I'll make damn sure he doesn't,' she added in a threatening tone. 'What's more, you can stop coming round here pestering me. There's nothing here for the likes of you and I don't want anything more to do with you.'

Julia decided that trying to put matters right between herself and Mrs Reynolds only made matters worse. She even wondered if Bob's mother had written damaging things about her to Bob because before he had been injured his letters had become more and more terse.

Eventually, he started writing to her again, explaining the silence by a brief account of his injuries. What she found very distressing was that he seemed to be in such low spirits, and she began to wonder exactly how serious his injuries were and how much they had affected his personality.

She still had no idea where he was and she worried about him endlessly. She always tried to write bright, newsy letters to him, but it wasn't easy. An air of gloom seemed be everywhere. So many things were in short supply. Most people seemed to have a relative on active service who had been either killed or injured or who was missing.

So many ships were being sunk that the usually brisk trade in Liverpool had declined and the Darnley, like all the other hotels and most of the big stores in the city, found that business was suffering as a result.

As the months passed she missed him more and more. His letters were so short and brusque that if she hadn't known him so well and knew how shy he was about revealing his feelings, she would have been upset by how formal they were.

She tried to keep hers light-hearted, which meant that the only things she could find to write to him about were all related to Amanda; telling him what a lovely little girl she was becoming and how much she enjoyed every minute she spent with her.

It was the beginning of 1918 before Julia saw Bob again. His broken arm had healed but his left leg had been amputated and he needed crutches to get around. As a result, he had been invalided out of the army.

The first Julia knew about it was when he hobbled into the hotel on his crutches.

'Bob! I had no idea you were home,' she

gasped, her eyes shining sapphire stars as she came rushing from behind the reception counter to greet him.

Her initial joy dimmed when he merely pecked her on the cheek. She consoled herself by telling herself that of course he couldn't take her in his arms and hug her when he was standing on only one leg.

She was shocked at how thin and haggard he looked. She grew even more concerned when they started talking and she realised that he was far more bitter and depressed than she'd gathered from his letters.

At first they were like strangers and she found herself struggling to find things to talk to him about.

'If only you could have let me know where you were, I would have come and visited you,' she remarked with a sigh.

'Like the way you visited my mother.' He frowned. 'I doubt if I'm ever going to live that down.'

'I was only trying to help,' she explained. 'When I heard you'd been wounded I knew she'd be dreadfully upset, like she was when your father was killed.'

He looked puzzled. 'So what were you hoping to do about it if she was?'

'I thought she might find it comforting to have someone to talk to about what had happened to you, someone who cared about you like she does.'

'I told you she doesn't approve of gossiping.'

'I didn't intend that we should gossip about you,' Julia protested. 'I simply wanted to try and ease her mind of some of her worry.'

He shrugged but said no more about it.

'So what are you planning to do now that you are at home?' she asked brightly.

'What the hell do you think I am going to do? I've lost one of my legs and I'm hobbling round on crutches so there's not very much I can do, now, is there?'

'Aren't you going to try and get your window-cleaning business going again?'

'Are you taking the mickey? I'm a sodding cripple. I've only one leg. What do you think I am, a bloody circus act? I can't shin up a ladder using just one leg!'

'No, I don't think you will ever be able to go up a ladder again,' Julia sighed, 'but you could always get someone else to do that for you. You could still clean the ground-floor windows yourself and organise the rounds, things like that,' she suggested. 'It would be far better than being on public assistance.'

'To hell with that! I lost my leg fighting for my country so it's up to those buggers to keep me from now on.'

'Well, if that's the way you want it then I suppose there's nothing more to be said,' Julia sighed. 'I thought you had more guts than that,' she added caustically.

'That's the way things have got to be. Anyone

with a grain of common sense would see that. I'm a cripple so I've no choice in the matter.'

'That's up to you, isn't it?' she persisted, her lips tightening as she blinked back her tears. She realised how upset Bob was, but he was reacting more and more like his mother.

She loved him so much that she was desperate to help him come to terms with the situation. So far, though, everything she'd said had met with his disapproval. She hated to see him so despondent. In the past, when she'd been the one who'd had problems he'd always been so optimistic and so determined to find ways of solving them.

'It's taken me over half an hour to walk from Skirving Street to here. Before, it would have taken me about ten minutes, even less on my bike,' he grumbled.

'You'll be able to walk much faster with practice,' she said encouragingly.

'Oh, will I! Well, thank you for telling me,' he muttered sarcastically.

Julia felt at a loss. She didn't know what to say next; everything she said seemed to upset him.

'Are we going to go out on Saturday night like we always used to do?' she asked cautiously.

'Yes, I'll take you dancing, shall I? If I jig around on one leg, and you hold out my cap, we might collect a fortune.'

'If that's how you feel, then perhaps we ought to leave it for a week or two. In actual fact, I was thinking that we could go to the pictures, not dancing,' Julia said mildly.

'So how am I going to manage when we get in there?' he asked bitterly. 'Where do I put my crutch? Do I stick it under the seat and hope no one falls over it, or do I nurse it all night? I certainly won't be able to stand up if someone wants to push past. Still, perhaps I wouldn't need to stand up since I've only got one leg blocking their way.'

Julia felt dismayed. Everything she said or suggested seemed to rub Bob up the wrong way. All she'd meant was that they should go for a quiet drink so that they could be on their own. Bob had lost more than a leg; he'd lost his happy outlook on life. He'd become sour and caustic and ready to take umbrage, whatever was said to him.

'Perhaps we ought to stop seeing each other for a while, until you are feeling better about things,' she suggested.

'Right, if that's the way you feel about things we'll do that. I should have known that you wouldn't want to be seen out with a one-legged man hopping along at your side like a bloody kangaroo,' he added bitterly.

'Oh, Bob!' She placed a hand on his arm. 'How can you say things like that? You know I want to be with you and to help all I can!'

Bob shrugged her arm away and limped off without a word, his crutches tapping rhythmically as he headed for home.

Paul Hawkins had been listening to their exchange and was full of sympathy for Julia after Bob left.

'Bob's making one hell of a fuss about things, isn't he?' Paul commented in astonishment.

Julia sighed. 'He's certainly taking the fact that he's lost his leg very much to heart.'

'That's understandable, but it's not the end of the world.'

'He's upset because it means he's lost his livelihood.'

'Not necessarily. I thought your idea that he should find some young lad who can shin up the ladder and clean the top windows was the perfect answer.'

'Really?' She looked both surprised and pleased. 'Bob didn't seem to like the idea,' she murmured ruefully.

'I don't think you should worry about it, my dear,' he told her, smiling consolingly. 'I can't see why he couldn't go with you to the pictures, either. You could always pick a seat at the end of a row and people would be able to get past quite easily.'

'Is that what you'd do?'

'No, if I was taking you to the pictures then I'd make sure I chose one of the double seats on the back row,' he told her, his eyes fixed on her face as if waiting for her reaction.

Julia felt the colour rushing to her face. When Paul Hawkins's hand moved over the top of the desk and clasped hers she immediately jerked it away, but she was not quick enough. Eunice had walked into the office holding Amanda in her arms and was standing there, a look of suspicion on her face.

'I was going to ask you to look after Amanda for me, but I'm not so sure if that is a good idea after all,' she said, raising her eyebrows questioningly and looking first at her husband and then at Julia.

'Paul was just acting the fool,' Julia told her as she held out her arms for the child.

Eunice stared at her coldly. Then, because Amanda was gurgling excitedly and eager to be with Julia, she said no more, but her lips tightened ominously.

As Julia took the child into her arms she felt a sense of unease. She'd done nothing wrong, but it was obvious from her manner that Eunice was upset.

'Shall we pop you into your pushchair and go for a little walk?' Julia asked, addressing herself to Amanda.

'Exactly where were you thinking of taking her?' Eunice demanded.

Julia hesitated. 'I was going to walk round to Skirving Street to see if Bob got home all right. He was rather upset when he left here. Being a cripple is tearing him to pieces,' she added by way of explanation.

The atmosphere between Julia and Bob seemed to deteriorate as the weeks went by. He seemed to be perpetually moody and depressed and so prickly that he seemed to take offence at everything she said or suggested.

Whenever she visited him at home his mother made sure that she never left them alone together for more than a couple of minutes. She fussed over him all the time like an old hen with a single chick. She waited on him hand and foot, not allowing him to try and do anything for himself.

Mrs Reynolds even discouraged him from going out. If the weather was damp, she pointed out that he might slip on the wet pavements. As the weather became colder, it was in case he caught a chill because he moved so slowly. Finally, she began to worry in case he lost control of his crutches when early morning frosts left a film of ice on the roads.

'Have you asked when they are going to fit you with an artificial leg?' Julia asked him.

'What does he want one of those horrible things for,' Mrs Reynolds butted in. 'He's much better off with his crutches, so why go through all the agony of having something like that fitted?'

'If Bob had an artificial leg, then no one would even know that he was crippled,' Julia pointed out.

'Yes, but when he's walking around on crutches then everyone can see what he's done for his country,' Mrs Reynolds declared proudly.

'Bob knows he's done his bit, and so do we,

so what does it matter what other people think?' Julia asked bewildered.

'It reminds them of the sacrifices some families have made,' Mrs Reynolds stated obstinately.

'I think most families have done their bit,' Julia retorted. 'I've lost the man I was going to marry as well as my younger brother,' she reminded her.

'Dead and gone, though, aren't they? They're at peace. They're not having to hobble around for the rest of their life like my poor son. His life has been completely ruined, he's not even able to earn a living any more.'

'He doesn't have to hobble around either,' Julia told her heatedly. 'If he had an artificial leg fitted, then apart from a possible slight limp he'd be as right as rain.'

'He'd still be an invalid. He'd still be unable to climb up a ladder and do his job as a window cleaner.'

'I've already suggested a way he could get round that problem,' Julia reminded her. 'All he has to do is to hire a fit young chap who can climb ladders to clean the windows he can't reach. That way he can run his business in the same way as he used to, before he was called up.'

'Oh yes, and where is the money coming from? How is he going to pay this young bloke?' Mrs Reynolds snapped.

'The same way as his father paid him when they worked together.'

'His father had plenty of customers, that's why he took Bob on when he left school; he needed the extra help.'

'Bob could soon regain all those old customers and more as well,' Julia pointed out.

Bob sat slumped in an armchair, listening to their exchange in moody silence. Afterwards he told Julia he thought it might be better if they met somewhere else. 'I'd rather you didn't call round here any more as all these arguments only upset my mother,' he told her gloomily.

'Well, why does she have to disagree with everything I say?'

'After you've gone home she goes over everything you've said time and time again. She doesn't like you criticising me, she gets very hurt and upset about it.'

'I'm not criticising you,' Julia protested. 'I'm only putting forward ideas to help you. Can't you see, Bob, that she's stopping you from getting back on your feet? She's making you believe you are an invalid instead of encouraging you to overcome your disability so that you can revive your business and get back on your own two feet.'

'I've only got one foot, so I'm hardly likely to ever get back on two feet, Julia,' he corrected her bitterly.

'Oh, for heaven's sake! You're as big a pessimist as she is,' Julia exclaimed exasperatedly.

She felt so hurt and annoyed by the fact that

300

Bob would listen to his mother, but not to her, that she did as he asked and stopped visiting them. Occasionally she saw him in the street, painfully limping along on his crutches and stopping every few yards as if he was finding it extremely difficult.

Occasionally they stopped and exchanged a few words. There was a barrier between them, though, which made her feel very uncomfortable. She felt convinced that if he would only put his mind to it he could pick up the threads of his own life again and make a success of things.

She had done her best to persuade him, but she couldn't do any more. She was still desperately in love with him and ached to feel his arms around her, holding her close, his lips on hers. She yearned to once again experience the joys their loving had brought both of them.

She missed the wonderful times they'd had together, but those seemed to have gone for ever. She tried not to think about them because she now had other problems. Things were not going too smoothly for her at the Darnley. For several days there had been an uneasy atmosphere between her and Eunice after she'd seen Paul holding her hand, although she had assured Eunice that there was nothing going on between them. Paul was much too familiar for her liking and she did all she could to discourage his attentions even though it didn't seem to have very much effect.

He was always paying her compliments, either about the way she had done her hair or commenting on what she was wearing. It was flattering and confidence-boosting, but sometimes he rather overdid the praise and left her feeling embarrassed.

He was also prone to touching her more than she liked. Nothing very suggestive, just the friendly arm around her shoulder, the occasional pat on the back, or holding on to her hand when she passed something to him.

Julia could understand why Eunice resented Paul's behaviour, but she felt she must see that she was not interested and that she didn't respond in any way.

Eunice must surely realise that the difference in their ages was so great that she couldn't possibly be interested in Paul, Julia thought exasperatedly. Paul was almost sixty; Julia was only twenty-one.

It wasn't as though he was all that attractive. He was only of medium height, and quite portly. His hair was not only thinning, but quite grey at the temples.

What was more, he was very overbearing and Julia had always made it quite clear that she didn't like men who were self-opinionated because they reminded her too much of her own father and his bombastic manner. Paul Hawkins, she had been quick to realise, was from a very similar mould.

Eunice, despite her buxom figure and soigné

appearance, had a similar temperament to her own mother in that she let her husband dominate her. In her case it was both when she was working in the hotel and in running her domestic life.

I need to be careful, though, Julia reminded herself, because Eunice obviously has a very jealous nature. She suspected that Eunice also resented the fact that little Amanda was always eager to be with her and was so happy in her company.

Whatever happens, I don't want to lose my job, she thought worriedly, because that would mean I wouldn't be able to see Amanda any more.

Chapter Twenty-five

In November 1918, the War was over and peace was declared. Pleased though she was by the news, Julia felt it was sad that so many young men's lives had been taken from them or been ruined. Bob was not only crippled physically, but mentally as well.

He had been such a bright, laughing, happy young man when she had first met him, she reflected. She would never forget how kind and considerate he had been towards her. It was thanks to him that she had survived her first few weeks in Liverpool and not gone running back home with her tail between her legs.

Now that he was facing his own nightmares she longed to be able to do more to help him, but his mother made that impossible. She was so fiercely possessive that it was difficult to offer advice or to even talk things over with him without her interceding.

With his walking disability he seemed to get out of the house less and less so there was not even the chance of bumping into him in the street and having a chat these days.

Her own life was also still fraught because of the strained atmosphere between her and

Eunice, which was steadily getting worse because Eunice was apparently not feeling well and was becoming more and more erratic in her behaviour.

Sometimes she would remain in the office for hours at a time whilst Julia looked after Amanda. At other times she simply vanished for the day, or turned up in the office when she was least expected.

Julia suspected that these tactics were deliberate and that Eunice hoped to surprise Paul and herself in some sort of compromising situation.

From sheer boredom, Julia sometimes toyed with the idea of satisfying Eunice's suspicions; then she would look again at Paul Hawkins and feel a shudder of revulsion. She might be in her twenties and still unattached, but she certainly didn't fancy a romantic encounter with a man like him.

She wished so much that she and Bob were still as close as they used to be. Their friendship had come to mean so much to her, she'd enjoyed talking to him and their outings together had always raised her spirits.

Lonely, often depressed and constantly irritated by Eunice's jealous attitude, she began to look round for companionship and amusement.

In the past she had always turned down any invitations from the commercial travellers who were regular clients at the Darnley. Now she no longer did so, although she was quite choosey about the sort of man she went out with. They had to be under forty, good-looking and well-spoken. She had money to spend on clothes and now that the War was over, fashionable clothes were gradually coming back into the shops. She always made sure that she looked attractive, and she expected whoever dated her to be equally smart and well turned out.

She always waited until her prospective escort told her where they intended to take her, to make sure that it was going to be a good night's entertainment, before she accepted an invitation. She was not easy to please and the travellers vied with each other to come up with something different.

She was happy to go to the theatre, cinema or a restaurant, but it took a great many outings before she even permitted her date a chaste goodnight kiss.

Even so, because commercial travellers were away from home, lonely, and usually able to stretch their expense account to accommodate her tastes, she was never short of company.

After every encounter she felt a sense of disappointment because the men were all so shallow. The majority of them were married, some even had young families in some other part of the country, and she knew that her behaviour, as well as theirs, was despicable.

Even so, she enjoyed the conquests because there was so little else in her life. She never felt as close to any of them as she had to Bob

Reynolds, though. She couldn't believe that it was all over between them. She still loved him intensely and felt a tug of emotion whenever his name was mentioned.

Often when she found herself in an embrace at the end of an evening out, she let herself believe that it was Bob's arms around her, his warm breath fanning her face as the man's lips sought hers. Then resentment and humiliation about the way she was cheapening herself by her crazy flirtations swamped her mind and turned her frigid.

It all came to a sudden end when the wife of Andy Jackson, one of the commercial travellers she frequently went out with whenever he was in Liverpool, turned up unexpectedly at the Darnley.

When Julia and Andy walked into the hotel, after a late-night show at the Empire, Eunice watched the confrontation with undisguised satisfaction. She had been at school with Brenda Jackson and she had made it her business to inform Brenda about her husband's regular bouts of infidelity.

The row that ensued between Julia, Paul and Eunice Hawkins the next day was of astronomical proportions and ended in Julia losing her job and Eunice telling her that she was setting such a bad example to Amanda that neither she nor Paul was prepared to tolerate it any longer.

Julia's appeal to Paul to reconsider his hasty

decision was scuttled by Eunice. She wouldn't even permit her to wait until Amanda arrived home from school so that she could say goodbye to the little girl. This upset Julia far more than any of the harsh things Eunice said about her, or the fact that she was being turned out into the street with nowhere to go.

For one, wild moment, Julia thought of going along to Skirving Street and asking Bob to help her. He would be able to tell her where she could get a room; he'd done it in the past and his knowledge of the Scottie Road area was so much better than hers. The only trouble was that they hadn't been in touch for such a long time that he mightn't want to have anything to do with her, she thought sadly. That, and the thought of facing his mother again, deterred her from taking the risk. No, she resolved, this time she would find her own solution.

She wasn't desperate; she had money saved and, with her background knowledge of hotel work and experience at the Darnley, she would have no difficulty in finding another job. Liverpool as well as the surrounding area was full of hotels if she wanted to stay in the city, or she could move further away and really start afresh. Chester, Edinburgh, Manchester or perhaps south to London, Brighton or Eastbourne, the world was her oyster, and she could take her pick.

She decided that before she left Liverpool for good she'd make one last attempt to see Bob Reynolds. She owed him that for old times' sake, she told herself. He had done so much for her when she'd first arrived in Liverpool and, until he went into the army, they had meant a great deal to each other. He was the only man, apart from Bernard, who had ever touched her heart and she still constantly thought of him with love and affection and regretted that they hadn't married before he'd been called up.

Bob's mother didn't recognise her, and if it hadn't been that she was calling at their house, Julia wasn't sure that she would have recognised Mrs Reynolds either.

She'd always looked frail, but now her hair was snow white and her face was ravaged with pain.

'Mrs Reynolds, are you all right?' Julia asked hesitantly.

The older woman looked at her blankly.

'It's Julia . . . Julia Winter, you remember me. I wanted a word with Bob.'

Mrs Reynolds shook her head. 'Bob . . . he's not here. Who did you say you were?'

'Not here? Where is he, then?'

'Out working. He's a window cleaner. If you're a friend, then you should know that.'

'I knew he used to be a window cleaner, but—' She stopped as Mrs Reynolds was seized with a spasm of coughing which left her shaking and leaning on the door for support.

'You're not well, Mrs Reynolds. Let me help you inside . . . somewhere where you can sit down.'

Gently she put her arm round the painfully frail body and guided her back down the hallway into the living room. As she helped her into an armchair, she looked round and saw that all the photographs had been removed and that the room was no longer a shrine to Bob.

'Sit here,' she said, settling her in an armchair by the fire. 'I'll go and make a cup of tea.'

'No no!' Mrs Reynolds struggled to stand up. 'You won't know where to find anything. Leave me be. Bob will be home soon, he'll look after me.'

'I'm going to make you a drink and sit with you until he comes home,' Julia insisted.

'I said no!' Mrs Reynolds's voice rose hysterically. With a supreme effort she pulled herself out of the chair and tottered towards the kitchen. 'Go on, get out! I remember you now. You were the one who came here interfering when Bob came home from the army after he'd been injured.'

'I was only trying to help,' Julia explained. 'I'm very fond of Bob . . .'

'I know you are, but he doesn't need you hanging around him, he's got me. I can look after him quite well without any interfering bint poking their nose in. Next thing, you'll be trying to move in and I'll find myself pushed into the background or else out on the street,' she muttered.

'Of course you won't,' Julia protested. 'I don't want to take Bob from you. He is my friend, though, even if I haven't seen very much of him lately.'

'So whose fault is that?'

Taken by surprise, Julia swung round, her colour rising, her heart thudding rapidly. She hadn't heard Bob walk in and she was taken aback to see him standing there in the doorway of the living room.

For a moment they stared at each other in silence, weighing each other up cautiously. As their eyes met Julia felt a tingling anticipation. For one, wild moment she wanted to throw herself into Bob's arms, but she restrained herself, waiting for him to make the first move. She'd never stopped loving him and more than anything she wanted them to get back together again.

When he walked towards her and merely gave her a chaste kiss on the cheek, she did her best to hide her disappointment behind a bright smile, conscious that Mrs Reynolds was watching them.

'I was about to go to the pub for a bevvy, fancy coming along with me?' Bob asked.

Julia nodded.

'I won't be long, Mam,' he said firmly as he led the way down the hallway.

Julia gave him a grateful smile. 'You're no longer using your crutches,' she exclaimed in surprise as they went out into Skirving Street.

He laughed and waved his walking stick in the air. 'That's right, and I won't be using this either for very much longer, not once I've got used to this artificial leg I've had fitted.'

'You are looking well,' Julia told him.

'Yes, almost back to normal,' he told her confidently. 'I've got the business going again and it's picking up nicely.' His eyes twinkled. 'I suppose I should say thank you to you for that. I did what you told me and hired a lad to help and now I've got two men working for me as well.'

'That's wonderful!'

'Yes, my biggest problem these days is that my mam is going downhill fast. I wanted to get a woman in to look after her, but she's so stubborn she won't hear of it. She says there's no one she knows well enough to trust and she doesn't feel well enough to follow them round the house all day to make sure they're not snooping amongst her things.'

'I can see she's not well,' Julia agreed. 'Is there anything I can do to help?'

'Not unless you want to become our housekeeper and move in here and take care of her,' he chuckled.

'Yes, I can do that, as long as you can persuade your mother to agree,' she told him.

Bob looked at her in wide-eyed disbelief as he pushed his floppy brown hair back from his forehead.

'Do you really mean that?'

'I've never been more serious in my life.'

'She won't be easy to live with and do things for, you do know that.'

'I know! She doesn't really like me. She didn't even want me to wait to see you because she's afraid I'm going to take you away from her or come between you both in some way. I told her I have no intention of doing either. I only came to see how you were getting on because you are a friend.'

'And did she believe you?'

'No, of course she didn't. She had asked me to leave when you walked in.'

'So how do you think you are going to be able to look after her, then? She's got tuberculosis and she needs nursing as well as general care, you know.'

'I can handle that. I was a nurse in a military hospital before I worked at the Darnley, if you remember.'

He nodded, pushing back his hair again. 'Yes, I do remember, so I'm sure you would be perfect.'

'What's more I can start right away.'

'Really! What's happened to your job at the Darnley?'

'I was sacked this morning. It was Eunice's idea. She seemed to think that I was getting too friendly with her husband.'

'And were you?'

Julia laughed contemptuously. 'What do you think? Have you seen him lately? He's old, he's bald and he's gross. Hardly my idea of a Romeo, I can tell you.'

'I have seen him several times over the past

few months when I've called to see you,' Bob said stiffly.

'You've come to the Darnley?' Julia looked puzzled. 'No one has ever mentioned it to me.'

'Every time I called, Eunice told me you were out with some bloke or other. I left a message each time, but when you didn't get in touch I thought you weren't interested in seeing me any more,' Bob said grimly.

'That's not true! You've no idea how much I've missed you . . .' her voice broke and she blinked back her tears.

'Probably not half as much as I've missed you!'

'You resented everything I said to you when you first came home,' she reminded him.

'Yes, I know! I had a huge chip on my shoulder and I was out of step with the whole world,' he admitted shamefacedly.

'I can understand that; I should have been more tactful and patient,' Julia sighed.

'I was so bitter about losing my leg that I hated the whole world and everybody in it. I was a pain in the arse and a right pig to you and I'm sorry. I've tried umpteen times to pluck up the courage and let you know, in the hope that you'd forgive me.'

'Forgive you? Of course I do,' Julia exclaimed fervently.

'Nothing would make me happier than if we could be together again,' Bob assured her.

'Me too!'

'Well, that's a relief.' Bob grinned, stopping to take her into his arms and holding her so close that she thought he would squeeze her to death.

Awkwardly she freed herself. 'It's eight years since you went into the army; we're probably both different people now,' she said cautiously.

Bob's face fell. 'Are you trying to say that we've left it too late?' He groaned. 'Does that mean you won't even consider coming back to Skirving Street?'

'Of course I'll come back, if you really want me to . . . and if your mother will agree to me being there and looking after you both.'

Bob's beaming smile, followed by a deep, lingering kiss, told her more about his feelings than words ever could.

Julia found that moving into Skirving Street and looking after Mrs Reynolds was not exactly a bed of roses. Although it was obvious that she was too weak to undertake the running of the house herself, or to prepare meals for Bob when he came home from work each day, Mrs Reynolds made it abundantly clear that she resented the intrusion. Bob did everything he possibly could to smooth matters between them, but it wasn't easy.

More and more Julia took over all the household duties until after a couple of months she was completely in charge and Mrs Reynolds spent most of the day in bed.

Julia ministered to her needs and tried to ignore her grumbles and protestations, but the more she did for her, the more Mrs Reynolds seemed to resent her.

Bob continually remonstrated with his mother about her attitude, reminding her that Julia was devoting every moment of her time to looking after them both.

'Prying into everything, you mean,' Mrs Reynolds grumbled weakly. 'I found her messing about in that back bedroom that you use as an office and where you keep all your business papers the other day,' she told him. 'She was in there prying into all your affairs while you were out.'

'No, Mam, Julia wasn't prying, she was doing the books for me,' Bob corrected her. 'After all her experience at the Darnley I can assure you that Julia's far more efficient at bookkeeping than I am,' he explained.

'You shouldn't let her know all your business,' his mother warned.

'Why not, what does it matter?'

'She'll be trying to latch on to you when she knows what you're worth,' she told him.

Bob laughed and patted her shoulder. 'Don't you worry about it, Mam. You rest and take advantage of having someone to care for you,' he told her.

Mrs Reynolds shook her head disapprovingly, but as the weeks went by, and she became weaker, she made less fuss about things. She even went as far as to remark to Bob one night when he went into her room to say goodnight to her, 'It's lucky we have that Judy you call Julia living here. I don't think I'm up to looking after you any more.'

Mrs Reynolds's health deteriorated very slowly. She spent more and more time in bed, sometimes in a deep sleep, at other times hovering between waking and sleeping, content to simply lie there and be waited on.

As time passed, there were days when she didn't feel like getting up at all. At other times she insisted on being dressed and in her armchair in the sitting room, waiting for Bob to come home from work.

Julia took it in her stride, adjusting what she was doing to Mrs Reynolds's whimsical lifestyle.

Although she and Bob were now as close as they'd ever been, they kept this fact hidden from his mother; especially the fact that they were sleeping together.

'She'd have a fit if she knew,' Bob admitted.

'I shan't tell her and I don't think you will,' Julia teased.

'No, but if she ever came looking for one of us and walked in and—'

'Ssh!' Julia pressed a finger on to his lips silencing him. 'It's not likely to happen; she's finding it more and more difficult to get out of bed on her own.'

'I know,' Bob sighed. 'I hate to see her in such a state. She's fading away, there's no doubt about that.'

Bob was right, but it was a long slow process. Several times when Julia took her breakfast tray in she thought that the end had come. The bedclothes barely moved and she was sure Mrs Reynolds had stopped breathing. Then she'd stir and Julia would give a sigh of relief – for Bob's sake, knowing how much he worried about his mother.

Sometimes Julia felt she was living in a time warp as month after month went by and Bob felt unable to go ahead with the plans they had for their marriage.

'I'm afraid it would upset my mother if we did anything about it at the moment,' he explained, 'and since the doctor says that she has only a short time left, we'll have to go on being patient.'

Although Julia understood the problem, it sometimes seemed as though Mrs Reynolds was clinging on to life solely to prevent them marrying.

Whenever this thought came into her mind she wondered why she was letting it worry her since apart from having a document to make it legal, they were as closely united as they could ever be.

Chapter Twenty-six

In January 1926, Mrs Reynolds died quietly in her bed in Skirving Street. Bob was completely devastated even though he knew he'd done everything possible to make her final years as comfortable as he possibly could.

It was left to Julia to take charge. She made all the funeral arrangements, and she also undertook to prepare a meal for the few neighbours who attended the funeral.

Bob was grateful that she had taken this load off his shoulders, but he was concerned when she refused to let the Homer Street Funeral Parlour make the final arrangements.

'Danny is going to be very cut up when he finds out; he's known my mam for most of his life,' he said worriedly.

'Surely you don't expect me to use them, not after what happened and remembering what I know goes on there!' Julia exclaimed exasperatedly.

'You're not working there now, though, are you, so what does it matter?' he asked, running his hands through his hair in a bewildered manner.

'It's a question of principle, isn't it? Paddy is

a rogue and I'm pretty sure Danny knows all about the things he does and simply turns a blind eye to what is going on. If you want them to handle the funeral arrangements, then you will have to be the one to go and see them, I certainly won't.'

Once the funeral was over their life went on very much as it had before. Julia cleaned the house, did the shopping and had a hot meal on the table waiting for Bob when he came home at night. She also kept the books for him and listened to his daily accounts of how the business was progressing.

She waited expectantly for Bob to realise that there was now nothing to stop them getting married. They'd known each other for over ten years and she waited hopefully for him to say that it was time she was something more than merely his housekeeper and that they should get married.

The weeks became months and still Bob said nothing; he simply seemed to accept matters as they stood. They lived like a staid married couple, resuming their weekly outings to the pictures or, occasionally, if they had something to celebrate, he would take her out to a restaurant for a special meal.

Five months after Mrs Reynolds died, Julia received a letter from Paul Hawkins asking if she would call in at the Darnley as there was something he wished to discuss with her.

From the tone of his letter it seemed likely

that he was going to offer her the chance of having her old job back and she was intrigued. She decided to say nothing to Bob until she'd been to see Paul and found out what it was all about.

She decided to wear a black suit and a plain white blouse, similar to what she had always worn when she had worked there. She was slightly taken aback to find how tight the skirt was around the waist. When she put the jacket on and the buttons would barely fasten she was shocked at how much weight she'd put on.

I've let myself go since there has been no one to notice what I look like, she told herself crossly as she brushed her auburn hair into a sleek chignon in the nape of her neck. Perhaps a job where I have to look smart because other people notice my appearance is exactly what I need.

It seemed strange to be walking into the foyer of the Darnley, a place she had vowed she would never set foot in again. Everything seemed exactly the same as it had when she'd last been there, almost as if time had stood still in the intervening years. Paul's hair looked thinner and a little more grey than she remembered but apart from that he hadn't changed very much either.

'Eunice is unwell and we need someone we can trust to help with running the hotel,' he explained after a cordial greeting and a warm handshake.

'I shouldn't think for one minute that Eunice

will want me to come back,' Julia said dryly. 'She was the one who sacked me, if you remember, because she didn't trust us to work together.'

'That's all been forgotten a long time ago,' Paul said dismissively. 'Blame the illness; it made her paranoid. It still does to some extent, but she'll be the first to admit that she was in the wrong and that she had nothing to worry about.'

'Even so, I can't see myself coming back here to work.' Julia frowned.

'If you don't want to help with running the hotel, then at least spare some time for Amanda,' he pleaded. 'She keeps asking for you; she's done so ever since the day you left.'

Once again Julia shook her head. How could she ever forget the abrupt way Eunice had dismissed her, refusing to even let her stay until Amanda came home from school so that she could explain that she was leaving?

'She's missed you so much, Julia,' Paul pleaded again. 'She's growing up and she needs a woman around her, one she can confide in. Eunice is so sick that she has very little time for her these days.'

'And you think I'm the right person to be there for her?' Julia asked wryly.

'I don't only think it, I know it,' Paul told her earnestly. 'I'm begging you to come back, Julia,' he pleaded.

'I'll think about it,' she promised. 'You'll have to give me a few days.'

'So that you can ask Bob Reynolds to give his permission?' he said scornfully.

Julia didn't answer, but merely smiled non-committally.

Bob's reaction would certainly determine her decision, but not in the way Paul was suggesting. She needed time to think, to reassess what was happening to her life. This might be exactly what was needed to rouse Bob from his complacency about how things stood between the two of them.

They'd lived together as though they were man and wife for so long now that Bob accepted it. She'd agreed to this arrangement because they both knew that it would distress Bob's mother if they said they were going to be married.

They both knew that Mrs Reynolds had worried in case Julia might take Bob away from her, which was why they'd made sure that she was unaware that they shared the same bed and were man and wife in almost all respects.

'So you'll let me have your answer in a couple of days?' Paul Hawkins persisted.

'Yes. If I do decide to come back, I shall want to talk to Eunice about it first though.'

He shrugged impatiently. 'If you must, but you'll have to be very tactful in order not to upset her.'

'I want her to be the one to ask me to come back,' Julia told him. 'You seem to have forgotten why I left here. I don't want Eunice to feel that this is some sort of devious plot you and I have cooked up between us.'

'She won't! I've already told you it is her idea. She is desperately hoping you will agree to come back, for Amanda's sake if nothing else.'

'Let her ask me to do so, then.'

Paul didn't seem to understand her reticence, but in the end he went upstairs to explain the situation to Eunice and to see if she felt well enough to talk to her.

Julia was shocked by the change in Eunice. Her face looked drawn, her hair was lank and her eyes had a flat dullness as though their light had gone out. She seemed to find it hard to concentrate on what was being said and had little interest in what was going on around her. All her thoughts and energy seemed to be focused on her own wellbeing and survival.

Julia found that Bob didn't seem to be too enthusiastic about her returning to the Darnley.

'Why not? I've plenty of time on my hands.'

'Rubbish! You've enough to do keeping house and doing my books.'

'I can do those in half a day each week and now, with only the two of us living here, running the house is child's play.'

'Well, it is up to you, of course.' He shrugged. 'But I hope you are not thinking of living there again.'

'Why not?'

'This place would be empty without you, that's why.'

Julia didn't answer immediately. She thought

it was the ideal opportunity for him to suggest they should get married, but it didn't seem to enter his head.

Why should it, she thought angrily, when he's got all the comforts of a wife without any of the responsibility of marriage? She knew it was a problem of her own making and she decided that by returning to the Darnley her absence from Skirving Street might help to force the issue. Left on his own, Bob might realise how very much a part of his life she had become.

Paul seemed to be delighted to have her back. She made it clear right from the start, however, that she was only doing it for Eunice and Amanda. He was equally quick to point out that since there was a full-time, fully trained nurse looking after Eunice, and Amanda was at school for most of the day, she would have plenty of time to help him if he needed her.

'You told me you'd already got a very efficient bookkeeper and full-time receptionist,' she reminded him, 'so why do you need me here? What else is there that has to be done?'

'I was hoping you would take over some of the work that Eunice used to do, supervising the staff and checking that everything is running smoothly.'

'Are you sure that Eunice will want me to be doing that sort of thing?'

'I think she will be relieved. It will stop her

worrying because she can't be on hand to do it herself.'

For the first few months everything went like clockwork. Julia made a point of spending some time each day with Eunice, reporting to her what she was doing and keeping her abreast of all that was happening in the hotel.

At first Eunice asked questions and made suggestions. As her illness grew worse, and she was in constant pain, so her interest in what was going on lessened.

Julia also made sure that Amanda spent some time with Eunice every day when she came home from school. Gradually, this had to be abandoned because Eunice complained that Amanda's chatter made her head ache.

To compensate for her mother's lack of interest Julia found herself spending more and more time with Amanda. She took her shopping for clothes and she attended school whenever a parent's presence was needed and Paul wasn't free to go. From time to time, she took her to the pictures or on some other little outing.

Paul seemed to encourage these jaunts and often expressed the wish that he could accompany them.

'Why don't you come as well, Daddy? I'd really like that,' Amanda asked, beaming.

'Your daddy needs to stay here in case your mummy needs him,' Julia told her firmly.

She had noticed the interested gleam in Paul's eyes when Amanda had asked him and she was already aware that since she'd returned he was gradually becoming more and more friendly. Remembering what had happened in the past, she had no intention of letting too much familiarity cause unpleasantness between them all again.

When it became necessary for Eunice to go into hospital for treatment Julia found Paul turning to her more and more for sympathy and she didn't know how to handle the situation.

She began to wonder if perhaps the time had come for her to leave, but Amanda was so desperately unhappy about her mother being so ill that she hadn't the heart to desert the child. Instead, even though Bob was very much against it, she agreed to move back into the Darnley so that she was there for Amanda.

'She's having terrible nightmares, Bob. She's so frightened now that her mother has had to go into hospital.'

'What about me, have you ever thought that I might be scared living on my own?' he jested.

'I doubt if you will even notice I'm not here, as long as I leave a tasty hot meal waiting in the oven, ready for when you come home at night.'

Once again she hoped that he would pick up on their relationship and suggest that they should get married. When the moment passed she felt rebellious and decided to move back into the Darnley to see if that would jog him out of his lethargy.

Paul took advantage of the situation that she was there most of the time. Whenever she planned to do something with Amanda, Paul would suddenly decide to go with them. It made no difference whether it was to take Amanda to the hospital to visit her mother, or whether it was something to do with the school, or even a trip to the pictures to take the child's mind off all that was happening. He frequently came as well.

Amanda's face would light up with pleasure and although Julia didn't want Paul with them she found it was difficult to deter him without upsetting Amanda, so she hadn't the heart to object.

In the end, she started saying that she didn't think it was necessary for her to go with them as well. At this, Amanda would look so woebegone, begging her to change her mind and to come as well, that usually she hadn't the heart to refuse.

With Eunice no longer under the same roof, Paul began to throw caution to the wind. Julia's attempts to avoid being alone with him were constantly being foiled and although his methods were devious in the extreme she was concerned that other members of the staff might be aware of what was happening.

Apart from the fact that she had no feelings of any kind whatsoever for him, she despised him for behaving in such a manner when his wife was so seriously ill. She felt that it showed a lack of respect both towards her and for Eunice. When she told him this he gave a great belly laugh and it took all her self-control not to smack him across the face and wipe away his smug, self-satisfied smile.

Her irritation and rebuffs, far from discouraging him, or making him desist, only seemed to increase Paul's ardour. He openly flirted with her, even in front of Amanda.

Amanda was now eleven, and even though she was young for her age she was very observant, which made Julia feel increasingly uncomfortable with Paul's constant attentions. Finally she felt forced to face him with an ultimatum.

'I can't go on like this,' she told him. 'Either you behave yourself and leave me alone or else I shall have to leave.'

'Leave?' He raised his eyebrows and gave her a supercilious smile. 'That's rather an idle threat, Julia, since you have nowhere else to go!'

'Oh, but I have,' she told him quietly.

'You'd give all this up and go back to live in that slum in Skirving Street with your one-legged window cleaner again,' he taunted.

When she didn't answer and he saw the anger in her eyes, he tried to retract what he'd said. 'I didn't mean that,' he apologised. 'You upset me and I spoke without thinking. I couldn't bear the thought of losing you. You've no idea how much I missed you when you left here last time. It was absolute hell, Julia. I never stopped thinking about you.'

'You mean when you sacked me?' she asked coldly.

'It was Eunice who sacked you, not me,' he defended.

'True! And we both know why she did it.'

Paul chewed his lip thoughtfully, watching her warily, and then he changed his tactics.

'You can't walk out on me, Julia. Not while Eunice is in hospital,' he pleaded. 'You must stay for the present, for Amanda's sake.'

'You've said all this once before,' she told him wearily. 'I only agreed to come back because of Amanda.'

'Then you can't break your promise to her, can you? It would upset her terribly.'

'I don't want to, but I shall unless you alter your ways,' she told him firmly.

'Please stay. She's finding it so hard to come to terms with her mother being so ill and in hospital. She doesn't confide in me anything like she does in you. If you vanish from her life, then I really don't how she will cope . . . or how I will, either, if it comes to that,' he added plaintively.

Julia felt herself weakening, She knew what he was saying about Amanda was very true. She was very vulnerable. The visits to see Eunice always upset her a great deal. Afterwards she was angry and depressed and often sobbed her heart out after she went to bed. Julia was well aware that she was the one Amanda turned to, the only one who seemed to be able to comfort her.

It didn't make Paul's behaviour any more acceptable, though. Even though he kept assuring her that he was going to mend his ways Julia didn't have a great deal of confidence that he would keep his promise.

If she left, she kept reminding herself, Eunice would be bound to suspect the reason why she had done so. The extra worry would be bound to take its toll on her already deteriorating condition.

Each time they visited Eunice the devastating illness she was suffering from seemed to have a greater hold on her and Julia knew she couldn't bring herself to cause her any additional distress.

Against her better judgement Julia agreed to stay on at the hotel. She insisted on new locks on her bedroom door; locks to which she was the only one who had keys, as well as a bolt on the inside of the door.

Chapter Twenty-seven

Eunice Hawkins died in August 1928. She left behind a twelve-year-old daughter, Amanda, and a sixty-nine-year-old husband, and Julia felt concerned about Amanda's future. Since she had returned to the Darnley to care for her, they had grown even closer than they'd been when Amanda was a small child.

The day of the funeral was cold and dank with a fine misty drizzle falling. As they clustered at the graveside, the eerie sound of ship's hooters and klaxons, warning each other of their position in the Mersey, added a mournful dirge.

As she watched the twelve-year-old, looking pale and wan in a black coat, black stockings and a black felt hat standing by her father's side at the graveside, battling so hard to control her tears, her heart went out to the child.

Most of those attending the funeral were strangers to Julia. They included family members who had never been near the hotel all the time Eunice had been so desperately ill. Amanda seemed to have no idea who they were and she shrank away from them after a polite handshake and a watery smile.

Paul seemed to know them all. From the

conversations that ensued Julia assumed that for many of Eunice's relations the last occasion they had all been together had been when Eunice and Paul had married.

After the service ended they all returned to the Darnley to take part in the lavish buffet meal and the liberal supply of drinks that had been prepared by the hotel staff. Amanda stayed close by Julia's side as if she had some premonition that her entire life was about to change.

As they stood together in a corner of the dining room, Julia wished that she had tried harder to persuade Bob to be there, but he had refused to take a day off work to attend the funeral of someone he barely knew.

Like Amanda she was also concerned about the future and her ongoing relationship with Paul. When Eunice had been taken into hospital Paul had made it patently clear that as his wife was no longer under the same roof he no longer felt that there was any need for any further restraint between the two of them.

'Come on, Julia, relax! I know your conscience has stopped you from showing your true feelings for me in the past in case Eunice found out, but now that she is no longer here there's absolutely nothing to worry about.'

She'd been so angry and confused that she couldn't speak. She'd listened in silence as he poured out his heart, telling her how much he cared for her ever since the time when she first came to the hotel to work as a receptionist.

'You were attractive then, but as a mature woman you are more desirable than ever now,' he told her.

When she remained silent he looked at her pleadingly. 'You must have always known how I felt.' He sighed. 'I know you have principles and that you didn't feel happy about us having an affair while Eunice was around, but everything is different now. I still want you, I'm desperate for you, and there is nothing to stop us being together at last.'

Julia had clamped her hands over her ears to shut out his pleading demands. She found him repulsive. She didn't want him, she never had. She should have listened to Bob and never come back, but with Eunice so ill she had felt that Amanda needed her. Perhaps now was the time to leave before she found herself caught up in an ugly situation; but could she bring herself to desert Amanda at such a vulnerable time?

All this went through Julia's mind as a tearful Amanda clung to her, begging her to promise that whatever happened she would never leave her.

Her feelings of disquiet grew stronger when a stout middle-aged woman with her hair piled up in a beehive style, strutted over to where she and Amanda were standing.

'So, you're Amanda,' she exclaimed in a loud, overbearing voice. 'Well, I'm your Aunt Polly. Your mother was my sister. You don't look very much like her – or your father, if it comes to that,' she commented, looking Amanda over speculatively.

Amanda clutched tightly to Julia's hand and smiled nervously, but made no reply.

'My goodness, you are a shy little thing!' the woman boomed. 'How old are you?'

'I was twelve last December, Aunt Polly.'

'My sister was such a pretty girl when she was your age and she had long, very pale fair hair halfway down her back,' the woman observed. 'Perhaps you take after your father.' She frowned, studying Amanda's mop of golden curls. 'Rather a job to tell now, since he seems to have lost most of his hair,' she observed, looking across the room to where Paul was talking to a group of men. 'If I remember correctly, though, when I first met him it was very dark, almost black in fact.' She sighed sadly. 'You must be a throwback, I suppose. Every family has them from time to time. Even the colour of your eyes is different from his or from those of anyone in our family.'

'I think Amanda is a very pretty girl,' Julia said quickly.

'You do!' Aunt Polly selected a glass of wine from an attentive waiter. 'Exactly who are you, then?' she asked as she raised it to her lips.

'This is Julia, she's our friend and she helps look after me,' Amanda replied before Julia could do so.

'I see. You mean she's your nanny, do you?'

'No, I am not Amanda's nanny, I'm—'

'No matter,' Amanda's aunt interrupted, waving her hand dismissively. 'It's of no great importance.' She took hold of Amanda's arm and drew her away from Julia. 'Has your father told you that you will be coming back home with me to Tarvin?'

'You mean for a holiday?'

'No dear, to live there permanently.' She helped herself to a canapé and bit into it. 'You need someone to look after you now that your mother is dead.'

'I can't come with you, I have to go to school here,' Amanda protested, wriggling away from her aunt and trying to get back to Julia.

'There are some very good schools in Chester and you will be going to one of them from now on,' her aunt told her firmly.

'I don't want to go to a different school. I like it where I am. I want to stay here.'

'Well, that's not possible! Your father has far too much to do running this hotel to be able to look after you,' Aunt Polly told her sharply.

Amanda's eyes filled with tears. 'Julia will look after me. She's been doing so all the time my mam has been ill.'

'You said she wasn't your nanny.'

'She isn't. I told you, she's a friend. She lives with us in the hotel and helps Dad in the office. She's always been here, ever since I was little. I've known her all my life and she does look after me properly,' Amanda defended Julia fiercely.

'She's not family, though, Amanda, and now that your mother is dead it is my duty as her sister to take care of you,' Aunt Polly stated as she reached out for another glass of wine. 'Your father agrees with me, so there's no point in arguing about it.'

Julia shared Amanda's dismay. She couldn't believe what was happening. Drawing Paul to one side she asked him what was going on.

He looked at her in surprise. 'Polly is Eunice's sister and she feels that Amanda is reaching the age where she needs a woman's guidance,' he said evasively.

'So what do you think I am?' Julia demanded indignantly.

His eyebrows lifted sardonically. 'I'm not too sure. I certainly don't want her turning into a frigid spinster. I want her to have the benefit of a normal family life.'

'You can't do this, Paul. Amanda needs me,' Julia argued. 'She's known me ever since she was born. Eunice's sister is not only a complete stranger, but lives miles away. How can you expect Amanda to be happy living with her and never seeing you?'

'Polly has raised a son and two daughters; she'll know how to handle her.'

'They're strangers,' Julia repeated stubbornly. 'I've taken care of Amanda for years, why change things?'

Paul looked uncomfortable. 'Let's face it, Julia, if Amanda goes to live with Polly, she will be in the heart of a united family,' he blustered. 'If our relationship was more amicable, if you showed the same sort of affection towards me as you do towards Amanda, then things would be different. Then I might feel you were the right sort of person to bring up Amanda.'

'You are utterly contemptible!' Julia told him, her lip curling as she looked at him with distaste. 'What you are suggesting is nothing short of blackmail.'

Paul Hawkins shrugged. 'The choice is yours. It's not too late to change the arrangements.'

Julia shook her head. 'No, Paul, as much as I care about Amanda I am not willing to take you on as well.'

'That's very short-sighted of you, Julia. In that case perhaps you'd like to go up and pack your things now. I want you to vacate your room immediately.'

'You want me to go now this very minute, in the middle of your wife's funeral?' she exclaimed in a shocked voice.

'Correct!' His eyes narrowed. 'And before you tell me that you have nowhere to go, let me remind you that you can always go back to Skirving Street, to your window-cleaner lover. I'm sure he'll take you back,' he added bitterly.

Julia's eyes were so blurred by tears that she could hardly see to pack her suitcase. She felt so unhappy about deserting Amanda, knowing she would have to face living with her aunt, especially at a time like this when the child was grieving for her mother, that she was almost tempted to capitulate and give in to Paul Hawkins's demands.

The thought of having to share a bed with him, when she couldn't even bear him to touch her, filled her with revulsion. She couldn't do it, not even for Amanda, she decided.

She didn't know how she could explain the situation to Amanda, so she decided to use the service stairs in the hope of avoiding being seen by either her or the crowd of relatives who were still there, noisily gossiping and drinking.

Amanda had overheard the bitter exchange and sensed the unpleasant atmosphere between her father and Julia and came looking for her.

'Why are you packing your suitcase?' she demanded. 'Where are you going?'

'I'm leaving.' Julia reached out and drew the child into her arms. 'You're going to live with your Aunt Polly, so I'm no longer needed here.'

Amanda pulled away, her face angry. 'I don't want to live with Aunt Polly. I don't know her, and I don't like her. I've already told my dad that.'

'I'm afraid you'll have to, it's what your father has decided is best for you,' Julia told her gently. She kissed the top of Amanda's curls.

'So where are you going?'

'I'm going back home . . . to Skirving Street.'

'Can't I come with you just for a few days while Dad thinks about it?' Amanda wheedled.

Julia shook her head. 'Your Aunt Polly is

taking you back with her now so that you have time to get settled in before you have to start at a new school in September.'

'I like the school I go to now,' Amanda persisted. 'All my friends are there. I don't want to go and live with Aunt Polly; I want to stay here with you.'

'That's not feasible, Amanda!'

They both jumped at the sound of Paul Hawkins's voice.

'I thought I might find you'd lured Amanda up here and that you'd be filling her head with all sorts of rubbish,' he said in a hard, reproachful voice.

'Daddy, I don't want Julia to leave, and I don't want you to send me away to live with Aunt Polly. I want things to go on the same as they've always done,' Amanda pleaded, her blue eyes bright with unshed tears.

'You heard what Julia said. She's decided she is leaving so I'm afraid you'll have to do as I say because there's no one here to look after you,' Paul said.

'Can't you persuade her to change her mind?'

'I've tried very hard to make Julia change her mind, my dear, believe me I have, but she doesn't want to be here with us any more. Isn't that right, Julia?'

Julia felt too choked to answer or to defend herself against the way Paul was twisting her words. She felt as if she was being torn in two. She wanted so much to stay and look after

340

Amanda, but how could she when she was only too aware of what personal sacrifice she would have to make in order to do so?

Bob Reynolds couldn't settle. He'd come home from work early, hoping that perhaps as soon as the funeral was over Julia would come straight home from the cemetery. It was now almost four o'clock and there was no sign of her so he assumed she must have gone back to the hotel.

He knew he should have gone to the funeral with her but he didn't think it was his place to do so. He knew Paul Hawkins well enough, but he had only spoken to Eunice three or four times in his life, so to go to her funeral seemed to be all wrong.

He wondered what changes her death was going to make to them. He hadn't wanted Julia to go back to work at the Darnley and certainly not to move back in there like she had done.

He sighed and stared round the comfortable living room. After his own mother had died he and Julia had got rid of all the old-fashioned furniture and furnishings and they'd turned the place into something that was more to their taste. Now it was a bright friendly room with light paintwork and pretty curtains.

He'd thought Julia was so happy there that for the life of him he couldn't understand why she had wanted to move back to the Darnley.

'It's for Amanda's sake, she needs me,' Julia

had explained. 'Poor child, she needs someone who understands her and who takes an interest in what she's doing.'

'She's got her father,' he'd argued, but Julia had shaken her head.

'He's so old! He acts more like her grand-father than her father. He hasn't the patience he should have and he doesn't seem to understand her at all.'

'Eunice is still able to care for her, surely.'

'Eunice is so involved with her own illness that she isn't as interested in Amanda as she should be. She can't go shopping with her and things like that, either.'

Bob had given in reluctantly and only because he understood what Julia meant and because he knew how very fond she was of the little girl.

What he hadn't counted on, though, was Julia moving back in there to live after Eunice went into hospital. It wasn't as though Amanda was a little kid. She could surely put herself to bed and get herself ready for school in the morning without having Julia there to cosset her.

Julia had remained adamant, though. She even went as far as to tell him that he didn't own her and that she was nothing more than his housekeeper.

That really hurt. They'd been living as man and wife for so long that he'd taken it for granted that she regarded him exactly the way she would if they were properly married.

He realised too late that their not being legally married was the nub of the problem. He didn't see that a piece of paper made any difference to the way they felt about each other, but obviously Julia felt differently.

They'd intended to get married, but had postponed it because his mother was so much against the idea and they didn't want to upset her knowing how ill she was. He realised now that he should have fixed a date as soon as possible after she'd died, but it had never entered his head to do so.

Now, the minute Julia got home, it would be the very first thing he'd do. He'd even go down on one knee and propose to her in the traditional manner, he told himself. In fact, he'd do just about anything to make sure that Julia didn't go gallivanting off ever again.

He'd loved her since that first moment he'd seen her standing outside Exchange Station looking so young and innocent and so utterly lost.

After that, their paths had crossed so many times that he became convinced that destiny intended them to be together. He had been worried for a long time, though, whether a smart girl like her, with her posh Wallasey accent, would even look twice at a slummy window cleaner.

She had, though, and they'd had some memorable times together. It was a shame that his mother had been so very much against her, but

343

then his mam had always taken a dislike to any girl he'd claimed was a friend.

After his dad was killed she'd become even more possessive and dependent on him. He knew he owed it to his dad to look out for her. He'd promised her that he'd take care of her no matter what happened, even though by then he had told Julia that he loved her and wanted them to be married.

He might even have managed to pull it off if he hadn't been called up. Then he knew they'd have to postpone marriage because his mother was insisting that she was his next-of-kin and, to pacify her, he promised to make his army allowance out to her so that she had something to live on.

Julia had understood that and stuck by him. Even after he'd been injured and had been sent home crippled she'd still been there, trying to help and offering sound advice.

He'd spoiled it all with his pent-up anger and bitterness, saying he didn't want her telling him what he should do to get his life together again.

After they'd parted, though, he'd done every one of the things she'd suggested and found that she'd been right about everything she'd said.

Yes, he reflected, Julia was one in a million and they were meant to be together. Look how she had helped out when his mother was dying, nursing her right to the very end.

Well, that was all in the past and now he

wanted Julia to come home. He'd told her she had to choose between the Darnley and Amanda and being with him.

He prayed she would choose him and then he'd make sure that the first thing they'd do would be to get married. This time it really would be the start of a whole new life for them.

Chapter Twenty-eight

For several months after she returned to Skirving Street, Julia felt so lethargic that she couldn't bring herself to take very much interest in anything that was going on around her.

Much of the time Julia found that her thoughts revolved around what had happened to Amanda. She felt guilty knowing that to some extent it was her fault that Amanda had been forced to go and live with her Aunt Polly in Tarvin, even though she didn't want to do so. It was all because she had refused to go along with Paul Hawkins's request.

Several times she'd tried to tell Bob all about it, but at the last minute had changed her mind. There was something shameful about being asked to do such a thing and she wasn't sure how Bob would react. Deep down she was afraid he might think that she had given Paul some encouragement for him to think she would be agreeable to his suggestion. She should have taken Bob's advice and never have agreed to move back to the Darnley when Eunice was taken ill. Would Bob still believe her when she said she'd only done it for Amanda's sake?

What made the situation even more difficult was that Bob had welcomed her back so enthusiastically. Furthermore, he was eager for them to get married just as soon as it could be arranged, but she wasn't sure that she could marry Bob until it was all out in the open as to why she'd left the Darnley.

She was no longer a young, starry-eyed romantic. She was over thirty, a mature woman. She still loved Bob deeply, but it was no longer a heady, frothy, filled-with-excitement kind of feeling. Now it was a much deeper, far more satisfying kind of love that would stay with her for ever.

She tried to explain all this to Bob, but she could see that it left him bewildered so she told him she that she didn't want to rush things.

'Leaving the Darnley has given me a sense of freedom that I've never had before. I want to enjoy not having any responsibility or commitments,' she told him.

Bob seemed more than a little taken aback by her attitude, but he was so eager to please her that he agreed, rather reluctantly, that they would wait until she felt she was ready to name the day.

'I thought you might be worried about what the neighbours thought about us living together when we aren't married,' he said worriedly, running his hand through his thick hair in a bewildered fashion.

Julia raised her eyebrows. 'And about what

they might be thinking about my recent absence?' she asked cynically.

He nodded. 'Even though you still visited regularly they must have thought that we'd quarrelled or something,' he admitted sheepishly.

'Well, as your mother always used to say when she was alive, people have to gossip about something. If they're talking about us, then they're leaving someone else alone.'

'You're right! What does it matter what they think?' Bob laughed. 'Let them surmise what they like, and gossip as much as they want to; as long as we are happy, that's all that matters.

And they were happy, Julia realised. Being back with Bob was like settling down in a comfortable armchair. When he finished work they shut the front door on the rest of the world and enjoyed each other's company.

While she had been at the Darnley, Bob had concentrated all his efforts on trying to expand his window-cleaning business. At the back of his mind he had the idea that once they were married they could move right away from the Scottie Road area if Julia wanted to do so.

With the General Strike causing a blockade at the docks, however, he found that it became increasingly difficult to even hold on to his existing customers. More and more shipping firms found themselves in trouble and losing business because of the effects of the strike. One of the many economies they made was to stop having their office windows cleaned.

Countless men found themselves out of work and they were no longer able to hand over a regular pay-packet to their wives. As a result, those living in the mean streets around Scottie Road either cleaned their windows themselves or left them, hoping that the rain would do the job instead.

Bob's other customers, the local shopkeepers, were also finding that their sales were down and that times were hard. Now, instead of having their windows cleaned every week, it became once a fortnight and, in some cases, only once a month.

One by one Bob found he'd had to get rid of the men and boys he employed. Now he was trying to manage with only one man working full time and a couple of young lads who came along after school and again on Saturday mornings.

When Julia eventually realised that Bob was barely making enough money to make ends meet, she told him she thought it was time she found herself another job. Having once tried factory work she was reluctant to do anything like that ever again, but she had no idea what else was available.

'Why don't you try to get a job as a book-keeper or receptionist at one of the other hotels in Liverpool?' Bob suggested when they talked the matter over. 'You've had plenty of experience at that sort of work and I'm sure Paul Hawkins would give you a reference, if you needed one.'

Julia agreed with him, but although there were countless hotels she couldn't find anyone willing to employ her and she wondered if perhaps Paul had spread some adverse criticism about her.

In desperation she started applying to the shipping offices in the dockside area. To her delight and relief she finally managed to get taken on as a clerk at Alison & Company. They were general importers and they had offices in Old Hall Street.

It was quite a small office run by a middle-aged man who was in the office full time and two shipping clerks who spent most of the day at the dockside arranging transportation of various cargoes and having meetings with the captains and customs officials.

Her duties consisted in checking their documents and writing out invoices. It was far from exciting but the pay was good; far more than she'd earned at the Darnley.

It meant that not only was she able to contribute towards her keep and not feel completely dependent on Bob, but she was also able to save so that she had money of her own.

They slipped back into their old way of life with ease. Since he'd come out of the army Bob had taken an interest in cooking, though he hated domestic chores, so Julia undertook most of those.

Their evenings were spent dealing with either household matters or doing the books for his business. They still enjoyed their occasional outings to the pictures, but, Julia reflected, despite her need to feel independent, they were very settled and in as comfortable a rut as if they were married.

Bob seemed to think the same, and as the two of them celebrated the quietest Christmas ever he suggested that perhaps they really should do something about tying the knot in the new year.

Julia didn't feel in the least bit excited but couldn't think of any valid reason why they shouldn't. Even so, it was St Valentine's Day 1930 before they finally set a date and agreed to get married on the first Saturday in June.

To celebrate their decision Bob suggested that they should have a day out in Chester.

'Mam used to take me there as a special treat when I was a kid,' he laughed.

'Then that's what we'll do,' Julia agreed. 'I used to love going to Chester, too. There're some lovely shops there and if it's a nice day, we can walk along the walls.'

'If you can get a day off work, then we can go in the middle of the week,' Bob suggested. 'It won't be as crowded on a Wednesday or Thursday as on a Saturday.'

It was a cold but bright and sunny February day when they set out the following Wednesday. They decided to make a real jaunt of their day, an occasion to remember, so they crossed over to Birkenhead on the ferry boat and then took a bus from Hamilton Square to Chester.

'Shall we take that walk around the walls first, while the sun is shining?' Bob suggested as Julia kept stopping to look in the shop windows.

'All right,' she agreed, 'and then we'll have something to eat and then I want to do some window shopping. I might even see an outfit to wear for our wedding.' She smiled, taking his arm.

The whole day went perfectly. They both enjoyed themselves and the time seemed to fly past.

'We could round things off by going to the Music Hall by the Cathedral,' Bob proposed.

Julia shook her head. 'I'd sooner go to the pictures than the theatre,' she demurred.

'It *is* a cinema. It used to be a theatre a great many years ago, that's why it's called the Music Hall. Let's find out what's on there, shall we?'

'Can we stop and have a cup of tea first? I'm gasping,' Julia protested.

'Of course! We'll have a proper afternoon tea, if you like, at one of the teashops in the High Street.'

'Well, what's it to be?' Bob asked when they found a table in the window and settled down to watch the world go by. 'Tea and fancy cakes or tea and toast?'

'They do a special cream tea,' Julia told him as she studied the menu, 'why don't we try that.'

Julia was biting into a scone spread with raspberry jam and topped with a generous blob of thick yellow cream when she let out a gasp and grabbed at Bob's arm.

'Look! Look out there!' she gasped, pointing through the window towards the busy street outside. 'It's Amanda!'

Before Bob could stop her, she'd run from the café and was out on the pavement, waving her arms and calling frantically to a group of schoolgirls who had walked past.

A few minutes later she was back inside the café, holding a tall, leggy schoolgirl by the hand and insisting that she must sit down with them.

'Ask them to bring another cup and some more scones, Bob,' she urged.

While they were waiting, she turned to Amanda. 'Come on, tell me all about what has been happening since you've been living with your Aunt Polly.'

As they listened to Amanda's account of the sort of life she was now living, Bob and Julia exchanged uneasy glances. Both of them felt dismayed by how unhappy she seemed to be.

'Your Aunt Polly certainly sounds rather a martinet for order and cleanliness,' Bob commented.

'Yes, and I'm the one who has to do all the work!' Amanda agreed with him gloomily. 'She saves up as many jobs as she can all week for me to do on Saturdays and Sundays. I'm

353

expected to do scrubbing, cleaning and polishing as well as washing and ironing,' Amanda sighed.

'She's fanatical,' she went on. 'Every single thing in the house has to be polished every week, from the brass letter box on the front door, to the furniture in every room in the house. Even the mirrors and windows have to be sparkling. Everything is so shiny and so tidy right through the house that you'd think no one lived there.'

'Apart from that, though, you are well looked after?' Julia pressed as Amanda paused and tucked into the scones that Julia had spread thickly with jam and cream and placed in front of her.

Amanda pulled a face. 'I suppose so. I'm not allowed to go out on my own, except to school.' She stopped speaking and stood up. 'I must go, I'll be in awful trouble because I'm going to be late home. There are two other girls who live in Tarvin and we are supposed to stick together and catch the five minutes past four bus from the Square.'

'I'm afraid you've missed that,' Bob exclaimed.

'Your friends will have gone on ahead and caught the bus, will they?'

Amanda nodded.

'So what will happen now if you wait for the next bus?' Julia asked worriedly.

'I don't know. I'll probably be sent to my room immediately after tea for the rest of the week. That's what happened when we all missed the bus and were late home the first week I was at the school.'

'It looks as though the best thing we can do is to get you to Tarvin before the bus reaches there,' Bob said quickly. He stood up and walked over to the cash desk and spoke to the woman in charge.

'Come on,' he called to them. 'Hurry up!'

As they reached the door a taxicab drew up outside and Bob bundled Julia and Amanda into it.

'Do you know where Tarvin is?' he asked the driver. 'As fast as you can go.'

'Don't worry, Amanda, we'll get you home almost as fast as the bus,' he told her as he settled in the front seat beside the driver, leaving Julia and Amanda on their own in the back and free to talk to each other for the four-mile journey.

As they reached the village they saw the green Crosville bus was only a short distance ahead of them.

'Could you stop wherever that bus does so that we can let the girl out?' Bob asked the driver.

'Anything you say, guv.'

Amanda was already standing on the pavement when the two other girls alighted from

355

the bus. Julia felt very relieved that they were in time for Amanda to walk down the village street with her two friends.

All the way back to Chester Julia reflected on the things Amanda had told her about her new home and school. It was obvious that she wasn't happy or settled and Julia wished she could do something to help her.

'I'm afraid that's the end of our day out,' Bob told her when they reached the city centre. 'That taxi ride has cleaned me out so we won't be able to go to the pictures.'

'That's fine, I don't think I want to watch a film now, anyway,' Julia told him.

On the way back to Birkenhead on the bus Julia talked non-stop about all the things Amanda had told her.

'She certainly doesn't sound very happy,' Bob agreed, 'but I don't see that there is anything you can do about it. It's what her father wants for her, isn't it, and I suppose he has the final say about where she lives and who looks after her.'

'She was always so bright and bubbly and yet today she looked so much older that for a moment I wasn't even sure it was her,' Julia said sadly.

'She looked older, I must admit, but then she's growing up. What is she now, twelve?'

'More than that, she was fourteen last December.'

'Are you sure?' Bob asked in surprise.

'I should know,' she told him dryly. 'I lost my baby the same week as Amanda was born.'

He nodded solemnly. 'Of course, you would remember the date.' He squeezed her arm. 'I haven't forgotten. It seems a lifetime ago to me, but I suppose it will always be fresh in your mind.'

'I do think about it from time to time,' she admitted. 'That's probably why I am so concerned about Amanda's happiness. Being with her since she was only a few weeks old has made us very close, almost as if she was my own child.'

He held her hand tightly and kissed her on the cheek. 'I think I understand. I'm sorry you can't change anything for her, but Paul Hawkins has taken his decision about who he wants to bring her up and that's that.'

'I know, but it would be nice to see her from time to time. She is so lonely without me. She says it's impossible to talk to her Aunt Polly like she used to confide in me.'

Bob nodded thoughtfully. He often felt resentful of the way Amanda seemed to come between them and wished Julia wasn't so involved with her. He also realised that Amanda meant so much to Julia that she would always have a place in her heart and he had to learn to accept it. 'I've an idea,' he said tentatively. 'Why don't you ask Amanda to come to our wedding, surely Paul would permit that, knowing how close you've been?'

'That's a wonderful idea,' Julia agreed. Then her face clouded. 'Would he let her come, though?'

'I think he'd feel he would have to if you said that you wanted Amanda to be your bridesmaid,' Bob chuckled.

Chapter Twenty-nine

All Bob and Julia's carefully laid plans about asking Amanda to their wedding in June went out of the window when they received a surprise visit from Paul Hawkins.

Julia was shocked by his appearance. He had aged considerably since she'd last seen him. He was still overweight, but now his jowls were slack like a turkey's crop, and his skin looked grey and unhealthy. His close-set eyes were bloodshot. His hand was quivering so much when he extended it to shake hands that she wondered if he was drinking heavily or if there was something seriously wrong with him.

'You probably both think it strange that I've come round here,' he told them, 'but you are the only ones who I think might be able to help. It's about Amanda . . .'

'Is she ill or something?' Julia interrupted.

Paul ran a trembling hand over his receding hair, shaking his head from side to side as he did so. 'I don't know . . . you see we don't know where she is; she's run away! Polly has no idea where she's gone.' He chewed his lip. 'I was wondering if you knew,' he said awkwardly.

'Why on earth do you think we would know where she is?' Bob frowned.

'Well,' he hesitated uncomfortably, 'Amanda was always very fond of Julia and I wondered if she had taken it into her head to come here to see her.'

'No,' Julia replied. 'We haven't seen anything of her. I've only seen her once since you sent her to live with your sister-in-law in Tarvin.'

'So you have seen her! Where? When?' His eyes darted from one to the other of them enquiringly.

'We saw her very briefly in Chester earlier in the year,' Bob explained.

'Yes, it was only a matter of about half an hour, though. She was on her way home from school . . .'

Paul Hawkins stood up and paced the room. 'When was this?' he snapped.

'Sometime in February.'

'That's almost three months ago! And you've not spoken to her since?' he asked suspiciously as he flopped back down in his chair.

'No, of course not.'

'So what did she say to you? What did you talk about? Did she say anything that would make you think that she might do something like this? Oh come on,' he begged when they both shook their heads, 'tell me all you know, anything that might give me some clue about what has happened to her.'

'Well, we both thought she looked very thin and she certainly didn't look happy.'

'Did Amanda give you any clues as to why she looked unhappy? Did she say anything to make you suspect that she might be thinking of running away?'

'She mentioned that her aunt kept a very spick and span home and that she was expected to do a great deal of cleaning on Saturdays and Sundays ...'

'Cleaning! Amanda wouldn't know how to start,' Paul guffawed. 'She never lifted a finger when she was at the Darnley. She didn't need to, of course. I always employed women to do that sort of thing. She didn't even have to keep her bedroom tidy; you know that, Julia, as well as I do!'

'Yes, but it seems it's a very different picture now,' Julia told him sharply. 'From the few words we managed to have with her I gathered that she is expected to do cleaning, polishing, washing and ironing on Saturdays and Sundays. What is more,' she added heatedly, 'Amanda seemed to be scared stiff when she realised that stopping to talk to us meant that she might be late home and that she would be punished if she was.'

'Utter rubbish!' Paul defended his sister-in-law. 'You're making it all up to try and upset me.'

'Not at all,' Bob assured him. 'Amanda missed her bus and we had to get a taxi to get her back to Tarvin so that she'd be there when her mates got off the bus and she could walk down the village street with them, otherwise she'd have been for it.'

'Meeting up with you again is what has unsettled her,' Paul exclaimed accusingly. 'Did you suggest that she could come back to Liverpool?'

'Of course not! I wouldn't dream of trying to influence her,' Julia exclaimed hotly.

Paul looked unconvinced. 'Are you quite sure she hasn't been here, or written to you, or tried to get in touch with you since that day?' he persisted.

'We've told you everything we can. If she does get in touch with us then you will be the first to know,' Bob told him. 'Have you been to the police and reported her missing?'

Paul Hawkins shook his head. 'I was hoping that wasn't going to be necessary,' he said wearily.

'Didn't you suspect that she was unhappy the last time you saw her?' Bob frowned.

'No, of course I didn't! I would have done something about it long before now if I had.'

'When exactly was the last time you saw Amanda?' Julia asked pointedly.

'Some little time ago,' he said evasively, avoiding Julia's icy stare.

'You mean at Christmas!' she commented in exasperation.

He nodded. 'I went to Tarvin and saw her briefly over Christmas. I thought it was better if she didn't come home. I was afraid it might revive too many memories being the first Christmas since Eunice died,' he explained.

'And I bet her Aunt Polly made sure that she didn't spend any time alone with you,' Julia commented.

'It was Christmas, and there were several other people there . . .' his voice trailed off uncertainly, 'I didn't have much time alone with her so I couldn't really ask her anything personal. Polly said she had settled in well.'

'Yes, indeed! Mostly as an unpaid servant,' Julia observed tartly.

'I had no idea that anything like that was going on,' Paul insisted.

'You haven't spoken to Amanda at all since then?'

Paul shook his head. 'I've been caught up with work at the hotel. Now the blockades are over business has been very busy and I've had a great deal to do. I haven't worried too much about Amanda because I was sure that she was in very safe keeping. I thought the reason I hadn't heard from her was because she was working hard at school and probably had a lot of homework.'

'What about her school friends? Have you spoken to them, can't they help in any way?' Julia probed.

'No.' Paul shook his head again. 'It seems she didn't have any friends.'

'Oh, yes she did! She went to and from school

with two other girls who lived in Tarvin. She told us so. She was with them the day we saw her in Chester.'

Paul shook his head again. 'They're not really her friends. It seems their mothers belong to the same church group as Polly does so there has been some sort of agreement that Amanda was to travel to and from school with them. They're in a class higher than Amanda; as I understand it, the two of them are long-standing friends and, apart from travelling on the bus with Amanda each day, they have nothing to do with her.'

'Isn't there anyone in her class at school who she's become friendly with?' Bob asked in surprise.

Paul hesitated. 'No, not at school, but she was friendly with some lad who lives in the village.'

'Well, have you asked him if he knows anything about where she might be?'

'That was the first thing Polly did, but his family told her that he was away visiting friends and had been with them for a couple of weeks.'

'In that case we seem to have drawn a blank for the moment,' Bob murmured.

'Yes, and I must be going,' Paul exclaimed, checking the time on his gold watch. 'If Amanda should contact you, then you will let me know?'

'Of course we will, but I still think you ought to alert the police to the fact that she's missing,' Bob advised as he showed Paul Hawkins to the door. 'She's your responsibility, not mine and Julia's.'

Julia couldn't stop thinking about the news Paul Hawkins had brought them. She kept remembering how worried and unhappy Amanda had looked when they'd seen her in Chester. She felt that in some obscure way it was her fault that Amanda had run away and she wanted to do something positive to help find her.

Amanda had been such a bonny baby and had grown into such a bright, intelligent and lovable little girl. She had loved school. Every night she'd been bubbling over with news of all the things she'd done there. She was quick to learn, and had mastered reading and writing with no trouble at all. She'd made friends readily and was so well liked that she was never without companions. The moment she went in through the school gates, other children ran up to greet her, wanting her to play with them.

Comparing that bubbly child with the world-weary fourteen-year-old she'd seen in Chester puzzled her. Even if her Aunt Polly was a hard taskmaster and expected Amanda to undertake an overwhelming amount of chores, Julia felt surprised that she had let it depress her so much that she should run away. It was out of character. She was far more likely to be resentful or mutinous, difficult and outspoken, even, but not simply to take off.

Amanda was no longer a young child, Julia reflected, so it was possible that she might have other problems apart from those at home.

Exactly what those could be Julia had no idea. She wondered if she was being bullied at school. Usually it was boys who were bullied, but when girls were picked on, they could suffer even more than boys. With boys it was usually physical violence that was involved. Girls could be viciously spiteful with their remarks and insinuations.

If Polly was restricting her from doing the things which other girls of her age were usually allowed to do, then Amanda might be having to put up with taunts and sneers. Perhaps it was something to do with her clothes. At fourteen, Amanda would be very sensitive about what she looked like. She'd want to dress like the other girls, but was she allowed to do so, Julia wondered? Amanda had been wearing school uniform when they'd see her in Chester so Julia had no idea what she wore at the weekends.

The more she thought about it, the more Julia worried, especially as Amanda had said she couldn't confide in her Aunt Polly.

Bob stared at Paul Hawkins in disbelief. 'Have you any idea what you are asking us to do?' he said angrily.

'Of course I have,' Paul blustered, 'that's why I've gone to the trouble of meeting up with you on your own. I wanted the chance to talk to you and see how you felt about it, before I said anything to Julia.'

Bob ran his hands through his hair in exasperation. 'You think she's going to say yes, do you?'

Paul shook his head. 'I'm not sure. All I know is that Amanda thinks the world of Julia and I'm pretty sure she would be a lot happier if she was living with her.'

'You didn't think that when Julia offered to look after Amanda after your wife died!' Bob reminded him sharply. 'You preferred to send her off to live with her Aunt Polly.'

'I know, I know. I was wrong to do that, but at the time I had my reasons.'

'You did? So what were they?'

Paul waved a hand dismissively. 'Nothing that you need trouble yourself about. I made the wrong decision and, believe me, I've regretted it ever since.'

'Are you saying that you knew Amanda hadn't settled at her aunt's place, and that she was unhappy, and yet you did nothing about it?' Bob asked incredulously.

Paul shrugged. 'It's not exactly been easy facing up to all this or coming here to ask for your help,' he blustered. 'I knew she was missing Julia because she kept saying so, but I thought she'd get over that. Young girls often get crushes on people but they don't last for ever. I thought that with the new school and everything she'd have so much else to occupy her mind that she'd soon forget all about Julia.'

'You may be right or you may be wrong, I've no idea,' Bob told him. 'She's run away from her aunt, that's for sure, but she hasn't come looking for Julia, has she?'

'I know,' Paul admitted helplessly, 'that's what I can't understand. I'm convinced, though, that she will turn up at your place sooner or later.'

'And when she does, you expect us to keep her there and to look after her?'

'Well no, not exactly,' Paul said hesitantly. 'I want her to come back here. This is her home! She'll want to be here, with me, her father.'

Bob shrugged. 'If you say so, but what has that to do with us?' He frowned.

'Like I keep saying, I want Julia to look after Amanda, at least until she finishes school.'

Bob stared at him in astonishment. 'Are you saying that you want Julia to give up all her plans for us to be married and to move back to the Darnley? She can't do that! Everything is settled for us to get married in a couple of months' time.'

'For God's sake,' Paul exclaimed angrily, 'this is an emergency! You can postpone your wedding for a bit longer. You've been saying you are going to get married for the last ten years, so what difference does another few months make?'

'Yes, we have been putting it off, but this time we're going to do it, come hell or high water.'

'Another few months won't matter, surely, Bob,' Paul wheedled. 'Look, Julia need only stay until Amanda has settled back down again.'

'Oh yes, and how long is that going to take?'

'Three months, six months, how the hell do I know?' Paul snarled, his colour rising. He began pacing the room, picking things up and putting them down again as his agitation increased. 'If you had kids of your own, you'd understand!' he barked angrily.

'Not much chance of having any if I put off our wedding day again, is there!' Bob said.

'I knew I should have gone straight to Julia and not to you,' Paul blustered. 'She'll say yes, I know she will.'

'Will she? If you are so positive about that, then why didn't you ask her when you came to the house to tell us that Amanda was missing?'

'Knowing that it might disrupt your plans, I thought I'd do the decent thing and speak to you first.'

'Oh it would be doing that all right, but it won't happen because I don't intend saying a word to Julia about her looking after Amanda and I don't want you doing so either.'

Paul was not so easily placated. He argued, he begged, he threatened, but Bob remained steadfast.

'It's over a year since your wife died,' he told Paul. 'You've had plenty of time to get over your grief and to make a home for Amanda. She's not a little kid; she could have come back to live with you again long before this, especially when you knew she was unhappy living with her aunt. The truth is, you didn't want the responsibility of that, did you?'

'It's not like that at all, Bob—'

'It most certainly is. Now you're trying to foist the responsibility of looking after Amanda on to Julia. Well, it won't work. I'm not standing for it.'

Chapter Thirty

Bob and Julia exchanged puzzled glances when, two nights later, as they were about to sit down to their evening meal, there was a loud knocking on the door.

Julia's heart thudded. 'It might be Amanda,' she exclaimed, her eyes lighting up hopefully. Pushing back her chair she headed towards the door, but Bob grabbed hold of her arm and stopped her. 'I'll go,' he said quickly.

His mind was still buzzing with the conversation he'd had with Paul Hawkins and he half expected to find him standing there on the doorstep.

As he pushed past Julia into the small hallway, the banging sounded again, this time even louder. Before he could reach the door, Julia was already at his side.

Neither of them knew the young boy who stood there, but Julia recognised the Darnley uniform.

'It's someone with a message from Paul Hawkins,' she said breathlessly. 'Have you come to tell us that they've found Amanda?' she demanded.

The boy glanced from one to the other, a

puzzled look on his freckled face as if he had no idea what they were talking about. 'I've been sent to ask Miss Winter to come back to the hotel with me right away,' he told them.

'Who has asked you to do that? Was it Mr Hawkins?' Bob frowned.

'No! He didn't send me, but it's Mr Hawkins who is asking for her,' the boy muttered.

'Then tell him she's busy and can't come,' Bob told him, pulling Julia away from the door. 'Who the hell does he think he is?'

'Bob, please! It must be something important.' She turned to the young boy who was looking at them in bewilderment. 'Have you any idea what he wants to see me about?'

'Not really. You don't seem to understand – he's very ill,' he persisted as Bob made to shut the door.

'Oh, I understand all right,' Bob muttered, 'but remind him that she has a life of her own and can't dance attendance on him. Get it?'

'Mr Hawkins has had a heart attack, miss,' the boy explained, ignoring Bob and speaking directly to Julia, 'and the doctor who's with him sent me here and said to tell you to come right away.'

Julia felt close to tears as she stood at Paul Hawkins's bedside. She had no idea what to do or say as she reached out and took his almost lifeless hand in her own and looked at the grey, sunken face and half-closed eyes.

'He's very anxious to talk to you,' the doctor said in a low voice, his face very grave. He didn't want me to administer any drugs in case it robbed him of the chance to speak.'

Although she strained to hear what Paul was saying, Julia couldn't understand a word because his voice was so weak and faint and his breathing so laboured. She could see from the anxious expression in his eyes, though, that it was something he thought to be very important. She bent down and placed her face as close as she could to his, trying hard to catch his words.

'It's no good,' she said as she straightened up, her eyes misted by tears, 'he seems to have drifted off.' She took a deep, steadying breath. 'He will get better?' she asked anxiously.

The doctor pursed his lips. 'I'll do whatever I possibly can,' he assured her.

Julia recognised the caution in his voice and felt a lump in her throat. She had never really felt at ease in Paul's company, but she didn't like to think of him dying.

'Have you any idea what it is that he is trying to tell me?' she asked, frowning.

The doctor shook his head. 'I'm not too sure, but it seemed to be something to do with his daughter, Amanda.'

'You do know that Amanda is missing?'

The doctor looked startled. 'No, I didn't know. When did all this happen?'

'Amanda's been missing for almost two weeks now,' Julia told him.

'I see! This upset could well be what has brought on his heart attack.'

'He will certainly have been under a tremendous amount of stress for the past two weeks,' Julia agreed.

'I was under the impression that Mr Hawkins sent his daughter away to boarding school after his wife died,' the doctor murmured thoughtfully.

'No, she's been living with his sister-in-law in Tarvin, just outside Chester.'

'Well, well. He's never said a word about that to me. And now you say she is missing. Do you mean she has run away?'

Julia nodded. 'Apparently. I understand she wasn't very happy about living there.'

'And no one knows where she is, or has any news about where she might be? Not even after all this time?'

'Not a word, as far as I know. No one seems to have heard from her or seen her.'

'Have the police been informed?'

Julia shook her head. 'I don't know about that either, but I don't think so.'

'Perhaps you'd better have another attempt at trying to understand what it is that Mr Hawkins wants to tell you. I'm sure it will ease his mind if he can talk to you. He's been asking for you ever since he was taken ill.'

'So why didn't you send someone to fetch me sooner?' Julia questioned.

The doctor shook his head. 'It was necessary to treat him first. You're here now, though, and surely that's all that matters.'

Paul Hawkins died later that night, but not before he'd extracted a solemn promise from Julia that she would do all she could to find Amanda. She also agreed to his request that when she did find Amanda she would look after her and give her a home. At least having given up her job to concentrate on helping Bob out with his business she would be able to devote more time to finding the young girl.

Bob was angry when she told him. 'He should never have made you promise to do something like that. It's burdening you with far too much responsibility.'

'I suppose you'd sooner Amanda was sent back to live with her Aunt Polly even though she's been unhappy there?' Julia blazed.

'No, you know I wouldn't want that to happen. All I meant was that we don't want to be saddled with a young girl, not now when at long last we are going to get married.'

'What difference will it make to us?' Julia asked in surprise. 'She'll be at school every day so we're hardly going to notice she's around.'

'We'll be newlyweds, though, and we'll need some privacy,' he insisted.

'Oh do try and talk sense, Bob,' Julia exclaimed scornfully. 'If we do get married, all we'll be doing is legalising a long-standing relationship. We've been living together as though we were man and wife for years!'

'Except for whenever you've packed your bags and gone dashing back to live at the Darnley when Paul Hawkins has snapped his fingers,' he retaliated.

She faced him angrily. 'That's not fair. The first time I went back there it was because your mother didn't want to have anything to do with me. She was determined to have you all to herself, and you know it.'

'Don't blame her, she's dead and can't defend herself,' he retorted huffily.

Julia sighed and placed a hand placatingly on Bob's arm. 'Instead of wasting our time and energy arguing about the past, shouldn't we be trying to find Amanda?'

They looked at each other in despair. 'The trouble is, neither of us have any idea where to start,' Bob groaned, running his hand through his hair.

'Because Paul's been the manager of the Darnley for so long there's bound to be a piece in all the papers about him dying,' Julia said thoughtfully. 'If Amanda reads it, then I'm pretty certain she will come back home.'

'Perhaps,' Bob said non-committally. He looked at her helplessly. He knew how worried she was, but he didn't see any sense in raising her hopes. Even if Amanda did come home, it wouldn't be the end of the problem, he thought gloomily. Julia would still feel responsible for her, especially now that Paul was dead.

'No doubt Paul's sister-in-law Polly and all the rest of the horde will see it as well, and all turn up like they did for his wife's funeral,' she went on.

'Yes,' he agreed gloomily, 'they'll all be here hoping they're going to benefit from whatever Paul Hawkins leaves.'

'I suppose I ought to go back to the hotel for a few days to help sort out his papers, since I know where everything is,' Julia ventured.

'Why get involved? Surely he has a solicitor who will be able to do that?' Bob said irritably.

'I don't know. Mr Markham, his solicitor, will certainly have Paul's will and all that sort of thing. There are a lot of private papers kept in the office, though, which he might know nothing about and which he might not be able to find.'

The next few days were extremely hectic for both Bob and Julia. All thoughts of their wedding were pushed to one side, as Julia concentrated on helping Mr Markham to sort out Paul Hawkins's affairs and arrange the funeral.

Her knowledge about Paul's business matters was extensive and Mr Markham kept telling her that her help was invaluable. For some reason that she couldn't understand, however, he insisted that the contents of Paul's private papers, which had been in the office safe, should be held in abeyance until after the funeral when all his family were present for the reading of the will.

*　*　*

Bob Reynolds knew that although Julia felt it her duty to give whatever help she could to sort out business matters at the Darnley, she was deeply worried about Amanda.

There had been wide coverage in all the local newspapers and even in the national and hotel trade papers of Paul's death, but Amanda had not turned up at the Darnley as they'd all hoped. Nor, or so it seemed, had she returned to her aunt's house in Tarvin. In fact, she'd not made any contact whatsoever with anybody.

The police had now been notified. They had visited everyone who'd known Amanda and taken statements from them. They'd put her on their missing list and this had been widely circulated. Even so, there was still no news of her.

Without mentioning anything to Julia about what he intended to do, Bob decided to take a day off and do some scouting around himself. His plan was to go to Chester and see if he could find the two schoolgirls who'd been with Amanda on the day they'd seen her there.

He didn't know their names or where they lived in Tarvin. He reasoned, though, that all he had to do was to wait for the five minutes past four bus from Chester to Tarvin and then travel on it and he'd be sure to see them. After that it would simply be a matter of speaking to them and seeing if there was anything they could tell him which might help him find Amanda.

His plan worked well. At first, the two schoolgirls were rather nervous about talking to him. To break the ice he reminded them of the way Amanda had missed the bus and how he had hired a taxi to take her from Chester to Tarvin.

'That's right! You arrived there at the same time as the bus did! Yes, and then she walked home with us and her Aunt Polly never knew anything about it,' one giggled.

After that both of them relaxed and were happy to talk quite freely and tell him all they knew about Amanda.

'We have no idea at all where she is,' they both told him. They did confide one nugget of news, though, which made Bob sit up and take notice.

'Amanda was ever so friendly with Jimmy Holman, a boy who lives in the village,' they told him.

'Do you know if he's been asked if he knows where she might be?'

'Jimmy's been away on holiday ever since she went missing,' one of them told him. 'His mum says he's gone to stay with friends in Southport.' They looked at each other and giggled. 'We wondered if Amanda had gone with him.'

'Were they that close?' Bob asked in surprise, remembering how strict Amanda had said her Aunt Polly was.

'They were ever so lovey-dovey,' the girls tittered. 'They were always sneaking kisses and holding hands when they thought no one was looking.'

As he travelled back to Liverpool Bob chewed over everything the two girls had told him. He pondered on the importance of all the things they'd told him about Amanda and Jimmy Holman.

She was fourteen, he reminded himself, and it certainly sounded as though she and this boy had quite a crush on each other. Since she was so unhappy about living with her aunt, and they didn't seem to get on, this probably made her friendship with Jimmy Holman much deeper and more important to her than it would otherwise have been.

He wondered if the boy's parents knew anything about their close friendship. If they did, would they even suspect for one minute that Amanda was with him? On the other hand, perhaps they did know that the two of them had run off together and didn't want to be involved in any scandal so that was why they were saying that he was away visiting friends in Southport.

Bob wondered if Amanda's aunt suspected that something like this might have happened and knew more than she was saying. Though if she did, why was she was keeping it to herself?

Bob pondered over this for a long time and eventually came to the conclusion that it might be because the boy's mother was one of Polly's friends and neither of them wanted what had happened to be known in the village.

He wasn't sure whether to say anything about all this to Julia or not. It was merely surmising on his part, because he had no real proof that this was what had happened or where Amanda might be now.

It had been rather a wasted journey, he reflected. Even if he and Julia faced Aunt Polly with all the information he'd gathered from the two girls, she could deny all knowledge. Furthermore, Jimmy Holman might genuinely be on holiday. Even though he'd been a close friend of Amanda's, he mightn't know that she was missing.

Julia seemed to be utterly exhausted when she arrived home that night. After one or two false starts Bob decided that the best thing to do was to keep his theories to himself and to say nothing. It would be better to tell her about his futile search after the funeral was over, he resolved.

He still held out the hope, just as Julia did, that Amanda would have read about her father's death in one of the newspapers. If so, she would know when the funeral was taking place and she would turn up at either the Darnley or the cemetery on the day of his funeral.

All he could do now, he thought gloomily, was to try and support Julia as much as he could and to make things easier for her if that was at all possible.

Although he hated attending funerals he decided that this was one he really ought to go to in case Amanda turned up. He felt that although Julia would be pleased and very relieved if she did, she would also be quite over-whelmed, knowing that it meant that the onus for Amanda's future now rested on her shoulders.

Chapter Thirty-one

The Darnley was packed and every room taken with people attending Paul Hawkins's funeral. It had taken the new manager, Stanley Albright, all his organising skills to accommodate regular long-standing guests and ensure that they were as comfortable as possible under the circumstances. Commercial travellers, who were regulars, were even sharing the twin-bedded rooms.

He'd also found that it was a major operation to oversee the arrangements for all the extra food and drink that everyone would be expecting when they returned to the hotel after the funeral.

In the week leading up to it he had also tried to get to grips with the books and routine. Julia Winter, an ex-employee and friend of Mr Hawkins, had helped enormously, but there were still some books and papers in the hands of Mr Markham, the solicitor, which she'd explained would not be released until after the will had been read.

Stanley Albright would be glad when the funeral was over and he could get on with re-organising the day-to-day running of the place to suit his standards.

At the moment, the hotel was swarming with gloomy-faced men and various members of Paul Hawkins's family. There were about twelve of them and they were causing more fuss than the thirty-odd commercial travellers who seemed to know the place inside out and needed no special looking after at all.

A tall, thin man in his late forties, Stanley Albright was the exact opposite of his predecessor both in appearance and manner. He had an abundance of energy and moved so quickly that he seemed to be everywhere at once. He was always charming to guests and crisp and authoritive when dealing with his staff. Although he was pleasantly surprised at the number of people who'd turned up for the occasion and who, he could tell from the books, were regulars and would be coming back time and time again, he was anxious to put his own stamp on the place.

The Darnley was near the Exchange Station and the docks were not far away, and so he was hoping to expand the place into a specialist hotel accommodating businessmen.

To do this he planned a complete refubishment. It wasn't only that the place was shabby, but also that the colours and styles were Edwardian and not what he considered right for the thirties.

For now, though, his duty was to make a favourable impression so that there wasn't any dropping off in numbers, and to do this he was determined to convince everyone there that he provided an excellent service.

He was well aware that commercial travellers were his bread and butter – for the moment, at any rate – and he was anxious to see that their needs took preference over the temporary influx of relatives since, after today, he'd probably never see any of them ever again.

On the day of Paul Hawkins's funeral Bob Reynolds made sure that he stayed in the background. Julia was kept busy introducing the new manager to the countless regular guests who were there to pay their last respects and most of whom knew her extremely well. She was also fending off questions from various members of Paul's family about what had happened to Amanda and whether she was going to be there.

Although she was doing it with tact and efficiency, Bob was well aware of the strain Julia was under. She frequently glanced towards the door and he knew that she was hoping, or possibly even expecting, that at any moment Amanda would walk in and join them.

Bob's heart ached for her because he felt it was highly unlikely that her hopes would be fulfilled. There had been no news at all from Amanda, not a word. They were as mystified by her disappearance now as they'd been three weeks ago.

He knew she must be somewhere, but he was

beginning to wonder if she had left Liverpool on a boat for Ireland, or somewhere even further afield. It could account for why she hadn't seen the reports of her father's death in any of the newspapers. If she had, then he was sure she would have come back. Julia had told him that Paul Hawkins had doted on his daughter as she was growing up and that she'd returned his affection.

Amanda had been at her mother's funeral so they were quite sure she would want to be at her father's.

'Amanda was much closer to him than she was to her mother,' Julia had assured him when they were trying to figure out where she might be.

He was still thinking along those lines when the hearse arrived. It was drawn by a pair of black horses, their coats gleaming and their harnesses sparkling. The light breeze made the black plumes on their heads wave majestically.

Bob scanned the crowd that had gathered in the street outside, anxiously searching for a sight of Amanda as Paul's coffin was loaded, but his vigil was to no purpose.

Along with the others he watched as the countless wreaths and floral tributes that had been brought to the hotel were carefully arranged. Some were placed on the top of the gleaming oak coffin, others were stacked along the sides.

There were so many of them that some had

to be transported in the boot of the large limousine that was to follow behind the hearse and carry close members of the family. Bob and Julia were to follow in the third car, along with Mr Markham the solicitor and Stanley Albright.

When the service ended and they filed out to the graveside Bob hung back, but there was still no sign of Amanda. Still alert, Bob stood behind the many black-coated men and the dozen or so black-garbed women, Julia amongst them, who gathered at the graveside for the final ritual. He felt that Amanda was somewhere close by. It was an uncanny feeling, but one he couldn't dispel.

If she was there, then this was the time when she would come forward, he told himself. With only half an ear on what was happening at the graveside his eyes darted from side to side, alert, watching and waiting.

He had almost decided that his vigil was hopeless when he sensed a movement from the shrubbery near the lyche-gate. For a moment he wasn't sure what it was that had attracted his attention. It might only be a bird, or a stray dog, he told himself.

Out of respect to the dead man he tried to remain facing the grave, leaning on his walking stick, but with his head tilted ever so slightly to one side so that he could keep watch. He saw the movement again and this time he was convinced that he'd also seen a face; a young girl's face.

Cautiously he moved closer to the bushes, one step at a time, shuffling backwards as noiselessly as he possibly could. He hoped that whoever was there would be so intent on watching what was going on at the graveside that they wouldn't observe his stealthy approach.

As the interment ended and people began to disperse, picking their way over the grass on to the gavel path, he made a quick decision about what he must do.

He wished he could sprint across the intervening space, but even though he now walked with only the trace of a limp, his artificial leg was still something of a handicap. He needed a walking stick to ensure he didn't lose his balance, especially when he was walking on uneven ground.

Before he could reach the bushes, whoever was hiding there became aware of what he was doing and realised they'd been discovered. There was a sudden movement as they tried to make their escape.

By then Bob had seen the face more clearly and even though it was partly hidden by the bushes, he was certain that it was Amanda. Shouting her name he hobbled after her.

Hearing Bob calling out Amanda's name, Julia turned around and it took her only a moment to grasp what was happening. She immediately began to run as fast as she could in the direction he had taken.

Finding herself hindered by her black high-heeled shoes she paused to take them off then ran as fast as she could in her stockinged feet towards the hedge.

Regardless of the fact that she was ruining her smart black coat she pushed her way through the bushes and chased after the figure fleeing down the road. As she overtook Bob she yelled at him to ask one of the drivers to use their car to head the girl off.

'I'm sure it's Amanda,' she panted. 'I can't see her face, but I recognise the school uniform.'

A hue and cry followed although half the people had no idea what was happening. Bob explained the situation to one of the commercial travellers who had come to the church in his own car and they gave chase, catching up with Amanda before she reached the end of the road.

Leaving the engine running they jumped out of the car and grabbed hold of her arm, insisting that she wait until Julia reached them.

Julia was so breathless that she couldn't speak. Panting, she held her arms wide open and with a howl of distress Amanda flung herself into them. They clung to each other, both of them sobbing with relief.

They didn't try to talk as they were driven back to the Darnley.

Julia was far too breathless, and Amanda was still sobbing. Julia held her close and gradually the girl's tears stopped, but her sobs turned to convulsive gulps that racked her body.

Julia wiped the tears from Amanda's face, murmuring words of comfort. When they arrived at the hotel she took her upstairs to her old bedroom and waited while Amanda bathed her eyes and regained her composure.

'Do you feel you can face your family now?' Julia asked gently after they'd both tidied themselves up.

'You mean Aunt Polly?' Amanda shivered. 'She's going to be furious with me.'

'You don't have to speak to her if you don't want to,' Julia assured her.

Amanda looked at her wide-eyed. 'Are you saying that I won't have to go back to her place?'

Julia hesitated, remembering what Paul had said about her being the one to take care of Amanda in the future. She didn't want to say anything until she knew for certain that it was still going to be possible, so she didn't answer.

'I think we should be going downstairs now; Mr Markham is waiting to read your father's will.'

Amanda shuddered. 'Do you know what it says . . . about me, and who will be looking after me?' she persisted.

Julia bit her lip; she didn't want to lie. 'Let's go and find out,' she suggested, taking Amanda's hand and holding on to it as they went downstairs.

Mr Markham was waiting for them in the foyer and there was a look of relief on his face as he saw them.

'Thank heaven you've calmed her down,' he said quietly. 'I've asked all the family to assemble in the dining room, so are you ready?'

Julia put an arm around Amanda's shoulders and gently propelled her forward. 'Yes, Mr Markham, we're both ready, so shall we get on with it?'

Paul Hawkins's will was quite straightforward. He had left small legacies to various members of his family, and then the rest of his estate was left in trust for Amanda. She was to be under the supervision of Mr Markham and Julia Winter until she reached the age of twenty-one.

Julia squeezed Amanda's hand and turned to smile at her. She felt confident that Amanda would be delighted by the news, especially since it would mean that she need have nothing further to do with her Aunt Polly unless she wanted to. To her surprise, Amanda avoided her eyes. She was biting her lips as if she was distressed by what she had heard.

Mr Markham brought the meeting to a close and reminded everyone that food and drinks were waiting for them in the lounge and suggested they should all make their way there.

'There are some further personal papers to be finalised in due course, Miss Winter,' he told her.

'What sort of personal papers?'

Mr Markham hesitated. 'I think we've all had enough of such matters for today, don't you?'

he said evasively. 'Amanda seems to be far too upset to take in anything more. In fact, she looks as though she needs a good night's sleep. Will you be taking her home with you?' he asked.

'Oh yes, I'll certainly be doing that,' Julia confirmed, giving Amanda a hug, 'but we'll come and see you tomorrow, if that is what you wish.'

'There are quite a lot of things which have to be gone into so perhaps you could be at my office at ten o'clock and we'll talk about it all then. Can you manage that, and bring Amanda with you?'

'We'll be there,' Julia assured him.

Mr Markham nodded but he was still frowning. 'I think it might be a very good idea if Mr Reynolds came with you,' he added cryptically.

Bob and Julia discussed the day's events late into the night, even after they went to bed and long after Amanda was tucked up and deep in an exhausted sleep.

'Has she said anything to you about where she's been or who she's been with for the past three weeks?' Bob asked.

'Not a word, and I haven't asked her. All she's told me is that she read in the papers about her father's death and when the funeral was taking place.'

'So that was why she turned up today like she did,' Bob murmured thoughtfully.

'It's amazing that you spotted her.'

'I had a feeling she would come,' he said quietly. 'I was watching out for her even before we left for the church.'

'It's a pity you didn't spot her a bit earlier so that she could have come into the church and been there when the service was taking place.'

'I'm not at all sure that she could have faced up to that,' Bob said gravely. 'Look how much watching the graveside ceremony distressed her.'

'Yet she still tried to run away.'

'I can understand that. She knew she was in trouble with her Aunt Polly and didn't want to have to face her.'

Julia sighed. 'I suppose you're right. I'm sure there's still something troubling her, though. Let's hope she tells us the whole story in the morning.'

'Yes, and let's hope that Mr Markham is able to sort all the other things out.'

Julia frowned. 'Yes, I wonder what papers he's talking about and why he feels it is necessary for all three of us to go to his office tomorrow?'

Bob yawned. 'Legal types like him enjoy making a mystery out of things. It helps to justify their fees.'

'True!' Julia chuckled.

'Paul's left her in your care until she's twenty-one, but I suppose Mr Markham will want to explain that he will still be her legal representative until then.'

'You're right. I suppose he'll be the one who has to manage and administer the money that Paul's left for her upkeep and so on. There're probably various papers to be signed in connection with that,' Julia reasoned.

'Go to sleep; it'll all be sorted out tomorrow,' Bob said drowsily. He leaned over and kissed her and then pulled the bedclothes higher around his shoulders as he settled down himself.

Chapter Thirty-two

Julia didn't sleep at all well; Bob tossed and turned and kept muttering as though he was having some unpleasant dream, and she could hear sobbing coming from the adjoining room where Amanda was sleeping.

Once or twice she wondered if she should get up and go and see if Amanda needed anything. Each time, though, she thought better of it, deciding that perhaps Amanda needed privacy in order to grieve for her father.

Julia was glad when the hands on the illuminated alarm clock on her bedside table reached seven o'clock. She felt that at last it was a reasonable time to get up.

As she crept downstairs to make a pot of tea she wondered if she should take one up for Amanda, as well as Bob, or whether it would be better to let her go on sleeping.

She shivered as she drew back the kitchen curtains and looked out and saw that it was a grey misty morning with overcast skies. Although it was not raining, it looked as though it might quite soon. A fitting day for what lay ahead, she thought gloomily, remembering that they had to be at Mr Markham's office at ten o'clock.

While she waited for the kettle to boil she wondered what else there was that Mr Markham had to tell them. He had mumbled something about the conditions attached to Amanda's care and that both puzzled her and made her feel apprehensive.

She knew Bob wasn't too pleased that she had been made Amanda's guardian. He felt that Paul's close relations should be the ones to undertake such a responsibility.

'Why should it be you?' he had grumbled the previous night. 'You were the hotel's receptionist, that's all.'

She'd reminded him that Paul and Eunice had been very kind to her when she'd first started work there. They'd not only let her live in at the hotel, but had taken care of her when her baby was born, even paying their own doctor to look after her.

'Only because they wanted to make sure you were fit enough to return to work because his wife wanted to be able to take time off after her own baby was born,' Bob pointed out.

At that point she'd decided that they were both far too tired to discuss it any further. She now hoped that everything would be cleared up quickly and amicably this morning so that both of them could get back to work.

She couldn't understand, though, why Mr Markham had been so insistent that Bob come to his office with both herself and Amanda. Bob thought it might be a legal thing. Possibly, since they were planning to be married, Paul Hawkins had stipulated some kind of joint agreement, she thought uneasily. Personally, she didn't think he would do that unless it was absolutely necessary.

In another couple of hours' time we'll all know what he wants to see us about, she told herself as she poured out three cups of tea and took Bob's and Amanda's upstairs. Everything will be cleared up and we can get on with our plans for the future.

'What time is it? I intended to be up and make *you* a cup of tea,' Bob said drowsily as she placed it down on his bedside table. 'Brought yours up as well, have you?'

'No, this is for Amanda,' Julia said. 'She's been sobbing half the night, but there doesn't seem to be a sound coming from her room now.'

'Then why don't you drink it and let her go on sleeping,' he suggested.

'I was going to let her lie in, but we have to be at Mr Markham's office at ten o'clock this morning.'

Bob yawned and closed his eyes.

'Come on, that means you as well,' Julia reminded him, pulling back the bedclothes.

'Why the hell do I have to be there?' he grumbled.

'I don't know, that's something I don't understand, but it's what Mr Markham told us yesterday, so you'd better come along.'

Half-heartedly Bob sat up and drank his tea. 'Don't I get a kiss and a cuddle?' he asked.

'No, not this morning, there isn't time! Why don't you cut along and get washed and shaved before I wake Amanda.'

'Does that mean we can have breakfast on our own?' he asked hopefully.

'We can try.'

They had almost finished their meal when they heard Amanda stirring. Julia immediately jumped up to get another cup and saucer. 'I'd better take her up a fresh cup of tea, the one I made earlier will be stone cold by now.'

As she reached the bottom of the stairs Julia could hear a horrible retching sound and she stopped and looked enquiringly at Bob.

'It sounds as though she's being sick!'

'Poor girl! It must be all the strain of yesterday,' Julia agreed worriedly.

'Do you think you should take in that tea or would it be best to leave her to get over it?'

'She may not want the tea, but I'm sure she needs someone to comfort her,' Julia said as she hurried up the stairs.

Amanda was sitting bent double on the edge of the bed. When she looked up her face was drained of all colour and she looked so unwell that Julia's heart went out to her. Placing the cup and saucer down on the chest of drawers, she went and sat on the bed beside Amanda and placed an arm around her shoulders.

'Sorry, did I wake you up?' Amanda apologised.

'No luv, I've been up ages. Bob and I have

had breakfast; I was coming up to tell you it was time to get dressed. I've brought you up a cup of tea, but I'm not sure if you want it. Something seems to have upset your stomach, by the sound of things. Would you like me to get you a dose of Andrew's Liver Salts?'

'No!' Amanda shuddered and rubbed a hand over her face, pushing back her mop of golden curls. 'I'll be quite all right in a minute.'

'Are you sure?'

Amanda nodded. She stood up and walked over to where Julia had placed the cup of tea and began sipping it.

Julia looked at her in disbelief. The colour was already back in her cheeks and she looked as if nothing at all was the matter with her. She was on the point of asking her what had caused the upset, but Amanda forestalled her.

'I'm as right as rain now,' she said brightly. 'I'd better get dressed. You said that we have to see the solicitor again this morning, didn't you?'

'Yes, we are due at Mr Markham's office at ten o'clock, but before we go there I think you should tell me where you've been hiding out for the last three weeks.'

'What do you think I ought to wear? Will he expect me to be wearing black?' Amanda questioned, completely ignoring what Julia had said.

'I shouldn't think so, but it's up to you,' Julia murmured. 'There was a plain black skirt amongst the things you brought from the

Darnley, wasn't there? Anyway, what you wear isn't nearly as important as you telling me where you've been all this time.'

'Does it matter? I'm back now,' Amanda stated with a petulant shrug.

'It certainly does matter . . . to me, at any rate. Come on, spill the beans and tell me where you've been. I won't say anything if you don't want me to. Promise!'

Amanda pulled a face. 'You probably will. You'll tell old Markham, for a start, if he asks you, and I'm sure you'll tell Bob because you seem to tell him everything.'

Julia remained silent, waiting as patiently as she could. In some ways, it probably didn't matter where Amanda had been. The main thing was that she was back safe and sound.

'All right, I'll tell you if I must,' Amanda sighed, walking over to the wardrobe and opening the door. 'I ran away to Southport.'

'Not on your own?' Julia said quietly.

'What's that supposed to mean?' Amanda asked defensively, riffling feverishly through the clothes hanging there.

'You went with a boy, didn't you?'

Amanda's blue eyes darkened in shock as she whirled round and stared at Julia. 'How did you know that?'

'We made enquiries of everyone we could think of in Tarvin who might know you, including the two girls we'd seen you with in Chester. One of them mentioned Jimmy Holman and said that he was a friend of yours. They also said that he was away on holiday in Southport.'

'He wasn't on holiday. He wanted to go to sea but his mum wouldn't let him, so he was planning to run away. I asked him if I could go with him.'

'You weren't thinking of going to sea, I hope?' Julia commented, trying hard not to smile.

'Of course I wasn't!' Amanda scowled indignantly. 'Jimmy's grandmother lives in Southport and he wanted to go and see her and say goodbye before he joined his ship. He said she would let me stay there for a while and I thought I might be able to get a job and go on living there with her.'

'It didn't work out, though?'

'I saw the bit about Dad in one of the papers and then I didn't know what to do. I didn't want to go back to Aunt Polly's . . .' suddenly Amanda's air of bravado was gone and she was in floods of tears. Once again, she was a young girl who felt the whole world was against her.

By the time the three of them reached the solicitor's, Amanda was looking perfectly composed despite her bout of crying after she'd explained to Julia where she'd been.

Even though she was concerned about what Amanda had told her, Julia pushed it to the back of her mind in order to concentrate on what the solicitor had to tell them.

After waiting for them to sit down in the three chairs he'd already placed facing his desk, Mr Markham shuffled the pile of papers in front of him uneasily.

He cleared his throat twice before he started to speak and Julia was surprised at how hesitant he was. Any dealings she'd had with him in the past had been conducted in a brisk, efficient way, but now he seemed almost reluctant to speak out.

As they waited patiently, trying hard not to fidget, he finally started speaking. In a low, hesitant voice, and avoiding their eyes, he detailed the careful arrangements Paul Hawkins had made for Amanda.

Julia and Bob exchanged puzzled glances as they listened in silence to the legal jargon, indicating to each other that neither of them was completely clear about what was involved.

'Do you think you could put all that into words that we can understand?' Bob asked bluntly.

'Yes, of course, Mr Reynolds. Basically, it applies to Miss Winter—'

'So what the devil am I doing here listening to it all for, then?' Bob interrupted.

'Well, there is a codicil to Mr Hawkins's will that concerns you. It is to deal with the situation in the event of you and Miss Winter marrying . . .'

Mr Markham paused and sorted through his papers again. 'I believe there is a possibility of that happening,' he commented, looking up at them enquiringly.

'That's right! We are getting married in less than two months' time,' Bob assured him.

'I see. Well, the situation, then, is this; Miss Winter has been appointed Amanda's guardian and one of the conditions is that Amanda will make her home with Miss Winter until she reaches the age of twenty-one.'

'Bloody hell!' Bob looked shocked.

'For that length of time,' the solicitor went on, ignoring Bob's outburst, 'Miss Winter will receive a very generous regular monthly sum to cover all expenses involved in looking after Amanda, together with a personal gratuity.'

He paused and looked at Julia from over the top of his glasses. 'Both of these will be paid to you monthly from a trust fund which I have been instructed to administer and over which I have complete control,' he explained. 'This trust fund is linked to a portfolio of investments which have been set up by the late Paul Hawkins. When Amanda reaches twenty-one then control of all monies held in trust for her will revert to her.'

'You mean I'll be able to do what I like with it? Spend it exactly as I like?' Amanda questioned.

Mr Markham removed his spectacles and pursed his lips. 'Yes, Amanda, that is so. However, your father has expressed a wish that you will retain my services, or those of my successor. He hopes that you will continue to let us oversee your investments and to advise you on how to handle your income so that you remain financially solvent for the rest of your life.'

Amanda's eyes widened. 'How much has he left me, then?' she gasped.

'A very considerable sum. He was a very successful businessman and he invested wisely. Until you are twenty-one, the only monies which will be paid out, apart from what is spent on your upkeep during the ensuing years, will be annual fees for administration. When you reach maturity the remaining capital will be entirely yours apart from a special one-off gratuity to Miss Winter which will not be paid to her until that date.'

'I can't have any of it until then, not even if I need money for something special?'

'You will receive a regular allowance of pocket money. A quite generous amount, in my opinion,' Mr Markham stated.

Amanda's face clouded, but she offered no comment, nor did she show any real pleasure in the details of her inheritance.

'I have prepared a copy of all these details for you to study,' Mr Markham told Julia, patting a folder in front of him.

'So why have I had to be here?' Bob enquired.

'Ahh!' once more Mr Markham shuffled the papers on the desk in front of him and brought out a separate document which he passed across the desk to Bob.

'As you will see from this, Mr Reynolds, my client was aware that you and Miss Winter were planning to be married and he has left you an extremely generous wedding present.'

Bob scanned the paper in his hand and his lip curled. 'Looks like bribery to me!' he stated.

'Bob, what on earth do you mean?' Julia reached out and took the paper from him. 'Heavens! How very generous!' she exclaimed, her eyes widening.

'Too generous,' Bob snapped. 'Look at the conditions attached to it. It's his way of ensuring that I don't raise any objections to Amanda living with us.'

'Well, you don't mind, do you?' Julia smiled.

'No. I suppose not.' Bob shrugged. 'It is such a large sum, though, that I feel as if I'm being paid to agree.'

'I think you are being over-sensitive,' Mr Markham said dismissively.

'Perhaps!' Bob shrugged again but he still looked slightly discomfited.

'Is that everything, then, Mr Markham?' Julia asked.

'Almost. There are some papers to be signed before you leave and . . . and one other little matter.'

'So what is that?' Julia looked at him enquiringly.

Mr Markham hesitated and he had an uneasy

look on his face. Picking up a sealed envelope he turned it over in his hands before passing it to Julia.

'This is Amanda's birth certificate,' he stated, his face impassive. 'Mr Hawkins requested that it was to be handed to you personally, Miss Winter, for safe-keeping.'

Julia smiled as she took it from him and put it into her handbag. 'Right, I'll take good care of that.'

'I think you should look at it very carefully as soon as you have the time to do so,' Mr Markham pronounced.

Puzzled, Julia opened her handbag to take the letter back out, but Mr Markham held up his hand, signalling her to stop.

'Not now, Miss Winter. I think it would be better if you read it later when you have more time. There are documents now that you all have to sign—'

'We're not signing any papers until we have had the chance to read them all through and study exactly what they say,' Bob interrupted.

'Well, really!' Mr Markham looked taken aback. 'I have explained everything in detail. What is it you don't understand? What else do you want to know?'

'We want the time to go over them and to discuss the contents between ourselves before we sign them,' Bob insisted stubbornly. 'There's far too much involved. I don't want to take on something that is going to prove to be more than we can handle.'

'Surely it's only a question of letting Amanda make her home with us until she reaches twenty-one,' Julia intervened. 'Isn't that right, Mr Markham?'

The solicitor avoided Julia's eyes. Standing up, tugging at the points of his waistcoat, he cleared his throat and then began gathering up the papers in front of him.

'I'll see all three of you again tomorrow morning, then. Shall we say the same time, ten o'clock?'

Chapter Thirty-three

Amanda felt so depressed that she was almost in tears by the time they got back to Skirving Street. She wasn't sure what it was that had upset Bob and made him sound so bad-tempered when they'd been in the solicitor's office, but she felt sure it was to do with her living with them.

She'd tried to see the pieces of paper with all the details on, but Mr Markham had stopped her from doing so.

'Not now, my dear,' he'd said firmly. 'Take them away and study them as Mr Reynolds suggests and then come back tomorrow and you can sign them then.'

She'd tried to talk about it on the way home, but Bob had insisted that she should wait until later.

'Julia needs time to read all the papers through first and then she will explain all the details to you, Amanda,' he told her, and his voice was so cold and hard that she hadn't liked to argue.

The first thing Julia did when they got in was to ask Bob to make a pot of tea. As they sat drinking it she took the envelope Mr Markham had given her before they'd left his office out of her handbag and opened it.

Amanda waited for her to say what it was all about. Instead, after scanning it, Julia suddenly complained of a headache and said she was going upstairs to lie down. She'd looked so white and drawn that Bob said he'd bring her tea up for her and insisted that she took a couple of aspirins and went and had a sleep.

Julia had left a casserole in the oven ready for when they came home from seeing the solicitor. Bob dished it up, but neither he nor Amanda had very much appetite.

Bob kept running up and downstairs to check that Julia was all right and each time he came back down he looked more upset than before. Julia stayed upstairs for most of the afternoon and Amanda found that no matter how persistent she was Bob refused to discuss either the details of her father's will or to tell her what was the matter with Julia.

His prolonged silence made her spine crawl. Her mind was filled with all sorts of dread because she was sure that Julia's headache, like everything else that seemed to be happening, was all her fault.

Once again Bob and Julia talked late into the night. They waited until Amanda had gone up to bed and made sure that she was sound asleep before they felt free to do so.

'If you hadn't seen Amanda's birth certificate,

would you ever have credited that such a thing could happen?' Julia asked, her voice full of disbelief.

Her sapphire gaze blazed with dismay as her eyes met his questioningly. 'I feel so stupid that I've let myself be duped by all the lies. It's so outrageous that I can hardly believe it is true.'

Bob looked at it in a very different light to her. 'I wouldn't have believed that anyone could be so bloody devious or so wicked and cruel,' he said angrily.

'To have kept it secret all these years,' she exclaimed.

'They had no choice. They were probably well aware that they'd committed a crime. If you'd found out and gone to the police, they could have ended up in prison.'

Julia shook her head. 'That Dr Wiseman who attended me must have been in on it with them,' she mused.

'Of course he was, that's why he admitted you into his special clinic. You probably didn't need to go there at all. I'm quite sure you had a normal, healthy baby, but you being in his clinic provided the opportunity to switch the two babies.'

'So really it was Eunice's baby that was still-born?' she said sadly.

'Well, that's quite obvious, isn't it!' Bob fumed, running his hands through his hair.

'They took a tremendous risk.'

'Not really. They knew you'd fallen out with

your family and that you were on your own in Liverpool. When they realised you were living in what was little better than a slum they planned ahead.'

'You mean they actually thought that there was the possibility that Eunice might lose her baby!' Julia gasped, looking at him in wide-eyed disbelief.

'Yes, of course they did! She was middle-aged and she'd already had three miscarriages. You were young and fit, so why should you lose your baby?'

'So mine was born healthy and their baby was stillborn,' she repeated, gritting her teeth in frustration.

'That's right! They made sure you were well looked after because you were their insurance if anything went wrong for Eunice. It must have seemed unbelievable when you walked into the Darnley and they realised you and Eunice were not only both pregnant, but that your babies were due at almost exactly the same time.'

'So they switched the babies over.'

'That seems to have been what happened. I bet that crooked doctor demanded a sky-high fee to keep his mouth shut,' Bob added cynically. 'The bugger should be strung up.'

'I wonder if Mr Markham was involved as well. I'm sure he was their solicitor at that time.'

'Probably. They were all in it together. They hoodwinked you good and proper into believing you'd lost your baby, luv. And at the time you thought they were all being so kind and considerate,' he added bitterly.

'Eunice took an incredible risk in letting me look after Amanda and grow so fond of her.'

'She probably did that because she felt so guilty about taking the kid away from you.'

'Paul must have known!'

'Yes, and it didn't stop him from sacking you, did it? I never really understood why he did that.'

'Water under the bridge,' Julia said evasively. 'I don't want to talk about it.'

'I think we should,' Bob said quietly. 'Let's get all the skeletons out of the cupboard and have everything out in the open. There have been too many secrets and underhand dealings. Why did he sack you?'

'He wanted me to be more than a receptionist or bookkeeper.'

'You mean . . .'

'He wanted an affair,' she said bluntly. 'I kept him at arm's length and while Eunice was alive he was afraid of pushing me in case I made a scene or she suspected anything. After she died then he thought there was no longer anything to stand in his way. Only I still didn't see it like that!'

'So you were sacked again, this time by him!'

'Yes, and far worse than that, he sent Amanda away to her Aunt Polly. He did that even though he knew it would break her heart to be parted from me after we'd been so close for all those years; ever since she could remember, in fact.'

'The bastard! That was to punish you, of course.'

'Looking back I realise now that the bond between me and Amanda was much greater than was normal,' Julia reflected. 'We both loved each other, there was no doubt at all about that. I was flattered that Amanda seemed to prefer to be with me rather than with her mother ... but of course, even though I didn't know it at the time, I was her real mother.'

'Come to think of it, you are very alike,' Bob pointed out. 'And she does have the same-shaped face, and her smile is very much like yours.'

'I'd always thought it was a coincidence that Amanda's hair is the same colour as Bernard's was as well. Her eyes are the same as his too,' she added thoughtfully.

'In many ways she is very like you were when we first met; the day you first came to Liverpool.'

Julia smiled dreamily. 'I was only a few years older than Amanda is now when we met, wasn't I?' She reached out and caught Bob's hand and pressed it against her cheek. 'What would I have done if I hadn't bumped into you that day?'

'You probably wouldn't have been deprived of your child for all these years,' he said wryly.

Julia frowned uncomprehendingly.

'I sent you to the Darnley, didn't I?'

'Yes, you did, but I could only afford to stay there for a few nights.'

'I was the one who later on told you that Paul Hawkins was looking for a receptionist.'

'That's true as well.'

'So, if I hadn't done that, and you hadn't gone to the Darnley to work, then you might have been a mother for the past fourteen years.'

'Would Amanda have had such a good life, though?'

'You would have managed.'

'Yes, I probably would have done, but it would have been pretty tough for her.'

'And probably for you as well,' Bob agreed.

Julia pulled away from Bob and sat bolt upright. 'I suppose in some ways we've both been very lucky and I've had the best of all worlds,' she said philosophically. 'I've probably spent almost as much time with Amanda as I would have done if she'd been my own child from the beginning, but I've had none of the responsibilities of providing for her upbringing.'

'Mm! and now she's been left a small fortune!'

'Yes, I wonder what she will think about that, though, when I tell her who she really is?' Julia questioned thoughtfully. 'Perhaps I shouldn't tell her. Maybe we should go on letting her think that Paul and Eunice Hawkins really were her parents.'

Bob looked at her incredulously. 'You can't do that, it's a downright lie . . . you're her mother. She knows you and she loves you, so she deserves to be told.'

'Will she go on feeling the same way about me once she knows the truth?'

'Come here!' Bob put his arms around Julia and hugged her. 'Of course she will, she'll be over the moon, luv.'

'I'm not so sure. Not when I tell her about my background and how I was an unmarried mother and such a disgrace to my family that I ran away from home because they were so ashamed of my behaviour.'

Bob shrugged. 'The decision is yours, of course, I can't force you.'

'I wonder if perhaps it would be better to wait until Amanda is twenty-one. What do you think?'

He ran a hand through his hair like he always did when a problem was too great for him, then shook his head from side to side helplessly. 'I don't know,' he admitted. 'I really don't know. I'm not even going to try and tell you what to do. Remember, though, Amanda knows there is something she hasn't been told. She probably still wants to know why you got so upset after we came home and you opened the envelope that Mr Markham handed you.'

Julia still hadn't decided what she ought to do about telling Amanda the facts about her birth and her true parentage as they got ready to go to the solicitor's next day to sign all the relevant papers.

'Are you feeling sick again?' Julia asked anxiously as Amanda pressed her hand over her mouth and the colour drained from the girl's face as she sat down to breakfast. For a moment Julia thought Amanda was going to be sick like she'd been the previous morning and tried to reassure her that there was absolutely nothing for her to worry about.

'It's all going to be plain sailing; you can live here with Bob and me and even go back to your old school if you wish,' she told her, hoping to take her worried look away.

Amanda nodded, but said nothing.

Mr Markham seemed relieved to see the three of them back. He laid out the documents and indicated where he wanted them to sign.

As Julia took the pen he held out, Mr Markham gave her an intense look. 'You have talked this through and feel you can comply with the terms set out?' he asked.

Julia nodded and bent over to sign the paper then held out the pen to Bob so that he could add his signature.

'Stop! There is something you should both know,' Amanda said quickly. White-faced, she looked from one to the other of them, and then gulped. 'You may not want to have me living with you when I've said my piece.'

'What do you mean, Amanda?' Mr Markham frowned.

'Well,' she hesitated as if lost for words. For a moment Julia wondered if she already knew that Paul and Eunice weren't her real parents and felt that she was an impostor.

Impulsively, she caught Amanda's hand. 'We're very happy to have you live with us, aren't we, Bob?'

'You don't understand. I can't live with you . . . you won't want me to when I tell you . . .' Again Amanda hesitated, looking wildly from one to the other of them.

'For God's sake, tell us what's wrong and put us out of our misery,' Bob snapped. 'What the hell have you done that is going to upset us so much?'

Amanda gulped in a huge breath. With her hands clenched so tightly that her knuckles were white she blurted out, 'I'm pregnant. It's Jimmy Holman's baby, but he doesn't want to have anything to do with it.'

'Pregnant!'

Three voices repeated the word 'pregnant' in varying tones of astonishment.

'There you are, I knew this would be how you'd all feel about me,' Amanda said hysterically, looking at the dismay on all their faces.

Pushing back her chair she stumbled towards the door. 'Don't worry, I understand, I never expected any of you to want to have anything to do with me once I told you.'

She'd wrenched open the door and was out into the street before any of them realised what was happening.

Julia was the first to recover. 'Amanda,

Amanda!' her voice rose to a scream. 'Come back, it makes no difference at all.'

Catching up with Amanda she held her close, burying her face in the girl's golden curls, sobbing and murmuring words of love as she did so.

Amanda struggled against her. 'Please, Julia, let me go.'

'No, never! I'll never let you go. You need me now more than ever before. We'll bring up this baby together . . . as a family.'

'Bob won't want to do that! He wants to marry you and for you to have children of your own. He doesn't want to have me and my little bastard living with you as well!'

'Of course he wants you living with us – we'll both take care of you.'

Amanda looked at her scornfully. 'Why should he? Why should you?'

Julia held her even tighter. 'I'll tell you why,' she whispered. 'I was pregnant and unmarried when I was very young. My baby's father had been called up in the army and he was killed before the baby was born, so I know what you are going through at this moment.'

Amanda looked at Julia in astonishment. 'So what happened to the baby? If you are telling me all this to try and persuade me to have mine adopted, you can forget it. It won't work,' she said firmly, not waiting for Julia to answer.

'I can understand that, and I wouldn't dream of expecting you to have your baby adopted,'

Julia assured her. 'Don't worry, I will always be there to help you.'

'We both will,' Bob declared, catching up with them. Spontaneously he put an arm around both of them. 'We'll bring up the baby together, all three of us,' he affirmed, hugging them close.

Julia smiled up at him, gratitude and love shining in her eyes for the man who had stood by her through everything.

'So what happened to your baby?' Amanda persisted. 'Did you have it adopted?'

'I'm holding her in my arms right now,' Julia murmured tenderly.

Amanda looked taken aback. 'I don't understand,' she protested.

Julia smiled. 'I'm still not sure that I do, either. I didn't know myself until yesterday.'

'It's a very long story, but Julia really is your mother, Amanda,' Bob assured her. 'Come on, let's go back inside; we'll sign the papers, then go home and Julia will tell you all the details over a cup of tea. It's a little bit like a fairytale.'

Chapter Thirty-four

Amanda listened, dumbfounded, as Julia related the story of her own past and everything that had happened since she'd run away from her home in Wallasey and had come to live in Liverpool.

'So that means that Bob isn't my real father,' she said in dismay, her eyes filling with tears.

'No,' Julia agreed hesitantly, 'but he is very fond of you. Surely you must realise that.'

'Only because I'm your daughter and he loves you,' Amanda sniffed. 'Now you've told me the truth he won't want me hanging around here, not when you are about to get married and everything.'

'Rubbish! You heard what he said about the three of us bringing up your baby,' Julia reminded her firmly.

Amanda shrugged resignedly but she still looked doubtful.

'Anyway, that's a long way off,' Julia told her cheerfully. 'Before that happens there's our wedding to be arranged and we want you as our bridesmaid.'

'Bridesmaid!'

'That's right.'

Amanda shook her head. 'Can you imagine it! I'd look like an elephant, standing there alongside the two of you,' she said scornfully.

'No you won't; not if we hurry up and fix the date as soon as possible,' Julia insisted.

'Having me as your bridesmaid would be enough to make Bob turn tail and run,' Amanda persisted.

'Not at all. It's what Bob wants. He suggested it ages ago; after we saw you in Chester, as a matter of fact.

'And afterwards we'll all live together, happy ever after,' Amanda exclaimed cynically.

'We'll all go on living together though whether we are happy or not depends, a great deal on you,' Julia said quietly.

Julia and Bob's wedding took place, to their great delight, on a golden, balmy day.

Being such a wonderful day, their spirits were lifted and they were filled with feelings of optimism for the future.

After the simple wedding ceremony at the Liverpool register office, with Mr Markham and Stanley Albright as witnesses, they all went back to the Darnley for a celebratory meal.

Because there had been so many adjustments and surprises lately, and because they didn't want to leave Amanda on her own, they had decided not to have a honeymoon.

'Next year, after you've had your baby, we'll all go away on a real family holiday,' Bob stated as the three of them returned to Skirving Street.

They'd settled into an amicable routine and Amanda hoped that it wouldn't change too much once the baby arrived. Because Julia was working, Amanda did as much as she could to keep the house clean and to do the shopping. At least twice a week she spent the evening in her bedroom. It was so cosy that it was no hardship and she was sure that Bob appreciated the opportunity to be on his own with Julia.

Amanda still couldn't believe that they really wanted her living with them, so in an attempt to prove how much they meant it Bob decided that they ought to put everything on a legal footing.

'I've had a word with Mr Markham about it,' he told Amanda and Julia, 'and he's handling it.'

'Handling what?' Julia asked in a puzzled voice.

'The papers and so on.'

Julia shook her head. 'I don't know what you are talking about. Are you going to explain?'

'I'll go on up to my room and leave you two to sort out your problem, whatever it is,' Amanda said as Bob ran his hand through his hair in an exasperated way.

'No, no, stay here!' he ordered sharply. 'It concerns you.'

Amanda stared at him wide-eyed, her insides churning. She'd been afraid all along that the three of them living together, like one happy family as Julia put it, was too good to be true.

Tensing, biting down on her lower lip and vowing to herself that when Bob said he wanted her to move out she wouldn't cry, she waited for him to go on.

His next words took her breath away, but not for the reason she had expected.

'I've been to see old Markham and have arranged for us to become your legal guardians, Amanda. It means you can change your name to Reynolds, Amanda Reynolds. That's if you want to, of course.'

Amanda stared from him to Julia, open-mouthed, wondering if she had heard correctly. 'Can . . . can you do something like that?' she stuttered, her face flaming.

'If you are happy about it . . .'

'Happy!' She let out a long sigh. 'I'd like nothing better – as long as both of you agree about it.'

Amanda's baby was born on a cold, blustery Saturday.

After the three of them had enjoyed a leisurely late breakfast, she'd insisted on going out to do the weekend shopping, even though both Julia and Bob warned her against risking it.

Her pains started when she was in the butcher's and she was alarmed in case she couldn't manage to get home again, but Julia had been so concerned about her that, at Bob's suggestion, she had followed her along Scotland Road and was on hand to help her home again.

Five hours later, Robert Julian Reynolds made his appearance.

'He's never going to know his real father,' Amanda murmured sadly, 'but at least he'll be able to call you Gran and Granddad.' Amanda smiled as she looked proudly at the baby in her arms. 'I wonder how he is going to like that? I'll probably have to spend all my time trying to stop the two of you from spoiling him,' she added with a cheeky grin.

'I'm not sure how Robert Julian is going to like the situation or, more importantly, how he is going to react to having an uncle who will be a few months younger than him,' Julia countered.

'An uncle?' Amanda stared at her uncomprehendingly, then her face broke into a huge smile 'You mean . . .' She hesitated, as if afraid to say the words.

'That's right!' Julia smiled brightly. 'Robert Julian is going to have a little playmate in a few months' time.'

'And then we really will be a big happy family.' Bob grinned, his voice husky with satisfaction at how well things had turned out for all of them.